THE TEA PLANTER'S WIFE

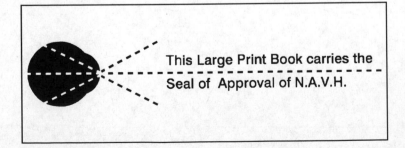

THE TEA PLANTER'S WIFE

DINAH JEFFERIES

THORNDIKE PRESS

A part of Gale, Cengage Learning

GALE
CENGAGE Learning·

Farmington Hills, Mich • San Francisco • New York • Waterville, Maine
Meriden, Conn • Mason, Ohio • Chicago

GALE
CENGAGE Learning·

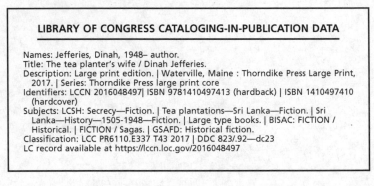

LIBRARY OF CONGRESS CATALOGING-IN-PUBLICATION DATA

Names: Jefferies, Dinah, 1948– author.
Title: The tea planter's wife / Dinah Jefferies.
Description: Large print edition. | Waterville, Maine : Thorndike Press Large Print, 2017. | Series: Thorndike Press large print core
Identifiers: LCCN 2016048497| ISBN 9781410497413 (hardback) | ISBN 1410497410 (hardcover)
Subjects: LCSH: Secrecy—Fiction. | Tea plantations—Sri Lanka—Fiction. | Sri Lanka—History—1505-1948—Fiction. | Large type books. | BISAC: FICTION / Historical. | FICTION / Sagas. | GSAFD: Historical fiction.
Classification: LCC PR6110.E337 T43 2017 | DDC 823/.92—dc23
LC record available at https://lccn.loc.gov/2016048497

Published in 2017 by arrangement with Crown, an imprint of Crown Publishing Group, a division of Penguin Random House LLC

Printed in Mexico
1 2 3 4 5 6 7 21 20 19 18 17

In memory of my son Jamie

PROLOGUE

Ceylon, 1913

The woman held a slim white envelope to her lips. She hesitated for a moment longer, pausing to listen to the achingly sweet notes of a distant Sinhalese flute. She considered her resolve, turning it over as she would a pebble in her palm, then sealed the envelope and propped it against a vase of wilting red roses.

The antique ottoman stood at the end of the four-poster bed. It was made from dark wood, its sides covered in satin moiré with a padded leather lid. She lifted the lid, took out her ivory wedding dress, and draped it over the back of a chair, wrinkling her nose at the sickly scent of mothballs.

She selected a rose, broke off the bloom, and glanced at the baby, glad that he still slept. At her dressing table she raised the flower and held it against her fair hair; such fine threads of silk, *he* had always said. She shook her head and let the flower go. Not today.

On the bed the baby's clothes were already placed in random piles. With the tips of her fingers she touched a freshly laundered matinee jacket, remembering the hours she'd spent knitting until her eyes had stung. Lying beside the clothing were sheets of white tissue paper. Without further delay she folded the little blue jacket, placed it between two sheets of the paper, and carried it to the zinc-lined ottoman, where she laid it at the bottom.

Each item was folded, placed between tissue and then added to the other layers of woolly hats, bootees, nightgowns, and romper suits. Blue. White. Blue. White. Last of all were the muslin squares and terry napkins. These she folded edge to edge, and then, when it was done, she surveyed her morning's work. Despite what it meant, she did not blanch at the sight.

Another glance at the baby's fluttering lashes signaled that he would be waking soon. She'd need to be quick. The dress she had chosen for herself was made from oriental silk in vivid sea green, slightly raised above the ankles and with a high-waisted sash. This had been her favorite dress sent over from Paris. She'd worn it the night of the party, the night she was certain the child had been conceived. She paused again. Might wearing it be viewed as a bitter attempt to wound? She couldn't be sure. She loved the color. That's what she told herself. Above all, it was the color.

The baby whimpered and began to fret. She glanced at the clock, lifted the child from his crib, and sat in the nursing chair by the window, feeling a light breeze cooling her skin. Outside the sun was high in the sky and the heat would be building; somewhere in the house a dog barked and from the kitchens came the heady scents of cooking.

She opened her nightgown to reveal a pale marbled breast. The baby nuzzled and then latched on. A fine strong jaw he had, so much so that her nipples were cracked and raw and, in order to bear the pain, she was forced to bite her lip. To distract herself she glanced around her room. In each of its four corners, memories had attached themselves in the form of objects: the carved footstool that had come from the north; the bedside lampshade she had sewn herself; the rug from Indo-China.

As she stroked the baby's cheek, he stopped feeding, lifted his free hand, and, in one heartbreakingly beautiful moment, his delicate fingers reached for her face. That would have been the moment for tears.

When she had winded him, she laid him on the bed wrapped in a soft crocheted shawl and, once dressed, she cradled him with one arm and took a last look round. With her free hand she closed the lid of the ottoman, threw the abandoned rose in a lacquered wastepaper basket, and then ran her palm over the remaining flowers in the vase, loosening the bruised petals. They floated past the white envelope to fall like splashes of blood on the polished mahogany floor.

She opened the French doors and, glancing around the garden, took three deep breaths of jasmine-scented air. The breeze had dropped; the flute silenced. She had expected to feel afraid, but instead was filled with a welcome sense of relief. That was all, and it was enough. Then, with firm footsteps, she began to walk, one inevitable step after another, and as she left the house behind, she pictured the palest shade of the color lilac: the color of tranquillity.

PART ONE:
THE NEW LIFE

1

Twelve Years Later: Ceylon, 1925

With her straw sun hat in one hand, Gwen leaned against the salty railings and glanced down again. She'd been watching the shifting color of the sea for an hour, tracing the shreds of paper, the curls of orange peel, and the leaves drifting by. Now that the water had changed from deepest turquoise to dingy gray, she knew it couldn't be long. She leaned a little further over the rail to watch a piece of silver fabric float out of sight.

When the ship's horn sounded — loud, prolonged, and very close — she jumped, lifting her hand from the rail in surprise. The little satin purse, a farewell present from her mother, with its delicate beaded drawstring, slid over her hand. She gasped and reached out, but saw it was too late as the purse dropped into the ocean, swirled in the dirty water, and then sank. And with it her money, and Laurence's letter with his instructions folded neatly inside.

She looked about her and felt another stirring of the unease she hadn't been able to shake off since leaving England. You can't get much further from Gloucestershire than Ceylon, her father had said. As his voice echoed in her head, she was startled when she heard another voice, distinctly male but with an unusually honeyed tone.

"New to the East?"

Accustomed to the fact that her violet eyes and pale complexion always attracted attention, she turned to look and was forced to squint into bright sunlight.

"I . . . Yes. I'm joining my husband. We're only recently married." She took a breath, just stopping herself from blurting out the whole story.

A broad-shouldered man of medium height, with a strong nose and glittering caramel eyes, gazed back at her. His black brows, curling hair, and dark polished skin stopped her in her tracks. She stared, feeling a little unnerved, until he smiled in an open sort of way.

"You're lucky. By May the sea would normally be a great deal wilder. A tea planter, I'm guessing," he said. "Your husband."

"How did you know?"

He spread his hands. "There is a type."

She glanced down at her beige-colored dress: drop-waisted, but with a high collar and long sleeves. She didn't want to be a "type," but realized that if it weren't for the chiffon scarf knotted at her neck, she might appear drab.

"I saw what happened. I'm sorry about your purse."

"It was stupid of me," she said, and hoped she wasn't blushing.

Had she been a little more like her cousin, Fran, she might have engaged him in conversation, but instead, imagining the short exchange to be over, she turned back to watch as the ship slipped closer to Colombo.

Above the shimmering city, a cobalt sky stretched into distant purple hills; trees gave shade and the air was filled with the cries of gulls as they swooped over the small boats massing on the water. The thrill of doing something so different bubbled through her. She had missed Laurence and, for a moment, allowed herself to dream of him. Dreaming was effortless, but the reality was so exciting it set butterflies alight in her stomach. She took a deep breath of what she'd expected would be salty air and marveled at the scent of something stronger than salt.

"What is that?" she said as she turned to look at the man, who, she rightly sensed, had not shifted from the spot.

He paused and sniffed deeply. "Cinnamon and probably sandalwood."

"There's something sweet."

"Jasmine flowers. There are many flowers in Ceylon."

"How lovely," she said. But even then, she knew it was more than that. Beneath the seductive scent there was an undercurrent of something sour.

"Bad drains too, I'm afraid."

She nodded. Perhaps that was it.

"I haven't introduced myself. My name is Savi Ravasinghe."

"Oh." She paused. "You're . . . I mean, I haven't seen you at dinner."

He pulled a face. "Not a first-class passenger is what you mean, I think. I'm Sinhalese."

She hadn't noticed until now that the man stood on the other side of the rope that separated the classes. "Well, it's very nice to meet you," she said, pulling off one of her white gloves. "I'm Gwendolyn Hooper."

"Then you must be Laurence Hooper's new wife."

She fingered the large Ceylon sapphire of

her ring and nodded in surprise. "You know my husband?"

He inclined his head. "I have met your husband, yes, but now I'm afraid I must take my leave."

She held out her hand, pleased to have met him.

"I hope you'll be very happy in Ceylon, Mrs. Hooper."

When he ignored her hand, she let it fall. He pressed his palms together in front of his chest, fingers pointing upward, and bowed very slightly.

"May your dreams be fulfilled . . ." With closed eyes, he paused for a moment, then walked off.

Gwen felt a little disconcerted by his words and the odd departing gesture, but with more pressing matters on her mind, she shrugged. She really must try to remember Laurence's lost instructions.

Luckily, first class disembarked first, and that meant her. She thought of the man again and couldn't help but feel fascinated. She'd never met anyone so exotic and it would have been much more fun if he'd stayed to keep her company — though, of course, he could not.

Nothing had prepared her for the shock of

Ceylon's scorching heat, nor its clashing colors, nor the contrast between the bright white light and the depth of the shade. Noise bombarded her: bells, horns, people, and buzzing insects surrounding her, swirling and eddying, until she felt as if she were being tipped about, like one of the pieces of flotsam she'd been watching earlier. When the background noise was eclipsed by loud trumpeting, she spun round to stare at the timber wharf, mesmerized by the sight of an elephant raising its trunk in the air and bellowing.

When watching an elephant had become quite normal, she braved the Port Authority building, made arrangements for her trunk, then sat on a wooden bench in the hot steamy air with nothing but her hat to shade her, and with which, from time to time, she swatted the clusters of flies that crawled along her hairline. Laurence had promised to be at the dockside, but so far there was no sign of him. She tried to recall what he'd said to do in the event of an emergency, and spotted Mr. Ravasinghe again, making his way out of the second-class hatch in the side of the ship. By avoiding looking at the man, she hoped to hide her flush of embarrassment at her predicament, and turned the other way to watch the haphazard load-

18

ing of tea chests onto a barge at the other end of the docks.

The smell of drains had long since overpowered the spicy fragrance of cinnamon and now mingled with other rank odors: grease, bullock dung, rotting fish. And as the dockside filled with more disgruntled passengers being besieged by traders and hawkers peddling gemstones and silk, she felt sick with nerves. What would she do if Laurence didn't come? He had promised. She was only nineteen, and he knew she'd never been further from Owl Tree Manor than a trip or two to London with Fran. Her spirits sank. It was too bad her cousin hadn't been able to travel out with her, but straight after the wedding Fran had been called away by her solicitor, and though Gwen would have entrusted Laurence with her life, all things considered, she couldn't help feeling a bit upset.

A swarm of seminaked brown-skinned children flitted among the crowd, offering bundles of cinnamon sticks, and with enormous, imploring eyes, begged for rupees. A child who couldn't have been more than five pulled out a bundle for Gwen. She held it to her nose and sniffed. The child spoke, but it was gobbledegook to Gwen, and sadly she had no rupees to give the urchin, nor any English money either, now.

She stood and walked about. There was a brief gust of wind, and from somewhere in the distance came a troubling sound — *boom, boom, boom.* Drums, she thought. Loud, but not quite loud enough to identify a regular beat. She didn't wander far from the small case she'd left by the bench, and when she heard Mr. Ravasinghe call out, she felt her forehead bead with perspiration.

"Mrs. Hooper. You cannot leave your case unguarded."

She wiped her forehead with the back of her hand. "I was keeping my eye on it."

"People are poor and opportunistic. Come, I'll carry your case and find you somewhere cooler to wait."

"You're very kind."

"Not at all." He held her by the elbow with just his fingertips and forged a path through the Port Authority building. "This is Church Street. Now look over there — just at the edge of Gordon Gardens is the Suriya, or tulip tree as it is known."

She glanced at the tree. Its fat trunk folded deeply like a woman's skirt, and a canopy studded with bright orange bell-shaped flowers offered an oddly flaming kind of shade.

"It will provide a degree of cool, though with the afternoon heat coming on so strong, and the monsoon not yet arrived, you will find little relief."

"Really," she said. "There's no need for you to stay with me."

He smiled and his eyes narrowed. "I cannot leave you here alone, a penniless stranger in our city."

Glad of his company, she smiled back.

They walked across to the spot he'd indicated, and she spent another hour leaning against the tree, perspiring and dripping beneath her clothes, and wondering what she'd let herself in for by agreeing to live in Ceylon. The noise had amplified, and though he stood close, hemmed in by the crowds, he still had to shout to be heard.

"If your husband has not arrived by three, I hope you won't mind my suggesting you retire to the Galle Face Hotel to wait. It is airy, there are fans and soft drinks, and you will be infinitely cooler."

She hesitated, reluctant to leave the spot. "But how will Laurence know I'm there?"

"He'll know. Anyone British of any standing goes to the Galle Face."

She glanced at the imposing façade of the Grand Oriental. "Not there?"

"Definitely not there. Trust me."

In the fierce brightness of the afternoon, the wind blew a cloud of grit into her face, sending tears streaming down her cheeks. She blinked rapidly, then rubbed her eyes, hoping she really could trust him. Perhaps he was right. A person could die in this heat.

A short distance from where she stood, a tight bundle had formed beneath rows and rows of fluttering white ribbons strung across the street, and a man in brown robes, making a repetitive high-pitched sound, stood in the center of a group of colorful women. Mr. Ravasinghe saw Gwen watching.

"The monk is pirith chanting," he said. "It is often required at the deathbed to ensure a good passing. Here I think it is because great evil may have transpired at that spot, or at the very least a death. The monk is attempting to purify the place of any remaining malignancy by calling for the blessings of the gods. We believe in ghosts in Ceylon."

"You are all Buddhists?"

"I myself am, but there are Hindus and Muslims too."

"And Christians?"

He inclined his head.

When by three there was still no sign of Laurence, the man held out a hand and took a step away. "Well?"

She nodded, and he called out to one of the rickshaw men, who wore very little more than a turban and a greasy-looking loin-cloth.

She shuddered at how thin the man's brown naked back was. "I'm surely not going in that?"

"Would you prefer a bullock cart?"

She felt herself redden as she glanced at the heap of oval orange fruits piled up in a cart that had huge wooden wheels and a matted canopy.

"I do beg your pardon, Mrs. Hooper. I shouldn't tease. Your husband uses carts to transport the tea chests. We would actually ride in a small buggy. Just the one bullock and with a shady palm-leaf hood."

She pointed at the orange fruits. "What are those?"

"King coconut. Only for the juice. Are you thirsty?"

Even though she was, she shook her head. On the wall just behind Mr. Ravasinghe, a large poster showed a dark-skinned woman balancing a wicker basket on her head and wearing a yellow and red sari. She had bare feet and gold bangles on her ankles and she wore a yellow headscarf. MAZZAWATTEE TEA, the poster proclaimed. Gwen's hands grew clammy and a flood of sickening panic swept through her. She was very far from home.

"As you can see," Mr. Ravasinghe was saying, "cars are few and far between, and a rickshaw is certainly faster. If you are unhappy, we can wait, and I'll try to obtain a horse and carriage. Or, if it helps, I can accompany you in the rickshaw."

At that moment, a large black car came hooting its way through the crowd of pedestrians, bicyclists, carts, and carriages, only narrowly missing numerous sleeping dogs. *Laurence,* she thought with a surge of relief, but when she looked in through the window of the passing vehicle, she saw it contained only two large middle-aged European women. One turned to look at Gwen, her face a picture of disapproval.

Right, Gwen thought, galvanized into action, *a rickshaw it is.*

A cluster of thin palms stood waving in the breeze outside the Galle Face Hotel, and the building itself sided the ocean in a very British way. When Mr. Ravasinghe had given her the oriental manner of salutation and a very warm smile, she was sorry to see him go but walked past the two curved staircases and settled herself to wait in the relative cool of the Palm Lounge. She instantly felt at home and closed her eyes, pleased to have a small respite from the almost total invasion of her senses. Her rest didn't last long. If Laurence were to arrive now, she was only too aware of the sorry state she was in, and that was not the impression she wanted to create. She sipped her cup of Ceylon tea, and then looked across the tables and chairs dotted about the polished teak floor. In one corner a discreet sign pinpointed the location of the ladies' powder room.

In the sweet-smelling, multiple-mirrored room, she splashed the repeated image of her face and applied a dab of Après L'Ondée, which luckily had been safely stowed in her small case and not in her drowned purse. She felt sticky, with sweat running down under her arms, but pinned up her hair again so that it coiled neatly at the nape of her neck. Her hair was her crowning glory, Laurence said. It was dark, long, and ringleted when unpinned. When she'd mentioned she was considering having it cut short like Fran's, flapper style, he'd looked horrified and tugged loose a curl at the back of her neck, then leaned down and rubbed his chin on top of her head. After that, with his palms placed on either side of her jaw, his fingers gathering up her hair, he'd stared at her.

"Never cut your hair. Promise me."

She'd nodded, unable to speak, the tingle from his hands so delicious that all manner of hitherto unfelt sensations arose in her.

Their wedding night had been perfect and so had the following week. On their final night neither of them had slept, and he'd had to rise before dawn in order to reach Southampton in time to board the ship for Ceylon. Though he was disappointed she wasn't coming with him, he had business in Ceylon and they agreed the time would soon pass. He hadn't minded her staying on to wait for Fran, but she had regretted the decision the moment he was gone and hardly knew how she would bear to be apart from him. Then, when Fran had been delayed still further in London over a property she was letting out, Gwen decided to travel alone.

With her captivating looks, Gwen had never been short of beaux, but she'd fallen for Laurence from the moment she spotted him at a musical evening Fran had taken her to in London, and when he had grinned at her and charged over determined to introduce himself, she was lost. They'd seen each other every day after that, and when he proposed, she'd raised a burning face

26

and, with no hesitation, said yes. Her parents had been none too pleased that a thirty-seven-year-old widower wanted to marry her, and her father had taken a little persuading but was impressed when Laurence offered to leave a manager in charge of the plantation and return to live in England. Gwen would not hear of it. If Ceylon was where his heart belonged, it was where her heart would belong too.

As she closed the powder room door behind her, she saw him standing with his back to her in the large entrance hall, and her breath caught in her throat. She touched the beads at her neck, adjusting the blue droplet so that it sat in the center, and, awed by the intensity of her feelings, stood still to drink in the sight of him. He was tall, with a good broad back and short, light brown hair, flecked with early gray at the temples. A product of Winchester College, he looked as if confidence ran in his veins: a man who women adored and men respected. Yet he read Robert Frost and William Butler Yeats. She loved him for it, and for the fact that he already knew she was far from the demure girl people expected her to be.

As if he had felt her eyes on him, he spun round. She took in the relief in his fierce brown eyes and the wide spreading smile as he came striding toward her. He had a square jaw and a cleft chin, which, along with the way his hair waved at the front and went crazy at the double crown, she found utterly irresistible. Because he was wearing shorts, she could see that his legs were tanned, and he looked so much more dusty and rugged here than he had done in the chilly English countryside.

Full of energy, she ran across to meet him. He held her at arm's length for just a moment, then wrapped her in a bear hug so tight she could hardly breathe. Her heart was still racing when he'd finished swinging her round and finally let her go.

"You have no idea how much I've missed you," he said, his voice deep and a little gruff.

"How did you know I was here?"

"I asked the harbormaster where the most beautiful woman in Ceylon had gone."

She smiled. "That's very nice, but of course I am not."

"One of the most adorable things about you is that you have no idea how lovely you are." He held both her hands in his. "I'm so sorry I was late."

"It doesn't matter. Someone looked after me. He said he knew you. Mr. Ravasinghe, I think that was his name."

"Savi Ravasinghe?"

"Yes." She felt the skin at the back of her neck prickle. He frowned and narrowed his eyes, increasing the fan of fine lines that were prematurely etched into his skin. She longed to touch them. He was a man who had lived and, to her, that made him even more attractive.

"Never mind," he said, quickly recovering his good humor. "I'm here now. The darned car had a problem. Luckily, Nick McGregor managed to sort it out. It's too late to drive back, so I'm just booking us rooms."

They walked back to the desk, then, finished with the clerk, he reached for her, and as his lips brushed her cheek her breath escaped in a little puff.

"Your trunk will go up by train," he said. "At least as far as Hatton."

"I know, I talked to the man in the Port Authority building."

"Right. McGregor will arrange for one of the coolies to fetch it from the station in a bullock cart. Will you have enough in that case until tomorrow?"

"Just about."

"Do you want some tea?" he said.

"Do you?"

"What do you think?"

She grinned and suppressed the urge to

laugh out loud as he asked the clerk to send the bags up double quick.

They walked to the stairs arm in arm, but once round the bend in the stairwell she felt unexpectedly shy. He let go of her and went on ahead to unlock and then throw open the door.

She took the last few steps and gazed in at the room.

Late-afternoon sunlight spilled through tall windows, tinting the walls a delicate shade of pink; the painted lamps either side of the bed were already lit and the room smelled of oranges. Looking at a scene so clearly set for intimacy, she felt a burst of heat at the back of her neck and scratched the skin there. The moment she had imagined over and over was finally here, and yet she stood hesitating in the doorway.

"Don't you like it?" he said, his eyes bright and shiny.

She felt her pulse jump in her throat.

"Darling?"

"I love it," she managed to say.

He came across to her and let loose the hair that was pinned up. "There. That's better."

She nodded. "They'll be bringing the bags."

"I think we have a few moments," he said,

and touched her bottom lip with his finger-tip. But then, as if on cue, there was a knock at the door.

"I'll just open the window," she said, stepping back, glad of an excuse not to let the porter witness her stupid anxiety.

Their room faced the ocean and as she pushed the window ajar she looked out at ripples of silvery gold where the sun caught the tips of the waves. This was what she wanted, and it wasn't as if they hadn't spent a week together in England, but home felt very distant and that thought brought her close to tears. She closed her eyes and listened as the porter carried in their bags, then, once the man had gone, she twisted back to look at Laurence.

He gave her a crooked smile. "Is something wrong?"

She bowed her head and stared at the floor.

"Gwen, look at me."

She blinked rapidly and the room seemed to hush. Thoughts raced through her mind as she wondered how to explain the sensation of being catapulted into a world she didn't understand, though it wasn't just that — the feeling of being naked under his gaze had unnerved her too. Not wanting the embarrassment to ambush her, she looked up and, moving very slowly, took a few steps toward him.

He looked relieved. "I was worried for a moment there."

Her legs began to shake. "I'm being silly. Everything is so new . . . You're so new."

He smiled and came to her. "Well, if that's all, it's easily remedied."

She leaned in toward him, feeling light-headed as he fumbled with the button at the back of her dress.

"Here, let me," she said and, reaching behind, slipped the button through the loop. "It's a knack."

He laughed. "One I shall have to learn."

An hour later and Laurence was asleep. Fueled by the long wait, their lovemaking had been intense, even more so than on their wedding night. She thought back to the moments when she first arrived in the country; it was as if the hot Colombo sun had sucked the energy from her body. She'd been wrong. There was abundant energy lying in reserve, although now as she lay listening to the threads of sound drifting in from the outside world, her arms and legs felt heavy and she wasn't far from sleep. She realized how perfectly natural lying beside Laurence was beginning to feel and, smiling at her earlier nervousness, shifted a little so that she could look at him while still feeling the strength of his body in the places where he seemed to be glued to her. Now that her love had somehow distilled into this perfect moment, she felt blanched of all other emotion. It was going to be all right. For another minute or two she breathed in the muskiness of him while watching the shadows of the room lengthen and then rapidly darken. She took a deep breath and closed her eyes.

2

Two days later Gwen woke early to sunlight streaming through her muslin curtains. She was looking forward to breakfasting with Laurence and then being taken on the grand tour. She sat on the side of the bed and undid the plaits in her hair, then swiveled round to sink her feet into a sleek fur rug. She glanced down and wriggled her toes in its whiteness, wondering what animal it had belonged to. Out of bed, she slipped on a pale silk gown someone had draped over a nearby chair.

They'd arrived at the plantation in the hill country the night before, just as the sun went down. With a head aching from exhaustion, and dazzled by the violent reds and purples of the evening sky, Gwen had fallen into bed.

Now she marched across the wooden floorboards and went to the window to pull the curtains apart. She took a deep breath when she looked out on the first morning of her new world and, blinking in the brightness, reeled at the barrage of buzzing, whistling, and chirping that filled the air.

Below her, gentle flower-filled gardens sloped down to the lake in three terraces, with paths, steps, and benches strategically placed between the three. The lake itself was the most gloriously shining silver she'd ever seen. All memory of the previous day's car journey, with its terrifying hairpin bends, deep ravines, and nauseating bumps, was instantly washed away. Rising up behind the lake, and surrounding it, was a tapestry of green velvet, the tea bushes as symmetrical as if they'd been stitched in rows, where women tea pickers wore eye-catching brightly colored saris and looked like tiny embroidered birds who had stopped to peck.

Just outside her bedroom window, there was a grapefruit tree beside another tree she didn't recognize, but that looked as if it was laden with cherries. She would actually pick some for breakfast, she decided. On the table out there, a small creature stared back at her with round saucerlike eyes, looking half monkey and half owl. She glanced back at the enormous four-poster bed, surrounded by a mosquito net. The satin spread was barely crumpled and she thought it odd that Laurence hadn't joined her. Perhaps, wanting her to have an uninterrupted sleep after the journey, he had gone to his own room. She looked round, hearing the door creak as it opened. "Oh, Laurence, I —"

"Lady. You must be knowing, I am Naveena. Here to wait on you."

Gwen stared at the small, square-shaped woman. She wore a long blue-and-yellow wraparound skirt with a white blouse and had a long graying plait that hung all the way down her back. Her round face was a mass of wrinkles and her dark-ringed eyes gave nothing away.

"Where's Laurence?"

"Master is at work. Since two hours going now."

Deflated, Gwen took a step back and sat on the bed.

"You wishing breakfast here?" The woman indicated a small table in the window. There was a pause as they stared at each other. "Or verandah?"

"I'd like to wash first. Where is the bathroom?"

The woman walked across to the other side of the room, and as she moved, Gwen noticed her hair and clothes were infused with an unusual spicy fragrance.

"Here, Lady," the woman said. "Behind screen is your bathing room, but latrine coolie not coming yet."

"Latrine coolie?"

"Yes, Lady. Coming soon."

"Is the water hot?"

The woman waggled her head. Gwen was unsure whether she had meant yes it was or no it wasn't, and realized she must have shown her uncertainty.

"There is wood-burn boiler, Lady. Albizia wood. Hot water coming in, morning and evening, one hour."

Gwen held her head high and attempted to sound more self-assured than she felt. "Very well. I shall wash first and then take breakfast outside."

"Very good, Lady."

The woman pointed at the French doors. "They open to verandah. I will go and come. Bring tea for you there."

"What is the creature out there?"

The woman turned to look, but the creature had gone.

In complete contrast to the sweltering humidity of Colombo, it was a bright but slightly chilly morning. After breakfasting she picked a cherry; the fruit was a lovely dark red, but when she bit, it tasted sour, and she spat it out. She wrapped her shawl round her shoulders and set off to investigate the house.

First she explored a wide, high-ceilinged corridor that ran the length of the house. The dark wooden floor gleamed and the walls were punctuated by oil lamps along its length. She sniffed the air. She'd expected the place to smell of cigar smoke, which it did, but it also smelled strongly of coconut oil and aromatic polish. Laurence called it a bungalow, but Gwen noticed a sweeping teak staircase that led off from an airy hall to another floor. On the other side of the stairs, a beautiful chiffonier inlaid with mother of pearl leaned against the wall, and next to that was a door. She pushed open the door and walked into a spacious drawing room.

Surprised by its size, she took a deep breath, opened one of the brown shuttered windows from a bank of windows running across the entire wall, and saw that this room also fronted the lake. As light filled the room she glanced around. The walls were painted the softest blue-green you could imagine and the general effect of the place was refreshingly cool, with comfy-looking armchairs and two pale sofas piled high with embroidered cushions depicting birds, elephants, and exotic flowers. A leopard skin hung across the back of one of the sofas.

Gwen stood on one of two navy-blue-and-cream Persian rugs and twirled round with her arms held out. This would do nicely. Very nicely indeed.

A deep growl startled her. She glanced down to see that she'd trodden on the paw of a sleeping short-haired dog. A glossy black Labrador she thought it might be, though not quite the usual kind. She took a step back, wondering if it might bite. At that moment a middle-aged foreign man almost soundlessly entered the room. A narrow-shouldered man, with small features and a saffron-brown face, he wore a white sarong, a white jacket, and a white turban.

"The old dog's name is Tapper, Lady. Master's favorite dog. I am butler, and here is tiffin." He held out the tray he was carrying, then deposited it on a small nest of tables. "Our own Broken Orange Pekoe."

"Really? I've only just had breakfast."

"Master will return after twelve. You will hear the workers' horn, Lady, and then he will be here." He indicated a wooden rack beside the fireplace. "There are magazines for you to read."

"Thank you."

It was a large stone-surround fireplace, with brass tongs, shovel and a poker, the usual trappings of a fire, and beside them an enormous basket piled high with logs. She smiled. A cozy evening lay ahead, with just the two of them curled up beside the fire.

She had just an hour before Laurence returned, so, ignoring the tea, she decided to explore the outside of the house. It had been dusk when they'd arrived in Laurence's new Daimler, and she hadn't been able to see what the front of the house really looked like. She found her way back along the corridor and into the main hall, then pushed open one of the dark double doors, with a pretty decorative fanlight above it, and found herself on the front step, under a shady porch. A gravel drive, lined with flowering tulip trees, and interspersed with palms, led away from the house and then twisted upward into the hills. A few of the blooms lay scattered like large orange tulips, bright against the grassy verge.

She longed to walk up into the hills but first went round to the side of the house, where a covered but wall-less room fronted the lake, though at a slightly different angle from her own room. This outdoor room or portico had eight dark wooden pillars, a marble floor and rattan furniture, and the table was already set for lunch. When a small striped squirrel raced up one of the pillars and disappeared behind a beam, she grinned.

Retracing her steps to the front of the house, she began to climb the gravel drive, counting the trees. The further she climbed, the stickier she felt, but she didn't want to look back until she reached twenty. As she counted and smelled the scent of Persian roses, the heat was building up, though thankfully still nothing like the blistering hub of Colombo. Either side of her, lush verges were carpeted with bushes crammed with large heart-shaped leaves and peachy white flowers.

At the twentieth tree she threw off her wrap, closed her eyes, and spun round. Everything glittered. The lake, the red roof of the house, even the air. She took a deep breath as if by doing so she might absorb every particle of the beauty before her: the scented flowers, the thrill of the view, the luminous green of the plantation hills, the sound of the birds. It was heady stuff. Nothing kept still, and the air, filled with vivid bustling life, buzzed in continuous motion.

From her vantage point the shape of the

house was clear. The back elevation was parallel with the lake, with the outdoor room on the right, and at one side of the house it looked like an extension had been added, thus forming an L. Beside it was a courtyard and a path that disappeared through a wall of tall trees. She took several more deep breaths of clean air.

The ugly loud hooting of the midday horn shattered the tranquillity. She had lost track of time, but her heart skipped a beat when she picked out Laurence with another man as they strode from the tall trees toward the house. He looked in his element, strong and in charge. She threw her shawl over her shoulder and made a dash for it. But running down the steep slope was more awkward than climbing up, and after a few minutes she slid on the gravel, caught her toe in a root, lost her footing, and fell forward so hard it forced the air from her lungs.

When she was able to breathe and attempted to stand, her left ankle gave way. She rubbed her grazed forehead and felt so dizzy she sat back on her behind, already feeling the start of another headache, set off by the sun's heat. It had been so cool earlier, she hadn't thought to wear a sun hat. From beyond the tall trees she heard a frightful shriek, like a cat or a child in pain, or perhaps a jackal. She didn't want to wait to find out, so she forced herself to stand again, this time managing not to yield to the pain, and began to hop back down to the house.

Just as she was in clear sight of the front door, Laurence came back out and hurried toward her.

"I'm so pleased to see you," she called out as her breath quickened. "I went up to see the view but I fell."

"Sweetheart, it isn't safe. There are snakes. Grass snakes, tree snakes. Snakes that rid the gardens of rats. All kinds of biting ants and beetles. Better not go off on your own. Not yet."

She pointed at where the women had been picking tea. "I'm not as delicate as I look, and those women were in the countryside."

"The Tamils know the land," he said as he came across to her. "Never mind, hold on to my arm and we'll get you inside, and I'll ask Naveena to strap that ankle up. I can get the local doctor down from Hatton if you like."

"Naveena?"

"The ayah."

"Oh yes."

"She looked after me as a child and I'm

fond of her. When we have children —"

Gwen raised her brows and gave him a slow smile. He grinned, then finished his sentence: "She'll look after them."

She stroked his arm. "What will I have to do?"

"There's plenty to do. You'll soon find out."

On the way back down to the house, she felt the warmth of his body against hers. Despite the pain in her ankle, she experienced the familiar tingle and lifted a hand to touch the deep cleft in his chin.

Once her ankle had been bandaged, they both sat down together in the outdoor room.

"Well," he said, with a sparkle in his eyes. "Do you like what you see?"

"It's perfect, Laurence. I'm going to be very happy here with you."

"I blame myself for your fall. I'd intended to talk to you last night, but your headache was so bad, I decided to wait. There are a few little things I need to mention."

She glanced up. "Oh?"

The furrows on his forehead deepened, and when he narrowed his eyes, it was clear how the sun had enhanced the wrinkles there.

"For your own safety, steer clear of work-force matters. You don't need to bother yourself with the labor lines."

"What on earth are they?"

"They're where the plantation workers and their families live."

"But that sounds interesting."

"To be honest, there's nothing much to see."

She shrugged. "Anything else?"

"Best not to wander about unaccompanied."

She snorted.

"Just until you're more familiar with things."

"Very well."

"Only allow Naveena to see you in your nightgown. She'll bring your morning tea at eight. Bed tea, they call it."

She smiled. "And do you stay with me for bed tea?"

"Every chance I get."

She blew him a kiss across the table. "I can't wait."

"Me neither. Now don't worry about a thing. You'll soon pick up on how things are done. You'll meet some of the other planters' wives tomorrow. She's a funny old bird, but Florence Shoebotham may be a great help to you."

"I haven't got anything left to wear."

He laughed. "That's my girl. McGregor

has already sent someone in a bullock cart to pick up your trunk from Hatton station. Later, I'll introduce you to the staff, but apparently there's a crate waiting for you from Selfridges too. Things you ordered before you came out, I'm guessing?"

She stretched out her arms, feeling suddenly brighter at the thought of the Waterford crystal and a wonderful new evening dress. The dress was just the thing, short with several layers of fringes in silver and pink. She remembered the day in London when Fran had insisted she have it made. Only ten days and Fran would be here too. A large jackdaw swept across the table and, quick as a wink, snatched a bread roll from the basket. She laughed and Laurence did too.

"There's a lot of wildlife. I saw a striped squirrel run into the verandah roof."

"There are two. They have a nest up there. They do no harm."

"I like that." She touched his hand and he lifted it to kiss her palm.

"One last thing. I'd almost forgotten, but it's probably the most essential point. Household matters are entirely your affair. I won't interfere. The household staff answer to you and only to you."

He paused.

"You may find things have gone a little awry. The staff have had their own way for far too long. It might be a struggle, but I'm sure you'll pull them back into shape."

"Laurence, it'll be fun. But you haven't really told me much about the estate itself."

"Well, it's a large Tamil workforce. The Tamil are excellent workers, unlike most of the Sinhalese. We house at least fifteen hundred. Provide a school of sorts, a dispensary, and basic medical aid. They have various benefits, a shop, subsidized rice."

"And the actual tea making?"

"That's all done in our tea factory. It's a long process but I'll show you one day, if you like."

"I'd love it."

"Good. So now that's settled, I suggest an afternoon rest," he said, standing up.

She looked down at the remains of their luncheon and hugged herself. She took a deep breath and let it out slowly. Now was the time. When Laurence bent down to kiss her forehead, she closed her eyes and couldn't stifle the sensation of pleasure, but as she opened her eyes, she saw he had already moved off.

"I'll see you this evening," he was saying. "I'm so sorry, darling, but I have to see McGregor now. The tea factory horn will sound at four, and I'll be away from the house then, but do sleep on."

She felt tears warm the back of her lids but wiped her eyes with her table napkin. She knew how busy Laurence was and, of course, the plantation had to come first, but was she only imagining that her lovely, sensitive husband was being just a teeny bit distant?

3

The next evening Gwen stood at her window looking at the sunset. The sky and water had turned almost the exact same shade of gold, and the lake was framed by hills in varying shades of sepia. She moved away and dressed carefully, then studied her reflection. The woman had helped thread silver beads through the heavy coil of hair at the nape of her neck, but Gwen teased out a ringlet at the side. Laurence had arranged a little supper party to launch her as the new mistress of Hooper's Plantation. She wanted to look her absolute best, though she'd decided to save her new dress for when Fran arrived. Then they could practice dancing the Charleston together.

Her dress tonight was pale green silk with a trim of lace at the neckline, and lower than she normally wore. It was, of course, drop-waisted, with chiffon godets hanging in points at the dangerously short hem. There was a knock at the door.

"Come in."

Laurence pushed open the door and stood with his legs slightly apart as they stared at each other.

He wore a black dress suit, white shirt, white waistcoat, and a white bow tie, and had attempted a parting in his hair. Gwen felt herself tremble under his prolonged gaze and held her breath.

"I . . . You . . . My God, Gwendolyn!" He swallowed.

"You look very handsome yourself, Laurence. I'd rather got used to you wearing shorts."

He came across, put an arm round her, and kissed her neck just below the hairline at the back. "You look ravishing."

She adored the feeling of his warm breath on her skin and knew the night was going to be wonderful. Who could doubt a man like Laurence? He was so strong, you just had to be near him to feel wanted, and so safe that nothing could ever go wrong.

"I mean it. You'll put all the others to shame in that dress."

She glanced down at her shimmering dress. "It is quite short."

"Maybe we all need a bit of a shake-up now and then. Don't forget your stole. Even with a fire it can be a little cool after sundown, as you probably gathered last night."

The night before Laurence had been busy with estate business, so the cozy time together beside the fire had not materialized. At nine, the servants had come in singly, and in strict order of importance. First, the turbaned butler, who was in charge of the whole house, then the head cook, or *appu* as he was known, who either was bald or had shaved halfway back to his crown, the remaining hair tied up in a fancy knot. He had slightly oriental features, as if somewhere in the past there had been an ancestor from Indo-China, and he wore a long white apron over a blue-and-gold sarong. Then Naveena had brought in hot goat's milk, sweetened with bee honey as opposed to jaggery, she had explained, before saying good night with a charming smile. She was followed by the five houseboys, who stood in a line and wished her good night in unison, and then, finally, it was the turn of the kitchen coolies, who simply gazed at their bare feet and bowed. Soon after the elaborate household-staff ritual had taken place, Gwen had gone to bed alone, claiming a painful ankle. Now she smiled at the thought of how strange it had been.

"What's so funny?" Laurence said.

"I was just thinking about the staff."

"You'll soon get used to them."

Laurence kissed her on the lips and she smelled soap and lemons on his skin. Arm in arm they left the room to go to the drawing room, where they were to enjoy cocktails before dinner.

"What is the scent the serving woman has about herself?" Gwen asked.

"Are you speaking of Naveena?"

"Yes."

"I don't know. It's probably a mix of cardamom and nutmeg. For as long as I can remember she has had it."

"How long has she worked here?"

"Since my mother ferreted her out to be my ayah."

"Poor Naveena. I can just imagine you as a boy, thundering about the place."

He laughed. "Mother assembled a family history of sorts: letters, photographs, birth certificates, wedding records, you know the kind of thing. Anyway, I think there may have been some photos of Naveena when she was younger."

"I'd love to see. I want to know everything about you."

"I haven't seen it all myself. Verity keeps a

box of that stuff in England. I am so looking forward to you meeting her, by the way."

"A shame she missed our wedding. Maybe she could bring the family albums over next time she visits?"

He nodded. "Of course."

"Was Naveena Verity's ayah too?"

"No, Verity had a younger woman as her ayah, until she went to boarding school, that is. It was hard for her when our parents died, poor girl. She was only ten."

"What happens when Naveena's too old to work?"

"Then we look after her," he said, and flung open the tall French doors. "Let's go via the verandah."

She took a step forward and laughed. Outside, the sounds were deafening. *Rat-tat-tat. Twee twee. Tap tap.* The rustles, whistles, and guttural croaks rose to a crescendo before dying back and starting over. Then came a *whoosh* of running water and a loud *scree scree scree,* and the singing of cicadas filling the humid air. Over in the dark bushes minute flashes of light darted and swooped in their dozens.

"Fireflies," he said.

Gwen glimpsed flaming torches down by the lake.

"I thought afterward we'd take a midnight

stroll," Laurence said. "The lake is gorgeous lit only by torches and the moon."

She smiled, unable to contain her pleasure at the raucous night.

"And there's less danger of running into a water buffalo at night. They have poor eyesight, so tend to stagger into the water in the middle of the day when it's hot."

"Goodness, do they?"

"Make no mistake, they are dangerous, and will gore or trample you if they're feeling particularly aggressive. Don't worry, we don't get many here. It's up on Horton Plains that they're prolific."

Back in the drawing room, Florence Shoebotham and her husband, Gregory, were the first to arrive, and while Laurence and Mr. Shoebotham talked over by the drinks cabinet, Gwen sipped a sherry and made small talk with his wife. The woman was large, with the typical wide hips and narrow shoulders of an Englishwoman. She wore a pale yellow floral dress almost to her ankles and had a high-pitched, squeaky voice, which sounded odd coming from someone so large.

"Well, you are a little young thing, aren't you?" Florence said, her chins wobbling as she spoke. "I do hope you'll be able to cope."

Gwen tried her best not to laugh. "Cope?"

Florence plumped the cushion that had been behind her on the sofa, then held it on her lap as she shifted closer to Gwen. The woman had a low forehead and her hair was a faded salt-and-pepper color, wiry and hard to control by the look of it. Gwen smelled a mix of gin and body odor.

"I'm sure you'll soon grow used to our ways. Take my advice, girl, and whatever you do, don't become over friendly with the servants. It doesn't do. They don't like it and they will not respect you for it."

"I was always friendly with our maid in England."

"It's different here. The dark races are different, you see. Kindness does them no good. No good at all. And the mongrel are even worse."

As more couples were announced, Gwen felt disturbed. She knew the word *mongrel* but hated hearing it used like that.

"Treat them like children, and keep your eyes on your *dhobi*. Only last week I found my silky Chinese pajamas had been swapped for some old things that must have come from the street market in Hatton."

Gwen was now completely at sea and beginning to panic. How could she keep her eyes on the *dhobi*, when she didn't even know who — or what — a *dhobi* was?

She looked around the room. This was supposed to be a small supper party, but there were more than a dozen couples already, and plenty of space for more. She tried to catch her husband's eye but had to laugh when she saw Laurence absorbed in conversation with a bald man whose ears stuck out at right angles from his head. A teapot man.

"Probably talking about the price of tea," Florence said, seeing her look.

"Is there a problem with tea prices?"

"Oh no, dear. Quite the opposite. We're all doing rather swimmingly well. Your husband's new Daimler should be enough to convince you of that."

Gwen smiled. "It is rather splendid."

A white-coated houseboy, positioned by the door, sounded a brass gong.

"Now don't worry, if there's anything, just ask. I'm happy to help. I can remember how it felt to be young and newly married. So much to take in." Florence discarded her cushion, then held out her hand. Gwen recognized it was a command, so she stood to help the woman up.

The dining room looked pretty with all the silver candelabra lit. Everything gleamed or sparkled, and the air smelled fresh from sweet peas arranged in shallow glass vases dotted about. Gwen spotted a trim, youngish woman smiling broadly at Laurence. She had green eyes, pronounced cheekbones, and a long neck. Her blond hair was styled so that it looked like a waving bob from the front, but when she turned sideways, Gwen saw that her hair was long and knotted elegantly at the back. She was heavily laden with rubies and dressed, quite simply, in black. Gwen tried to catch her eye, hoping they might soon become friends.

The mild-looking, bespectacled man sitting on her left introduced himself as Partridge. She took in his slightly jutting chin, the small bristly mustache, and the kind look in his gray eyes. He hoped she was settling in and told her she should call him John.

As they spoke a little longer, all eyes were on her, but soon the conversation turned to the latest gossip from Nuwara Eliya — who was who and what they'd done, to whom, and why. Most of it went over Gwen's head. She didn't know any of the people concerned and found it hard to care. Only when the table went quiet and the teapot man banged his fist on the table did she pick up and take notice.

"Bloody disgrace if you ask me. Should

have shot the lot of them."

There were a few "hear hears" from one or two others as the man continued with his diatribe.

"What are they talking about, John?" Gwen whispered.

"There was a skirmish in Kandy recently. The British government acted rather brutally with the offenders, it seems. Now that has caused uproar. Thing is, there's word on the street that it wasn't a protest against the British at all, but something to do with remembrance flowers."

"So we're not in any danger?"

He shook his head. "No. It just gives some of the old colonels something to bang on about. It all began about ten years ago when the British shot at a gathering group of Muslims. It was all a bit of a blunder, as a matter of fact."

"It doesn't sound very satisfactory."

"No. You see, the Ceylon National Congress are not actually asking for independence yet, just for more autonomy." He shook his head. "But if you ask me, we need to tread more carefully. What with everything going on in India, it won't be long before Ceylon follows suit. It's still early days, but mark my words, trouble is brewing."

"Tell me, are you a socialist?"

"No, my dear, I'm a doctor."

She smiled at the amusement in his eyes, but then his look grew serious.

"The trouble is that only three Kandyans were elected to the council, so this year some of them left the Ceylon National Congress and they've created the Kandyan National Assembly instead. That's what we've got to keep an eye on, that and the Young Lanka League, who are beginning to promote opposition to the British."

Gwen glanced over to Laurence at the other end of the table, hoping he might give her the sign they'd agreed on for the ladies to withdraw, but he was looking into the distance with narrowed eyes.

"We feed them," another of the men was saying, "look after them, give them a roof over their heads. We more than meet all the required standards. What more do they want? Personally —"

"But there is much more we could do," Laurence said, interrupting him while clearly controlling his temper. "I've built a school, yet hardly any of the children attend. It's time we found a solution."

His wave of hair was sticking up at the front, a sure sign he had been raking his fingers through it, and she realized it was something he did when he felt uneasy. It made him seem younger than he was, and she desperately wanted to hug him.

The doctor tapped her hand.

"Ceylon is . . . well, Ceylon is Ceylon. You'll form your own impression soon enough," he said. "Change is still a way off, but we won't remain immune to Gandhi's message of *swaraj* forever."

"*Swaraj?*"

"Self-governance."

"I see. Would that be a bad thing?"

"At this stage, who knows."

After all the guests had gone, she was thrilled when Laurence came to her room and fell spread-eagled on her bed. With a log fire blazing, the room was too warm. Would they be going down to the lake together now?

"Come on, darling," he said. "Come and join me."

She went across to him and lay down on top of the counterpane, fully dressed. He sat up, resting his weight on one elbow, and grinned.

"God, you're lovely."

"Laurence, who was the blond woman in black? I didn't get a chance to talk to her."

"Black?"

"Yes. There was only one."

He frowned. "You must mean Christina Bradshaw. She's an American widow. Her husband was the banker Ernest Bradshaw, hence all the jewels."

"She doesn't look like a grieving widow." She paused and looked at his intelligent, well-shaped face. "Laurence, you do love me, don't you?"

He looked surprised. "What's brought this on?"

She bit her lip, wondering exactly how to say it. "But you don't . . . what I mean to say is, I've felt a bit lonely since I arrived at the plantation. I want to spend time with you."

"You're with me now."

"That's not what I meant."

There was a brief silence, during which Gwen felt a little unsure of herself. "What's the tree outside my window?" she said. "It looks just like a cherry tree."

"Oh Christ, you didn't try one, did you?" She nodded. "Bitter fruit. They make chutney out of it. I never touch the stuff." He rolled on top of her suddenly, then, pinning her down, kissed her on the mouth. She liked the slight smell of alcohol on his breath and, flushed with expectation, parted her lips. He traced the outline of her mouth with his finger and she felt her muscles lose all their tension, but then something odd happened. As he drew in his breath and stiffened, she caught a glimpse of something disturbing in his eyes. She touched his cheek, wanting to make it go away, but he stared at her — almost stared through her — as if he didn't know who she was. Then he swallowed rapidly, got up, and walked away.

She froze for a moment, then ran to the door to call to him, but after a few steps along the corridor, she saw he was already heading up the stairs. Rather than allow any of the servants to catch her chasing after her husband, she turned back to her room and, once inside, leaned against the door to steady her breath. She closed her eyes and gave in to a hollow, lonely feeling. Her vision of the torchlit midnight lake was over too. What on earth was the matter with him?

She undressed and climbed into bed. Accustomed to straightforward emotions, she felt confused, and while longing to feel Laurence's arms round her, a wave of homesickness swept over her. Her father might have patted her hand and said, "Chin up," and her mother would probably shoot her a commiserating look as she brought in a mug of cocoa. Cousin Fran, with a hopeless pretense at a stern face, would simply tell her to toughen up. She wished she were more like Fran. Nobody approved when Fran went to see that medium, Madame Sostarjinski, but Fran went all the same, and who could blame her when her parents had died so tragically when the *Titanic* sank.

With her worries over Laurence thwarting any attempt to sleep, and feeling she'd probably stay awake all night, Gwen lay on her back with her eyes wide open. He must have his reasons, she thought, but surely nothing that would explain that strange look in his eyes?

4

A whole week had passed, and Gwen was sitting in the drawing room. Now more accustomed to the unobtrusive, light-footed servants appearing and disappearing, she waited for those she had summoned to meet her. She had been watching the workings of the household and preparing notes on what she'd seen. But still Laurence had not shared her bed. There always seemed to be some reason she could not contradict. She had learned not to look at Naveena's face as she carried in her bed tea on a silver tray. It would be obvious to the woman that Gwen slept alone, and Gwen, cringing at the prospect of becoming an object of pity, knew she'd have to sort this out alone.

She squared her shoulders and, though it upset her, she decided she wouldn't think about it, at least not for the time being. Laurence was probably worrying about plantation affairs, and she felt sure he would come round soon. In the meantime, she would keep busy and get on with being the best wife she could be. Of course, she didn't feel in direct competition with Laurence's first wife, Caroline; she just wanted Laurence to be proud of her.

She heard a knock on the door and wiped her slightly clammy palms on her skirt. Naveena, the *appu,* the butler, and a couple of the houseboys came in.

"Are we all here?" she said with a smile, and clasped her hands together so as to conceal her nerves.

"Kitchen coolies are busy," Naveena said. "And other houseboys too. This is all are coming."

The butler and Naveena were Sinhalese. The rest of the group were Tamil. She hoped they all understood English and got along well with each other.

"Well, I've called this little meeting so that you might all understand my plans."

She glanced at each one in turn.

"I have made a list of the different areas of your work, and I have some questions."

Nobody spoke.

"Firstly, where does our milk come from? I see no cows on the estate."

The *appu* raised his hand. "The milk is coming every day, from buffalo, down in

65

the valleys."

"I see. So the supply is plentiful?"

He nodded. "And we have two nanny goats, isn't it."

"Excellent. Now my next question is which day does the *dhobi* come?"

"You are arranging with him, Lady."

"Does he speak English?"

"He speaks English also, not very good."

"But enough?"

The man waggled his head.

She still wasn't sure whether that meant yes or no, but at least she'd already discovered that the *dhobi* was the man who took care of all the laundry. She also knew he was employed by more than one estate, and she wanted to know if she might employ him exclusively.

She looked at their expectant faces. "The next thing is that I am planning a little kitchen garden."

They looked at each other uncertainly.

"A garden coming in the kitchen?" the *appu* asked.

She smiled. "No, a garden for growing vegetables for the kitchen. We have so much land it is only sensible. But I will need workers to tend it."

The butler shrugged. "We are not gardeners, Lady. We have a gardener."

"Yes, but it will be too much for just one man." She had seen the gardener: an unusually fat little man, with a small head framed by frizzy black hair, and a neck as wide as his head.

"He is every time coming, but, Lady, ask to Mr. McGregor," Naveena said. "He may be giving men from the labor lines."

Gwen smiled. She still had not been formally introduced to Nick McGregor, and this would be the ideal opportunity to make friends with him. She rose from her seat.

"Well, thank you all. That will do for today. I shall speak with you individually about changes to your daily routine."

They each stood and bowed, and she left the room, pleased with how it had gone.

Apart from the Labrador, she'd also discovered two young spaniels, Bobbins and Spew, with whom she'd made friends, spending hours throwing sticks and chasing about. As they followed her down the corridor now, her thoughts returned to Laurence. She sucked in her breath and pressed her lips together. What was she going to say to Fran, who was due any day now? She could hardly force her husband to make love to her, although she'd have a good try. Before their wedding, when they'd talked about having a family, he'd said the more the merrier, five at least; and recalling the wonderful time they'd had in England, and in the hotel when she first arrived, she couldn't figure out what had gone wrong.

It was almost time for lunch, and she decided to tempt Laurence to her room straight afterward and insist on an explanation. It was his day off and he couldn't possibly use work as an excuse.

And so, after lunch as they wiped their mouths with the embroidered linen napkins, she stood and, with fingers aching to touch him, held out her hand. He took it and she pulled him up to her, noticing his palms were cool, then she tilted her head and batted her lashes.

"Come."

In her room she closed the shutters but left the window glass open so that air could still pass through. He stood absolutely still with his back to the window and they stared at each other without speaking.

"I won't be a moment," she said.

His face gave nothing away.

She walked into her bathroom, slipped out of her day dress, unbuttoned her silk stockings and rolled them down — in the heat of Ceylon she had abandoned her corset before she'd even left the ship — then removed her lacy French chemise and

68

matching knickers, and took off her suspenders and earrings, leaving only the rope of pearls at her neck. Totally naked, apart from the pearls, she glanced in the mirror. Her cheeks were flushed from three glasses of wine, and she added color to her lips by dabbing on a touch of Rigaud rouge in Persian Blush. She watched herself in the mirror as she smoothed it over with a finger and then rubbed a little on her throat. Munitions: that was what Fran called powder and rouge.

Back in the room, Laurence was sitting on the bed with closed eyes. She tiptoed across and then stood in front of him. He didn't open his eyes.

"Laurence?"

When her breasts were level with his chest she pressed herself against him. He put his hands on her waist and held her away for a moment, then opened his eyes and gazed up at her. She watched as he took one nipple in his mouth and, feeling her knees about to give way, almost passed out at the current that ran through her, intensified by the sight of him observing everything that must be showing on her face.

They stayed like that for a short while, and then he let her go. As he kicked off his shoes, unbuttoned his braces, then removed his trousers and undergarments, she felt her heart thump. He pushed her back on the bed and the hairs on the nape of her neck rose as he straddled her, then adjusted his position. When he entered her, she gasped at a sensation that made her heart knock against her ribs and seemed to swallow her breath. Excited by a complete loss of inhibition, she dug her fingernails into his back. But then something changed; his eyes glazed over and he was going too fast. She had encouraged this, but now she couldn't keep up, and with the sudden absence of connection between them, it felt wrong. How could he have become so quickly consumed by something that didn't feel as if it was anything to do with her? She asked him to slow down, but he didn't seem to hear and then, after just a few seconds, he groaned, and it was over.

He straightened up but turned his head away as he recovered his breath.

There was silence for a moment or two as she struggled with her feelings.

"Laurence?"

"I'm so sorry if I hurt you."

"You didn't. Laurence, look at me." She turned his head toward her. The truth was he had hurt her a little, and, shocked by the emptiness in his eyes, her own filled with tears.

"Darling, tell me what the matter is. Please," she said.

She wanted him to say something, anything that would bring him back to her.

"I feel so . . ."

She waited.

"It's being here," he eventually said, and looked at her so wretchedly that she reached out, wanting to comfort him. He lifted her hand, turned over her palm, and kissed it.

"It's not you. You are utterly precious to me. Please believe that."

"So what is the matter?"

He let go of her hand and shook his head.

"I'm sorry. I can't do this," he said, then pulled his clothes on quickly and left the room.

Completely bewildered, and feeling as if her heart might break at the change in him, she pulled the pearls from her neck. The clasp broke and they clattered across the floor. *Why* couldn't he do this? She wanted him so much and, in the certain belief of his love, had pinned everything on being a good wife and mother. She knew that he had wanted her, really wanted her — look at how he'd been in Colombo! But having come all this way, now she didn't know

71

where to turn.

She must have fallen asleep, because she didn't hear Naveena enter the room, and jumped when she opened her eyes and saw the Sinhalese woman sitting in the chair beside the bed, her soft round face looking composed, with a jug cradled in her lap and all the pearls collected in a saucer on the bedside table.

"I have lemonade, Lady."

The expression in her dark eyes was so kind that Gwen burst into tears. Naveena held out a hand and put her fingertips on Gwen's arm, just a light touch. Gwen stared at the woman's rough brown-skinned hand, so dark against her own whiteness. Naveena looked as if she had the wisdom of the ages in her eyes, and Gwen was drawn to her composure. Though longing to have Naveena hold her and gently stroke her hair, she remembered Florence Shoebotham's words and turned away. Best not become too friendly with the servants.

A little later, anxious to get out of the house to try to salvage something of the day, Gwen dressed quickly but couldn't stop the turmoil in her mind. She remembered her hat and decided to explore what might lie beyond the tall trees at the side of the house. It was quiet and the air hung lazily in the solid afternoon heat. Even the birds were sleeping and the only sound came from the hum of insects. She walked out of the back door and passed by the lake. A pale lilac haze had spread over it for as far as she could see. Laurence had told her she could only swim under supervision, so she ignored her inclination to peel off her dress and slip into the water.

The usually green hills on the other side of the lake were now blue, and it was harder to pick out the colorful shapes of the women pickers. Her first impression had remained, however. Exotic birds they were, with a basket hung over their shoulders and their saris of every hue. She now knew that all the laborers on the estate were Tamils; the Sinhalese thought it shameful to work for a wage as laborers, though a few were happy to work indoors, and so the plantation owners had turned to India. Some Tamils had actually lived on the plantation for generations, Laurence said. And though she had been told not to, Gwen wanted to see what the labor lines looked like. She imagined cozy cottages and soft, round-bellied children sleeping in hammocks hanging from the trees.

She reached the courtyard, bordered by

the kitchens on one side. The trees marked the end, and the house and terraces to the lake formed the other two sides of the square. Just as she was about to cross the gravel yard, a man wearing little more than rags shuffled to the open kitchen door. She watched as he held out two hands and wobbled his head. A kitchen boy came out, shouted, and then pushed the man away. In the kerfuffle, the man fell to the ground. The kitchen boy gave him a kick, then marched back indoors, slamming the door.

Gwen hesitated for a moment, but as the man still lay groaning on the gravel, she plucked up her courage and ran across to him.

"Are you all right?" she said.

The man looked at her with black eyes. His hair was scruffy, he had a broad and very dark-skinned face, and when he spoke, she had no idea what he was saying. He pointed at his bare feet and she saw a suppurating sore.

"Gracious, you can't walk around on that. Here, take my arm."

The man gazed at her blankly, so she held out her hand to assist him. Once he was firmly holding on, she encouraged him with gestures to move back toward the kitchens. He shook his head and tried to pull away.

"But you must. That wound needs washing and treating." She pointed at his foot. He attempted to pull away again, but owing to his condition, she was the stronger of the two.

Once they managed to reach the kitchen door, she turned the handle and pushed. Three pairs of eyes watched as they entered the room. None of the three people moved. As Gwen and the man reached the table, she pulled out a chair with one hand and then settled the injured man onto it.

The kitchen boys were muttering in what she assumed was Tamil, because the man on the chair seemed to understand and attempted to rise. Gwen placed her hand on his shoulder and pressed, then glanced around. She could smell kerosene and noticed that two meat safes and several cream-colored cupboards had their legs standing in bowls of the stuff; to kill the insects, she assumed. There were a couple of low sinks and a cooking range, clearly fed from the great pile of wood stacked neatly at its side. The whole room smelled of a mixture of human sweat, coconut oil, and the curry they'd had for lunch. Her first curry.

"Now," she said as she pointed at two large water tubs next to the sinks. "I need a

75

bowl of lukewarm water and some muslin."

The kitchen boys stared at her. She repeated her request, adding, "Please." Still, nobody moved. She was wondering what to do when, at that moment, the *appu* walked in. She smiled, thinking she might get somewhere with him; after all, he regularly wished her good night and had been pleasant at their meeting. But one look at his face showed he was not happy.

"What is this?"

"I want them to bring water so that I can clean this man's wound," she said.

The *appu* picked his teeth, then made an odd whistling noise through them. "You cannot."

Gwen felt her skin prickle. "What do you mean, I cannot? I am mistress of Hooper's and I must insist you get them to do as I ask."

He looked as if he was tempted to stand his ground, but then, seeming to remember his place, he turned to one of the kitchen coolies and, with a scowl, muttered and pointed at the sink. The boy scurried off and a minute later came back with a bowl of water and some scraps of muslin. She could see that Laurence was right. Some of the staff had clearly had their own way for too long. Gwen dipped a piece of muslin in the water and then cleaned for as long as the man was able to bear it.

"This man's foot is badly infected," she said. "If it is not treated he could lose it."

The *appu* shrugged, and she could see the opposition in his eyes. "The factory and field workers are not coming to the house."

"Do you know what happened to him?" she asked.

"A nail, Lady."

"Where is the iodine?"

The kitchen boys looked at the *appu,* who shrugged again.

"Iodine, man, and be sharp about it," Gwen said, the tension knotting between her shoulder blades.

The man went to a cupboard on the wall and took out a small bottle, and Gwen could see he bristled with ill-concealed resentment as he did so. It didn't matter what the cook thought, she told herself; what mattered was helping this poor man.

"And bandages?" Gwen added.

The cook took out a roll of bandage, then passed it and the bottle of iodine to a kitchen boy, who passed it to Gwen.

"He injure hisself, Lady," the cook said. "Very lazy man. Make trouble."

"I don't care. And while you're at it, give him a bag of rice. Does he have a family?"

"Six children, Lady."

"Then give him two bags of rice."

The cook's mouth fell open in protest, but he seemed to think better of it, shrugged, and ordered the kitchen coolie to fetch the rice.

When Gwen had finished her work on the man's foot, she helped him to his feet as the *appu* and the coolies stared. It wasn't easy getting the man through the door, and she could have done with a helping hand. But together they managed to leave the house and walk toward the screen of tall trees. She heard a commotion break out behind her in the kitchen but held her head high and continued along the well-trodden path between the trees, with the man leaning on her as he hopped. When he attempted to disengage in order to put his bandaged foot to the ground, she shook her head.

It was densely wooded, with roots spreading across the path. Not only was she taking his weight on one arm, with the other hand she was batting away a million winged creatures. They walked maybe half a mile, through watery green light with patches of brightness and an intense smell of leaves, earth, and rotting vegetation, their progress so slow she lost any accurate sense of distance.

After a while, where the trees thinned and then opened out into a clearing, she heard the sound of children shouting. Farther along the dirt path, she saw a row of about a dozen wood-planked huts with tin roofs, all attached to each other like a sort of shanty terrace. Among the trees other similar lines of huts — some with tin roofs, some with palm leaf — could be seen stretching in every direction. Each had a row of rooms opposite, clearly sawdust lavatories that stank to high heaven. Bright saris of red, green, and purple hung on washing lines, and litter fluttered about on the compacted earth. Several old men, wearing only loincloths, were sitting cross-legged outside their huts, smoking foul tobacco, with scrawny hens pecking the ground around them.

A woman came out. Seeing Gwen, she raised her voice to the man and called three of the children in. The rest of them gathered around Gwen, chattering excitedly and pointing at different parts of her clothing. One of the bolder ones touched her skirt.

"Hello," she said, and held out her hand, but the child stepped back as if suddenly shy. She made a mental note to bring sweets next time she came.

They all looked the same, very dark and

shiny skinned, with black waving hair, thin bodies, and large stomachs. They gazed at her with beautiful brown eyes, eyes that didn't seem like the eyes of young children. One or two didn't appear well, and they all looked undernourished.

"Are these your children?" she asked the man.

Clearly unable to understand her, he shrugged.

As Gwen watched a solid little bird pecking in search of worms and insects, the woman who had called out came up to Gwen and bowed but kept her eyes lowered. Her hair was parted in the middle and she had wide nostrils, pronounced cheekbones, and long-lobed ears. The man passed her the two bags of rice. The woman took them and this time glanced at Gwen, with something in her eyes that Gwen could not fathom. It seemed like dislike, or maybe fear. It may even have been pity, and if it was pity, that was something far less easy to comprehend. The woman had so little and she, Gwen, had everything. Even the Tamil's jewelry consisted of just a row of red seedpods. The woman bowed again, then pulled aside the ragged curtain covering the front of the hut and disappeared inside. Each hut was about ten foot by twelve, not as big as

Laurence's boot room, and must be cold at night.

In not much more than an instant, the sky turned red. She heard the crickets clicking and, from down by the lake, the chorus of frogs starting up. She let go of the man's arm and took a step away, then turned and ran back toward the trees, just as night was falling in the sudden way it did.

It was dark along the path, the tall canopy of trees blocking the scant remains of daylight. She felt a shiver of fear. There were sounds in the woods: rustles and creaks, the patter of feet, heavy snuffling. Laurence had told her there were wild boar and they had been known to attack. She wondered what else there might be. Deer maybe, certainly snakes. Tree snakes, grass snakes. They didn't sound too bad. But what about hooded cobras? She picked up her pace. Laurence had warned her, and she hadn't listened. What had she been thinking? It became hard to breathe in the suffocating darkness and impossible to see the path ahead. She had to find her way by touch alone, and as her feet tangled in trailers, she faltered and grazed her forehead and arm on a coarse tree trunk.

Her heart was racing by the time she saw the twinkling lights of the house, and only when she eventually stumbled through the last of the trees and into the courtyard did she breathe more freely.

But then, as she crossed the dark yard, a voice called out in an imperious tone. It wasn't the night watchman.

Darn it, she thought, recognizing the Scottish accent. Of all people. And she'd wanted to make a good impression.

"It's me, Gwendolyn," she said as she reached him at the door and turned her face to the light.

"What the dickens were you doing coming out of the trees like that?"

"I'm so sorry, Mr. McGregor."

"You may be in charge of the household, but I think you will find everything that happens on this estate is my affair. You, Mrs. Hooper, are not expected to be anywhere near the labor lines. I take it that's where you were coming from?"

Stung by a sense of injustice, she spoke up. "I was just trying to help."

She looked at the broken veins in his cheeks. He was a beefy-looking man with reddish hair, thinning at the temples, and a heavy neck that would turn to jowls. His mustache was sandy, his lips thin, and his eyes were steely blue. He took hold of her grazed upper arm quite roughly.

"You are hurting me," she said. "I'll thank you to remove your hand, Mr. McGregor."

He gave her an unpleasant look. "Your husband shall hear of this, Mrs. Hooper."

"You're quite right," she said, with more poise than she actually felt. "He will."

At that moment Gwen was enormously relieved to see Laurence come out of the house. He smiled but there was a moment of strain as he and McGregor stared at each other without speaking. The moment passed and Laurence reached out a hand to her. "Let's get you fixed up."

She felt shaken but gave him a weak smile and took his hand.

Laurence turned to McGregor. "Come on, Nick, there's no harm done. Gwen will soon get the hang of things."

McGregor looked fit to explode but didn't speak.

"It's still early days. We must make allowances." Then Laurence put an arm round her. "Here, lean on me."

Her dash through the dark trees had made her feel vulnerable, and she recognized she had wrong-footed McGregor with Laurence. Something about the man alarmed her, though it wasn't just him — the deprivation of the labor lines had bothered her too. And though not quite as comfortable with Laurence as she had been before the bedroom incident, she still felt intensely glad to have his arms round her and hoped there might be a chance to talk about what had happened between them.

The next morning, after drawing up a new plan for the cleaning roster and trying to make sense of the household accounts for more than two hours, she consigned them to the back of her mind. McGregor's attitude was more difficult to ignore, and the trouble was that she needed his help to find her some gardeners.

She picked up a small drawing of her plan for her scented arbor; maybe white jasmine woven through a decorative metal trellis, she thought, as she went out through the French doors.

The lake shimmered under a bright blue sky, deep navy in the shade but almost silver in the sunshine, with little flecks of green. She walked past the blue jacaranda tree and smelled some unknown blossom in the air. A couple of magpies took off from a lawn composed of stiffer grass than one found in England, though it was well kept and neatly mown. She wanted somewhere to make her mark yet didn't want to upset the old Tamil, who regarded the lawns and flower beds as his own. She would have to ask Laurence about a location for the kitchen garden, but for the time being she'd look out for the best spot to create her arbor.

Bobbins and Spew were getting under her feet, in the way they did. She threw the ball hard and it vanished into the bushes, near where the magpies had been pecking at worms.

"There," she said. "Find that one!"

Spew was the daring one and wherever the ball would go, there would go Spew. She watched as he shuffled on his belly, through a gap, into an overgrown part of the garden.

She was feeling irritable. When she had gone in search of Laurence that morning, she'd bumped into Naveena, who told her she'd just left a note on her dressing table, a note from the master.

On tearing it open, Gwen had seen, in Laurence's strong forward-sloping hand, that he was letting her know she wouldn't see him for another two days. They hadn't even had a chance to talk. Now she read that he'd gone to Colombo to fetch Fran; and as a justice of the peace and unofficial police magistrate, he also had a report to file at the court in Hatton. Tempers had frayed in a local village, so he'd had to pacify the natives and decide on the true culprit.

Gwen felt a burst of homesickness. She gave herself a talking-to but couldn't help feeling annoyed that he hadn't told her himself, nor had he asked if she wanted to accompany him. Though he had mentioned it would be hot as hell in Colombo with the monsoon now overdue. At least here, high up in the central hills at Dickoya, it remained quite cool and, now that she was hoping to spend the rest of the day outside, she was glad of that.

As she called Spew, Mr. Ravasinghe came to mind again. She realized she had found herself returning to their encounter on several occasions. He'd been the soul of consideration, but she'd felt a hint of something more than could be explained away by his nut-brown skin, his long wavy hair, or his dark, glittering eyes.

There was no sign of the spaniel.

Bobbins was digging, backside in the air, exactly where Spew had vanished after the ball, next to a bank of anthuriums with the heart-shaped leaves and peachy flowers that she'd noticed on her first morning. Gwen walked over and patted the little dog.

"Where's he gone, eh, Bobbins?"

She heard a bark and peered through a

small gap in the shade of a large tree, but the light was too dim to see much. She pulled at a tangle of some kind of creeper. It gave way surprisingly easily, and once she'd yanked away more of it, she found a sort of overgrown tunnel between the trees. A tunnel had to lead somewhere. She made an opening large enough to squeeze through, scratching her forearm on some vicious thorns, but once through, could almost stand upright.

"Spew, I'm coming to get you," she called.

The tunnel curved round a bend and then led to a flight of moss-covered stone steps leading downward. She glanced back at the light coming from the entrance of the tunnel. *It's safe enough,* she thought, though there might be snakes. She stood absolutely still and glanced around at the ground; nothing moved, and with no breeze in the enclosed space, not even the leaves were rustling.

She carried on, hearing only her own footsteps, the whine of mosquitoes and Bobbins panting.

At the bottom of the slippery steps she came to a very small clearing, though she guessed it might once have been larger. Here, the bushes and creepers had encroached in such a way that there was only just space for her to sit on a slab of stone resting across a couple of tree stumps. It was almost like the childhood den she and Fran had built in the woods at Owl Tree; the light was shadowy, and all exterior sounds were muffled by trees. It was peaceful, and Bobbins lay silently at her feet. She sniffed, recognizing honeysuckle, but also a bitter leafy smell.

The quiet was broken when Spew crawled back into the clearing on his belly, his pink nose covered in earth and carrying something in his mouth.

"Drop it, Spew!" she said.

The little dog growled and stood his ground.

"Come here, you naughty dog, and drop!"

He didn't obey.

Gwen stood up, caught him by his collar, and took hold of one end of the thing. She pulled and saw it was part of a wooden toy. A ship, she thought, a ship with no sail.

The little dog had lost interest in the argument. He wagged his tail and dropped the remainder of the toy at Gwen's feet.

"I wonder who this belonged to," she said aloud, and grinned at the dogs. "No use asking you two, is there?"

Both dogs went back to the spot where Spew had appeared. Gwen followed, thinking that if all this area was cleared, it might be the perfect place for her arbor, and, in order to see more clearly, pulled at a branch heavily laden with some kind of berry. She carried on pulling at the creeper, breaking off small branches and twigs. A pair of pruning shears was what she really needed, and some gardening gloves.

She sat back on her haunches, her hands stinging from cuts and scratches. Ready to give up, she decided to come back later, properly equipped.

Spew carried on digging, then barked again. She recognized the excitement in that bark; Spew had found something. She pulled away another layer of overhanging leaves and stooped to look. In front of her, a flat, upright, moss-covered stone leaned very slightly to the left. The ground in front of it was rounded and covered with pale forest flowers. She breathed in the damp woody smell around her and felt hesitant. This looked like a small grave. She looked round when she heard something scurry among the leaves, and then, unable to control her curiosity, scratched at the moss, tearing a fingernail in the process.

When she had finished, she traced the letters with her index finger. There was only a name, nothing more. Just THOMAS BENJA-

MIN, engraved in the stone. No date. No indication of who he had been. He might have been a brother of Laurence's perhaps, or a visitor's child, though Laurence had never mentioned a dead child. Other than asking Laurence, there was no way of knowing why Thomas Benjamin had been hidden in this inaccessible place and not buried properly at the church graveyard. And the fact that Laurence had never mentioned anything of the sort made her think he might not be pleased that she had found it.

5

Two days later, at the sound of Laurence's car pulling up, and despite a trace of anxiety, a pleasant feeling of anticipation ran through her. It had been a cool, misty day, and she'd occupied herself with the household accounts once again. They did not tally, and she couldn't work out exactly what was wrong, but at least she'd managed to organize a message to be taken to the *dhobi,* telling him that she wanted to see him the next day. Apart from that, she hadn't even been able to complete a garden walk, and the lake itself had remained annoyingly hidden behind the mist.

She threw on a tasseled wrap to cover the scratches on her arms and ran down the corridor, then out through the front door.

Fran was climbing out of the back of the Daimler with an enormous grin on her face. Gwen ran straight to her, wrapped her arms round her, and hugged her fiercely. Then she pulled back to scrutinize her cousin.

"Heavens, Fran, look at you!"

Fran tore off her very nearly brimless cloche hat, yellow with a red felt flower, and did a twirl, pointing to her hair. "What do you think?"

Fran's shiny chestnut hair was shingled at the back, cut in an even sleeker bob than before, and with a long fringe. In the sunlight, the lighter threads in it showed up like gold. She had circled a black outline round her eyes and she wore bright-red lipstick. And from under her fringe, her blue eyes sparkled.

She laughed and spun round again.

The spin showed off her curvaceous figure, loosely enveloped by a sleeveless cotton voile dress. A band of lace at the hem and a rope of jet beads hanging to her waist completed the look. Her gloves, which came to just below her elbows, perfectly matched her yellow dress and her hat.

"It's a bit chilly, isn't it?" she said. "I thought it would be hot."

"I have plenty of warm wraps you can borrow. It will be quite a bit cooler when the monsoon comes. They say it's due any day now. What was it like in Colombo?"

"Ghastly. Humid as hell. And everybody seems to be so cross. But what an amazing journey. I have never seen anything like it. We must have climbed thousands of feet. And the views from those iron bridges!"

"The views are marvelous but they gave me a headache," Gwen said, and turned round to Laurence. "How high are we up here, Laurence?"

"Hello, darling." His happy grin and obvious pleasure at seeing her was enough to momentarily wipe away the memory of their last time in bed. He paused for a moment, then bent down to help another woman climb out of the front passenger seat.

"And in answer to your question," he said, straightening up, "nearly five thousand feet."

"It's his sister," Fran whispered, and pulled a face. "She was already in Colombo, staying at the Galle Face. We picked her up. Barely said a word to me all the way here."

The tall woman standing on the gravel on the other side of the car threw back her head and laughed with Laurence about something he'd said.

"Gwendolyn," Laurence called out as he moved toward her. "Say hello to my dearest sister, Verity."

Laurence and his sister came round and Verity held out her hand. Like her brother, she had deep-brown eyes and the same cleft in the chin. Her face was long and rather sallow, and Gwen couldn't help think that the Hooper features didn't sit half so well on a woman. When she leaned forward and kissed Gwen's cheek, Gwen smelled stale scent on her skin.

"What's that graze?" Laurence said, and touched Gwen's arm.

She smiled. "Just where I bumped into a tree. You know me."

"Dear Gwendolyn," Verity said. "I have so been looking forward to meeting you. Laurence has told me everything."

Gwen smiled again. She knew Laurence and his sister were close but sincerely hoped Laurence had not told her everything.

"I am so sorry I missed your wedding. Unforgivable, I know, but I was in darkest Africa." She gave a little laugh, pursed up her thin lips into a pout, then turned to Laurence. "Am I in my old room?"

He grinned and took her arm. "Where else?"

She kissed him on the cheek twice. "My darling, darling brother, how I have missed you." Then they both walked, arm in arm, up the steps and into the house.

"Oh, Gwendolyn," Verity twisted her head and called back. "Have one of the servants bring up my bag. The trunk's not arriving until tomorrow."

94

"Of course," Gwen said as she stared after them. A trunk. How long was Laurence's sister planning on staying?

Fran was watching her face. "Is everything all right?"

"Absolutely marvelous," Gwen said, and smiled. *Well, it will be marvelous,* she thought. "But I am so pleased you are here, at last."

"I expect to hear everything," Fran said, and nudged Gwen. "And I do mean everything." They both laughed.

The next morning Gwen got up early to catch Laurence at breakfast. Full of anticipation at the prospect of surprising him and finally being able to talk, she smiled and flung open the dining room door.

"Oh," she said at the sight of Verity tucking into kedgeree, the smell of the fish turning her stomach.

"Darling," Verity said, and patted the chair next to her. "Laurence has just left, but this is perfect, we can spend the morning getting to know each other."

"That would be nice. Did you sleep well?"

"Not brilliantly, but I'm the world's worst sleeper. Though I can see the same can't be said of your cousin Fran."

Gwen laughed but noticed the dark circles

round Verity's eyes that hadn't seemed so obvious the day before. "You're right," she said. "Fran does like a good long lie-in."

"I thought a walk might be a treat, just for the morning. What do you say?"

"I do have to see the *dhobi* at half past eleven. I think a couple of Laurence's better shirts may have gone missing from the laundry."

"Oh, we'll have acres of time before then, darling. Do say you'll come. I shall be perfectly miserable if you don't."

Gwen glanced at Verity. She wasn't unattractive exactly, but she lacked warmth; the permanent frown lines between her brows might have had something to do with that. She must have been aware of them, as every now and then she deliberately raised her eyebrows to smooth out the skin. This, unfortunately, rounded her eyes and gave her a slightly owl-like appearance. But apart from the circles under her eyes, this morning she looked brighter, less sallow. The hill country air must suit her, Gwen thought.

"All right," she said. "We can't have you being miserable, but I'll only go on condition that I'm back in time to see the *dhobi* before lunch. And I'll have to change my shoes."

"I promise. Now come and sit down. This

96

kedgeree is divine. Or you might try the buffalo curd with jaggery. It's the syrup they extract from *kithul* trees."

"I know."

"Of course you do."

Gwen glanced at the bowl of buffalo curd. It looked rather like clotted cream with brown treacle drizzled over it. "Not today. Just toast for me."

"Well, no wonder you're so tiny, if that's all you eat!"

Gwen smiled but felt slightly unsettled by her sister-in-law, who was now drumming her fingers on the table with a nervous kind of urgency. The prospect of a walk with her was not really what Gwen had planned for the morning, especially as straight after lunch they'd all be going to Nuwara Eliya, and she still hadn't packed her case.

When she went to change into her walking shoes, she found Naveena tidying her bedroom.

"You are walking with the sister, Lady."

"Indeed."

For a moment Naveena looked as if she wanted to speak, but did not, and simply handed Gwen her shoes.

Once out in the early sunshine, Gwen felt more enthusiastic about the outing. It was a glorious morning and still cool, although the mists were burning off rapidly. You could see for miles and only small white clouds flecked the sky. In the trees the birds were singing and the air smelled sweet.

"We'll head down to the lake and then walk on round it for a while. I'll lead the way. Does that suit you?" said Verity.

"Absolutely. I really don't know anything about the walks yet." Verity smiled and linked arms with her.

Gwen gazed at the nearest tea-covered hills, bright green and shining in the sun. Intrigued by the women's fingers flying over the tips as they picked, she pointed at the pathways zigzagging between them and traveling upward to the top.

"I wouldn't mind walking along those paths. I'd love to see the pickers close up."

Verity frowned. "Pluckers, darling, not pickers. But no, not today. You might fall in one of the irrigation channels. I have a better idea. We'll branch off from the lakeside in a minute and head toward my favorite woods. They're absolutely magical. Laurence and I used to play hide-and-seek there in the summer holidays."

"Did you both go to boarding school in England?"

"Oh yes, though not at the same time. I

was at Malvern. Laurence is much older than me. Of course, you know that."

Gwen nodded, and they continued to walk on the path round the lake for about half an hour. The lake was calm in the center and very dark. At the edge it rippled white against the rocky banks, where gray birds with white breasts and cinnamon bellies stretched their wings and preened.

"Water hens," Verity said. "Here's where we turn off." She pointed at a track.

The woods were sparse at first, but as they went deeper, the air was chock-full of smells and the sound of creatures shifting about. Gwen stopped to listen.

"It's just lizards," Verity said. "And birds, of course, and maybe the odd tree snake. Nothing to worry about, I promise. It's a bit wild and woolly, but keep up with me and you'll be fine. Single file now. You follow."

Gwen reached out to touch the branches of a stumpy tree, but the leaves pricked her and she quickly withdrew her hand. The woods felt wilder than anything she had known before, though not in a threatening way. She rather liked the feeling it gave her of a bygone time. Twigs cracked underfoot and the air seemed to be tinged with green in the damp spots where the sun did not reach.

Verity smiled. "If there's anything you need to know, do just ask. I'm sure you're going to fit in wonderfully well."

"Thank you," Gwen said. "There is something. I wondered about the storeroom keys. There are two sets. Should I keep them both?"

"No, that would be an awful nuisance for you. Give one set to the *appu*. Then he doesn't have to bother you for every little thing." She pointed to some violet flowers at the edge of the path. "Aren't they lovely! I wish I'd brought a basket."

"Maybe next time."

"Put one in your hair," Verity said, and bent down to pick one of the flowers. "Here, I'll do it for you."

She threaded the flower through one of Gwen's escaped ringlets and then stood back. "There. Perfectly lovely. It matches your eyes. Shall we go on?"

They walked on, Verity chatting and seeming so pleased to be out with her that Gwen relaxed and lost all track of time. The smell of the lake was long gone when she suddenly remembered her meeting with the *dhobi*.

"Oh Lord. I had forgotten. Verity, we must

turn back." She began to turn round.

"Of course, but don't go back the way we came. It'll take ages. There's a shortcut just along here. Laurence and I used to use it all the time. It'll get you back much sooner." Verity pointed at the path then took a step in the other direction.

"Aren't you coming?"

"I think I'll go back the long way, if you don't mind. It's such a beautiful morning and I'm not pushed for time. See that track? Just go down it for about fifty yards then turn right, where there's a little crossroads. There's a fig tree in the middle. You can't miss it."

"Thank you."

Verity gave her a beaming smile. "It'll take you straight home. Just follow your nose. See you back at the house."

Gwen walked on in the direction Verity had indicated, then turned where the fig tree grew in the middle of a small open patch. She had really enjoyed the morning and came to the conclusion that her sister-in-law was a lot friendlier than she had first thought. She was glad. It would be lovely if the two of them became good friends.

She walked on, expecting to soon see the glittering water of the lake, but after some distance she noticed the path was disappearing deeper and deeper into the woods. Large boulders blocked her way and now even the birdsong had stopped. She looked about her, but a sense of direction had never been her strong point.

A little farther on, the path sloped steeply downward. That couldn't be right. She glanced back and saw that she'd been heading slowly downward for some time, when, to get back to the house, she felt sure she needed to be heading upward.

She sat on a mossy boulder, ran her fingers through her hair and wiped away the line of sweat, then decided to turn back and retrace her steps. She wasn't frightened, she was annoyed with herself for getting lost, and the trouble was that the farther she went, the less she recognized the path. A drooping branch caught in her hair, and when she pulled it out, her hair tumbled from its clip. A little farther on she tripped and fell on her bottom, ripping her new cotton voile dress.

With grazed hands, she picked the leaves from her clothes, but when she stood, the backs of her thighs were stinging. She twisted round to check them and saw that the normally pale skin was bright red. Something had bitten her. She glanced around and noticed swarming ants just where she'd been sitting.

At least it was a bright sunny day. She started moving again and, after several wrong turns, eventually found the fig tree. It meant going the long way round and she had no option but to make a beeline for the path she and Verity had originally taken. She would be late, very late.

When she emerged at the lake, her heart lifted at the sight of her new home in the distance. She ran back, not caring about the state of her hair and clothes. Nearing the house, she saw Laurence pacing up and down at the edge of the lake, using his hand to shield his eyes from the afternoon sun. He saw her and stood still, watching as she ran up to him.

She was so pleased to see him, she felt her chest might burst with happiness.

"Nice walk?" he said, looking serious, and then, with his mouth turning up further on one side and his eyebrows very slightly raised, he smiled.

"Don't tease. I got lost."

"What am I to do with you?"

"I didn't mean to get lost." She scratched the back of her legs. "I bloody well got bitten too."

"By what?"

She pulled a face. "Just ants."

"There are no 'just ants' in Ceylon. But, seriously, I would never forgive myself if you were to get hurt. Promise me you'll take more care."

She arranged her face to look suitably solemn but, unable to maintain it, broke into a grin and they both ended up laughing.

"You sound like my father."

"Sometimes I feel like him." He pulled her closer. "Except for this."

The kiss was long and deep.

At that moment Verity came out. "Oh, there you are," she called out breezily. "Sorry to interrupt. I've been back for ages. We were terribly worried."

"But I took the path you said. I got bitten by ants."

"Did you take the path to the right? You remember, at the fig tree."

Gwen frowned.

"Never mind. You're here now." Laurence put an arm round her and took out a clean handkerchief to rub the dirt from her cheeks. "You've missed lunch, of course, but you can thank Verity for seeing the *dhobi* in your place."

Verity nodded and smiled. "No need for thanks. I'll tell the *appu* to prepare some sandwiches for you, shall I? And I'll find some lotion to soothe the ant bites."

"Thank you."

While Verity turned and headed back into the house, Laurence took Gwen's hand. "And then, darling, we need to prepare to go to the ball."

"Laurence," she said, squeezing his hand. "I've been wanting to say . . . about the other day."

His face clouded. "I'm sorry I was rough."

She stared at the ground for a moment. This was a conversation she wanted to have but not right now with his sister possibly in earshot. Maybe after the ball they would have a better chance to talk in private.

"Let's forget that, shall we, for now?" she said. "But what I meant was that I wanted to explain why I went to the labor lines."

He interrupted. "McGregor has already told me."

"You do know the man was hurt?"

"You are kind, Gwen, and very caring, but he's a known troublemaker. The belief is that he injured himself."

"Why would he do that?"

"To try to force our hand over sickness pay."

"Well, if people are injured, of course we must help them."

"Not if it's self-inflicted."

She thought for a moment. "I didn't much like the way McGregor spoke to me."

"It's just his manner. Nothing personal."

Gwen sighed and, remembering McGregor's steely eyes and thin lips, she wasn't sure.

"Just leave the plantation workforce to McGregor. He does resent his authority being challenged, I'm afraid, and especially by a woman. He's a stalwart of the old-school type."

"There seem to be rather a lot of those around."

He shrugged. "There's so much still to do, but with the different factions at work in Ceylon, we can't afford to alienate people by rushing through change. We need a consensus to make any sizable difference to the country as a whole."

"And if there is no consensus?"

He looked very serious as he replied. "There has to be, Gwen." There was a pause.

"You're fond of McGregor?"

"I suppose I am. I left him in charge during the war, with just two assistant managers. He couldn't fight, you see."

"Oh?"

"You might have noticed his slight limp. But he managed the thousand-strong labor force admirably, and I'd trust him with my life."

"I shall have to learn to like him."

"Strictly speaking, as I mentioned before, it's more like fifteen hundred now that I've taken over another estate. There have been some teething problems with some of the coolie laborers who've been transferred. There's a lot more going on than just the plucking of the leaves."

"Why is it always women who pick?"

"Nimble fingers. We call it plucking."

"Verity said. And the men?"

"There are plenty of jobs that need brawn. Digging, planting, fertilizing, drain clearing, and, of course, pruning. We have gangs of pruners, and their children run along collecting the trimmings to take home for the fire. Just remember, while you acted out of pure decency, McGregor's job is to ensure your safety."

She nodded.

"You might have noticed that the household staff think themselves a cut above the estate staff. We don't want to upset them either. How are you getting on? Nobody causing too much trouble?"

She considered telling him about the accounts but decided against it. The household was her responsibility and she would find a way to understand what was going wrong.

As he kissed her on the lips she caught the trace of soap and lemons again. "Now come on, my gorgeous wife," he said. "Isn't it time we had some fun?"

The golf club's Annual Ball was to be held at the Grand Hotel in Nuwara Eliya. Exactly like an Elizabethan manor house, it was surrounded by immaculate gardens with buffalo- and blue-grass lawns covered in daisies. Gwen had been looking forward to this for days. Now she'd have the chance to wear her new flapper dress in pink and silver, and she and Fran would finally dance the Charleston.

It was a three-hour drive to the town, embracing steep mountain roads, and Gwen felt slightly nauseated. But when they eventually arrived, she climbed out of the car and, in air smelling of mint, she soon revived. The town looked as if it could have been in Gloucestershire, with a clock spire, steps up to an imposing war memorial, and an English-looking church.

Earlier, as Gwen stepped out of the house, she had been surprised to see that Verity had installed herself in the front passenger seat next to Laurence. There was a flicker of annoyance on his face, but he didn't tell her to get out.

Verity had twisted round. "You don't mind, do you, Gwen? I haven't seen him for ages."

Gwen's vanity was a little injured — after all, the front seat should have been hers — but she understood that Verity and Laurence might want to catch up.

Laurence had already booked them all hotel rooms, and when they reached the foyer she stood at the reception desk with him.

"I've arranged for you and Fran to share a room," he said. "You'll enjoy the time together."

She looked at the people milling about and tried to swallow the words she wanted to say.

"It'll be like old times," he said, his tone a little defensive. Then he turned to talk to the clerk.

"That's not the point," she hissed. "For goodness' sake, Laurence —"

"Not now, Gwen, please. Here's the key."

She caught hold of his sleeve. "This isn't settled!"

He didn't reply. She bit her tongue, choking back the sudden burst of emotion, and, not wanting to be seen crying in a hotel foyer, started to turn away.

He reached out a hand. "I'm sorry, I know we need to talk. I'm afraid I haven't been entirely —"

On the point of saying more, he took a sharp breath as Verity swept toward them. With a friendly look at Gwen, she wrapped herself round her brother and leaned her head against his shoulder. He gave Gwen an apologetic look, but, flushed with anger, she turned on her heels and went in search of Fran.

Their room was large and comfortable, with a sofa, two mosquito-netted beds, a wardrobe, two little bedside tables, and a matching dressing table, where three pale orchids had been tastefully arranged. Fran peeled off her dress and the warm woolen wrap Gwen had lent her and immediately slid under the crisp sheets of one of the beds. She held out her hand and a bracelet tinkled on her wrist. "Look, it's a Buddhist temple. I bought it in one of those noisy bazaar streets in Colombo."

Gwen examined the new charm on Fran's bracelet.

"So how are you enjoying married life?" Fran said, with raised eyebrows.

"It's very nice."

"Nice? It should be a lot more thrilling than that." Gwen pretended ignorance and shrugged.

"Come on, spill. You know what I'm talking about." Gwen's face fell and she looked down.

Fran sat up immediately. "Oh, Gwennie, what is it?"

There was a short silence as Gwen fought the need to tell all while still remaining loyal to Laurence.

"You're scaring me. Has he hurt you?" Fran held out a hand.

Gwen shook her head and looked up. "He didn't mean to."

"You're covered in scratches."

"The scratches were my own stupid fault."

"Good. Laurence seems far too nice for that."

Gwen frowned. "He is nice."

"Then why are you looking so unhappy?" She paused. "That's it, isn't it? He actually is nice, far too nice. You're not having any fun, are you?"

Gwen swallowed a lump in her throat and felt her neck grow hot. "We were. Then —"

"Oh, that's no good at all. What's the point of being tied to one man if you aren't having a whale of a time. Does he know what to do?"

"He was married before. Of course he knows."

Fran shook her head. "Doesn't always follow. Some men just aren't cut out for it."

"It was wonderful in England." Gwen felt the blush spread. "And in Colombo."

"There's something troubling him, then."

"Actually, I think there *is* something worrying him, but he won't talk."

"Talk won't do it. Let's make you look so utterly irresistible, he won't be able to keep his hands off you. That's the way to a man's heart!"

Gwen laughed. After Fran had gone back to London the last time, and before her marriage to Laurence, Gwen had tried to talk to her mother about intimate matters. The attempt had ended in hopeless stuttering. Her mother had probably never heard of orgasms, and the thought of her handlebar-mustached father enabling her mother to have one was enough to make a person cringe, or die laughing. Mother hadn't even come out with the "men have needs" guff they all used to laugh about at boarding school.

Fran interrupted her thoughts. "I forgot to tell you. I thought I might get a job when I go back home."

"You don't need a job. You've got your

rental properties."

"I don't need one for the money, but I was getting bored with parties and champagne. You've always had your smelly old cheesemaking, so why shouldn't I have something?"

The memory hit home. It hurt how much she missed her parents and the ramshackle old manor they lived in. After her mother had converted an old barn to take up cheesemaking, the whole place had become infused with the smell of it. She shook her head. She was here now, in the land of cinnamon and jasmine, and there was no point looking back.

"Shall we get ready now?" Fran said.

After they'd both bathed, Gwen put on a pearl-beaded hairband, and Fran helped her arrange her hair so that her dark ringlets fell loosely at the nape of her slim neck. Fran's own chestnut hair, short and chic, swung about her head, shining beneath a red headband and matching feather.

Fran looked Gwen up and down.

"Will I do?"

Fran grinned. "Let operation seduction begin!"

By eleven that night the ball was in full swing. The orchestra had taken a break and

113

Gwen looked around the room at the people dotted about. Most of the women wore old-fashioned pastel dresses, barely showing an ankle, and even the young ones were dressed like their mothers.

Laurence, handsome in a white tuxedo, hadn't been able to keep his eyes off Gwen, and they'd been enjoying a close waltz until his sister commandeered him. As Gwen stepped away he gave her a wry smile. Now, unable to spot Fran anywhere, she felt at a loose end. She was leaning against a column at the entrance, listening to the swell of voices and nodding at vaguely familiar faces, when a man spoke.

"Mrs. Hooper. How lovely."

She spun round and there he was, looking splendid in a dark dinner suit, with a rather extraordinary embroidered waistcoat in shades of red and gold. His eyes lingered a little too long on her face. She remembered the glittering caramel eyes from the day they'd met, and now, as then, when he smiled they warmed, transforming the look of his face. She felt ruffled and searched for a word to describe the man. Exotic, she had thought before, but it was more than that. Disconcerting, maybe? She tried for a smile but wasn't quite able to, though after remembering her manners, she offered her hand and his lips brushed over the silk glove that extended as far as her bare underarm.

"Mr. Ravasinghe. How are you?"

"You look very lovely tonight. Not dancing?"

"Thank you, and no, not dancing at the moment." This time, flattered to have caught his attention, she managed a smile but then instantly felt self-conscious. "Laurence is over there with his sister."

He nodded. "Ah yes. Verity Hooper."

"You know her?"

He inclined his head. "Our paths have crossed."

"I've only recently met her. She seems very fond of Laurence."

"Yes, I do recall that." He paused and smiled at her. "Would you care to dance, Mrs. Hooper, when the orchestra returns?"

"Please do call me Gwen. But I'm not sure if I should." She glanced around and saw Fran coming back into the room from the opposite entrance, carrying something under her arm. Fran, as usual, looked suitably dramatic in her scarlet swing dress, with little red button shoes to match.

"Oh, look. I must introduce you to my cousin, and best friend, Frances Myant."

As Fran came up, Gwen saw the instant attraction between Savi Ravasinghe and her cousin. They stared at each other for too long, and he seemed unable to speak. Fran glowed with health and glamour, and Gwen realized her cousin had never looked more beautiful, though more than anything it was Fran's zest for life that made her stand out. Her confidence seemed to draw people to her, as if by being close some of her shine might rub off on them. Either that, or they were disapproving.

For a moment Gwen felt a twinge of envy. Although on the two occasions that they'd met, Savi Ravasinghe had clearly admired her, he had not looked at her like that. And the truth was that when he had looked at her, she'd been ashamed to feel her skin flushing. Now she just felt silly. He'd looked after her, as an older brother might, taking her under his wing, and even his offer to dance, just now, she judged must have been made out of kindness. She coughed to get their attention and was then able to introduce them.

"Look, I've brought these," Fran said. She held out two recordings made by the new electric microphone process.

"I'm going to ask that young fellow to play them." She pointed to a dinner-suited man who was in charge of a wind-up gramophone. "Do you Charleston, Mr. Ravas-inghe?"

He shook his head and feigned dismay.

She grinned and took his arm. "Well, never mind, I'll teach you both."

Over Fran's shoulder, Gwen noticed that Laurence had been waylaid by Christina, the American widow. She was the sort of woman who drew a circle of men around her; the bias-cut, slinky black satin dress that clung in all the right placcs saw to that. Gwen looked at the wave at the front of Laurence's hair and wanted to march across and claim her husband. She raised a hand to signal but then noticed that Laurence hadn't even spotted her, his wife, and did not stop smiling at the woman. She suppressed the hot prickle of jealousy as she saw the woman reach up a hand and touch his cheek. When Laurence eventually glanced up and saw her looking, he nodded at Christina before making his way across.

"Gwendolyn. There you are."

"What were you saying to that woman?" She knew her voice sounded painfully petulant.

He pulled a face. "A bit of business."

She narrowed her eyes and took a deep breath. "Laurence, I saw her touch your face."

He laughed.

"It isn't funny —"

He wrapped an arm round her waist and, drawing her to him, he smiled. "I have eyes for only you. Anyway, she more or less owns a bank."

He'd spoken as if that explained it. Then his face darkened and he grew serious.

"More importantly, I saw you speaking to Ravasinghe. Look, have fun, dance the Charleston with Fran, do anything you want, but I'd rather you didn't spend time with him."

She unwrapped his arm. "Don't you like him?"

"It doesn't matter whether I like him or not."

"Then what? Surely it's not because he's Sinhalese?"

"I hope you don't think me that shallow."

"I don't, actually. But I do think Mr. Ravasinghe is a charming man."

Laurence shot her a troubled look. "Charming? Is that what you think?"

"Yes." She paused for a moment or two. "Do your Sinhalese acquaintances ever come to the house?"

"Occasionally."

"Do we go to theirs?"

"I know it must seem strange to you, but

no, not even the relatively well-off ones like Ravasinghe." He shook his head and when he spoke again the tone of his voice had changed. "He's painting Christina's portrait, as it happens."

"He's a painter? I didn't realize. You sound as if you mind."

"Why should I mind?" he said. "Now, there are some people I want to show you off to."

"Oh no. Fran is going to teach Savi and me how to dance the Charleston now." And, feeling annoyed with him, she turned her back and followed the other two to the gramophone.

After that, Laurence did not come near. While pretending to look the other way, Gwen watched him dance with Christina more than once. She was trying to be grown-up about it, but the sight of them together actually made her feel sick. The nerve of him, telling her who she should pass time with, when the woman was pressing herself against him and touching his face as if she owned him. After seeing that, and with a rising sense of devilment, Gwen drank several glasses of champagne straight off.

For about an hour, Fran, Savi Ravasinghe, and Gwen practiced the Charleston, to looks of barely disguised disapproval from some of the older onlookers, who were no doubt itching for the return of the orchestra and the chance to continue their waltzes and foxtrots. One or two younger ones had linked up, and for a while even Verity joined in, laughing so much that Gwen found herself really warming to her.

Afterward, when Fran had disappeared off somewhere and Verity couldn't be seen, Gwen wilted, her earlier bravado fading. She grabbed another glass of champagne from a passing waiter, left the ballroom, and went out to the hall, where she leaned against the wall behind the stairwell, feeling tipsy, and wondered how to dig Laurence out from the American woman's clutches.

When Savi Ravasinghe came across, her eyes were drooping.

"You wait here," he said. "I'll find your husband."

"I feel faint. Please don't leave me."

"Very well. Which is your room? I'll help you up the stairs."

She giggled. "I think I might be a little drunk."

He took the glass from her and put it on a table. "It's nothing that a glass of water and a good night's sleep won't cure. Come along. Lean on me."

He kissed her gloved hand and placed his hand under her arm. Through the silk of her dress, she felt the coolness of his hand against the warmth of her body. At the back of her mind she knew it wasn't entirely proper to allow a stranger to take her upstairs, but after the way Laurence had been dancing with Christina, she decided to throw caution aside.

"Have you the key?"

"In my purse." She paused to look at him. "You always seem to be helping me out of scrapes."

He laughed. "Well, if you will insist on getting into them."

"Actually, I feel a bit sick."

"Right. Upstairs with you now, Mrs. Hooper." He gave her a comforting squeeze and she felt her knees loosen. "Hold on to my arm, and once I've got you settled, I'll find your cousin."

As he helped her up a few steps, she heard the sound of footsteps. She glanced up and saw Florence Shoebotham approaching, her nose shining and her chins wobbling. How those chins could speak, Gwen thought as she waited for a pointed comment, but was surprised when none came and Florence shuffled off without a word.

"Drat! She'll probably tell Laurence."

"Tell him what?"

She waved her hands about and felt extremely woozy. "Oh, nothing. Just that I was tipsy."

Mr. Ravasinghe led her to her room and they went in together. When she felt his fingers on her ankles as he pulled off her shoes, she was flustered by his proximity. She bit her lip in an effort not to reveal that she'd felt something she shouldn't have. He helped her lie down on top of the bed. As she closed her eyes, he gently stroked her temple. It was comforting and she wanted him to go on doing it, but, feeling a little ashamed, she shifted slightly.

"I love Laurence," she muttered, the words slurring.

"Of course you do. Are you still feeling sick?"

"A bit. The room is wavery."

"Then I'll just stay until you fall asleep. I wouldn't want to leave you while you might be sick."

He was a lovely man, she thought between giddy spells, but then she said it out loud, hiccupped, and her hand flew to her mouth. "Ooops!"

He continued to gently stroke her face.

Part of her knew she should ask him to go, but she was feeling so alone and homesick, and had been longing for this kind of gentle contact so much, that any thoughts of genuine caution had disappeared with the last glass of champagne. A recurring image of Christina in her black dress, flirting with Laurence, made her eyes sting and she muttered to herself.

"I can help you get a little more comfortable, if you like."

"Thank you."

He held the glass while she sipped some water, then he slipped another pillow under her head. She threw off her wrap, feeling too warm, and then, falling in and out of a feverish sleep, seemed to burn up. As she lay on the bed with her arms stretched out, the back of her head hurt. Sometimes he was still there, or still seemed to be, and sometimes he was gone. And she had the most disturbing dreams of Mr. Ravasinghe touching her, and her own hands reaching for him, only suddenly he turned into Laurence and everything was all right. She was allowed to make love to her husband. When she woke properly she saw that she must have unfastened the buttons of her dress and rolled down her stockings in her sleep — she remembered feeling terribly hot — and her new silky French knickers lay on the floor. When Fran turned up in the middle of the night, she ordered Gwen to get under the covers.

"Look at the state of you, Gwen, you're half dressed and all crumpled. What on earth have you been doing?"

"I can't 'member."

"You stink of booze."

"Drinkin', Franny," Gwen said, still feeling groggy. "Drinkin' champagne."

Fran snuffed out their gaslight and climbed into the same bed, snuggling up close behind her, just as they had done as children.

The next morning, over breakfast, Fran was nowhere to be seen and Verity had gone for a walk. Laurence seemed in a good mood and asked if she had enjoyed herself. She replied that she had, but that she'd had rather too much fizz and had gone to bed early nursing a sore head.

"I looked for you, but when I couldn't find you, Verity said she thought you'd gone up and that Fran was with you."

"Verity was pretty blotto herself. Why didn't you come to check on me?"

"I didn't want to wake you." He paused and grinned. "I think you and Fran gave our staid group of friends something of a shake-up."

Gwen's face burned. Her memory of the night was somewhat fuddled, but she could remember feeling terribly light-headed, and then Mr. Ravasinghe had helped her up the stairs.

She looked at her husband and thought about what to say. "Did you enjoy dancing with Christina?" she asked, aiming for lightness, though what came out sounded tense.

He shrugged and buttered his toast, then spread the jam thickly. "She's an old friend."

"And that's all?"

He gazed at her and smiled. "That's all now."

"It didn't use to be?"

"No, before you, it didn't use to be."

Gwen bit her lip. She knew it wasn't fair, but couldn't help feeling stung. "And it's over now?"

"Completely."

"It didn't look over."

He frowned. "She enjoys being provocative. Take no notice."

"It isn't because of her, then?"

"What isn't?"

She took a sharp breath in. "The way you've been."

Did she imagine that his face clouded as he shook his head?

"It's all over for her as well, is it?"

125

"What is this, Gwen, the Spanish Inquisition? I've said it's over."

"And is this what you were about to tell me yesterday?"

He looked puzzled.

"In the foyer when we arrived."

"Ah, that . . . yes . . . yes, of course."

She decided not to pursue it further. She cast around for something different to talk about, and then she remembered. This was her first proper chance to raise the subject of the little grave she'd found. She drank her tea and dabbed at her mouth, then over the toast and marmalade — especially imported from Fortnum & Mason, she noticed — she gave him a quick half smile and spoke.

"Who was Thomas, Laurence?"

His body stiffened and he kept his eyes lowered.

In the time that he didn't speak, she heard the sounds of breakfast: the desultory early-morning murmurs, the light-footed waiters, the genteel clinks of cutlery on china. The time stretched out, extending uncomfortably. Was Laurence going to say anything at all? She felt an itch starting at the nape of her neck, and she couldn't help shifting slightly against the chair. She buttered another piece of toast, then reached out

126

across the table to give it to him.

"Laurence?"

He looked up, raising a hand, and as he accidentally knocked the toast out of her hand it was as if he had wiped his eyes of expression. "It would have been better if you had not poked around in there."

His voice was flat, but she felt the rebuke and frowned, partly in dismay and partly in anger. "I wasn't poking, as you put it. I was searching for the perfect spot for my arbor. And anyway, Spew had run in there and I had to fetch him. I had no idea I would stumble across a grave."

"Your arbor?" He took a deep shuddering breath.

"Yes."

There was another pause.

"Please tell me. Who was Thomas?"

As he exhaled, Laurence seemed to be looking over her left shoulder and not at her. She took a last bite of toast and watched him closely as he rubbed his chin.

"It seemed so sad that he was all alone there. Why wasn't he laid to rest at the church? People don't usually bury other people in their garden, even if it's just a child." She took another sip of tea.

"Thomas was not *just* a child. He was Caroline's son."

She almost choked on the tea.

There was silence as Laurence wiped his mouth, then after he had put the crumpled napkin down, he cleared his throat as if he was about to speak. When he did not, she decided to just come out with it.

"Do you mean *only* Caroline's son?"

"Caroline's son . . . and mine." He stood up and left the table.

She leaned back in her chair. All she knew of Caroline was what Laurence had told her when they first met. He had been married before; his wife had been ill and then she had died. No mention of a little boy. She felt awfully sorry for him, but why had he never said, and if it mattered so much, as it clearly must, why had he allowed his own child's grave to become so overgrown?

6

Fran had left a note at reception saying she might stay on at the Grand in Nuwara Eliya, and to go back without her. It worried Gwen because as they got in the car straight after breakfast, the massing thunderclouds and the strange light that came with them had tinted the sky yellow. If the rains came soon, Fran mightn't even be able to get back. Laurence said that the previous year parts of the road to Hatton had been washed clean away, and the only means of travel had been by canoe. Though Gwen was excited to experience her first monsoon, she'd be happier if Fran was safely back with them.

Once home, Gwen and Laurence skirted round each other for part of the afternoon, and then he went to the tea factory. Inside the house, the air had changed. It seemed full of moisture in a way that it had not before: hot and thick, so heavy you could almost slice it, and with an unfamiliar over-sweet smell. It was oppressively quiet too and, wanting to tell Fran about Thomas, Gwen was feeling miserable.

At teatime when she went to the kitchen to check on the rice supply, she found Nick McGregor sitting at the table with his pipe and a cup of steaming tea. Although he lived in his own bungalow, not far from theirs, he was often to be found in the main house kitchen resting his leg.

When she broached the subject of gardeners, he was surprisingly helpful, agreeing to allocate workers for the vegetable garden, who would work on a rotation basis. Gwen was delighted at the outcome. She had got McGregor completely wrong, it seemed. Perhaps pain in his bad leg made him irritable.

After that Gwen wondered whether to brave an early-evening walk by the lake with Spew. It was not such a good proposition with the prospect of imminent rain, and the resultant slippery steps and pathways back up to the house. Instead, she plumped up one of the tapestry cushions behind her head, sank back on the sofa, and closed her eyes.

The sound of Laurence coming in drew her attention. She always recognized the sound of him. She wasn't sure why. A sureness in his steps perhaps, a feeling in the air of the master having returned, or maybe it was just the sound of Tapper finally rising from his basket.

She went out and found Laurence standing in the corridor, staring at his hands, his white shirt soaked with blood. Her breath caught in her throat.

"What on earth has happened?"

He glanced at her for a moment, his brows drew together, and then he jerked his head in the direction of one of Tapper's three baskets. She looked around and saw that Tapper had not come into the hall.

"Where's Tapper?"

Laurence's jaw was working and it looked as if he was trying to control himself.

"Darling, tell me," she said.

He attempted to speak but the words came out too brusquely for her to make any sense of them. She picked up the little handbell from the hall table and rang it twice. While they waited she tried to comfort him, but he brushed her hands away and continued to stare at the floor.

Within minutes the butler arrived.

"Please ask Naveena to bring water and a fresh shirt for the master. Tell her she can take them to the master's room."

"Yes, Lady."

"Come on, Laurence," she said. "We're going to your room. You can tell me what has happened when you're ready."

She took hold of his elbow and he allowed her to guide him upstairs to his room at the end of the long corridor. She'd only been in Laurence's room twice before; on both occasions she'd been interrupted, once by a houseboy who came to dust and once by Naveena bringing up Laurence's ironed shirts.

He pushed open the door. A slight trace of incense hung in the air and the deep-blue velvet curtains were almost closed, with just a strip of late daylight showing.

"It's gloomy," she said as she turned on two of the electric lamps. He didn't seem to notice.

It was a room so sumptuous and so unlike Laurence it couldn't be imagined, not the masculine hideaway she had at first expected. There were two blue-fringed lampshades, some framed photographs on a table and a few china ornaments on the mantelpiece. A large Persian rug covered a part of the glossy floorboards and the bed was covered in a satin eiderdown the color of bitter chocolate. The mosquito net hung from a large ring attached to the ceiling and had been tied in a knot above the bed. The furniture, unlike her own, was dark.

There was a knock at the door and Naveena came in with a towel, a bowl of water, and a freshly laundered white shirt for Laurence. Though she must have seen the blood on his shirt as he stood by the bed, she didn't speak, just reached out a hand to pat his arm. He glanced up and a look passed between them. Gwen didn't understand what it meant but could see that the two understood each other.

"Right," Gwen said, once Naveena had left the room. "Let's get that shirt off."

She pulled back the bedcovers and Laurence sat on the edge of the mattress as she undid the buttons of his braces and his shirt, then gingerly slid the shirt away from his arms and back in case of injury. She wiped the blood from his hands, and he stood up to remove his trousers. When she examined him, she saw he did not appear to be hurt.

"Do you want to tell me what happened now?" she said.

He took a breath, then sat back on the bed and slammed his fists down on the mattress. "They killed Tapper. My Tapper. The bastards cut his throat."

Gwen's hand flew to her own throat. "Oh,

Laurence. I am so sorry."

She sat down next to him and he leaned against her. She watched his hands as they flexed and contracted in his lap. Neither of them spoke, but she could feel the pent-up emotion in her husband's hands, each movement as eloquent as if they were trying to communicate on his behalf. Eventually he went limp and she held him in her arms, stroking his hair and murmuring. Then he began to make great gulping, sobbing sounds that seemed to come from somewhere deep within.

Gwen had only ever seen her father cry once, and that had been when his brother, Fran's father, had drowned. Then, she had sat on the stairs with her head in her hands and been frightened by the sound of her brave, strong father sobbing like a baby. But at least it had taught her to wait for Laurence's sorrow to pass, as her father's had eventually done.

When he seemed to quieten, she wiped his face and kissed him repeatedly on the cheeks, tasting the saltiness of his tears. Then she kissed his forehead and nose, just as her mother used to do when she was hurt.

She cupped her hands round his face and looked in his eyes, and what she saw instantly confirmed that this was not only about Tapper.

She kissed him on the lips. "Come to bed."

They both partly undressed, then lay down on the bed, side by side, and didn't move for a stretch of time. She felt the heat of his body against hers and listened as his breathing steadied.

"Do you want to tell me why Tapper was killed?"

He moved onto his side and looked in her eyes. "There has been some trouble in the lines."

Gwen's brows shot up. "Laurence, why didn't you tell me?"

"I don't like to worry you."

"I'd like to be more involved. My mother and father always talk their problems over, and I want to do the same."

"It's a man's work, running a plantation. And you have enough to do, getting to grips with the household." He paused. "The thing is, maybe I allowed McGregor to treat the culprits too harshly."

"What will you do?"

He frowned. "I don't know, I really don't know. Attitudes are changing and I am making progress with some of the other planters, but it's hard going. Things used to be so simple."

"Why don't you start by telling me about

how it used to be? Right back to the beginning. Tell me about Caroline and Thomas."

There was silence for a while, and Gwen hoped she had not misjudged the moment.

"You must have loved Caroline very much."

A little on edge, she waited. Eventually he rolled onto his back and, staring at the ceiling, he paused to swallow. When he spoke again she had to strain to hear.

"I did love her, Gwen." There was a very long pause. "But after the baby —"

"Was that when she became sick?"

He didn't speak, but his breath shook, and she wrapped an arm round his chest, then kissed the side of his face, the stubble there prickling her lips.

"Where is she buried?"

"At the Anglican church."

She frowned. "But not Thomas?"

He paused again and seemed to be weighing his words, and then he turned to face her.

She watched him carefully and suddenly felt shaky.

"She would have wanted him to remain here, at home. I'm so sorry I didn't tell you about him. I know I should have. What happened was too painful."

She looked in his eyes and a lump came

in her throat. For someone accustomed to keeping his unhappiness hidden, he looked profoundly stricken, in a way she'd never seen before. It seemed as if something inaccessible underlined the sorrow, something more than grief, and it appeared to be tormenting him. Though she was curious to know what the sickness was that had caused Caroline and baby Thomas's deaths, she felt unable to press him.

She nodded. "It's all right."

He closed his eyes.

Lying next to him like this, Gwen felt a familiar craving and tried to ignore the flutter in her heart. But as if he had felt it too, he put a palm on her breast at exactly the spot, opened his eyes, and smiled at her. Then, with a very different look, he touched his thumbs to the hollows at the base of her neck and his lips brushed the corners of her mouth, tentative at first, but soon with more force. Her lips parted and she felt the warmth of his tongue. As he pressed her down against the mattress, she realized that the depth of his anguish had somehow triggered his desire. Without her even knowing how it had happened, he was pulling up her skirt, and she was helping him remove her underclothes. She moaned as he raised her body, bending her forward to remove her chemise. And then, when he laid her back down and she pushed her hips against his, they were making love. She had felt so lost without him, but now that Laurence was back to his old self she could hardly contain her joy.

When they were finished, there was the sound of breaking thunder, louder than gunfire, and of immense rainfall; the sky had uncurled its fist and was now releasing the entire contents on the earth below. Gwen lay listening with her back curled against him. She started to laugh and she could feel his body shake as he laughed with her, a free, happy sound, and it was as if everything that had been holding him back had fallen away.

"I'm so sorry, Gwen, about before. I don't really know what happened."

"Shhh."

He turned her round and put a finger to her lips. "No, I have to say it. Please forgive me. I haven't been myself. I was just so —"

She saw him hesitate and she watched a kind of struggle going on in his face. When he looked as if he was on the verge of saying more, she cast around for something to say that might encourage him.

"It wasn't because of Caroline?"

"Not exactly."

"Then?"

He sighed deeply. "Being here at the plantation with you . . . it just brought everything back."

The rain had cooled the air by quite a few degrees, and Gwen, energized, shifted in the bed, feeling as if the power of a tropical storm had taken root in her and was now flowing in her blood.

"I wish we could stay here forever, but it's probably time we went down," she said.

After they had dressed, just before she turned off the bedroom lights, Gwen glanced back at the photographs she'd seen on the side table earlier. One, of a woman sitting on a tartan rug in the garden, with Tapper's head on her lap, caught her eye. The woman was blond and smiling. Laurence didn't notice her looking.

"Thank you," he said, and took her hand as they walked along the landing.

"You don't have to thank me."

"But I do. You have no idea how much." He kissed her again, and then as they went down for dinner, hearing crows shouting, she looked out of a landing window. It was nightfall, but she could still see the white mist cloaking everything.

In the drawing room, Gwen was pleased to see Fran deep in conversation with Verity.

Both women turned to look as she and Laurence walked into the room, holding hands.

"Well, you two look positively radiant," Fran said.

Laurence grinned and winked at her. Gwen noticed that although Verity smiled, it didn't quite reach her eyes.

"You changed your mind. How did you get back?" Gwen asked, turning to Fran.

Though her cousin always showed a confident face to the world, Gwen knew it wasn't the whole story, and that she'd struggled to get over the death of her parents. It struck her that it was something Fran and Verity had in common, and wondered if it might bring them together.

"After a hair of the dog, I caught the train to Hatton," Fran was saying. "What a journey! But Savi was so kind. He lent me the money for the fare and arranged a lift to the station at Nanu Oya. I'd left all my wherewithal here at the house, you see."

Laurence's lips tightened. "Well, you must send Mr. Ravasinghe what you owe, immediately."

"No need. I'm meeting him in Nuwara Eliya next week, weather permitting. It's such a marvelous little country, isn't it? He's promised to show me more. Gwen, you're invited too. We're both going to have lunch

140

with Christina, and he's going to unveil her portrait. Isn't that jolly?"

Laurence turned his back and Gwen noticed his shoulders were tense.

"I hope I'm invited too," Verity said with a little laugh.

Fran glanced at her and shrugged. "They didn't mention you, I'm afraid. So, no, I think it's just Gwen and me."

Gwen felt sorry for her sister-in-law as she watched her turn away. She seemed rather alone in the world, apart from her brother, and Gwen couldn't help think there was something troubling the girl. She never seemed quite at ease, though the truth was she didn't make the best of herself. The short straight hairstyle didn't suit her long angular face and, apart from one rust-colored dress, she wore all the wrong colors. She should wear colors that complemented her brown eyes, not the drab fawns and acid colors she chose.

Gwen favored violet, not just because it matched her eyes, but because she loved and wore all the English summer colors. Sweet-pea colors, Fran called them. Her dress tonight was the palest green, and though she hadn't had a chance to change, she still felt fresh. A typical outdoorsman, Laurence didn't care what he wore, and liked nothing better than to stride about the estate in his shorts and an old cream short-sleeved shirt, with a battered hat on his head. Tonight, looking self-assured and happy, with no trace of that unsettling look in his eyes, he wore something resembling evening wear.

After supper Laurence threw a couple of logs on the fire, and Verity sat at the piano; on it a dozen or more photographs in silver frames showed Laurence gazing out, with a mixture of dogs around him, and silhouetted men in plus fours leaning on their rifles.

Verity played, singing quite tunefully and seeming to have recovered from Fran's slight. As Gwen read the words over Verity's shoulder, she noticed for the first time that her sister-in-law was a nail biter.

It was Fran who made them laugh when they began a game of charades and Gwen developed a knot in her throat from laughing.

"What to do about Fran" had been a constant refrain throughout Gwen's childhood. For as long as she could remember, Fran had liked to perform, either by constructing a puppet theater and using papier-mâché puppets to relate a tale, or by leaping onto a makeshift stage of orange boxes and flinging her arms about while singing an operetta. Her choice of clothes usually matched her dramatic performances: crimson dresses, sequined jackets, or sunflower-yellow gowns.

The family were used to it, and though Laurence was ready to accept Fran, it seemed Verity didn't quite know how to take her. Gwen knew Fran was, in reality, a sensitive and clever woman, and that her behavior was just a defense against an unjust world. But by the look of Verity's slightly raised brows, Gwen worried that her sister-in-law might think Fran brazen, especially when, with a small smile, she interrupted to speak to her brother.

"Laurence, shall we take a ride round the lake tomorrow? We could take the estate horses. I'm sure Nick wouldn't mind."

Laurence pointed at the rain.

"Well, we could swim, just you and me, remember, like we used to when we were children? I'm sure Gwen wouldn't want to come."

Gwen overheard. "Come where?"

"Oh, I was wondering about riding or maybe swimming." She smiled. "I thought you wouldn't want to come . . . but of course you must join us."

"We never swam during the monsoon," Laurence muttered.

Verity clung onto his arm. "We did swim. I'm sure we did."

Laurence's relationship with his sister was complex. Gwen knew that after their parents died, he had become responsible, giving her an allowance and generally protecting her. Gwen thought Verity, at twenty-six, should really be married and not relying on her brother. Yet from what Laurence had said, when a wedding had eventually been announced, Verity had called it off at the last minute.

Gwen couldn't help wonder how Caroline had got on with her. Her sister-in-law seemed friendly enough, but Gwen sensed that that might not always be the case. She went to the window and looked out. The rain was falling in silver sheets, lit by the sheen from the house lamps. There would be puddles in the dips and hollows of the lawn by morning, she thought as she turned back to face the room. Laurence winked at her. She couldn't resist and walked over, then seated herself on the arm of his chair. He unhooked Verity from him and put his hand on Gwen's knee, gently stroking, but as soon as no one was looking, slid his hand beneath her underskirt. It made her feel lightheaded and she longed to be alone with him. While Tapper's death had been terrible, because of it everything had changed. Laurence had opened up and was himself again, and she was determined to do everything she could to keep him that way.

7

In the mornings when she woke, and the light was pale and lemony, Gwen felt that life couldn't get any better. It had been over a week now, and every single night Laurence had stayed with her. Something had released its grip on him and he was as passionate as he'd been before they arrived at the plantation. They made love at night and they made love in the mornings too. While he slept, the sound of his breathing was comforting, and if she woke before him she just lay listening and marveling at her luck.

She heard the sound of a distant cockerel and watched as Laurence's lashes flickered.

"Hello, darling," he said, opening his eyes and reaching for her.

She snuggled in to him, luxuriating in the warmth.

"Shall we get food sent in and stay in bed all day?" he said.

"Really? Aren't you going to work?"

"No. This is a day entirely for you. So what would you like to do?"

"Do you know what, Laurence?"

He grinned. "Tell me."

She whispered in his ear.

He laughed and pulled a face. "Well, I wasn't expecting that! Bored with me already?"

She kissed him hard on the mouth. "Never!"

"Well, if you're serious, I don't see why you shouldn't see how the tea is made."

"I knew all about making cheese at Owl Tree."

"Of course, I've tasted it . . . so you really want to get up now?"

He stroked her hair and neither of them moved.

He began to bite her ear. Every day Laurence seemed to find a new part of her body, and once he'd found it, she experienced feelings she'd never known were possible. Today, from her ear his mouth traveled all the way down past her breasts, round her waist and to the place between her legs, where she felt the shock of wanting him. But he ignored her as she pushed against him, and carried on to the soft sensitive place at the back of her knees. When he'd finished kissing them, he examined the scars on the front of her knees.

"Heavens, girl, what have you done to yourself?"

"It was the Owl Tree. When I was a child, I used to look for the ghosts in the tree, but I kept falling out before I found them."

He shook his head. "You are impossible."

Whoever would have thought this would be so heavenly, she thought as they made love, and, feeling the warmth of his skin against her own, all thoughts of tea vanished from her mind.

Two hours later, with the rain holding off but a heavy mist still circling the land, Laurence walked her up the hill and along a track she hadn't spotted before. When they could see the lake, Gwen noticed the water was still brown where red earth had washed down. The woods were unusually hushed, the trees dripping and ghostly, and for a moment Gwen believed in the devils that Naveena said still took cover there. All along their route, the rain had intensified the scent of wild orchids and the smell of the grass. Spew, who had become singularly attached to Gwen, ran on ahead, sniffing and snuffling.

"What are those flowers?" she asked, looking at a tall plant with white blooms.

"Angel's Trumpets, we call them," he said, and then pointed at a large rectangular building with rows of shuttered windows, high up on the hill behind their house. "Look, there's the factory."

She touched his arm. "Before we go in, I've been wanting to ask if you'd found out who did that to Tapper?"

There was a flicker of distress on Laurence's face. "It's hard to prove. They close ranks, you see. It's not helpful when it becomes a question of us against them."

"So why was Tapper killed?"

"Revenge over an old injustice."

She sighed. It was so complicated here. She had been brought up to be kind to people and animals. If you were kind, people usually responded the same way.

When they finally reached the building she was out of breath, and watched dark-skinned men squatting on an exterior ledge and washing the multiple windows. Laurence opened the door to the sounds of Hindu worship in the distance, and ordered Spew to wait outside.

He showed Gwen in. There was the clunking noise of machines from the floor above, and a slightly medicinal smell.

He noticed her listening. "There are a lot of machines involved. Everything used to be

149

powered by wood, and on many estates still is, but here, I've invested in fuel oil. Was one of the first, in fact, though we have our wood-burning furnace for drying. Blue gum wood we use. It's a kind of eucalyptus."

Gwen nodded. "I can smell it."

"The building is on four floors," he said. "Do you want to sit down to catch your breath?"

"No." She scanned the spacious ground-floor room. "I didn't realize it would be so big."

"Tea needs air."

"So, what's happening here?"

His eyes lit up. "You really want to know?"

"Of course."

"It's a complicated process, but this is where the baskets of green leaves come in and get weighed. Though there are other weighing stations too. The women are paid by the pound, you see. We do have to keep an eye that they don't include anything they shouldn't to bulk up the weight. We only want the very tips of the bushes. Two leaves and a bud is what we say."

She noticed how warm and friendly he was with a man who came up and spoke in Tamil. After Laurence had replied, also in Tamil, he proudly put an arm round her shoulders.

"Gwen, let me introduce you to my factory manager and tea maker. Darish is in charge of the entire manufacturing process."

The man nodded rather uncertainly and bowed before heading off again.

"He's only ever seen one Englishwoman in here."

"Caroline?"

"No, actually, it was Christina. Come upstairs and I'll show you the withering tables. When there's a large amount of leaf, Darish and his withering supervisor will be working from two in the morning, but because of the weather it's quiet at the moment."

To Gwen it didn't seem quiet at all, but a medley of activity, movement, and background noise. Whether it was the mention of Christina that made her feel uneasy or the intoxicating smell of leaf, strong, slightly bitter, and rather strange, she didn't know. She told herself not to be silly. Laurence had said it was over.

They walked past piles of baskets and various bits of paraphernalia, tools, rope, and the like, and then went on up the stairs.

"These are the withering lofts where we allow the leaves to wither naturally," he said as they reached the top. "The tea plant is actually called *Camellia sinensis.*"

Gwen looked at the four long platform tables on which the tea was laid out. "How long does it take to wither?" she asked.

He put an arm round her waist and she leaned against him, enjoying being with him in his world.

"It depends on the weather. If it's misty, as it is now, it withers slowly. The leaves need warm air to circulate through, you see. The temperature has to be just right. Sometimes we have to use artificial heat from the furnace to dry the leaf. That's what you can hear. But in fine weather, if the shutters are properly adjusted, the wind coming through the open windows is enough."

"And what's on the floor below?"

"Once it's withered adequately, it will go under rollers to bruise the leaves. Do you want to see?"

She watched as the withered leaf was sent down large chutes and into another machine on the floor below. As Darish joined them again, Laurence rolled up his sleeves and, striding around, checked the machines, looking so much in his element she couldn't help smiling.

He said something in Tamil as he turned to Darish. The man nodded, then shot off to do as he'd been asked.

"Shall we go down?" Laurence took her

arm and they headed for the stairs. "The leaves will be compressed in the roll breakers."

"And then?"

"A rotor vane chops the tea, and then it will be sifted to separate the larger particles from the smaller."

She sniffed the air, which now smelled rather like dried mown grass, and gazed at tea that looked like chopped tobacco.

"It will be fermented in the drying room. It's the fermentation that turns it black."

"I never realized so much went into my morning cup of tea."

He kissed the top of her head. "That's not the end of it. It's fired to stop the fermentation, then it's sifted into different grades, and then, only after the final inspection, is it packed and sent off to London or Colombo."

"So much to do. Your man must be very skilled."

Laurence laughed. "He is. As you can see, he has assistant tea makers, and dozens of workers, but he's been on this estate since he was a boy. He worked for my father before me, and he really knows the job."

"So who actually sells the tea?"

"It's auctioned, either in Colombo or London, and my agent fixes up my financial affairs. Now, I think the midday horn will be going off very shortly and you'll find it unbearably loud from here."

He grinned and she couldn't help but see what a powerful man she had married. He wasn't just lean and strong from the physical work he did, he was also determined and very much in charge. And though he was having trouble implementing some of the changes he talked about, she had absolute confidence that he would succeed.

"I love it that you're interested," he said.

"Wasn't Caroline?"

"Not really." He took her arm and led her out.

The mists had lifted and the sky had cleared. It almost looked as if it wasn't going to rain.

"Laurence, I was wondering, why hasn't your sister married?"

He frowned, and a serious look came into his eyes. "I still have hopes."

"But why hasn't she?"

"I don't know. She's a complicated girl, Gwen. I hope you understand that. Men fall for her but then she pushes them away. It's a mystery to me."

Gwen didn't say that she thought Verity sometimes seemed to set herself up to look unattractive to men. She took a breath and sighed.

When they were a hundred yards down the track, the horn blew. She clapped her hands over her ears and tripped over a branch that had fallen across the path.

He groaned. "I did say."

She picked herself up and began to run. Laurence and Spew raced after her, then Laurence swooped down and lifted her into his arms.

"Put me down at once, Laurence Christopher Hooper. What if someone sees!"

"You cannot be trusted to get down a hillside without scratching, grazing, or cutting yourself, so I am going to carry you."

That afternoon the sound of shouting distracted Gwen from the postluncheon book she was reading. A nice little detective story. She reluctantly put the book down and got up to see what was going on.

She heard Laurence call for Naveena. Out in the hallway, he was attempting to comfort Fran, who was sitting with swollen angry eyes and tears streaming down her flushed cheeks.

Gwen went straight to Fran. "Darling, what on earth has happened? Is there bad news?"

Fran shook her head and gulped but, unable to speak, began to sob again.

"It's her charm bracelet," Laurence said. "It's gone missing. But I have no idea why she's so upset. I told her I'd buy her a new one, but it only made her cry the harder."

Fran stood, turned on her heels, and fled.

"See what I mean."

"Oh, Laurence. You are an idiot. That was her mother's bracelet. All the charms are individual and were collected over her mother's entire lifetime. Every charm meant something to Fran. It is utterly irreplaceable."

Laurence's face fell. "I had no idea. Is there nothing we can do?"

"Organize a search, Laurence. That's what you can do. Get all the servants to search. I'm going to comfort my cousin."

The next day, Fran had not turned up for breakfast, so Gwen knocked on her door and tiptoed in. In the room, the shutters were closed and the sour odor of overnight sweat hung in the air. She marched over to the window to let in fresh air.

"Is something wrong?" she said, glancing across at Fran. "You're not even up. Didn't you remember we're going out for lunch?"

"I feel awful, Gwen. Really awful."

Gwen glanced at Fran's full lips, her long lashes, and the two spots of pink on her otherwise flawless complexion. How was it that Fran still looked lovely even when she was unwell, whereas at the first sneeze of a cold, Gwen looked ethereal at best and ghostly at worst.

She sat on the edge of the bed and put a hand on her cousin's forehead. It was rare to see Fran looking sorry for herself.

"You're awfully hot," Gwen said. "I'll get Naveena to bring you some porridge and tea in bed."

"I couldn't eat a thing."

"Maybe not, but you must drink."

Gwen couldn't pretend she wasn't disappointed. This was the day she and Fran were due to go to Nuwara Eliya to lunch with Christina and Mr. Ravasinghe. She wanted to see Christina again, partly out of curiosity and partly to put her own mind at rest, but now that Fran had woken up feverish, they most certainly could not go.

"It's because you were so upset yesterday," Gwen said. "And the weather doesn't help."

Fran groaned. "I don't think my bracelet will ever be found. It has been stolen, I'm sure."

Gwen thought about it. "Did you still have it after the ball?"

"Definitely. You know I wear it almost every day and I'd have noticed if it was missing."

"I'm so sorry."

Fran sniffed.

"Well, don't worry about today. We can go another time."

"No, Gwen, you go. Savi is unveiling his painting. At least one of us must be there."

"You like Mr. Ravasinghe, don't you, Fran?"

Fran's face colored. "I do like him. Very much, as it happens."

"Trust you. I know he's attractive, and it might be fashionable in some circles to patronize artists, but the parents will have a fit." Though she had spoken with a smile, her words were scolding.

"Your parents, Gwen."

There was a short silence.

"Look," Gwen said. "I can't possibly go without you. I don't think Laurence would like it. I don't know why, but he's not too keen on Savi."

Fran made a small gesture of irritation. "It's probably just because he's Sinhalese."

Gwen shook her head. "No. I don't think it's that at all."

"Anyway, you don't have to tell him. It would be dreadful to let Savi down. Please say you'll go."

"And if Laurence finds out?"

"Oh, I'm sure you'll think of something. Can you get back by suppertime?"

"By train, possibly."

"Well then, you'll be back. He probably won't even notice."

Gwen laughed. "If it means that much to you. And Laurence isn't here for lunch today. But who'll look after you?"

"Naveena can bring me drinks and change the sheets. Other than that, the butler can call the doctor if need be."

"I suppose I could ask Verity to go with me."

Fran raised her brows.

"But then again, maybe not."

Fran laughed. "You're not telling me the angelic Gwendolyn Hooper is actually admitting to disliking someone?"

Gwen gave her a poke in the ribs. "I don't dislike her."

"Oi! I'm ill, you know. But if you are going, hurry up, or you won't make the train." She paused. "One last thing."

"Fire away," Gwen said as she leaned over to straighten Fran's bedclothes.

"Find out if he likes me, Gwen. Please."

Gwen laughed as she stood up, but she

had heard a pensive note in her cousin's voice.

"Please?"

"No, honestly, I can't. It's ridiculous."

"I'll be going back to England soon," Fran said, her voice firm again. "And I just want to know if I've got a chance, before I go."

"For what exactly?"

Fran shrugged. "That remains to be seen."

Gwen stooped over the bed and took Fran's hand. "Mr. Ravasinghe is very lovely, but you cannot marry him. Frannie? You do know that, don't you?"

Fran pulled her hand away. "I don't see why not."

Gwen sighed, and considered it. "For one thing, apart from me, nobody here would speak to you again."

"I wouldn't care. Savi and I could live like savages on a remote island in the Indian Ocean. He could paint me naked every day, until my skin turned brown in the sun, and then we'd be the same color."

Gwen laughed. "You are quite ridiculous. One minute in the sun and you look like a lobster."

"You're a spoilsport, Gwendolyn Hooper."

"No, I just believe in being practical. Now I'm off. Take care."

■ ■ ■ ■

Christina wore another black dress, with a plunging neckline, and black lace gloves that ended just past her elbows. Her green eyes glittered, and Gwen noticed how beautifully shaped her brows were. Her blond hair was barely pinned up but hung in loops down her back; interwoven with black beads, it gave the impression of effortless glamour. She had a heavily sequined silver ribbon that lay across her forehead, jet drop earrings, and a jet choker. Gwen, in a pastel day dress, felt eclipsed.

"So," Christina said as she waved her ebony cigarette holder in the air. "I hear you met our ravishing Mr. Ravasinghe before your feet even touched Ceylonese soil."

"I did . . . He was kind to me."

"Oh, that is like Savi. He is kind to everyone, aren't you, sweetie? I'm surprised you didn't head straight off into the jungle with him."

Gwen laughed. "The thought did cross my mind."

"But then again, you have hooked the most eligible man in Ceylon."

Savi turned to Gwen and winked. "Don't

take a blind bit of notice. Christina's whole aim in life is to get under people's skin, one way or another."

"Well, since darling Ernest popped off, what is there to do but make even more money, and annoy the hell out of everyone? He left me a bank, you know. How boring is that? Several years ago now, of course. But I shall stop right now. It isn't fair to our new arrival. I hope we shall become immensely good friends, Gwen."

Gwen said something vague in response. She had never met anyone quite like Christina, and it wasn't just the strange New York accent that made her different. She had an unsettling thought that perhaps it was that very difference that Laurence had found attractive.

"Why are you in Ceylon, Mrs. Bradshaw?"

"Oh, for heaven's sake, don't be bashful, call me Christina."

Gwen smiled.

"I've been here on and off for years, but I'm here now because Savi promised to paint my picture. I found him ages ago at a little exhibition of his work in New York. So intimate, his portraits. He draws the heart out of his sitter. I, for one, have fallen in love with him. We all do in the end. You must get him to paint you."

"Oh, I —"

"Now I do hope you like duck," Christina interrupted. "We are having curried *brinjal* to start with, and then the most beautiful honeyed duck."

As Christina led them into the dining room, Gwen stopped in front of a large mask hanging on the wall of the corridor.

"What is that?"

"A traditional devil dancer's mask."

Gwen gaped at the odious thing, took a step back, and bumped right into Mr. Ravasinghe, who patted her on the back. The mask was shocking. An abomination. Wild gray hair a foot long, a large open red mouth with bared teeth, and bright red ears that stuck out either side. It had ogling orange eyes, and the nose and cheeks were painted white.

"Your gorgeous husband gave it to me," Christina said. "A little gift. You know how appreciative he is."

Gwen was dumbstruck, both by the gift and by Christina's attitude.

She thought back to earlier on when, after taking a carriage from the small station at Nanu Oya, she'd met Mr. Ravasinghe at the Grand. She had waited for him outside in the street and had picked up the scent of eucalyptus drifting across from the cloudy

163

Pidurutalagala ranges. With things now going well with Laurence, she'd felt embarrassed by her previous interest in the
painter. Though she could remember little
of what had passed, she did feel ashamed
that she'd drunk so much champagne at the
ball.

Today, outside the Grand, he had smiled
deeply as if nothing had happened at all,
then he'd taken her arm to assist her across
a road crammed with bullock carts and
rickshaws. At that point a high-pitched voice
had called out.

"Hello. How are you?" the woman asked,
and stared with her nostrils flaring. Gwen
was beginning to think of Florence as the
voice of conscience.

"Very well, thank you," she said.

"I hope your husband is well, dear." The
word *husband* was pointedly emphasized.

"Florence, it is lovely to see you, but I'm
afraid we can't stop to natter. We're on our
way to luncheon."

Florence's nostrils flared again, and her
chins shook. "Without Laurence?"

"Yes, he's busy all day. Some business
about the rollers."

"No doubt God will take care of you,
dear," she added, narrowing her eyes at Mr.
Ravasinghe.

After that they'd passed a small photographer's shop. Gwen glanced in the window and, intrigued to see a photograph of a wedding ceremony between a European man and a Sinhalese woman in traditional dress, she thought of Fran.

Mr. Ravasinghe noticed her looking. "It wasn't unusual, you know, in the early days. Up until the midnineteenth century, the government actually encouraged mixed marriage."

"Why did it change?"

"A lot of reasons. In 1869, once the Suez Canal was open, that made it easier for Englishwomen to get here quickly. Up until then they'd been scarce on the ground. But even before that the government wanted to claw back power. They were worried the Eurasian offspring of mixed marriages wouldn't be so loyal to the empire."

Now, as they seated themselves at the small dining table and Gwen kept a watch on Christina, she wondered if she might have been a little sharp with Fran about Mr. Ravasinghe.

"Ah," Christina said and clapped her hands. "Here comes the *brinjal.*"

The waiter served something Gwen did not recognize.

"Don't look so worried, Gwen," Savi said.

"It's only aubergine. It absorbs all the garlic and spices. Delicious. Do try."

Gwen forked a piece up. The texture felt strange in her mouth, but the flavors were lovely, and she was suddenly ravenous. "It's very nice."

"How well mannered you are. We will have to change that, won't we, Savi?"

Mr. Ravasinghe gave her another warning look.

"Oh, all right. Savi, you are a bore."

Gwen concentrated on polishing off her *brinjal* while the other two talked. This foreign food was growing on her, but Gwen felt a little intimidated by Christina. A familiar sinking feeling took hold of her, and she found it hard to swallow the last forkful as she began to wonder about Laurence and Christina again. Devil dancing indeed! Had Laurence given it to her to mean something in particular, or did people in Ceylon just go around giving each other hideous presents? She didn't want to reveal her ignorance, but she did, however, decide on one vital question.

"You've known my husband for a long time?" she said.

Christina paused before answering, then smiled. "Ah, yes. Laurence and I go way back. You're a very lucky woman."

Gwen looked across at Mr. Ravasinghe, who just inclined his head. He hadn't looked especially put out when she'd turned up alone, and with his normal civility, they had set off together for the villa Christina was renting. His clothes were immaculate — a dark suit and white shirt that shone against the color of his skin — and he'd walked so close she could smell the cinnamon. Yet she wondered why he had stubble on his chin as if he'd risen late and not had time to shave or, indeed, as if he hadn't even been to bed at all.

"I am so very sorry about your cousin," he said, seeing her looking at him. "I do hope she makes a rapid recovery. I was thinking of inviting her for a boating trip on the lake at Kandy, now that the rain is holding off a little. Kandy is the Hill Capital."

"Fran would love that. I'll pass on the invitation."

He nodded. "Actually, if Fran is still here in July, you might both enjoy a candlelit, full-moon procession in Kandy. It's called the Perahera festival and is rather spectacular. They decorate the elephants in gold and silver."

Christina whistled. "Do come. The procession celebrates the tooth of Gautama Buddha. Have you heard the story?"

Gwen shook her head.

"Centuries ago, a princess is said to have smuggled the tooth over to Ceylon from India, hidden in her hair. And now it's carried through the streets, to the sound of drums and followed by garlanded dancers. Let's all go," Christina said. "Will you ask darling Laurence, Gwen, or shall I?"

"I will," Gwen said, and forced a laugh to mask her irritation at the way Christina was implying she still maintained a certain familiarity with Laurence.

After the pudding had been cleared away, Christina lit a cigarette, then stood. "I think it's time to unveil your canvas, Mr. Ravasinghe, don't you? But first, I need to powder my nose."

She came round to Savi's chair as he stood and Gwen caught a trace of Tabac Blond by Caron, an American perfume that Fran had worn. How appropriate it was here, muddled in with cigarette smoke. Christina kissed Mr. Ravasinghe's cheek, then raked his long wavy hair with her varnished nails. As Mr. Ravasinghe turned to Christina, Gwen studied his profile. He was a very good-looking man, perhaps made more so by the hint of danger behind his eyes. He lifted the American's hand from his hair and kissed it with such tenderness that it unset-

168

tled Gwen.

She had been avoiding the issue of asking Mr. Ravasinghe if he liked her cousin, but now that Christina had left them alone it seemed like the perfect opportunity. And though she had told Fran she wouldn't do it, now she felt it important that she did.

"Talking of Fran," Gwen said.

"Were we?"

"Earlier, yes."

"Of course. And what do you want to say about your delightful cousin?"

"What do you think of her, Mr. Ravasinghe?"

"You must call me Savi." He paused and smiled warmly, looking into her eyes as he did. "I think she is perfectly lovely."

"You like her, then?"

"Who could not? But then, I would like any cousin of yours, Mrs. Hooper."

She smiled, but his reply had only created more doubt. He did like Fran but would have liked any cousin. What kind of an answer was that?

As Christina came back into the room, he held out his hand for Gwen and they all walked through to a well-aired room at the back of the house. Two tall windows overlooked a terraced wall garden, and the canvas, covered by a sweep of red velvet, leaned on a large easel in the middle of the room.

"Now are we ready?" Christina said, and she pulled the drape of velvet away with a flourish.

Gwen gazed upon Christina's likeness, then glanced up at Mr. Ravasinghe, who smiled and held her gaze without blinking, as if in expectation of a comment.

"It's unusual," she said, feeling hesitant.

"It's more than that, darling Savi. It is sublime," Christina said.

The trouble was, Gwen wasn't sure. It wasn't that she didn't like his painting, but she had the feeling that he was somehow laughing at her. That they both were. He was a perfect example of polite well-bred manhood, but there was something about him, and it was more than the fact that he'd seen her in such a tipsy state, more than the fact that he had stroked her forehead and helped her into bed.

"It's not what you can see that's bothering you," Christina said.

Gwen looked at her and frowned.

"You're frightened of seeing what might happen next."

Savi laughed. "Or what has already happened."

Gwen looked back at the canvas, but a

second look only served to underscore her reservations. Christina's cheeks were flushed, her hair tangled, and all she wore was a black jet necklace and a knowing look. The portrait ended just beneath her naked breasts. She knew she was being ridiculous, but she hated to think that Laurence had seen Christina like that.

"Savi painted your husband's first wife, you know."

"I haven't seen it."

"I imagine Laurence might have taken it down after she died."

Gwen thought for a moment. "Did you know Caroline?"

"Not well. I got to know Laurence afterward. Savi was all set to paint Verity too, before her big day, had even made some preliminary sketches, but then she up and bolted back to England. Nobody knew why she ditched her poor intended chap. He was something in government, and rather sweet, I heard. What do you make of your sister-in-law?"

"I don't know her very well."

"What do you think of Verity Hooper, Savi? Do tell us."

Mr. Ravasinghe's slight frown was enough to communicate disapproval, though whether it was disapproval of Verity herself or simply disinclination to hear Verity as the topic of conversation, Gwen wasn't certain.

"Well," Christina continued, "in my opinion Verity is a troublemaker and, apart from her brother, horses are all she cares for. Or they were when she lived in England."

"She is a troubled soul," he said, and paused to take out a small sketch pad from his jacket pocket. "Would you mind if I made a sketch of you, Mrs. Hooper?"

"Oh, I don't know. Laurence . . ."

"Laurence isn't here, darling. Let him do it."

Mr. Ravasinghe was smiling at her. "You are so remarkably fresh and unspoiled. I'd like to try to capture that."

"Very well. How do you want me?"

"Exactly as you are."

8

The minute Fran was well again, she was up, dressed, and all set to take the train from Hatton for Nanu Oya, the station nearest to Nuwara Eliya. Her cases were going on ahead to Colombo, and Mr. Ravasinghe had promised to drive her to Colombo himself, after her little sightseeing tour up in Kandy. From Colombo she'd be returning to England. The two women hugged as McGregor brought round the car, muttering that he wasn't a bloody chauffeur. Gwen smiled, but she was really going to miss her friend.

"Now you be careful, Fran."

Fran laughed. "When am I not?"

"Just all the time. I will miss you, Fran."

"And I'll miss you too, but I'll be back, maybe next year."

Fran gave Gwen one more hug, then got into the car, and as McGregor steered them round and then up the hill, she hung out of the window waving until they disappeared over the brow of the hill. Gwen thought back to their breakfast together, when, blushing deeply, she'd confided her jealousy over Christina.

Fran had laughed. "Are you afraid Laurence might not be able to resist her?"

"I don't know."

"Don't be so silly. It's obvious he adores you, and he wouldn't put your love in jeopardy over an excessively made-up American."

Gwen stubbed her toe in the gravel, shook her head, and, hoping her cousin was right, hurried inside to write to her mother. Fran's departure had made her feel homesick.

The next morning, when Gwen awoke, she had to rush to the bathroom to be sick in the lavatory. Either it was that wretched brinjal or she'd caught whatever it had been that had made Fran ill, though Fran hadn't mentioned actually having been sick. The latrine coolie hadn't yet been, and as she threw in half a bucket of sawdust, the smell made her reel.

She rang the bell for Naveena and, while she waited, she opened the curtains on a summery sky with only fine trails of light cloud. Hoping that the rain might be over until October, when the second monsoon of the year would begin, she took deep breaths of sweet-smelling air.

Naveena knocked and brought in two boiled eggs on an ebony tray, with a silver spoon and two porcelain egg cups. "Good morning, Lady," she said.

"Oh, I couldn't eat a thing, I've been awfully sick."

"You must be knowing eating is good. An egg hopper maybe?"

Gwen shook her head. An egg hopper was a curious bowl-shaped biscuity thing, with an egg cooked in the bottom of it.

The woman smiled and waggled her head. "Won't you try the spiced tea, Lady?"

"What's in it?"

"Cinnamon bark, cloves, a little ginger."

"And our best Hooper's tea, I hope," Gwen added. "But as I said, I've been awfully sick. I think a cup of normal tea, don't you?"

The woman smiled again and her face lit up. "I have made it specially. And it is good for your condition."

Gwen stared at her. "For a tummy upset? My mother always said the blander the better."

The woman kept on smiling and nodding, and making funny little gestures with her hands, like birds' wings fluttering. Gwen couldn't think of the servants as people who did not feel or think, in the way Florence did, and often wondered what went on in their minds. This was the first time the woman's normally calm face had shown so much emotion.

"Well, what is it, Naveena? Why are you grinning at me that way?"

"You ladies! Master's first wife just the same. You are not observing your calendar, Lady."

"Why? Have I missed something important? I'll get dressed immediately. I feel much better now. Whatever it was seems to have passed."

The woman brought over a calendar from the small desk where Gwen kept her lists of household tasks.

"We will be needing to prepare the nursery, Lady."

The nursery? She felt a flash of heat and her face tingled as she scrutinized the dates. How could she have not realized? It must have been the day after the ball, the time Laurence had opened up, and they had made love properly, unless it had happened the time before. Still, what did that matter? This was what she had hoped for, what she had dreamed of, from the moment she set eyes on Laurence and thought, *That man is the father of my children.* She should have known. She'd felt queasy, there had been a languor about her too, some moments of intense hunger, and her breasts had felt unusually full. But, never regular, she hadn't even considered it. And with Fran ill, there had been so much going on, she hadn't kept track. Now that she knew, she couldn't wait to tell Laurence, and hugged herself in anticipation.

It had all happened so quickly that Gwen realized she had no idea where the nursery was. It seemed ridiculous that she still hadn't explored the whole house. There was Laurence's study on the ground floor; she had tried the handle once or twice when she was looking for him, but it had always been locked. His bedroom she had seen again when she'd gone to gaze at the photograph of the blond woman. She'd turned the picture over and noticed Caroline's name on the back, and then she'd looked for Savi's painting, but it was nowhere obvious. She'd also explored five guest rooms and two more bathrooms, but there were two other locked doors that she'd assumed must be storage cupboards, one in her bathroom and the other in the corridor. It was remiss. She should have asked to see inside them.

"Why don't you show me the nursery this morning?" she said, smiling at Naveena.

The woman's face fell. "I am not sure, Lady. It has not been touched since the day —"

"Oh, I see. Well, I'm not afraid of a little dust. I insist you show it to me, the moment I am fully dressed."

The woman nodded and backed out of the room.

When Naveena came back an hour later, Gwen was surprised that the woman led her straight to the locked door in the bathroom.

"It is through here, Lady. I have the key."

She unlocked the door, then pushed it open, and they walked into a short corridor, more of a passageway really, which Gwen realized must run parallel to the main corridor of the ground floor. It turned left at the end and into another room.

Inside the room, Gwen stood rooted to the spot, feeling uneasy. It was dark and the acrid smell made her nose sting.

Naveena opened a window and the shutters. "I am sorry, Lady. The master would not let us touch."

Now that there was light, Gwen scanned the room, startled to see cobwebs so dense the wall was barely visible behind them, and a thick layer of insect-encrusted dust lying over the furniture, the floor, a nursing chair, and the crib. What the smell actually was, she could not say. Decay certainly, not a smell you'd normally associate with a nursery, but more than that: the room smelled of sadness and she couldn't help imagine Laurence's crushed hopes.

"Oh, Naveena. It is so sad. How long ago?"

"Twelve years, Lady," Naveena said as she surveyed the room.

"You must have been fond of Caroline and little Thomas."

"We do not speak of it . . ." she said, her voice tapering off.

"Was it because of the birth that Caroline became ill?"

Naveena's face clouded. She nodded but said nothing.

Gwen wanted to know more, but seeing the old woman's distress she changed the subject.

"It certainly needs a good clean in here," she said.

"Yes, Lady."

Gwen knew that cleaning a room in Ceylon bore no resemblance to cleaning a room in Gloucestershire. Here, every single item was removed, and that included carpets, wall hangings, and heavy furniture. Then everything was piled up on the lawn. While the room was being cleaned and disinfected, another team of houseboys beat the rugs and polished the furniture. Nothing was left untouched.

"Once everything is outside, make sure they burn it."

Gwen looked at the end wall. On closer inspection, what she had first thought was mold was actually a mural, and you could just about make out the scene. Closer still, when she touched it, a light film of dirt came off on her fingers.

"Can you get me a rag, Naveena?"

The woman handed her a muslin from her pocket, and Gwen wiped a section of the wall.

She peered at it, her fingers tracing the images. "It's a fantasy land, isn't it? Look. Waterfalls and rivers, and here, look right here, there are beautiful mountains and . . . maybe a palace, or is it a temple?"

"It is Buddhist temple near Kandy. Painted by master's first wife. Picture is of our country, Lady. It is Ceylon."

"She was an artist?"

Naveena nodded.

Gwen inhaled, held her breath for a moment, then quickly exhaled. "Well, what are we waiting for? Let's get all this outside. And I think it would be best to paint over that mural."

While Gwen walked back to her room, she thought about Caroline. She had put so much effort into making the room beautiful, and Gwen wondered how much of the elegant house had been her doing too. She regretted her snap decision to paint over the wall. Maybe Mr. Ravasinghe could be persuaded to restore it, though Laurence's irrational dislike of the man might prevent that.

By the time Laurence was back for lunch, a fire was burning in the yard and the last of the nursery furniture was going up.

"Hello there," he said as he burst into the living room looking surprised. "Having a bonfire?"

She stared at him, a wide smile spreading across her face. "Darling," she said, and patted the sofa where she was sitting. "Come and sit down. I have something to tell you."

The next day, before Verity went south to stay on a friend's fish farm, with talk of possibly a visit to England after that, she, Laurence, and Gwen were sitting on the verandah finishing off breakfast.

"There's a horse I'm interested in buying," Verity said. "I've been missing having my own horse."

Gwen couldn't hide her surprise. "Goodness, how can you afford that?"

"Oh, I have my allowance."

Laurence turned sideways to fondle one of the dogs.

"I didn't realize it was so generous."

Verity smiled sweetly. "Laurence has always looked after me; why would he stop now?"

Gwen shrugged. If Laurence was always to be so generous, she'd probably never leave.

"But you must want to be married and set up a family home of your own?"

"Must I?"

Gwen didn't know what to make of her, but after her sister-in-law had gone, she decided to broach the subject with Laurence.

"I don't think Verity should remain under the impression that she may always live with us. She does have the house in England."

He sighed deeply. "She's my sister, Gwen. She's lonely there. What else can I do?"

"You might encourage her to make her own life. Once the baby is here —"

He broke in. "Once the baby is here, I'm

182

sure she'll buck up and be a great help to you."

Gwen pulled a face. "I don't want her to be a help to me."

"Without your mother at hand, you'll need someone."

"I'd rather ask Fran."

"I'm afraid I must put my foot down. Verity is already based here, and I'm not at all sure, charming though she is, that your cousin is the sort of person you'll need."

Gwen fought back angry tears. "I don't recall ever being consulted about Verity being 'based' here."

A muscle in Laurence's jaw was twitching. "I'm sorry, darling, but that was not your decision to make."

"And what makes you think Verity is the right sort of person? I don't want her help. It's my baby and I want Fran."

"I think you'll find it is 'our' baby." He grinned. "Unless, of course, the baby is the result of some kind of immaculate conception."

She flung her napkin on the table and, feeling much too tense, stood up. "It's not fair, Laurence, it really isn't!"

She ran to her room, took off her shoes, and, in a blaze of temper, threw them at the wall before bursting into loud sobs. She

183

closed the curtains and the shutters, took off her dress, then flung herself on the bed facedown and thumped the pillow. After a while, when he did not come, she crawled under the covers and, feeling sorry for herself, pulled them up over her head, just as she'd done as a child. The thought of home brought forth even more sobs and, curled up in a ball, she cried until her eyes were stinging.

She thought back to the day before when she'd asked Naveena why she hadn't been Verity's ayah too.

Naveena had shaken her head. "Younger woman. More strong."

"But you know Verity well?"

Naveena wobbled her head. "Yes and no, Lady."

"What do you mean?"

"You are facing difficulty with that one. Since she is a girl she is every time causing trouble."

Thinking of that now, Gwen felt even more strongly that she wanted Fran to be there when she had the baby.

A little later she heard a knock at the door, and then she heard Laurence's voice. "Are you all right, Gwendolyn?"

She wiped her eyes with the sheet but didn't speak. It really wasn't fair, and now she'd been made to look like a fool. She decided not to speak to him.

"Gwendolyn?"

She sniffed.

"Darling, I'm sorry I was brusque."

"Go away."

She heard him stifle a chuckle and then, despite her previous decision, found herself laughing and crying at the same time.

When he pushed the door open and came over to sit on the bed beside her, she reached out a hand.

"Gwen, I love you. I never intended to upset you."

He wiped her face and began kissing her damp cheeks, then pulled up her chemise and turned her onto her back. She watched while he removed his shoes and trousers. He was so tough and his skin so tanned from the outdoor life that the sight of him undressing never failed to excite her. As he pulled his shirt over his head she felt her breasts tingle and her stomach twist. The fact that she couldn't hide how much she wanted him seemed to drive him on and fired up even stronger feelings within her.

"Come," she said, unable to wait and reaching out her arms to him.

He smiled and she could tell from his eyes he was going to draw this out. He placed his warm palm on the barely perceptible curve of her belly, stroking softly until she moaned. Then he kissed her there and with small butterfly kisses carried on to the place where his head disappeared between her legs.

She was right, of course. He did draw it out and by the end she was almost crying with relief.

When her parents had rowed, her father seemed never to have heard of the word *sorry.* Instead he would make her mother a cup of tea and bring her a rock bun. She laughed out loud. This was so much better than a rock bun, and, if they were always to make up in this fashion, it might be worth falling out more frequently.

Apart from the argument over Verity, Laurence was the soul of consideration. She was only expecting a baby, she would repeat, though in reality she was delighted by his affectionate concern. In July, after only a minor battle with him over the advisability of traveling in her condition, they both went to Kandy with Christina and another friend, but not Mr. Ravasinghe. When Gwen asked Christina where Savi was, she just shrugged and said he was in London.

The procession was inspiring, though

186

Gwen clung to Laurence for fear of being trampled by the crowd, if not by the elephants. The air smelled of incense and flowers, and she had to keep pinching herself to check that she wasn't dreaming. While Gwen felt a bit drab in her maternity smock, Christina looked spectacular in floating black chiffon. Despite the American's continued attempts to draw Laurence aside, he appeared to show no particular interest and, hugely relieved, Gwen felt she'd been silly to suspect that he would not be able to resist the woman.

After that, despite some weeks of nausea, she seemed to float in a kind of perpetual haze. Laurence said she was blooming, and looked more beautiful than ever. And that was how she felt. Verity had stayed away and time had moved on. It was not until she was into her fifth month, on a day when Florence Shoebotham had been invited for afternoon tea, that her size was remarked on. Other people might have noticed it too, but it was Florence who pointed out that Gwen looked rather too big, and she offered to call Dr. Partridge.

When, the next day, John Partridge entered Gwen's room, his hand outstretched, she was delighted to see him.

"Oh, I am so glad it is you, John," she

said, and got up. "I do hope there is nothing wrong with me."

"No need to get up," he said, then asked how she was feeling as she perched on the edge of her bed.

"I am quite tired, and awfully hot."

"That is normal. Is there nothing else worrying you?"

She swung her legs up onto the bed. "My ankles do swell up a bit."

He smoothed his mustache as he pulled up a chair. "Well then, you must rest more often. Though in a woman as young as yourself, I don't think swelling ankles will be much of an issue."

"I get awful headaches, but then I always have."

He twisted his mouth around as he thought, then patted her hand. "You *are* big. I think the best thing would be to take a look at you. Would you like a woman with you?"

"Oh, there really isn't anybody. Only Naveena. My cousin Frances has been back in England for some time now." She sighed deeply.

"What is it, Gwen?"

She wondered what to say. Laurence would not budge from his view that Verity was the person to assist with the delivery, and with the baby. This was the one thorn in her side, and it was a big one. She had been feeling so content, but as the months rolled on and her confinement grew closer, she longed for her mother. She needed someone she felt comfortable with, and hated the thought that Laurence believed Verity should be that person. If she was honest, she didn't exactly distrust her sister-in-law, but the thought of having nobody she loved to turn to caused her deep misgivings. What if the birth was tricky, what if she couldn't cope? But whenever she broached the subject with Laurence, he dug in his heels and she'd begun to think she was being irrational.

She sighed and looked at the doctor. "It's just that Laurence has invited his sister to keep me company and to help, you know, with everything. She's on the coast at present, but may go back to their family place in Yorkshire for a bit. It's let out, but they keep a small apartment."

"Would you rather be confined in England, Gwen?"

"No. At least, not in Yorkshire. It's not that. It's just that I'm not sure about Verity being here." She pulled a face and her lower lip wobbled.

"I'm sure you have no need to worry. Your

sister-in-law will be a help, and perhaps some time spent with just her and your baby might assist you all to get to know each other a little better."

"Do you think so?"

"She suffered, you know, more than Laurence, I think."

"Oh?"

"When their parents died, she was still young, and Laurence was like a father to her. The trouble was he married so soon after their parents died and, of course, most of the year she was packed off to boarding school."

"Why didn't she come to live here after she left school?"

"She did for a while, she certainly loved it here, but all her old school friends were in England. I think Laurence thought she'd make a better life there. So when she was twenty-one, he gave her the place in Yorkshire."

"He does look after her."

"And that's a good thing. Rumor has it she was passed over by the one person she really wanted."

"Who was that?"

He shook his head. "All families have secrets of one kind or another, don't they? Maybe ask Laurence. But I think Verity could do with feeling useful to you. It might help her feel better about herself. Now lie back and I'll examine your tummy."

Once Gwen was lying flat on the bed, he opened his black leather bag and drew out something that looked like a horn. She wasn't sure that all families had secrets, and thought about her own family, but bringing her mother and father to mind only served to bring on an awful spasm of homesickness.

"I'll just have a listen," he said.

"Are there any other family secrets?" she asked.

The doctor just shrugged. "Who knows, Gwen? Especially when it comes to human relationships."

She stared up at the ceiling and, listening to the bumping and scraping going on overhead, thought about what he'd said about Verity. He glanced up too.

"It's just cleaning day. Laurence's room today."

"How are you and your husband getting on, Gwen? Looking forward to being parents?"

"Of course. Why do you ask?"

"No reason. Are there twins in your family, or perhaps in his?"

"My grandmother was a twin."

"Well, it looks to me that the reason for your advanced size is not due to anything being wrong. I think you might be carrying twins."

Her mouth fell open as she gasped. "Really? Are you sure?"

"I can't be sure, but it does appear to be the case."

Gwen glanced out through the window as she tried to unscramble her feelings. Two babies! That was a good thing, wasn't it? A furry langur was sitting on the breakfast table on the verandah, with a baby clinging to its tummy. The mother langur stared at Gwen with round, brown eyes and with fluffy golden hair standing up in a halo around its dark face.

"Is there anything particular I shouldn't do?" She felt herself turning red. "I mean with Laurence."

He smiled. "Don't worry about that. It's good for you. We just have to keep an eye on you, that's all, and you must take adequate rest. I can't stress that enough."

"Thank you, John. I was thinking of having a picnic before the rains, down by the lake. Would that be all right?"

"Yes, but don't go into the water, and watch out for leeches at the edge."

9

The picnic was timed to coordinate with Verity's arrival back from the south. Two of the houseboys had carried the hamper, along with the blankets, and had brought out a chair for Gwen from the weather-beaten boathouse at the edge of the lake. As Laurence, Verity, and her friend Pru Bertram made themselves comfortable on tartan rugs, they were watched by a long-tailed toque monkey in a nearby tree.

Gwen was wearing a green cotton over-dress, smocked at the top to create volume where she needed it, and was sitting with a large sun hat sheltering her face. Each morning, when she ran her hands over her breasts and belly after her bath, she gazed in wonder at her rapidly changing body, and carefully rubbed in a spoonful of nut oil infused with ginger. Now that the weeks of nausea were well and truly over, she hoped for some respite before growing even bigger.

Nick McGregor had been invited to join them but had refused, claiming a coolie problem.

"Is there another problem in the labor lines?" she whispered to Laurence.

"There are always minor disputes. Nothing to concern yourself with."

She nodded. Since the incident over the Tamil with the injured foot, McGregor had been cool with her. He'd helped her communicate with the new gardeners and had shown a mild interest in her cheesemaking plans, but other than that had remained distant. She'd tried including him in her ideas for the place, but he was only interested in tea.

It was a brilliant day, with the sun glittering on the lake and a light breeze to cool the skin. Gwen watched a cloud of pale butterflies float just above the surface of the water. Spew bounded in, jumping, splashing, and enjoying being a nuisance. Bobbins sat at the edge with her head resting on her paws. She was not as adventurous as her brother, added to which she was heavily pregnant. Gwen had been watching her with interest and felt a great deal of sympathy for the animal's huge distended abdomen.

"How funny," Gwen said. She leaned back to feel a little of the sun on her face. "Bobbins is the observer and Spew the doer. A bit like me and Fran. I do wish she were here, Laurence."

"We've been over that, sweetheart."

"I promise I'll do everything I can to help," Verity said. "That's why I haven't gone back to England."

"I'm sure Gwen is grateful."

Verity gave her a wide smile. "Darling, do let's open the hamper now."

Laurence undid the catches, pulled out two bottles of champagne and several glasses, which he handed round, and then three plates of sandwiches.

"Mmm," he said, taking the cover off one of the plates and sniffing. "These look like salmon and cucumber."

"What about the rest?" Gwen asked, feeling ravenous.

"Why don't you tell us what's in the other two, Pru?" Laurence said.

Pru was quiet and unassuming, a typically pale-skinned Englishwoman who under the Ceylon sunshine seemed to turn bright pink, and though a little older, she had been a loyal friend to Verity.

"Certainly." She took the two plates. "Egg and lettuce in these, and something I don't

195

recognize in these . . . Oh yes, of course, it's *brinjal*."

"*Brinjal* in a sandwich?" Gwen said, remembering her lunch at Christina's.

Verity nodded. "Absolutely! We always have one foreign dish on our picnics, don't we, Laurence? It's a family tradition. Don't you have family traditions in your own family?"

Laurence straightened his hat as he glanced at his sister. "We are Gwen's family now, Verity."

Verity colored. "Of course. I didn't mean . . ."

He uncorked the champagne, filled their glasses, then stood and held up his glass. "To my wonderful wife."

"Hear, hear!" Pru said.

When they had eaten their fill, Verity, who had polished off more than her share of the champagne, got up. "Well, as you know, Laurence, a walk round part of the lake is what follows. Are you coming?"

"I don't think I'll be able to manage that," Gwen said, reaching out a hand to Laurence.

"But you'll come, won't you, Laurence? You always do. Gwen will be fine with Pru."

"Nevertheless, I shall stay with Gwen."

Gwen shot him a thank-you smile and he

squeezed her hand.

"Keep an eye open for water buffalo," he said as Verity started to move off, looking a little miffed.

At that moment Spew came rushing out of the lake as he chased away a group of herons, then raced round Verity, showering her with water. Gwen looked round for Bobbins, who, it seemed, had disappeared.

"Dratted dog!" Verity said, brushing off her damp dress. As usual she'd chosen the wrong color, Gwen thought. Orange didn't suit a sallow complexion. And a yellow sun, reflecting its color onto her face, made her look quite acid.

"I'll accompany you, Verity," Pru said, and started to make a move.

"No. I'll take Spew for a run. You're not fit enough and you'll get too hot. Come on, Spew."

Pru looked deflated and settled down again. "No, of course, you're right. I'm not as energetic as you."

Gwen called out to Laurence, who had taken a few steps toward the lake. "Do you think I might just dip my toes in?"

Laurence twisted round. "I don't see why not. I wouldn't want to mollycoddle you."

"Do you want to come, Pru?" Gwen said as she took off her shoes.

When Pru shook her head, Gwen walked down to the bank with Laurence, then sat and rolled down her stockings with one hand while holding on to her sun hat with the other. He helped her up and they wandered a little farther along. The water was gently lapping the earthy edge and she wriggled her toes in the cool of it.

"This is so lovely, isn't it?" she said.

"It's you that makes it lovely."

"Oh, Laurence, I am so happy. I hope it never ends."

"There's absolutely no reason why it should," he said, and kissed her.

She watched a bird hop onto a rock nearby. "Do look at that robin," she said.

"It's a Kashmir flycatcher actually. Wonder what's brought it here. You usually see them on the golf course at Nuwara Eliya. It's the most beautiful place, sits between the town and the hills."

"You know a lot about birds."

"Birds and tea."

She laughed. "You must tell me what they all are, so that I can teach our baby."

"Our babies, you mean!"

As he wrapped his arms round her, she glanced up at him. His eyes were sparkling and he looked so proud and happy she felt her heart would burst.

But then, as he held both her hands and searched her face, he looked suddenly serious. "Gwen, if I could only tell you how much you've changed my life."

She drew back. "For the better, I hope."

He took a deep breath and she loved the way his whole face seemed to be smiling.

"More than you'll ever know," he said.

A gust of wind blew her hair into her eyes. He tucked a ringlet behind her ear. "After Caroline, I felt my life was over, but you've given me hope."

As the wind got up a little more, she took off her hat, then, leaning back against the warmth of his chest, turned to look at the lake again. He wasn't always able to say what he clearly felt, but as he stroked her hair, she understood how much he loved her. He dipped his head and twisted her round. She closed her eyes against the intense glare of a yellow sun reflecting off the waves, then felt his lips on her neck just behind her ears. A shiver ran through her. *If only I could fix this moment in my mind forever,* she thought.

They walked farther on for a while before turning back, but the peace was disturbed by frenzied barking. Gwen glanced across to see Spew scratching at the door of the boathouse.

"I'll bet Bobbins has got in there to deliver her puppies," Laurence said. He glanced back as the sound of an oar splashing the water drew his attention. "I don't believe it. What is he doing here?"

"It seems like Verity is with him. And Christina."

He muttered under his breath but went to lend an elbow to help Verity and then Christina out of the outrigger canoe. While Verity shook herself down, Christina grinned.

"Hello, darling," she said, before putting both palms on the sides of Laurence's head and kissing his cheeks. She took a step away, allowing her palm to trail down Laurence's bare arm, her fingers lightly tickling him as she did.

As Laurence reddened, Gwen bristled at this act of overt intimacy but forced herself to smile. "How nice to see you, Christina."

"My, you do look well, I must remember to get myself pregnant sometime." She winked at Laurence.

The nerve of the woman, Gwen thought. How dare she flirt with my husband in front of me. She moved closer to Laurence and pushed the hair off his forehead in a proprietary way.

"I came across them on my walk," Verity said. "He was sketching her with one of the islands as a backdrop. Their canoe was tied up nearby, so he offered me a lift. I can't resist a ride in a canoe with a handsome man."

Savi Ravasinghe seemed untroubled as he climbed out of the canoe, but Laurence looked tense.

"My apologies for intruding," Savi said.

"Not at all." Gwen held out her hand. "But I'm afraid we're just wrapping up here."

He smiled as he took her hand. "You look absolutely blooming, Mrs. Hooper, if I may say so."

"Thank you. I do feel rather wonderful. It's lovely to see you again. How was your trip to London? I sometimes think it's —"

"It's time we went in," Laurence said, interrupting and nodding curtly at Savi before turning his back on him and holding out a hand to Christina. "Would *you* like to come up to the house?"

Gwen frowned.

"Thank you, Laurence. I am, of course, deeply tempted," she said, and blew him a kiss, "but I think on this occasion I'll go back with Savi."

Laurence didn't speak.

"Actually, I have something for Mrs. Hooper," Savi said. He reached into a brown leather sketching satchel and pulled out a page of heavy cartridge paper protected by tissue paper. "I've been carrying this around for a while now. It's just a little watercolor."

Gwen held out her hand to receive it and removed the tissue. "Oh, it's beautiful."

"I painted it from that quick sketch I made of you at Christina's house."

Laurence's face darkened. He didn't speak, simply clasped hold of Gwen's arm and began striding up the bank toward the steps, where Pru stood watching. As they passed her and carried on up, Gwen glanced back at the others, feeling mortified. A little farther up she exploded.

"That was uncalled for. It was a gift. Why were you so rude? You could at least be civil to the man!"

Laurence folded his arms. "I will not have him here."

"What's wrong with you? I like Savi, and all he did was make a five-minute sketch of me."

Laurence was standing still, though she could almost feel him shaking.

"I don't want you to see him again."

Her eyes narrowed. "What about you and Christina?" she said, her voice rising dangerously.

"What about it?"

"You still find her attractive. I didn't notice you pushing her hand away. Don't think I can't see how she bewitches you."

He snorted. "We were talking about Mr. Ravasinghe, not Christina."

"It's because of his color, isn't it?"

"No. You're being ridiculous. And that's quite enough. Now come on."

"I'll decide what is enough, thank you very much, and I'll also decide who I choose to befriend."

He unfolded his arms and held out a hand. "Don't shout, Gwen. Do you want Pru to hear?"

"I don't give a damn if she does. Though if you bothered to look back you'd see she's already looking very uncomfortable." Her lip trembled, and she jutted out her chin. "And also if you cared to look you'd see your sainted sister has got back in the boat with Mr. Ravasinghe, as well as Christina, and Mr. Ravasinghe is checking their ankles for leeches. There's obviously something about *him* that women like!"

And no longer trying to control her anger, she stormed off as best as her size allowed.

She smarted for days but they didn't speak of the episode again, at least not then;

Gwen, because she didn't want to upset herself — her heart had raced abominably after their argument — and Laurence because he was pigheaded. The silences between them grew longer and her eyes stung with unshed tears. Neither apologized and Laurence continued to brood. She hadn't really meant to hurt him so badly with her parting shot, but it was clear she had, and relations between them suffered, which was exactly the opposite of what Gwen really wanted. It was bad enough that Verity was there again, without now also feeling cut off from Laurence. She longed to touch the cleft in his chin and make him smile again but was too stubborn to do it.

One gloomy evening, with the arrival of the migrating Himalayan blue-and-yellow pitta bird, the purple sky of the autumn monsoon took over their lives. Everything seemed to be damp. Drawers wouldn't open, and if they did you couldn't close them. Doors suddenly didn't fit. The ground was muddy, insects were multiplying, and on the few occasions that Gwen ventured into the garden, the air was white.

The rain dragged on into December, but once it had ended, Gwen was too heavily pregnant to stray far from the house. Dr. Partridge visited again and still diagnosed that twins were likely, but also said he couldn't be certain.

After ten weeks in the boot room, the puppies, five of them, had been allowed to scamper about the rest of the house. Gwen, unable to see her feet for the size of her bump, spent her life frightened she'd step on them. Either that or one of the bundles of fur would trip her up. But when Laurence suggested they might live in an outhouse, she shook her head. Homes had been found for four of them, and they'd be going soon, but her special favorite, the runt of the litter, was still unwanted.

One morning she answered a phone call from Christina.

"Can you tell Laurence that he left some papers here last time he was over," the woman said in a breezy voice.

"Where?"

"At my place, of course."

"Very well. Was there anything else?"

"Get him to call me, will you, or he could just drop by and pick them up."

Later, when Gwen mentioned that Christina had phoned, Laurence looked surprised.

"What did she want?"

"Papers. She said you'd left some papers at her house."

"I haven't been at her house."

"She said the last time you were over."

"But that was when I signed the agreements on the investments, months ago. I've already got everything I need."

Gwen frowned. Either he wasn't telling the truth or Christina was still playing games.

By the time January arrived, when Gwen was just into her ninth month, she stood on the front step of her home at dawn and glanced over toward the bushes where a thrush was whistling. She shivered, feeling lonely. A cool day was on its way, and the trees and bushes sparkled with dew.

"Now make sure you wrap up this evening. The temperature can drop, as you know." Laurence gave her a kiss on the cheek and took a step away.

"Do you have to go to Colombo?" she said, holding on to his arm and wanting more from him.

His face softened as he turned back to her. "I know the timing isn't good, but you still have a couple of weeks to go. My agent wants to talk finance."

"But, Laurence, couldn't you send McGregor?"

"I'm sorry, Gwen. I really have no choice."

She let go of his arm and stared at the ground, struggling to control her tears.

He tipped up her chin so that she had to look at him. "Hey, I'll only be gone two or three days. And you won't be alone. Verity will look after you."

Gwen's shoulders drooped as he got into the car, rolled up the window, and switched on the ignition. The car spluttered a couple of times, so a houseboy cranked the engine and she hoped for a minute that it might not start, but then it burst into life and Laurence waved as he drove past her and roared up the hill.

As she watched the car slip out of sight, she brushed away tears that continued to drip. Things had not been properly resolved since they'd exchanged cross words the day Mr. Ravasinghe had turned up with the watercolor, and even now a shadow still hung between them. That day had been a turning point of sorts. They had been polite with each other, but he remained a bit aloof and, although he shared her bed, he wasn't keen to make love. He said it was for the sake of the babies, but she missed the intimacy and felt very alone.

The one time they had made love was a couple of weeks before he left. She'd known there was only one way to bring him round so one night when he was sitting on the bed, she'd kissed him gently across the base of his neck while stroking his shoulders and then running her fingers down his spine. After that she got into bed with her back to him. He curled up behind her and she could feel how much he wanted her.

"You are sure it's safe?" she said.

"There is a way."

He helped her turn over onto her knees with her hands on the pillow taking the rest of her weight.

"Just tell me if it hurts," he said as he knelt behind her.

She was still amazed by what happened when they were together, and now he was so gentle that the sensations were even more intense. Maybe it was the pregnancy that had tipped her into another level of being a woman. Whatever it was, when it was over she fell asleep quickly and slept more soundly than she had in days. After that, things between them had lightened, though not completely, and when she'd asked what was the matter, he'd said nothing was wrong. She hoped very much it wasn't anything to do with Christina.

Now that he was gone, she missed him and wished she'd made more of an effort. She walked round the house to look at the lake. It was almost completely still, deep purple at the nearer edge, with a wide silvery streak in the middle. The lake always lifted her mood. She listened to the regular beat of a woodpecker for a minute or two and glanced up as an eagle flew above the house.

"Can you hear them, my little ones?" she said, and put a hand on her tummy. Then she quickly went indoors to warm up by the log fire. She had planned to carry on with her needlepoint but felt drowsy, and fell into a stupor in that semisleep way that is so seductive but leaves you more tired than you were. She was vaguely aware of Naveena tiptoeing in and out, and the butler bringing tea and biscuits, but could not rouse herself enough to pick up her cup. It was only when Verity came in and coughed that Gwen came round.

"Oh, darling, you are awake."

Gwen blinked.

"Look, I'm awfully sorry about this, but an old friend is throwing a party in Nuwara Eliya tonight. It's only one night. I'll be back tomorrow, or the day after at the latest, I promise. Will you be all right? I have missed so much this year."

Gwen yawned. "Of course, you must go. I have Naveena, and we have Dr. Partridge's phone number in Hatton. Go and enjoy yourself."

"I'll just take Spew for a trot by the lake, then I'll be off. I'll say good-bye now." She came across and kissed Gwen's cheek. "If you like, I can deliver the puppies to their new homes at the same time."

Gwen thanked her and watched as she left the room. It was true, by staying at home to keep her company, Verity had missed several seasonal dances. She had gone to the New Year Ball at the Grand in Nuwara, but that was all. Normally they would all have attended, Laurence said, but Gwen was too far advanced in her pregnancy. It was only fair that Verity should have a chance to let her hair down before the babies came. In any case, how would she find a husband if she never got out?

Gwen felt big and clumsy. It was awkward getting out of a chair now, but she struggled up to go to the window. Laurence's departure and the chillier weather had left her feeling homesick. Not only did she miss her parents but Fran too, though Fran's frequent letters kept her abreast of things. Fran had barely mentioned Savi in her letters but had hinted at a new romantic attachment, and Gwen sincerely hoped her cousin had found somebody to love her.

She glanced out at the garden. It was very still, and although she was so alone, it felt as if the whole earth was waiting with her. She spotted a large antlered *sambhur* moving between the trees. It must have come down from the cloud forests in the highlands of Horton Plains and lost its way. Laurence had promised a trip to Horton Plains, a forest wreathed in lilac mists that hung between gnarled squat trees with rounded tops. To Gwen it sounded magical and reminded her of Caroline's mural in the nursery. And with that thought she decided to go and check that everything was completely ready in there.

PART TWO:
THE SECRET

10

The mural had cleaned up beautifully, and Gwen was pleased she had decided to keep it, rather than paint it over. The colors might not be as bright as they once were, but the purple highlands were clear, the silvery blue lakes seemed to shine as if they were real, and luckily they hadn't needed Mr. Ravasinghe to retouch the paintwork.

She looked about her, holding Ginger, the one remaining puppy. The primrose-yellow room was ready. Two new white cribs stood side by side, and an antique satinwood nursing chair with cream embroidered cushions had been sent up from Colombo. A pretty locally made rug added the final touch. She opened the window to air the room, then eased herself into the chair and imagined how it would feel to hold her babies in her arms, rather than just a puppy. She patted her stomach and felt a little tearful. Being so young, she had suffered few of the

complications that carrying the next generation could bring, so it wasn't pregnancy
itself making her eyes water: it was her own
lonely, internal voice.

By the evening her head was throbbing
and she decided fresh air might help. She
felt a slight twinge and stood still, but then
threw on a jacket and left the house. The
nighttime lake was rarely black, but deep
purple, and shone when the stars and moon
were reflected. Tonight there was no shine.
As she moved she was halted by a pain that
sliced round her belly from her lower back.
When it eased, she managed to open the
door again before doubling over, almost crying in relief when Naveena arrived.

The woman's face was full of concern.
"Lady, I am looking for you."

With Naveena supporting her weight, they
reached the bedroom, where Gwen struggled out of her day clothes and pulled a
starched nightdress over her head. She was
sitting on the edge of the bed when she felt
warm liquid flow down her inner thighs. She
stood, horrified.

"Lady. It is only the waters."

"Phone Dr. Partridge," Gwen said. "Right
away."

Naveena nodded and went out to the hall.
When she came back in, her face was glum.

"Having no reply."

Gwen's heart began to race.

"Do not worry, Lady, I have delivered babies."

"But twins?"

The woman shook her head. "We will call doctor again later. I get warm drink."

She was only gone for a few minutes and returned with a glass filled with a strong-smelling brew.

"Are you sure?" Gwen said, wrinkling her nose as she sniffed the ginger and cloves.

Naveena nodded.

Gwen drank it, but a few minutes later felt herself overheat and was violently sick.

Nothing was easy now that she was so big, but Naveena helped her out of her night-dress then wrapped her in a soft woolen blanket. Frightened as the pain soared, all Gwen could hear was the sound of her own breathing. She closed her eyes and tried to picture Laurence as Naveena fetched clean sheets and remade the bed. The serving woman, accustomed to passivity, was a calming presence, but Gwen missed her husband and her eyes filled up. She wiped away the tears but then, as another tearing pain ripped her in two, she bent forward and groaned.

Naveena turned as if to go. "I ring the

doctor again."

Gwen clutched her sleeve. "Don't leave me. Get the butler to do it."

Naveena nodded, waiting by the door after giving the butler the instruction. As he made the call Gwen prayed, but with the door ajar she could hear that the doctor was still out. Her heart raced again.

Neither of them spoke.

Naveena stared at the floor and Gwen, feeling the panic rising, struggled to hold her nerve. What would they do if something went wrong? She closed her eyes and with an effort of will managed to calm her heart. Once it had slowed, she glanced up at Naveena.

"You were with Caroline when she gave birth?"

"Yes, Lady."

"And Laurence?"

"In the house too."

"Did she have a dreadful labor?"

"Normal. Like you."

"Surely this isn't normal!" At another searing contraction, Gwen choked back a sob. "Why did nobody say it would hurt like this?"

Naveena made soothing noises, helped her to her feet, and brought over a small stool to use as a step. Though she still felt

218

clammy, the pain lessened, giving Naveena time to help her back to bed. Gwen shuffled down a bit and, as she lay quietly under a sheet smelling of melons, her labor seemed to slow. The contractions dulled and became further apart, and the next few hours passed relatively easily. Gwen even began to hope that perhaps she might cope rather well.

Naveena had become more than a servant to her: not quite a friend, not quite a mother. It was an unusual relationship, but Gwen was grateful. She drifted for a while in a vaguely pleasant sort of haze, thinking of her actual mother and how it must have been when she gave birth.

Then a new agony sliced her back in two. She twisted onto her side and drew up her knees. The pain gnawed and pulled, and she felt as if a part of her was being torn away.

"I want to turn over again. Help me!"

Naveena helped her to crawl onto all fours on the bed. "Do not push — pant when the pain comes. It will pass, Lady."

Gwen parted her lips and blew out her breath in small puffs, but then the contractions came faster. She twisted as their sharp edge ripped her belly apart, and when she heard screaming as if it was coming from outside of her, she felt there were more than just two little babies wanting to be born.

Something far huger. Why would women inflict this torture on themselves? She fought it by trying to recall childhood fairy tales and screwed up her face in the effort of remembering: anything to take her mind off the hell that was boring through her. At each contraction, she bit her lip until she tasted blood. *This is all about blood,* she thought, *thick red blood.* Then, as she dripped moisture onto already sodden sheets and attempted not to scream, the brief respites grew even briefer.

More excruciating pain. Now she was in despair. She pounded her fists on the mattress, twisted onto her side, and cried for her mother, absolutely certain she was going to die.

"Jesus," she whispered, between gritted teeth. "Help me!"

Naveena stayed with her and continued to hold her hand, encouraging her all the time.

After a while, feeling too exhausted to speak, she exhaled slowly and rolled over to lie on her back again, stretched out her pale legs for a moment, then drew her feet up toward her bottom. As she lifted her head to look, something unbuckled in her and she parted her knees, any shred of dignity completely deserting her.

"Take deep breath when I start count,

Lady, and holding breath as pushing. At ten, take new breath, hold and pushing again."

"Where's the doctor? I need the doctor!"

Naveena shook her head.

Gwen inhaled deeply and did as she was told. Then, with her eyes closed and her hair wringing, she felt a stinging sensation. First there was the smell of feces, and Gwen, already too exposed to care, thought that was all, but then, with one excruciating push, she felt a burning sensation between her open thighs. She was about to push again when Naveena touched her wrist.

"No, Lady, you must not push. You must let baby slide out." For a few moments nothing happened, and then there was a slithery feeling between her legs. Naveena bent over to cut the cord, then pick up the baby. She wiped him down and grinned, her eyes swimming with tears. "Oh, my Lady. You have beautiful boy, that is what."

"A boy."

"Yes, Lady."

Gwen held out her arms and stared at the bruised and wrinkled red face of her first-born. She felt a moment of utter peacefulness, so powerful it almost erased everything she had just been through. The baby's hand contracted and expanded as if his fingers were trying to identify the place where he had arrived. He was perfect, and she, feeling like the first woman who had ever given birth, was so proud that she wept.

"Hello, little boy," she said, between her sobs.

The sound of his sudden shrieking filled the room.

Gwen looked up at Naveena. "Gosh, he sounds absolutely furious."

"It is good sign. Healthy lungs. Good strong boy."

Gwen smiled. "I feel so tired."

"You must rest now, the second one coming soon." She took the baby boy, wrapped him up, put a little hat on his head, and rocked him in her arms before laying him in his crib, where he mewed intermittently.

Soon after Naveena cleaned her up, Gwen delivered the afterbirth. Another hour and a half passed, and it was early morning by the time Gwen delivered her second baby. All her strength had deserted her and all she could think was thank God it was over. She pulled herself up to try to look at the second baby but collapsed straight back against the pillows, then watched as Naveena wrapped the baby in a blanket.

"What is it? A girl or boy?"

Seconds passed. The world hung still, finely balanced.

"Well?"

"It is a girl, Lady."

"How lovely, one of each."

Again Gwen struggled to raise her head to look, but when she did, she was only able to catch a glimpse of the baby before Naveena left the room without speaking. Gwen held her breath and listened. From the nursery there was only the faintest sound of crying. Too weak. Much too weak. The air suddenly became too thick to breathe. She hadn't seen her daughter properly, and wasn't sure, but the tiny baby had seemed to be a strange color.

Terrified the cord had strangled the tiny baby, she tried to shout for Naveena, but her voice came out as a screech. She tried again, then swung her legs round and attempted to stand, but, feeling hot, immediately fell back against the bed. She glanced over at her son. Hugh, they had agreed to call him. Their little miracle. He had stopped crying the moment his twin was born, and was now fast asleep. Using the stool, Gwen climbed into bed again, every muscle feeling raw. She closed her eyes.

When she opened them, Naveena's face swam into focus. She was sitting in the chair by her bed.

"I bringing tea, here for you, Lady."

Gwen sat up and wiped the beads of sweat from her forehead. "Where is the twin?"

Naveena lowered her eyes.

Gwen reached out and clutched the woman's sleeve. "Where is my daughter?"

Naveena opened her mouth as if it to speak, but no sound came out. Her face was calm, but the gnarled hands twisting in her lap gave her away.

"What have you done with her? Is something wrong with her?"

Still no reply.

"Naveena, bring the child now. Do you hear me?" Gwen's voice was shrill with fear.

The woman shook her head.

Gwen gulped for breath. "Is she dead?"

"No."

"I don't understand. I must see her, now. Get her for me! I order you to bring her to me, or you will leave this house this instant."

Naveena stood up slowly. "Very well, Lady."

As a world of imagined horrors grew to gigantic proportions, Gwen felt as if an iron band was constricting her chest. What had happened to her child? Was she hideously malformed? Sick in some terrible way? She wanted Laurence. Why wasn't he here?

After a few minutes, Naveena came back

into the room with a baby bundled in her arms. Gwen heard a weak cry and held out her arms. The ayah settled the child into them, shuffled back, and stared at the floor. Gwen took a deep breath and unwrapped the warm blanket. All the tiny baby girl wore beneath the blanket was a white terry-toweling napkin.

The baby opened her eyes. Gwen held her breath as she looked the child over. The little fingers, the rounded belly, the dark, dark eyes and her skin shining as if it was polished. Numb with shock, Gwen glanced up at Naveena. "This child is perfect."

Naveena nodded.

"Perfect."

The ayah bowed her head.

"But this is not a white child."

"No, Lady."

Gwen glared at the woman. "What kind of trick is this? Where is my child?"

"She is your daughter."

"Did you think I wouldn't notice that you've replaced *my* baby with this one?"

She began to cry, and her tears fell on the little girl's face.

"This is your daughter," Naveena repeated.

In a state of utter shock, Gwen closed her eyes, squeezing them tight to blot out the sight of the baby, then held out the child for the woman to take. It was impossible that something so dark could have come out of her. Impossible! Naveena stood by the bed, rocking back and forth while cradling the child. Gwen folded her arms round herself and, shaking her head from side to side, groaned. Overwhelmed by confusion, she could not meet the ayah's eyes.

"Lady —"

Gwen hung her head. Nobody spoke. It did not make sense. None of this made any sense. She stared at the lines of her palms, turned her hands over, ran a finger round her wedding ring. Several minutes passed while her heart thumped and jumped erratically. Eventually she glanced up at Naveena, and when she saw no judgment in the woman's eyes, it gave her courage to speak.

"How can she be mine? How can she?" she said, brushing her tears away with the back of her hand. "I don't understand. Naveena, tell me what has happened. Am I going crazy?"

Naveena's head wobbled. "Things happening. The willing of the gods."

"What things? What things happen?"

The old lady shrugged. Gwen tried to hold on to her tears, grew rigid with trying to keep her jaw firm, but it was hopeless. Her face crumpled and more tears spilled onto her sheets. Why had this happened? How could it have happened?

Until now the full impact had not hit her. Now it did. What was she going to tell Laurence? She struggled with it but, worn down by exhaustion and with a feeling of utter dread consuming her, she felt far from herself. What was right? She blew her nose and wiped her eyes again, and in her mind's eye saw the little girl open dark eyes and stare at her. Maybe something was wrong with the baby's blood, that was it, or maybe Laurence had some Spanish ancestors. Thoughts crowded her head. Air. That was what she needed. A night breeze. So that she could think.

"Can you open the window, Naveena?"

Naveena held the baby with one arm and went to the window to undo the catch, allowing a cool breeze into the room, and with it the scent of vegetation.

What could she do? Perhaps she could say that she had delivered only one child, or maybe she could pretend the baby was dead — but no, for that they would need a body. Gwen watched Naveena sitting by the window with the baby in her arms and wished herself far away from this awful country where a white woman could give birth to a brown baby for no reason. No reason at all. The air stilled and for a horrible fractured moment Savi Ravasinghe's face slid into her mind. No! Oh God. No! Not that. It couldn't be. With her breath knocked right out of her, she doubled over.

Utterly worn by her labor, she couldn't be thinking straight. Surely she would have known if the man had taken advantage of her? And then another thought almost tipped her over the edge. What about Hugh? Dear God. This couldn't be happening. If it was possible that the baby girl might be Savi's child — terrible, terrible thought — what about Hugh? Was it likely that two fathers could have been involved? She'd never heard anyone speak of such a thing. Was it possible? Could it be possible?

She looked over at Naveena again and, with a heavy heart, glimpsed the moon between breaks in the cloud where it was high in the fading night sky. Almost morning. What was she going to do? Time was running short. She had to decide before the servants started moving about the house. Nobody could know. The wind seemed to get up and then the sound of a car's tires crunching on the gravel sent blood pounding to her temples.

Both she and Naveena froze.

Naveena was the first to rise. "It is the master's sister," she said, and wrapped the covering blanket over the baby's tiny head.

"Oh God! Verity," Gwen said. "Help me, Naveena."

"I hiding the *baba*."

"Quickly, do it quickly."

"In nursery?"

"I don't know. Yes. In the nursery." Gwen nodded, then stared straight ahead in absolute panic. As Naveena hurried from the room, Gwen listened to the sounds of Verity entering the hall and then heading down the corridor. Within minutes there was a knock on the door. Gwen's breath was coming way too fast, her mind so frantic she could not think of a single coherent thing to say, and, as Verity swooped in looking flushed and over bright, she was certain she would give herself away.

"Darling, I am so sorry. Are you all right? Can I see them?"

Gwen inclined her head toward Hugh's crib.

"Where's the other one?"

Gwen's lips twisted slightly and she felt her chin tremble, but she took a breath and stiffened before speaking. "Dr. Partridge was wrong. There was only one. He's a boy."

Verity walked across and stooped over the crib. "Oh, isn't he gorgeous! May I hold him?"

Gwen nodded, but her heart was thumping so hard she pulled the bedcovers up to her chin to hide her chest. "If you wish. But please don't wake him, he's only just fallen asleep."

Her sister-in-law picked Hugh up. "My, but he's so tiny."

Gwen's throat felt strangled. She managed to improvise an answer, though her voice came out sounding thin. "I must have been carrying a lot of water."

"Of course. Has the doctor seen you yet?" Verity said as she put Hugh back in his crib. "You look awfully pale."

"He'll come when he can. He was out on another call last night, apparently." Gwen felt her eyes smart but did not say any more. The less she said about anything the better.

"Oh, darling, was it perfectly awful?"

"Perfectly, yes."

Verity drew up the chair and settled herself beside Gwen. "You must have been awfully brave to do this on your own."

"I had Naveena."

Gwen closed her eyes for a moment, hoping Verity would take the hint. She was acutely aware that in the rush, Naveena had not closed the door to the bathroom, and although she must have shut the door to the nursery from the bathroom, she wanted her sister-in-law to leave before the baby girl woke.

"Shall I tell you about the party to cheer you up?" Verity said.

"Well, actually —" Gwen began.

"It was wonderful," Verity continued, taking no notice. "I danced for so long I've actually got blisters, and can you believe it, but Savi Ravasinghe was there too, dancing most of the night with that Christina woman. He asked after you."

Dismayed by the turn the conversation had taken, Gwen raised a hand to fend off the woman. "Verity, if you don't mind, I need to rest before the doctor comes."

"Oh, of course, darling. Silly old me chattering on when you must be absolutely shredded."

Verity stood and took a few steps toward the crib. "He's still asleep. I can't wait for him to wake up."

Gwen shifted in the bed. "He will soon enough. Now, if you don't mind."

"You must rest, I see that. I had planned to see Pru in Hatton today, if that's all right with you. But I'll stay if you need me . . ."

So much for helping out, Gwen thought

but didn't say, although she was intensely grateful Verity would be leaving again.

"Go," she said. "I'm fine."

Verity turned and headed for the door. There was the faint sound of a baby's cry and then it stopped. As her sister-in-law spun round with a grin, Gwen went rigid.

"Oh, lovely, he's woken up," Verity said as she came back over to the crib, but when she saw Hugh she frowned. "That's odd, he's still asleep."

There was silence, and though it lasted for just a moment, for Gwen it was so fraught that it seemed to go on for a lifetime. As she closed her eyes, willing the baby girl not to cry again, she felt as if her skin was on fire. *Please God, don't let her make any noise while Verity is staring at Hugh.*

"They do cry in their sleep," she managed to say in the end. "Now do go to Hatton. I have Naveena."

"Very well, if you're sure."

As her sister-in-law closed the door behind her, Gwen leaned forward and hugged her knees. A sensation of being uprooted from the earth took over, and she felt so fragile that one gust of wind might lift her from the bed and carry her off. She rang the bell for Naveena.

When the ayah came back she sat at

Gwen's side and held her hand.

"Naveena, what am I going to do?" Gwen whispered. "Tell me what to do."

The old lady stared at the floor but didn't speak.

"Help me. Please help me. I've already told Verity there was only one baby."

"Lady, I do not know."

Gwen started to cry again.

"There has to be a way. There has to be."

Naveena seemed to struggle for a moment, then took a deep breath. "I am finding village women in the valley to look after *baba*."

Gwen stared at her and the woman met her gaze. Was she suggesting she should give the baby away to a stranger? Her own child?

"It is only way."

"Oh, Naveena, how can I just give her up like that?"

Naveena reached out a hand. "You must be trusting me, Lady."

Gwen shook her head. "I can't do this."

"Lady, you must."

Gwen bowed her head in desperation. Then she looked up and when she spoke her voice shook. "No. This can't be the only way."

"Just one other, Lady."

"Yes?"

Naveena picked up a pillow.

Gwen gasped. "You mean smother her?"

Naveena nodded.

"No! Not that. Under no circumstances."

"People are doing it, Lady, but it is not good."

"No, it's not, it's terrible," Gwen said and, horrified they'd even spoken of such a thing, she hid her face in her hands.

"I am thinking, Lady. Going to far valley with *baba*. You pay a little money?"

For a moment Gwen did not reply, but lifted her head and stared straight ahead with tears blurring her vision. She shivered. The truth was she could not keep the baby. If she did she would be cast out with a child that was clearly not her husband's. She'd probably never see her baby boy again. Where would she go? Even her parents might have no option but to turn their backs. With no money, no home, it would be a far worse life for the little girl than going to live in the village. At least there she wouldn't be too far away, and maybe one day . . . She paused. No. The truth was there never would be *one day.* If she sent the child away it would be forever.

She looked at the old woman and spoke in a whisper. "What shall I tell Laurence?"

"Nothing, Lady. I begging you. Like with

his sister we are saying only one baby."

Gwen nodded. Naveena was right, but she trembled at the thought of speaking such a terrible lie. Verity was one thing. With Laurence it would be so much harder.

Naveena's eyes filled with tears. "It is best. The master being scorned, if you keeping."

"But, Naveena, how could this have happened?"

The old lady shook her head and her eyes looked terribly pained.

The ayah's obvious emotion made Gwen feel even worse. She closed her eyes, but then all she saw were her silky French knickers lying on the hotel bedroom floor. She forced herself back to the night of the ball, tried to remember every detail, got to the point where Savi was stroking her temple, then . . . nothing. Trapped in a moment she could not recall, she felt violated. What had he done to her? What had she allowed him to do? She could only remember waking up half undressed when Fran came in. Again she wondered if it was even possible for there to be two fathers. The thought that it might not be only intensified her sense of violation and sent her heart beating wildly. Hugh had to be Laurence's son. He had to be.

"Lady, do not distress." Naveena took

hold of Gwen's hand and stroked it. "You wish to name the baby?"

"I don't know the right kind of name, for a child like —"

"Liyoni is a very good name."

"Very well." She paused. "But I must see her one more time."

"Not good, Lady. Better she go now. Do not be sad, Lady. It is her fate."

Gwen's eyes stung. "I can't just send her away without seeing her again. Please. Maybe if we lock the door to the corridor? I have to see her."

"Lady —"

"Bring her to me so that I can at least feed her, can't you, just once, and then later a wet nurse in one of the villages down in the valley can take over?"

With a sigh that seemed to give away her fatigue, Naveena took a step back. "First, we waiting for the sister to leave."

Neither spoke as they waited, but the moment they heard Verity's car take off, Naveena closed the bedroom shutters and brought the baby back.

There were no bruises, no red face, she was nothing like Hugh at all. A perfect baby the color of dark milky coffee.

"She is so small," Gwen whispered, and touched the softness of her silky cheeks.

The little thing latched on the moment Naveena put her to Gwen's breast. The sensation of the suckling was strange enough, but then, shocked once again by the darkness of the child's face against her own white skin, Gwen trembled. As she unlatched the child from her breast, the baby's eyes were huge; she shrieked once, sounding indignant, then sucked at the air. Gwen turned to face the wall.

"Take her. I cannot do it." And though her voice sounded harsh, the stark pain of knowing she was turning away her own flesh and blood was worse than the pain of her birth.

Naveena took the baby from her. "For two days I be gone."

"Let me know as soon as you're back. Are you sure you can find someone?"

Naveena shrugged. "I am hoping."

Gwen glanced over at Hugh, desperate to hold him tight and terrified he might be taken too. "They will look after her properly?"

"She will grow up well. I light a candle, Lady? It is peaceful. Will help you rest. Here is water. I will get hot tea and come. To ease the heart, Lady."

Thoughts sped through Gwen's brain as she reached for the glass of water, shaking uncontrollably. She tried to think if there was anyone who could act on her behalf, but looking for a different answer to explain the color of the child's skin would take time she didn't have. Right now she had given birth to a baby that was not her husband's, and if she were to talk about the night at the ball, nobody would believe she hadn't been intimate with Savi Ravasinghe willingly. She had allowed him up to her room, hadn't she? Laurence would reject her and Verity would have him to herself. It was as simple as that. And if she were ever to question anyone, she would have to admit the fact of Liyoni's birth. She couldn't do that. Not ever.

Although at first the baby's color had shocked her, it was what that color really meant that stopped her heart from beating. She felt lost. Godforsaken. Her hand shook so much that the water spilled, soaking her nightdress and trickling down her chest. She felt as if this terrible thing she had agreed to would mean peace and sleep were gone forever. And her guilt would surely destroy the return of those heavenly feelings she had discovered with Laurence. The girl's dark eyes came back to her — an innocent newborn baby needing her mother — and for a moment Gwen's longing to cradle both her babies grew stronger than her desire to keep her marriage intact. She picked up Hugh and rocked him; then she wept and wept again. But when she thought of Laurence's trusting smile and his strong arms wrapped round her, she knew she could not keep her tiny baby girl. As the grief bit into her heart, she realized she and her daughter would never enjoy happy memories. But worse — far worse — was that this poor little girl, through no fault of her own, would be forced to live with neither a father nor a mother.

11

They waited until almost dusk. Verity had not yet returned from Hatton, so Gwen kept watch as Naveena bundled up the baby and placed her in an old tea picker's basket. She climbed into a bullock buggy and put the baby in the back, but just as they were about to leave, McGregor stepped out of the darkness. Gwen hid in the shadows of the porch, holding her breath and listening as Naveena claimed she was going to visit a sick friend in one of the Sinhalese villages.

"The buggy is not for your own private purpose," McGregor was saying.

Gwen felt her jaw grow rigid.

"Going just one time, sir."

Please make him let her go.

"Do you have the master's permission?"

"The mistress say."

"What do you have in the basket?"

Panic swept through Gwen, the breath sucked right out of her.

"Just old blanket the mistress give."

McGregor moved to the other side of the buggy, and Gwen couldn't hear what he said. If he were to check the basket now, she might as well be dead. As a few more words were spoken, Gwen prayed, for the sake of all that she held dear, to please let McGregor leave. She couldn't hear what they were saying now, couldn't even hear if they were still talking, and in the darkness she couldn't see if McGregor was already looking inside the basket.

As the memory of her foolishness on the night of the ball overcame her, she longed to step forward and admit her wrong. If she hadn't been jealous of Christina she never would have accepted help from Savi Ravasinghe, so only had herself to blame. If she spoke now it would all be over . . . but then, hearing the sound of footsteps and the buggy starting to move off, Gwen slipped back into the house, dizzy with relief.

Poor Naveena had not wanted to go in the dark, but the difficulty of keeping the baby without her cries being heard was too great.

In the time that Gwen was alone she longed for sleep, but every few minutes she kept checking on Hugh. After an hour or so she heard Laurence's car. She threaded her fingers through her tangled hair to tidy it, then made her escape to the bathroom, locking the door behind her. She pressed her fists to the sides of her head and longed to sink to the ground. But knowing she could not, she splashed her face and tied back her hair, then sat on the edge of the bath and waited for her hands to stop shaking. When she heard Laurence enter the bedroom, she pinned a smile on her face, found her courage, and went through to the bedroom.

Laurence was standing motionless with a look of amazement on his face as he gazed at his son for the first time. She watched while he remained unaware of her presence, taking in his broad shoulders and the way his hair waved at the front. Struck by how happy he looked, she knew she couldn't bear to reopen the hole in his heart. It wasn't all about protecting Laurence — a selfish current ran through her too — but for both their sakes she had to go through with this.

She took a step forward and he turned at the sound. She realized that, along with amazement, there was also a look of what she could only call relief on his shining face. Unsurpassable relief. As they stared at each other, his eyes sparkled, but then he screwed up his face as if to stem the tears.

"He's like you, don't you think?" she said.

"He's perfect." He stared at her in awe. "You've been so brave. But where's his twin?"

She froze, unable to think or feel, as if every moment that had passed between them had never been. He was a stranger. She fought the urge to run and with an effort of great will walked across to him instead, somehow able to hide her distress.

"There was only one baby after all. I'm sorry."

"Darling girl, you have nothing to be sorry for. I couldn't love you more, but this . . . this means so much."

She forced herself to smile.

He held out his arms. "Come here. Let me hold you." He hugged her and as she leaned her head against his chest she felt his heart beating.

"Gwen. I'm so sorry I've been distant. Forgive me."

She stretched up and kissed him but felt torn. She ached to share this terrible confusion, get the truth into the open and stave off the lifetime of lies before they began, but his wide, spreading smile stopped her. After so many weeks Laurence was back, not just physically, but emotionally too. She was able to hold herself in and allowed him to continue hugging her, but she knew nothing could ever be the same again. Something was flowing out of her: safety, security, she wasn't sure what, but it left her feeling shaken and desperately alone. She listened to the harsh screech of birds taking off over the lake and felt the thump of his heart against her cheek again. She was drained, and not even the warmth of Laurence's smile could stop the crushing pain she felt.

Once the doctor had been to check Gwen over, she made up a string of excuses to explain why Laurence must leave her alone, but the truth was she could only grapple with her pain during his absence. The same thought kept recurring: could two men father twins? She'd wondered if she could pretend to be finding out for a friend, but because of her pregnancy she'd had no time to forge individual friendships here, so Laurence would see through that. For much of the time they lived in isolation and most social functions, like the Governor's Ball or the Golf Club Ball, they attended together. Who could she trust with this? Not her parents. They'd be horrified. Fran? Maybe she could talk to Fran, but it would be ages before she saw her again. The fact that she could not actually remember Mr. Ravasinghe making love to her didn't help. He had seemed to be so kind. He had stroked her forehead. He had stayed with her while she felt sick. But what more? Not knowing was driving her mad.

By Laurence's third night back at home, Naveena had still not returned from the village and Gwen hardly dared imagine what would happen if the woman had been unable to find a foster mother. As her anxiety increased, the child's dark eyes began to haunt her. She was on high alert, edgy, jumping at sudden noises, and the constant worry that Laurence might discover the truth made her feel ill.

He tiptoed into her room just as she was finishing off Hugh's late-night feed.

"Why are you always creeping up on me?" she said. "You gave me a fright."

"Darling, you look tired," Laurence said, ignoring her bad temper.

She sighed and wiped the curtain of ringlets away from her face.

Now that the milk had come in, Hugh was a voracious little feeder but had fallen asleep at the breast. Laurence adjusted her pillows, then sat on the edge of her bed and twisted round to face her. She shuffled her bottom up a little, then rotated her neck to ease the tightness that came from allowing the baby to feed for too long.

He took her hand. "Are you managing to get any sleep, Gwen? You look so pale."

"Not really. I take so long to fall asleep, and by the time I do, he's awake again."

"I am a little worried that you don't seem yourself."

"For heaven's sake, Laurence, I've just given birth. What do you expect?"

"Only for you to seem a little happier. I would have thought you'd be so tired from feeding Hugh that you'd fall asleep instantly."

"Well, I can't." She'd spoken abruptly, really barking at him, and felt shamed by the sad look on his face. "The baby doesn't sleep much either."

His brow furrowed. "I'll call John Partridge again."

"There's nothing wrong. I'm just tired."

"You'll feel much better if you have some decent sleep. Maybe you should limit the time you spend feeding?"

"Whatever you think," she said, but could not tell him that the times when Hugh was feeding were her only moments of internal peace. Something primal about the suckling infant soothed her. She could watch his soft curved cheek and fluttering lashes, and feel better; yet if he opened his blue eyes to stare at her, she could see only the dark eyes of the other.

When he wasn't feeding, he cried. Cried so much that all she could do was hide her head under her pillow and weep.

Laurence leaned across to kiss her, but she turned her face away and pretended to fuss over Hugh.

"I'd better put him in the crib or he'll be awake before I know it."

Laurence stood and reached over to squeeze her shoulder. "Sleep. That's what you need. I hope Naveena has been a help."

Gwen dug a nail into the fleshy part of her palm and kept her eyes lowered. "She's visiting a sick friend."

"*You* should be her priority."

"I'm all right."

"Well, if you're sure. Good night, my love. I hope you feel better in the morning."

Gwen nodded. She couldn't tell him she felt that she might never sleep again.

After he had gone, she blinked angry tears away. She tucked the baby in his crib and then looked herself over in her bathroom mirror. Her nightdress needed changing and her hair stuck to her neck in damp trails; the skin of her breasts and upper chest was almost translucent and marbled with fine blue veins, but it was her eyes that shocked her. Her usually bright, violet eyes had darkened to almost purple.

Back in her room, bereft of all hope, Gwen slumped in her chair. She wanted to cry but had to hold on to herself somehow. Naveena had been gone a day longer than she had expected, but at last she heard the sound of a bullock cart pulling up, followed by voices. Her mind emptied as she waited.

A few minutes later Naveena came into the room and Gwen sat up, sharply drawing in her breath.

"It is done," Naveena said.

Gwen let out her breath. "Thank you," she said, almost sobbing with relief. "You must never speak to anyone of this. You understand?"

Naveena nodded, then said that she had told the Sinhalese village woman who had taken the baby that Liyoni was the orphan child of a distant cousin, and that she, Naveena, could not look after her. She had arranged for messages to come up from the village. Once a month, on either the day after full moon or the day before, the foster mother, who could neither read nor write, would slip a charcoal drawing into the hand of the coolie driving the daily bullock cart that fetched milk for the plantation. The coolie would be paid a few rupees and told that the drawings were for Naveena. As long as the drawings arrived at roughly the right time, Gwen would know the child was well.

After Naveena had left, another chilling thought held Gwen in its grip. What if Naveena didn't keep her promise? What if she spoke of it? The accusing voices in her head would not stop going on and on, until she covered her ears and cried out against their words.

A God-fearing Englishwoman does not give birth to a colored child.

When Gwen opened her mouth, at first no sound came out, but then, as the loss of her baby girl tore at her heart, a deep moan began to rise from the pit of her stomach. By the time it reached her open mouth it had become a terrible growling animal sound over which she had no control. She had given her own tiny newborn baby away.

It was another day before Dr. Partridge managed to make a second appearance, and by the time he did, the afternoon was drawing to a close. Gwen looked out at the lengthening shadows in the garden and squeezed her hands together. She scanned the room and ran a palm over her towel-dried hair. Naveena had left the window ajar and placed a large vase of wild peonies on the table nearby, so at least the room smelled fresh.

Gwen sat up in bed waiting for the doctor, turning her hands over and over, examining her nails without seeing them as her fingers twisted this way and that. Wearing a newly laundered nightdress, she stilled her hands and, pinching her cheeks to bring back the roses, she muttered the words she must say. Inside she felt sick with nerves, but if she could just remember the right words . . . She heard the shriek of tires and tensed.

Then, through the open window, came Laurence's voice. She had to strain to hear but he was not a quiet man, and she thought she heard him say something about Caroline. Then came the doctor's quieter response.

"But damn it, man," Laurence said even more loudly, "Gwen is not herself. You should have come straight here. I know there's something wrong. There has to be something you can do."

Again the doctor's soft-voiced reply.

"Good God," Laurence said, and then continued in a hushed voice. "What if the same thing happens? What if I can't help her?"

"Childbirth affects some women badly. Some recover. Some do not."

Gwen could not make it out, but she heard Laurence mention Caroline's name again. She felt like a child, eavesdropping on her parents.

"How long has she been like this?" the doctor asked, and then the two men walked out of earshot. He'd taken the doctor to the lakeside, so that they would not be overheard by the servants. He already knew! Her throat dried and, just in time, Gwen stopped herself thinking that way, though every muscle throbbed with the tension of waiting. She cast around the room, wanting to hide, while sliding further down beneath the sheets. She heard a door bang, then footsteps in the corridor. The doctor would be in her room. Any moment now.

The door opened. Laurence came first and then the doctor, who approached with a hand stretched out in greeting. When she took it and felt the warmth of his palm, tears stung her eyes. He was so kind, she longed to tell him, to just blurt it all out and be done with it.

"So how are you now?" he said.

She gritted her teeth, looked him in the face, and, quelling the fear that he might smell the guilt on her, swallowed before

251

speaking. "I'm fine."

"Can I check the baby over again?"

"Of course."

Laurence went to the crib and lifted his sleeping son. Her heart constricted at his rapt attention.

"He's quite a chap. Feeds nonstop."

Gwen interpreted Laurence's comment as a criticism. "He's hungry, Laurence, and it soothes him. Surely you must hear him cry?"

The doctor sat in the chair beside Gwen and, taking the baby in his arms, looked him over. "A bit on the small side, but he does seem to be growing bonnier every day."

"He was early," Laurence said.

"Yes, of course. Yet I am surprised it wasn't twins. Must have been water retention after all."

Gwen took a sharp breath in.

"I'm sorry I wasn't able to be with you, though I'm sure you were very brave."

"I can hardly remember it, to be honest with you."

The doctor nodded. "That is what so many mothers say. And thank goodness for selective memory."

"Indeed."

Laurence, who had been standing at the end of the bed, spoke up. "Actually, John, it's Gwen I'm worried about. She's hardly sleeping and you can see how white she looks."

"Yes. She is pale."

"Well, then? What are you going to do?"

"Laurence, don't worry."

"Don't worry?" He balled a fist and slammed it into the palm of his other hand. "How can you say that!"

"I'll give her a good tonic, but I'm afraid a sleeping draft could harm the baby. It's thought that it might seep into the mother's milk. Give things another fortnight to settle, and if she is not improved, we'll rethink. Maybe a wet nurse."

Laurence puffed out his cheeks, then let the breath go. "If that's all you can suggest, that will have to do for now. But damn it, man, I want you to keep a strict eye on my wife."

"Of course, Laurence. Wouldn't have it any other way. Rest assured, Gwen is in safe hands."

"I'll leave you with her for a moment or two," Laurence said.

Had Laurence and the doctor concocted this plan between them?

"What's troubling you, Gwen?" the doctor said, once Laurence had gone. He laid

Hugh in his crib, then gave her a puzzled look.

As she stared into his friendly gray eyes, a lump came in her throat. But how could she tell him about Liyoni? And how could she tell him that by controlling her tears so they spilled only when she was alone, or with Hugh, she lived with the added fear that her son might grow up with her guilt running through his veins.

"Is it just lack of sleep? You can tell me, you know. It's my job to help." He patted her hand. "There is something else, isn't there?"

She swallowed the lump. "I —"

He ran his fingers through the thinning hair at his temple. "Is it resuming relations with Laurence that's bothering you? I can have a word."

She lowered her head, acutely embarrassed. "No, nothing like that."

"You seem so terribly unhappy."

"Do I?"

"I think you must know you do. It's normal for a woman to feel exhausted after a prolonged labor, and with a heavily feeding baby, it's no wonder, but it seems to me, well, it seems to me that there's something more."

Gwen bit her lip in an attempt to control

her emotions, and avoided looking at him. *A God-fearing white woman does not give birth to a colored child* — nor does she give a child away, she thought. Though she tried to convince herself that giving a baby away was better than smothering one, she felt so far beneath contempt that no words could ever lessen her wretchedness.

"Do you want to tell me?"

"Oh, Doctor, if —"

The door opened and Laurence walked in. "All done?"

The doctor glanced at Gwen. She nodded.

"Yes, all done, for now. I think if your wife tries to establish a regular feeding schedule and takes some gentle exercise, that might help. And remember, you can call me any time, Mrs. Hooper."

As Laurence showed the doctor out, he glanced back at Gwen.

"Would you like company? I'm sure Verity would be happy to sit with you. She wants to help."

"No thanks, Laurence," Gwen snapped. "I'm fine on my own."

He looked miserable as he turned away. At the door he looked back again. "We are all right, you and me, I mean?"

"Of course."

He nodded and went out. She had almost told the doctor, had really wanted to, and she had made her husband unhappy. Her lip trembled and she whimpered as a flash of pain seared through her temple. Another headache. When her head felt so swollen that she could not remain awake, she slept fitfully. As dawn spread a pale gray light across her room, she woke: thirsty, lonely, and wanting Laurence.

She imagined holding the baby girl in her arms, saw her lying in the cot beside Hugh, gazed so long that the line between what was real and what was not became blurred. She pictured the baby suckling, her lashes fluttering on her dark cheeks. The image seemed so real she felt compelled to run through to the nursery, fully expecting Liyoni to still be there, and hoping, half in terror and half in genuine hunger, that she would be fast asleep in the cot next to Hugh's. But when she got there she saw, straight away, that only one child slept in the nursery. She stood still, listening to Hugh — only one tiny breath where there should have been two — and felt as if her whole being had been sliced in two.

She clenched her fists, then turned and fled, knowing nothing would ever fill the aching void. It drove her to the mirror again, in search of her own real face. She stared at herself and screwed up her eyes in the effort of remembering what she had overheard Laurence say to the doctor. Until now, the words had seemed to dislocate. She didn't know what she'd expected them to be, but they had seemed important at the time. Suddenly they came back again, and this time the meaning was clear.

God willing, she's not going the same way as Caroline.

Yes, that was it. And Caroline was dead.

After that, she tried not to think. Not about what had happened to Caroline and not about her daughter. But she still wept, and sat for hours in the dark of her bathroom where she could hide her tears. Naveena brought her tea and toast, but the sight of food made her nauseated; she left it to grow cold on the bedside table.

Gwen knew she could not remain in her room forever, nor could she let what had happened ruin her life, or Laurence's. She had to find some inner resolve: the grit she'd never needed until now. Mechanically, she forced herself to wash.

At her dressing table she examined herself in the mirror. Her face had changed. It might not be obvious to others, but Gwen saw the damage. How long would it take for her face to reveal the guilt? Five years? Ten? She scanned the row of glass bottles, picked up her favorite, Après L'Ondée, and dabbed some behind her ears. As the lovely scent filled the air, she took her silver-handled hairbrush and, while she was brushing her hair, made a decision. She put the brush down and from between her silk scarves she took out the pretty little watercolor Mr. Ravasinghe had made of her.

She picked up the box of matches that Naveena used to light her fire, then looked out of the window. It seemed as if flickering coins of liquid gold floated on the lake, and with the sound of the household coming to life, the morning sky appeared brighter, the clouds fluffier, her heart a little lighter. She took the painting to the wastepaper basket, struck a single match, and watched the image curl as it burned and fell.

12

The doctor had suggested activity, so although she wanted to bury herself in her bed and never face another day, a few days later she forced herself up. She dressed, trying not to think about anything, then asked Naveena to take care of Hugh and to fetch her only for timed feeds. It wouldn't be easy as the baby cried so much, but for everyone's sake, she had to find a way. When she emerged from her room, nervous energy flooded her body and, as if awakened from a long slumber, the call to action took over from feelings of self-recrimination.

She had spotted a storeroom at the back of the house — a cool ground-floor room with thick walls in a shady part of the garden, and because it was situated next to the kitchen there would be access to water — a good place to make cheese. With her head held high, she walked through the house and out of the side door into the courtyard. A tiny purplish-black sunbird took off right in front of her and was followed by another as it rose into the big blue sky. It was a lovely sunny day, and as she glanced up to follow the flight of the birds, she heard a window open. Verity leaned out and waved.

"Hello. You're up and about, I see."

"Yes. Yes, I am." Squinting, she looked at her sister-in-law.

"Are you going for a walk? I'll join you. I won't be a tick."

"No, I'm actually going to sort out the storeroom."

Verity shook her head. "Get a houseboy to do that. You've just had a baby."

"Why does everybody keep treating me as if I were ill?"

"In that case, I'll give you a hand. I've got nothing to do today." Undeterred, Gwen attempted to smile. "There's really no need."

"I insist. I'll be right down. It'll be fun. Goodness knows what we'll find squirreled away. I'd really like to help."

"Very well."

As Gwen walked across the courtyard to the storeroom, she glanced up at the tall trees. Today they seemed bright and light, not the gloomy tunnel she had once rushed through in fear, and feeling the sun's warmth on her skin, she felt hope stirring. She'd already requested the key from McGregor, and though he'd been surprised that she really intended to go through with her plan to make cheese, he had not objected. He'd even smiled quite warmly and wished her luck.

"Here I am," Verity said as she came up behind her.

The padlock on the storeroom door came apart with a tug. Together they pulled the doors, the sudden draft of air sending dust motes swirling in a room that smelled of old, forgotten things.

"First, we need to get everything out," Gwen said as the dust gradually settled.

"I still think we need houseboys to lift the heavy stuff."

Gwen scanned the room. "You're right. There's some furniture back there we'd never be able to shift."

A couple of kitchen boys had come out to see what was going on. Verity spoke to them in Tamil and one of them went to fetch the *appu,* who nodded at Gwen when he came out, but smiled when he saw Verity. They chatted together as he smoked a cigarette and leaned against the wall.

"You seem to get on well with him," Gwen said as the *appu* went back in. "I always find him a little terse."

"He's nice to me. Well, he would be, I was the one who got him the job here."

"Oh?"

"Anyway, he says he'll call a couple of the houseboys. Though they won't be pleased to get their nice white clothes dirty. It's not a cleaning day today."

Gwen smiled. "I know that. I was the one who drew up their timetable, remember."

"Of course you were."

Gwen squeezed past an old chest of drawers that looked as if it had seen better days. "This piece is riddled with some kind of woodworm."

"It might be termites. It should go on the bonfire. Oh, let's have one. I do love a bonfire."

"Is the gardener around? I've rather lost track, what with the baby and everything."

"I'll go and look."

While Verity was gone, Gwen, driven by a jittery kind of energy, carried out the smaller items: broken kitchen chairs, a couple of cracked vases, a bent umbrella missing one or two spokes, a few dusty cases, some metal boxes. This stuff should have been chucked years ago, she thought, as she made a pile for burning. When the houseboys arrived, she pointed at the chest of drawers and the furniture at the back, and they began to shuffle it out, piece by piece. Dust flew about in clouds and their white clothes soon dirtied.

By the time they had almost finished, Verity still hadn't returned. There was just a large ottoman trunk left at the very back of the room. When the boys carried it out, she saw the sides were covered in fabric, now stained and ripped in places, and when she lifted the leather top, she saw it was a metal-lined container, the kind that they used in the house for storing linen. But there was no household linen in this trunk and she was shocked to see toweling nappies and dozens of immaculately folded tiny baby clothes, each one wrapped separately in tissue paper. Matinee jackets, bootees, woolly hats, all hand-knitted and lovingly embroidered. At the very bottom she spotted some yellowing lace. She reached for it and stood up to shake it out. It was long, perfectly preserved apart from the color, and Gwen's eyes stung as she realized that it must have been Caroline's bridal veil. She wiped her hands on her skirt, then brushed the tears away, wishing she'd never seen such sad reminders. She asked the boys to carry it all indoors, certain that Laurence would tell her what to do with it.

She was relieved to see Naveena coming across with Hugh in her arms, and feeling the fullness in her breasts and the dragging sensation as the milk began to seep, she went over to the ayah and reached for her child.

As Gwen went indoors, she took stock. For almost the whole morning she had not focused on the little baby girl, and apart from the moment when she had seen the contents of the trunk, she had not felt wretched. Encouraged by her progress, she saw that if she could only erect a wall around herself by keeping busy, the misery might fade.

At lunch, Laurence was in a jovial mood. Gwen was amazed that she'd been able to hide her unease so well that he hadn't noticed her true state of mind, but he joked with her and Verity and was delighted to hear that Hugh had smiled.

"Well, it might not have been a real smile," Verity said. "But he is such a darling and he didn't cry so much today, did he, Gwen?"

"Perhaps the doctor was right about scheduling his feeds," Laurence said.

Verity smiled. "I can't wait for him to grow up a bit."

Laurence turned away to look at Gwen.

"It's wonderful to see you looking so much better, Gwen. I can't tell you how happy it makes me."

"I've been helping Gwen sort out the old storeroom for her to make cheese there," Verity said.

"Really, Verity?"

"Yes."

"Well, I'm jolly pleased to hear it."

"What do you mean by that?"

Laurence smiled. "Exactly what I said."

"But you said it as if you meant something by it."

"Verity, I meant nothing. Come on. We were having a nice lunch. And I've got some good news as it happens."

"Tell us," Gwen said.

"Well, you know I was investing in copper-mining shares through Christina's bank, or rather the bank in which she is the major shareholder? They're doing rather well, and as long as things go on like this, in a couple of years I hope to be able to buy the neighboring plantation. My third. We'll be the biggest tea planters in Ceylon!"

Gwen forced a smile. "How marvelous, Laurence. Well done."

"It's Christina you have to thank. She persuaded me to invest even more during that ball in Nuwara Eliya. America, that's where the money is to be made these days. England's lagging behind."

Gwen pulled a face.

His brows drew together a little. "I wish you'd try to like her. She was very good to me after Caroline died."

"Was that when you gave her that devil mask?"

"I didn't know you'd seen it."

"I went for lunch the day Mr. Ravasinghe's painting of her was unveiled. I thought the mask was perfectly horrible."

He frowned slightly. "They're pretty hard to get hold of. The natives use them, or used to use them, for their devil dancing. Some still do, I believe. Caroline actually saw one take place."

"Where?"

"I don't quite remember the circumstances. They wear the masks and some grotesque outfit and lose themselves in wild primitive dancing."

"Sounds ghastly," Verity said.

"Actually, I think Caroline found it fascinating."

When they'd finished their pudding, Verity got up abruptly, claiming a headache.

Laurence held out a hand to Gwen after his sister had gone. She reached up to touch his cleft chin and fought to conceal her hesitation. If she wanted to keep her husband she had to get over this.

"I've missed you so much, Gwen," he said, lowering his head to kiss the soft skin at the base of her neck.

She shivered. Then, as he hugged her, she felt herself unbend a little and, despite her sorrow, had to admit that by sending the baby away she had managed to save her marriage. She buried her face in his chest, wanting everything he was and everything he would always be, but feeling heavy-hearted that she must now keep something of herself apart. She pulled back and looked into his eyes: eyes so full of love and longing that she held her breath. He was entirely blameless and must never know.

"Come on, then," she said with a smile. "What are you waiting for?"

He laughed. "Just you."

In the days and weeks that followed, Gwen kept busy by going through the baby clothes she had found, separating them into those that were damaged and those that had remained intact, and also worked hard to get the storeroom ready. But Liyoni's birth had opened up a seam in her and she felt it wouldn't take much for the fabric of her life to rip apart.

Still finding it hard to believe what had happened, she felt cut off from the household and trapped in her own confusion. Had Savi Ravasinghe really behaved so abominably? She tried to focus on Laurence's love for her, her love for Hugh and their lives together as a family, but whenever she thought of Liyoni, she felt as if part of her had died. Liyoni had to be the result of that night at the Grand, and because she and Laurence had made love the very next day, she prayed with all her heart that Hugh really was Laurence's child. She had no way of finding out if it was possible — she could hardly ask the doctor — and had no choice but to live with uncertainty. She told herself that as long as Naveena never spoke of what had passed, nobody would suspect.

Although Gwen thought she had managed to convince Laurence that all was well, he seemed to sense that really it was not, and on April 14 he decided that a trip to see the New Year celebrations in the afternoon would be just the thing to cheer her up. When he suggested it, they were standing at the edge of the lake looking at birds dive, pick off their prey, then swoop up into the air. It was a blazing afternoon, with a clear blue sky and a lovely smell of blossom in the air. Gwen glanced up as an eagle flew right across the sky then disappeared behind the trees.

"I thought it might do you good," he said. "It's just that you still don't seem very happy."

She swallowed the lump in her throat. "I've told you, I'm perfectly happy. It's just tiredness."

"The doctor did suggest a wet nurse if the tiredness didn't diminish."

"No," she snapped, and then felt awful for biting his head off.

"Well, let's celebrate this moment between the old and the new, when everything stands still and hope rises."

"I don't know. Hugh is still so little."

"It's not a formal religious festival. It's just about eating and wearing new clothes. A family occasion really."

She made an effort and smiled. "That does sound good. What else?"

"Lanterns and dancers, if we're lucky."

"If we go, we must take Hugh and I think Naveena should come too."

"Absolutely. You'll hear the brass drums. *Rabanas* they're called. Make a heck of a din, but it's fun. What do you think?"

She nodded. "What shall I wear?"

"Something new, of course."

"In that case, I'd better see what I've got."

She turned to go up to the house, but he caught hold of her hand and pulled her back. She glanced at her feet, then out at the lake again, and then he brought her hand to his mouth and kissed it.

"Darling," he said. "Please throw the old baby clothes away. I should never have kept them. At the time I just didn't know what to do."

"And Caroline's veil?"

Something flickered on his face. "Was that in there too?"

She nodded. "Naveena washed it and hung it out in the sun. It's still a bit yellow."

"It was my mother's veil, before Caroline."

"Then it's a family heirloom. We should keep it."

"No. There is too much darkness attached to it now. Get rid of it."

"What was the matter with Caroline, Laurence?"

He paused before speaking, then took a sharp breath in. "She was mentally ill."

Gwen stared at him for a moment before she voiced her thoughts.

"Laurence, how did that kill her?"

"I'm sorry . . . I don't think I can talk about it."

The thought of Caroline and Thomas brought tears welling up. She cried so easily nowadays. Everything set her off, and the strain of keeping the secret of Liyoni's birth was becoming harder. With Laurence near, she couldn't prevent the sadness bubbling up, but if she allowed the tears to fall, and if he was kind, the truth might spill out too.

He reached for her and she was horrified to find her mouth open of its own accord. A word escaped, she let go of his hand, made some excuse and then ran into the house and to her room, only just holding herself together.

In the bathroom she sat on the edge of the bath. Her bathroom was simple and beautiful. Green tiles on the walls, blue on the floor, and a silver-framed mirror. A good place to cry alone. She got up and glanced at her puffy eyes. She undressed slowly and looked down at the extra layer of fat on her breasts, stomach, and thighs, and once again she felt far from herself.

She'd been so happy when she'd believed her destiny was to be a wife to Laurence and a mother to his children. Naveena had said it was the child's fate; if so, had it been her fate to give birth to a baby after a night she could barely recall? And the more she tried not to think of what she might have done, the more Savi's dark eyes haunted her. She clenched her jaw and made a fist.

271

She hated Mr. Ravasinghe, with all her heart she hated him, and hated what he had done to her. She raised her fist and smashed it hard against the mirror. Besides the dozen fractured reflections of her naked self, it gave her the oddest sense of relief to see the repeated image of blood dripping from the cuts in her fist.

The festival was quite low key. The torches around people's houses sent smoke laced with incense to swirl in the evening air, and Gwen recognized the same drumming that she'd first heard on her arrival in Colombo. People drifted about in brightly dressed, happy groups. When they came across a troupe of dancers in the small square, they stopped to watch.

Gwen leaned back against Laurence with Hugh in her arms and attempted to relax. Naveena had bandaged her cuts and Gwen felt better than she had before. It had been a good idea, this outing. Verity seemed happy and Naveena spent most of the time grinning and nodding.

"They are Kandyan dancers," Laurence said.

She looked on as male dancers in long white skirts, with bells on their wrists and jeweled belts, were followed by turbaned men in red and gold, with drums tied to their waists. The beat was mesmerizing.

Women dancers followed, wearing delicate traditional dress and clapping their hands as they moved away. Then came a string of little girls. Gwen felt hot as she watched their slim brown bodies twist and turn. She watched the trancelike looks on their faces, the simple but dignified way they moved, the delicate flicks of their wrists and their lovely dark curling hair, allowed to fall free. They each had her daughter's face, her daughter's body, or the face and body she would one day have. As her longing for Liyoni took over, her throat closed and she could only gulp for air. *Breathe,* she told herself. *Breathe.* She took a step forward and felt her knees buckle. Laurence caught her just as she started to fall. Naveena took Hugh, then Laurence shepherded them through the crowd and over to a bench at the edge of the marketplace.

"Put your head between your knees, Gwen."

She did as she was told, as much as anything to hide her face from his scrutiny. She felt his palm on her back, gently stroking, and tears pricked her lids.

She fought to regain her breath, and once she had, and her head had stopped spinning, she sat up again, still trembling inside.

Laurence felt her forehead. "You're terribly hot, darling."

"I don't know what happened. I did suddenly feel hot, as if I might keel over. My head hurts."

Verity, who hadn't noticed until now that they'd left the crowd, came running up. "You missed the absolutely best bit. There was a fire-eater. One of those little kids, can you believe it?"

Gwen looked up at her.

"You look pale. What's happened? Is it Hugh?"

"We're all going home," Laurence said.

Verity pulled a face. "Must we? I was really enjoying myself."

"Well, there's no question, I'm afraid. Gwen has a headache."

"Oh, for heaven's sake, Laurence. Gwen and her headaches. What about me? Nobody considers what I want!"

Laurence took hold of Verity's elbow and pulled her a few steps away, but Verity's angry voice still reached Gwen.

13

At three in the morning, Gwen sat bolt upright in bed, drenched in sweat and shaking. Three in the morning was the hour when she used to wake as a child, fearing that the ghosts of the Owl Tree had come for her. She called out for Naveena, who came through from the nursery where she now slept. But Gwen could only stutter. In the dream something was wrong with both her children, and though she had tried her utmost, she'd only been able to save one of them.

In the morning, Gwen thought she heard the little girl cry. She wasn't sure if she had heard the cry in her sleep or if it had been at the moment of waking. Whichever it was, the shock remained the same.

After the fourth night of waking, trembling and breathless, she made a decision and called Naveena. As Gwen swung between flashes of anger and heart-stopping guilt, she knew Liyoni's absence was beginning to have more impact on her than Hugh's presence. She needed to put her mind at rest, and had decided that if the child was well cared for, she'd be able to let go. Naveena was less convinced by the idea and Gwen had to coerce the woman into agreeing to do what she asked. Once she had done that, all she could do was wait for a time when Laurence and Verity would both be absent. Until then the nightmares would go on, as would the sound of the little girl's cries.

She waited and on the appointed day, with Laurence and Verity finally having stayed overnight in Nuwara Eliya — Laurence to play a few hands of poker at the Hill Club and Verity to see her old chums — Gwen prepared herself to go. She thought about Laurence at the all-male club. She had peeked once and seen a gloomy interior with only boars' heads, hunting pictures, and stuffed fish for decoration. The contrast between that and what she was about to do could not have been greater.

"But, Lady," Naveena said as she wrapped Hugh up in a blanket, "it is a danger. What if it is going wrong?"

"Just do what we agreed."

The woman bowed her head.

Despite wearing an old cloak of Naveena's over her own clothes, Gwen shivered in the chilly early-morning air. In the hope of concealing her eyes, she pulled the hood down over her forehead, then wrapped a dark shawl round her shoulders and the lower part of her face.

"I have the buggy ready at the side of the house." A look of embarrassment reddened Naveena's face. "You have the money, Lady?"

Gwen nodded. "I think we'd better go now. It will be fully light soon. I've locked my door and left a note with the butler, telling him I am not to be disturbed at all today."

Gwen had sounded a great deal more confident than she felt, and as they slipped out through a side door she saw the bullock standing in the blue half light. She gritted her teeth and clambered up beneath a woven palm-leaf roof stretched over curved cane hoops. Her heart thumped against her ribs, she felt hot, and her hands began to shake; the buggy's rough planked seating was not welcoming. Naveena passed Hugh up in a basket, then sat in the front and flicked the reins. The bullock snorted, and they slowly moved off.

Nobody had seen.

The buggy smelled of sweat, smoke, and tea, and Gwen glanced back as they made their way up the hill. She picked Hugh up and held the sleeping baby to her, wanting to stop caring about the other. The lights in the house were coming on now, just visible in the mist that gathered around the place first thing. *Hurry,* she thought, *hurry.* But the bullock cart was not a speedy way to travel, and until they reached the brow of the hill, she would feel uneasy. Hugh gave a little cry and she murmured to him as a mother does.

Once they had reached the top, the grand house looked small and indistinct and then, as they started along the road, it disappeared completely. Daylight took over from night, the sky turned yellow, and the mist melted, revealing a clear fresh morning. As they went on, it seemed as if the rounded hills, with their rows and rows of startling green tea bushes, went on forever.

Gwen rolled her shoulders to release the tension, and when they drew away from the plantation her breath came a little more easily. As the birdsong started up, she began to enjoy the sweet smells of jasmine, wild orchid, and mint. She closed her eyes.

The day before, she had taken Hugh outside. After the usual damp start, the sun had shown up and the day had warmed. The poor little thing had needed warmth on his cheeks and, exhausted by the broken nights and frenzied days, so had she. But in the spaces of the garden where the light and shade met, she felt the little girl's presence too easily, and Hugh had begun to cry. He held out his little arms, and his fists opened and closed repeatedly, as if he was reaching for something that should have been there.

Gwen sighed and settled back as the buggy, despite its clumpy wooden wheels, ran fairly smoothly along the road. After a while, the drifting scent of lemons caught her attention. As she breathed in deeply, her distress began to ease and the tightness in her chest loosened. It felt like her first relaxed breath since the day the babies were born.

"We turn off now, Lady," Naveena said, and glanced over her shoulder.

Gwen nodded but was almost shaken from her seat as the buggy bumped and jolted down a dirt track. She leaned forward to look out at the small rocks and holes in the ground and saw on either side dark trees towering over the track, but with little undergrowth.

"Do not look into the trees, Lady."

"Why ever not? Is it the *Veddha*?" Laurence had told her about the ancient forest dwellers, known by the Sinhalese word *Veddha,* which, as far as she could tell, simply meant they were uncivilized. As she recalled the grotesque mask, the thought frightened her.

Naveena shook her head. "The uneasy spirits live there."

"Oh, for heaven's sake, Naveena! You don't believe in that, do you?"

Gwen watched the back of Naveena's head as she wobbled it.

Neither of them, it seemed, felt inclined to pursue this conversation. At the side of the track, Gwen spotted a *sambhur* raising its head in alarm, and then it stood stock-still. A large caramel-colored creature, it faced her full on, with warm eyes and beautiful antlers curving up on either side of its head. Tranquil and calm, it didn't look away as they passed.

The forest was quieter than she had expected, and only the sound of the buggy's squeaking wheels accompanied them. Lost in thought, she barely noticed when Naveena turned in a different direction. A new kind of tree came in sight, with trailing leaves, and as they carried on a monkey leaped onto the side of the buggy. It clung to the canvas and stretched its fingers as it stared. The hands and fingernails were black, but its fierce eyes were so human it shocked her.

"It is the purple-faced monkey. It will not hurt," Naveena said, glancing back.

Further on, where the trees thinned out, there was a smell of burning charcoal. She heard voices in the distance and asked Naveena if they were nearly there.

"Not yet, Lady. Soon."

Here there was shallow undergrowth, and their path became less disrupted by rocks and holes in the track. The going became a little faster, and eventually the path curved inward to follow the steep bank of the river. Gwen glanced down into the clear water, where soft dancing greens mirrored the trees on the opposite bank. The air smelled different here, not just of earth and vegetation, but also of something spicy. The land either side of the flattish path was studded with little daisylike flowers and, ahead of her, the trees were draped in unripe wild figs. Beyond them, where the river widened, two elephants seemed to be sleeping in water up to their ears.

Naveena stopped the buggy and tied the reins to one of the trees. "Wait here, Lady."

Gwen watched Naveena go and knew she could trust her. Naveena had been so accepting, so unjudgmental, that Gwen felt it must be something to do with the Buddhist faith and the ayah's belief in fate. Then she glanced down at Hugh, still asleep where she'd put him back in the basket. In the river, two sinuous brown men, with long hair knotted at the back of their heads, led two more elephants into the water. The elephants sat down with slow, lumbering movements, and the men began to wash their heads. When one of the elephants trumpeted, a huge spray of water arced from its trunk, almost reaching Gwen and making her cry out. One of the men looked up, slid out of the water, and came to investigate. She drew back and covered her face, so that only her eyes could be seen. He wore a loincloth, but a belt round his waist held a knife of sorts. Her heart was pounding as she placed a protective arm round Hugh in his basket, and she tried to tell herself the knife must be for opening coconuts.

The man drew out the knife and advanced toward her. She narrowed her eyes in fear. Naveena had all the money with her, so she had nothing to give him. The man spoke and gesticulated, waving the knife in the air.

Gwen spoke no Sinhala at all, so she shook her head. He stared at her for a moment without moving, and then Naveena returned, carrying a bundle in her arms. She spoke to the man and shooed him away, then climbed into the buggy. As Naveena passed the bundle over, Gwen longed to turn back. She did not look down at the child immediately, just held her wrapped up in the shawl and felt the warmth against her chest.

"What did that man want?" she asked.

"To know if you have work for him. He show you his knife, so you know he has own tools to cut the garden."

"Does he know who I am?"

Naveena shrugged. "He call you white lady."

"Does that mean he knows?"

Naveena shook her head. "Many white ladies. I am going through village. I cannot turn buggy here. Too narrow. Cover face. Put baby girl in basket with Hugh."

Gwen did as she was told, then looked out through the open back of the buggy as they passed through a village of thatch-roofed daub and wattle huts. Children played and laughed in the dirt, women carried packages on their heads, and from deep in the woods came the faintest sound of singing. They passed a man making earthenware pots by coiling mud round and round and upward. Outside another hut, a woman wove a blanket on a primitive loom; another was stirring a pot hung over a wood fire. The village seemed peaceful.

Once through, and safely on the other side, they stopped away from the glances of curious eyes. As Gwen unwrapped the baby girl her heart almost stopped. She stroked the baby's soft cheek and gazed in wonder at the precious sight. Liyoni was breathtakingly beautiful, so perfect that it brought tears to Gwen's eyes. Hugh had not cried at all since his sister had been in the basket with him, but now he began to whimper. A girl of about twelve had followed the buggy and Gwen caught sight of her standing a few yards away.

"You hold Hugh, while I check the baby girl," Gwen said. "And tell that girl over there to go away."

Liyoni was wide awake but silent, and staring up at her mother. The shock almost derailed her, but Gwen steeled herself. She was only there to see that the child was being cared for and was not suffering. That was all. With a mixture of longing and fear running through her, she examined the baby carefully, separating the child's fingers and toes, and looking at her legs, her arms, and her skin. She kissed her forehead and her nose but resisted the impulse to bury her face in the shiny dark hair. She took a deep breath, her eyes smarted and a tear drop fell on the child's cheek. The baby didn't smell of talcum powder and milk like Hugh, and the dampness on her skin already carried a trace of cinnamon. Gwen's stomach knotted and, swallowing rapidly, she drew back. She longed to keep on cradling the baby and never let her go but knew with absolute certainty that Liyoni could not be allowed to steal her heart.

At least she was thriving, Gwen told herself. She had fattened out a little and was clean, and that went some way to assuage her guilt.

"That's enough," she said. "The child is well."

"Yes, Lady. I am all the time telling you."

"Let the woman know we are happy and shall continue with the payments."

Naveena nodded.

"Very well, take her back and give Hugh to me."

Naveena and Gwen transferred their bundles and, as Liyoni was taken away, Gwen felt a lump develop in her throat. She listened to the wind getting up in the trees but this time did not look out as she waited. As the minutes passed, Gwen realized there was no point compulsively dwelling on how

Liyoni's conception had come about; what mattered was making sure that it never came to light. She determined never to breathe a word to Mr. Ravasinghe, or to anyone else, for as long as she might live.

"What do they survive on?" Gwen asked, when Naveena returned.

"They have *chenas*. Growing grain and vegetable there, isn't it. And in the forest, fruits. You have seen fig."

"But what else?"

"They are having goats and a pig. They are surviving so."

"But the money you gave her will help?"

"Yes."

On their way back through the village, Gwen glanced out, wondering if she might be able to guess which of the women was the one who would bring up her daughter. At the side of the track, a large land monitor lizard with razor-sharp claws raced up a tree. Gwen noticed one woman who seemed to be watching the buggy with intense dark eyes. She was small but had rounded breasts, wide hips, and a broad-cheeked, dark face. Her black hair was tied at the nape of her neck and a beaded plait hung down her back. The woman smiled as they passed by, and Gwen wondered if it had been a knowing smile or just the absent smile of a woman at peace with the world. For a moment she panicked over what she had done and longed to hold the baby again, but when a bright orange Peacock Pansy butterfly landed at the base of one of the bullock buggy's hoops, she steadied her breathing. Liyoni was being well cared for, that was what mattered, and it was better not to know by whom.

14

Florence Shoebotham's strong floral scent filled the room. She sat on the sofa and leaned back against the leopard skin. Gwen smiled inwardly at the unlikely combination of a wild animal skin and Florence's typical British restraint, the muted shades of blue no competition against even a dead leopard's dark energy. Florence raised the china teacup to her lips, and as she took a sip her chin wobbled. Poor Florence, with her fading hair and multiplying chin.

"It is nice to see you looking so well," Florence said.

Gwen's face fell into a well-rehearsed position. Since seeing Liyoni, she had lied to herself repeatedly in front of the mirror, until she had grown accustomed to knowing how to place her face, where to look, what to do with her hands.

She smiled now, and went on smiling until her jaw ached. "How are you, Florence?"

"I can't complain. Verity's been telling me all about the cheese."

Gwen glanced in Verity's direction. Her sister-in-law was studying her nails and taking no interest in the conversation, so it seemed unlikely that it had been she who had mentioned cheese. In fact, apart from the first day when she had helped clear out the store, Verity had expressed no interest at all.

"I've not made a lot of progress. We cleared the room out about a month ago. It has been cleaned and whitewashed, and we've got some basic furniture and utensils ready. We already had some bits and pieces, but I had to order a cheese thermometer and cheese molds from England."

"But it's a good idea. You are clever."

"My mother is sending over an old cheese press from our farm at Owl Tree."

"It's hard to get good cheese out here."

"It's not difficult to make, but you do have to know how to handle the milk."

"Are you actually planning to sell the cheese?"

Gwen shook her head. "No. I don't even know if we can make it work in this climate. I really just thought of making it for the household, and any friend who might enjoy it."

"Well, do please include me in that, my dear."

"Of course. As I said, cheese isn't difficult, it's the accounts that give me a headache. I'm afraid numbers are not my forte. I just can't get them to tally. I'll probably find it's my own mistake."

"Well," Verity said, interrupting. "It's thrilling that you take such an interest in the business side of things. I don't think Caroline bothered much."

Florence's voice dropped a little. "I'm so glad you've settled down here."

"Settled down?"

"I mean settled in. I was worried at first. You seemed to be spending a lot of time with that painter chap."

Gwen's heart lurched. "Do you mean Mr. Ravasinghe?"

"That's the chap."

"I've only met him on two or three occasions."

"Yes, but he's not British, you see. They do have a way of being rather more forward than we would consider correct."

Gwen faked a laugh. "Florence, I can assure you, he was perfectly correct with me."

"Of course, I didn't mean anything by it." She turned to Verity. "And are you helping your brother's wife make the cheese?"

Verity looked up again. "What?"

"Do stop biting your nails, dear." Florence paused. "I was talking about the cheese. Are you helping Gwen?"

Florence was always so eager to be involved, and keen to give unwanted advice. Gwen felt a moment of sympathy for her sister-in-law and came to her rescue.

"Oh, I'm sure Verity has her own plans," she said.

Verity sighed.

"Such a wonderful idea," Florence carried on saying. "You have such a clever new sister-in-law, don't you, Verity dear? Don't take this amiss, but maybe you should think up some kind of useful occupation too. Something that might help you appeal to the gentlemen."

"And what might you suggest?"

"Men like to have a resourceful wife, you know, like Gwen here. She manages the household, is a wife and mother, and now here she is, busy as a bee, making cheese no less."

Verity stood up, gave Florence a dirty look, and then swept out of the room, knocking over a side table. The teapot, milk jug, and sugar bowl clattered to the floor.

Gwen felt irritated. Her sympathy for Verity evaporating, she rang the bell for one of the houseboys. "I'm so sorry. I don't know what's got into her."

"She was a difficult child."

"How did Caroline cope?"

"Ignored her mostly. I don't think they got on particularly well. Verity was a lot younger then, of course, and still at school. Caroline was rather remote. Though I do remember Verity once went so far as to suggest that Laurence suspected his wife of having an affair."

"Surely not!"

"Verity said she'd heard them arguing about it during the school holidays and that Caroline denied it adamantly. I think Verity made it up. You know what girls are like."

Gwen inclined her head.

"And then, after she left school, Verity spent some time at the house in England, and when she came back she seemed to cling all the more to Laurence. It isn't healthy. That much I do know. I don't know what happened in England, but something must have."

"Caroline's death must have troubled her too?"

"Terribly."

A few days later, Gwen assembled her equipment on the long trestle table in the storeroom. The cheese press, newly arrived from England, sat on a table on the other side of the room. Various-sized colanders, several milk jugs, some wooden stirring spoons, a palette knife, and a large ladle occupied another smaller table. The cheese molds had been washed, dried, and neatly piled, and the cheese cloths hung on the line in the sunshine.

The larger-than-usual supply of buffalo milk had arrived just after dawn, and Gwen was up at half past six, ready for it. She had tied her hair up in a net and wore a large white apron that had been bleached and scrubbed. She was standing in the middle of the storeroom surveying her domain when Laurence popped in.

"I thought you'd gone already," she said.

"I couldn't go without catching a glimpse of our new dairymaid." He came over and studied her face. "And quite a picture she looks too. I could sweep her right off her feet and make away with her to the hayloft."

Pleased he was looking happy, she smiled. "We don't have a hayloft."

"Pity."

He pulled her to him, hugged her, then relaxed his hold. "Best of luck on your first day, darling."

She smiled. "Thank you. Now shoo. I'm busy."

"Yes, ma'am."

She watched him go. Whenever she saw him unexpectedly like that, he made her heart skip, just as he had the very first time. After carefully unwrapping the starter culture specially sent down from Kandy, she poured the milk into a large pan ready to be carried to the kitchen in order to heat it. She took a couple of steps, using both hands to carry the pan, but at the door she realized she didn't have a free hand to open it. She balanced the pan against one side of the door and was about to open the door with the other when the pan slipped and slid to the concrete floor, drenching her in milk.

Now she had to waste time changing her clothes.

By the time she was back in the storeroom, clean and ready to start all over again, Naveena turned up with Hugh, who was wide awake and screaming.

The *appu* stood at the kitchen door and watched the whole procedure with a wry smile. He couldn't voice his objection to what she was doing, but when she'd told him her plans, his disapproval had been plain to see. Her agreement with him was that she would disrupt the smooth running of the kitchen as little as possible, only using it at designated times. So far things were not going well.

Once Hugh was settled, Naveena took him to the nursery, and Gwen began again.

A kitchen boy carried the second batch of milk to the kitchen, while Gwen opened and closed the door. The *appu* oversaw the heating of the milk, and Gwen walked down the three terraces to the lake while she waited for the milk to cool. She sat on a bench at the bottom, glanced up at the fat white clouds, and then watched the water ripple as she listened to the birds. With a light breeze to cool the skin, it was a perfect day. She heard a door creak to her left and swung round to see Laurence emerge from the boathouse.

"What are you doing?" she called out. "I thought you'd be up at the factory, now that the weather's improved."

"It's a surprise."

"For me?"

"No, for the brigadier's wife!"

She frowned.

"Of course for you. Come and see." He flung the door of the boathouse open.

She walked over and glanced in.

It had been spruced up. The interior had

been freshly painted and the gloomy old place had been transformed from a rarely used storage space to a lovely outdoor room. The wide window that overlooked the lake sparkled, the new curtains fluttered, and fresh orange marigolds had been arranged on a small satinwood coffee table in front of a large, though rather threadbare, sofa. He stooped to kiss her cheek, then sat on the sofa, put his feet up on a newly covered footstool, and looked out at the water.

"And the boat?" she asked.

"Right underneath, patched, painted, and ready for us to sail into the sunset. It's my way of saying I'm a fool for not taking into account how tiring it is when you have a new baby. Do you like it?"

"It's lovely. But how did you get all this done without my noticing?"

He winked and tapped the side of his nose.

"Well, I am thrilled."

She came to sit beside him on the sofa and he put his arm round her. It was peaceful watching the water shining in the sunlight and listening to the birds through the open window.

"I wanted to talk to you, Gwen."

She nodded but, not knowing what was coming, felt a moment of anxiety.

"About Caroline."

"Oh?"

"I told you she was mentally ill but I don't suppose anyone has told you that she drowned?"

She inhaled sharply, covered her mouth with her hand, and shook her head.

He reached into his pocket and pulled out a single sheet of notepaper, unfolded it, and smoothed it out.

"I asked the servants not to speak of her death but I think you should see this."

He handed the sheet of paper to Gwen.

My darling Laurence,

I know you will not understand this, and that you may never forgive me, but it is quite impossible for me to go on bearing the pain that I've been in since Thomas was born. From the moment of his birth, I have lived as if a devil were inside me. A devil that blackens my thoughts and steals my equilibrium. It is a hell that I could never have imagined possible. I see no way out but this. I am so very sorry, my love, but I cannot leave poor Thomas without his mother to protect him. So, and this grieves me terribly, I have decided he must come with me, and that together we shall be at peace. May God forgive me. Once I am gone, find a new and better wife, Laurence dear, I shall not mind. In fact I shall pray for it.

Do not blame yourself.

Your Caroline

When she had finished reading it, Gwen swallowed the lump that had tightened her throat. This was not her tragedy, she told herself. She had to control her feelings and help Laurence.

"I haven't found it easy," he said and paused for a moment. "First my parents, then Caroline."

"And the baby," she added.

He nodded slowly but didn't meet her eyes. "And then the trenches, though in some ways the war was almost a relief. You just had to get on with it. No opportunity to dwell."

She fought back warm tears. "Caroline must have been very disturbed to kill herself."

He cleared his throat, then shook his head, for a moment seeming reluctant to speak.

"Did it happen at the lake?"

She waited.

"No. That would have been even harder to bear."

She understood that, though really it was equally awful wherever it had happened. It was just that the lake would have never seemed quite so beautiful again.

"Why did she do it, Laurence?"

"It was . . . complicated. Even the doctor didn't know what to do. He did say some women never seem to recover from childbirth — mentally, I mean. She wasn't herself. Could barely care for the child. I tried to talk, you know, to comfort her, but nothing worked. She just sat staring at her hands and shaking."

"Oh, Laurence."

"I felt so helpless. There was absolutely no way of getting through. Apart from the feeding, Naveena took over almost completely. In the end the doctor did suggest a mental hospital, but I was worried she might end up in some awful asylum. Afterward I couldn't forgive myself for not having sent her away."

She leaned against him. "You didn't know."

"I might have saved her life."

Gwen stroked his face gently, then drew away and held both his hands while she scrutinized his face. "I'm so sorry, Laurence."

"A baby is supposed to bring such joy,

but for us . . ." He stopped.

"You don't have to tell me."

"There's so much I wish I could say."

"One thing I don't understand. What did she mean — poor Thomas without her to protect him? Surely she must have known you would have protected him?"

He just shook his head. There was a long silence.

"Sometimes it is better just to cry, Laurence," she eventually said, seeing the pain on his face.

He blinked and his jaw trembled. The tears when they came were slow and silent. She kissed his wet lips and wiped his cheeks with her hands. Laurence was proud, and not a man given to crying easily, yet this was the second time she'd seen him weep.

"How does anyone recover after something like that?" she said.

"Time helps, and keeping busy, and now there's you and Hugh."

"But something must remain, surely?"

"Yes, I suppose it does."

His gaze fixed somewhere over her shoulder. Then he turned to look at her again. "It affected Verity badly. She was afraid to let me out of her sight."

"Afraid that you might die too?"

"No. I . . . I'm not sure."

He narrowed his eyes as if he was thinking, and seemed to want to say more, but did not know how. The moment of intensity passed.

She hugged him and swore to herself she would never do anything that might wound him further. While she was thinking that, he loosened the strings of her apron, then lifted it over her head. She lay back on the sofa and he carefully undid the tiny pearl buttons of her dress. She slipped it off and removed her underwear as he undressed himself.

Since Hugh's birth, apart from the one time, they had barely touched. Now that their bodies made contact, the fragility of love, and what that meant, came home to her. So easy for it to be ruined. So easy, it seemed, for it to break. She held her breath, not wanting the moment to pass, and as they lay together on the sofa, she felt a world apart from the usual plantation day.

"What if somebody comes?" she whispered.

"Nobody will."

When he stroked her thighs and kissed her toes, she felt the thrill as her body responded, until she could bear it no longer and wrapped her legs round him.

Afterward she lay folded in his arms, with

one pale arm curled round his chest. She lifted her hand to trace the contours of his face with her fingertips, intensely conscious of the warmth of his hand resting on her thigh.

"I love you, Laurence Hooper. I'm so very sorry about what happened to Caroline."

He nodded and took her hand.

She gazed at him and saw that his eyes were less pained than they had been a little earlier.

"Will I have spoiled the cheese?" he said.

"No. The milk has to cool anyway, but the boy will have carried the pan back to the storeroom by now, so I'd better get back." She smoothed down her damp, tangled hair. "I must look a fright."

"You never look a fright. But just one thing," he said.

"Yes?"

"This place is just for you and me. It's a place for us to come whenever either of us needs a sanctuary. Agreed?"

"Absolutely."

"And here we begin afresh, whenever the need."

She placed a hand over her heart and nodded.

Back in the storeroom she added the starter

302

culture to the milk, and left it for an hour or so while she fed Hugh. He grizzled when she tried to put him down inside, so Naveena wheeled out his pram, with a large parasol to shade him. Gwen rocked the pram, feeling the sun on her face and thinking of Laurence as she listened to the insects buzzing. Hugh quickly fell asleep and Gwen told Naveena she could take a well-earned rest. It was perfectly possible to hear if Hugh woke from where she was in the storeroom.

Inside the little room, Gwen added the rennet and stirred, then left the pan under a small window at the back of the room for the sun's warmth to help set the milk.

Though she felt terribly sad about what had happened to Caroline, today had been a good day's work. And at the back of her mind a brown baby girl slept peacefully in her hammock.

■ ■ ■ ■

PART THREE:
THE STRUGGLE

■ ■ ■ ■

15

Three Years Later: 1929

Gwen and Hugh sat on opposite sides of the table waiting for the others to arrive. Hugh looked angelic, dressed in a smart little sailor suit, and with his wild fair hair brushed and flattened for once. Gwen was wearing a dress Fran had bought as a present while she had been staying with her in London, a diaphanous blue chiffon with the new, slightly longer skirt, and she loved that it made her feel young and feminine.

After nearly four years in Ceylon without going home once, it had been a long-overdue trip to England. First she spent two weeks at Owl Tree with her parents, who had burst with pride at the sight of Hugh. With promises of picnics and rides on a train to Cheddar Gorge, they couldn't wait to have him to themselves for a week. Then Gwen had taken the train to London to stay with Fran. The apartment was situated on the top floor of a grand, architect-developed building, with wonderful views over the River Thames, though Gwen couldn't help but compare the gray expanse of water with her beautiful lake at home.

The two women had exchanged letters, planning exciting outings for almost every day, but on the afternoon of her arrival, she'd found Fran not quite her usual self. A little reserved, a little pale. After a much-needed cup of the best Ceylon tea, Fran asked Gwen if she'd like the maid to unpack her case, and linked arms with her.

"I'll do it myself, Frannie, if you don't mind."

"Of course."

Upstairs, in a well-aired, prettily decorated room, Fran went over to the window to close off the noise and dust of London. Gwen opened her case and started to take out her dresses, while Fran remained with her back to the room, gazing out of the window.

"Is anything the matter, Fran?" Fran shook her head.

Gwen picked up a French navy suit, suit-able for a shopping expedition to Mr. Selfridge's store later that day, and went over to hang it in a large mahogany ward-robe. In the gloomy interior of the wardrobe, she couldn't see much at first, but as she reached up for a hanger, her hand brushed against something. As she explored with the tips of her fingers, she realized it was a heavily embroidered silk garment and, judging by the size of it, not a woman's piece either.

She took it down by the hanger and held the garment to the light. It was the most gorgeous red and gold embroidered waistcoat and, Gwen was sure, the one Savi Ravasinghe had worn at the ball. Fran twisted back at that moment and stared at it.

"Oh," she said. "I didn't think he'd left it behind."

"Mr. Ravasinghe's been here?"

"He was staying while undertaking a commission. Rather an important one, actually. He's in great demand."

"You didn't say a word."

Fran shrugged. "I didn't know I had to."

"Is it serious?"

"Let's just say it's a bit up and down."

After that, Gwen had tried to encourage Fran to speak, but whenever she raised the subject, a closed look came on her cousin's face. For the first time, a gap had opened up between the women, and Gwen didn't know how to fix it.

By the penultimate day, the possibility of Fran being really serious about Ravasinghe left a bitter taste in Gwen's mouth and her stomach in knots. She had never seen her cousin lovesick and, as she sat on her bed thinking, she desperately wanted to tell Fran about Liyoni and warn her about Savi Ravasinghe. But now she did not dare. If she were to speak of it, Fran would be outraged and would certainly confront Savi. Who knew where that might lead? He might even insist on knowing his daughter, and that didn't bear thinking about.

So Gwen kept her silence and felt as if she had betrayed her friend. The two women spent their last day together with everything remaining unsaid, and after another bitter-sweet week with her parents, Gwen had been glad to set off on her homeward journey back to Ceylon.

Now, as Gwen smiled across the birthday table at her son, she felt so proud but was aware she felt something more than love, something ineffable that struck to the core of her. Hugh grinned at her, not at all able to sit still, and it brought her back to basics. Children did that. One moment they inspired such a surge of love that it sent you reeling and gasping for breath, and the next moment it was jelly and biscuits, or needing a number two.

It surprised her how quickly three years had passed, and that she had become so accustomed to living with what had happened that at times it almost seemed like a dream; almost, but not quite. She glanced out of the window toward the lake and then beyond to the rounded hills, carpeted with tea and dotted with tall, spindly trees. It was a lovely, cloudless, bright blue day. In the almost three years since their first trip to the boathouse, she and Laurence had revisited it often. Life had settled down. They had been happy, with the joys outweighing the sorrows, and in the end, as something toughened up inside her, Gwen had managed to suppress some of her regrets about Liyoni.

Laurence didn't understand why she hadn't conceived another child, despite, as he put it, his best efforts. He didn't know that Gwen had secretly done everything she could to prevent it. Remembering the heartbreak over giving Liyoni away, Gwen felt she didn't deserve another child, and used her douche bag every time. If she felt in any danger, she drank a large quantity of gin and took a hot bath. Naveena understood her reluctance and concocted bitter-tasting herbs that always brought the monthly cycle on.

A noise at the door interrupted her thoughts. She twisted round to see McGregor, Verity, and Naveena coming in together.

Verity clapped her hands. "This looks wonderful, doesn't it, Hugh?"

Today was Hugh's third birthday. The table was laid with fresh flowers, piles of sandwiches, two pink-and-yellow blanc-manges, and a space in the middle for the cake. As Laurence came through trailing a bunch of balloons, his arms loaded with presents, Hugh's little cheeks flushed with excitement.

"I open them now, Daddy?"

Laurence put them on the table. "Of course. Do you want the big one first?"

Hugh jumped up and down, squealing as he did.

"Well, you'll have to wait a minute, it's in the hall." Laurence went back out and a few minutes later wheeled in a tricycle, with a big yellow ribbon tied round the handlebar. "This is from Mummy and Daddy," he said.

Hugh stared at the gleaming machine, then ran over and needed help from Naveena to climb onto the seat. His face fell when his feet didn't quite reach the pedals.

"We can adjust the seat a little, but you might have to grow into it."

"Did we choose the wrong size?" Gwen said.

"It will be fine in a month or two," Laurence said.

Hugh was already tearing the paper from the rest of the presents: a giant jigsaw from Verity, a wooden fire engine from Gwen's parents, and a cricket bat and ball from McGregor.

Gwen sat back and watched her family, feeling blessed. Hugh was a whirlwind of energy, exuberant in the way only a three-year-old can be, and Laurence was beaming with pride as he watched his son. Even Verity seemed happy, though the fact that she was still with them was a thorn in Gwen's side.

After they'd polished off the sandwiches and blancmanges, Hugh shrieked when Laurence turned the act of extinguishing the lights and drawing the curtains into a matter of great solemnity. He squared his shoulders and, with a serious face, told them the moment had arrived.

Naveena brought in the cake and placed it on the table in front of Hugh. Hugh's rapt attention was a picture, and the innocence of his little face as he looked up at them all, while they sang "Happy Birthday," triggered a feeling of intense joy in Gwen. She would tear the head off a leopard to protect her little boy. She covered up the surge of emotion by fussing round the cake and shifting it slightly closer to her son. It was a large square cake with a spaniel made out of icing sugar on the top, made by Verity who, it turned out, had a distinct talent for sugarcraft.

"It's Spew," Hugh shouted at the top of his voice. "Spew is on the cake!"

"Blow out the candles, darling," Gwen said. "And make a wish."

As the child puffed out his cheeks and blew, Gwen thought of Hugh's twin and made a wish of her own.

"Did you make a wish?" Laurence asked.

"It's a secret, Mummy said. Didn't you, Mummy?"

"I did, darling."

As Hugh raised his face to his father, Gwen thought for the hundredth time how like Laurence he had grown. Hugh's eyes had changed soon after his birth and now they were the same color as his father's. They both had the same square chin, and the same-shaped head, with a double crown at the back that made his hair so difficult to tame. There was no doubt as to Hugh's parentage.

"There are secrets, Daddy."

"I suppose there must be," he said and pulled a face.

Hugh wriggled in his seat, unable to suppress his energy. "I got one."

"What is it, darling?" Gwen said.

"My friend, Wilfred."

Laurence grimaced. "Not this again."

"But, darling," Gwen said, "we all know about Wilfred, so it isn't a secret."

"Yes it is. You can't see him."

"That's true," Verity said.

"I can see him. And he wants a piece of cake."

"Naveena, please cut a piece of cake for Wilfred."

"Not pretend piece, Neena." Neena was the name Hugh used for her when he had first begun to speak, and the name had stuck.

"I don't think we should indulge him," Laurence said, and put an arm round Gwen's waist.

"Does it matter so very much?"

Laurence stuck out his chin. "An invisible friend will not help him at school."

She laughed. "Come on, Laurence, he's

only three. Let's not talk about this now. It's his birthday party."

"Me have 'nother slice too?" Hugh said in a wheedling tone of voice.

"Two is quite enough," she said.

Hugh stuck out his bottom lip. "Daddy?"

"Oh, let him have it, it is his birthday," Verity said. "Everyone should be indulged on their birthday."

"No more cake, old chap," Laurence said. "Mummy's always right."

"I'm glad that's clear."

He laughed, picked Gwen up, and spun her round. "But it doesn't stop me doing this."

Hugh giggled at the sight of his mother being twirled as if she was weightless.

"Laurence Hooper, put me down this instant!"

"As I said, Mummy's always right. That's something I've had to learn. So I better had put her down."

"No. No. Spin again!" Hugh cried.

"Laurence, if you don't put me down, I swear I will be sick."

He laughed and let her drop to the floor.

"Can we go to the waterfall, Daddy? We never go."

"Not right now. Tell you what, why don't you and I have a kick around outside? Have you got your new ball?"

Hugh grinned, the cake seemingly completely forgotten. "Yes, I have got the ball. I have. It's mine."

It was only as Laurence, Hugh, and Verity went out that Gwen noticed Wilf's empty plate. Hugh, the little monkey, had managed to pilfer his third slice of cake after all. Gwen shook her head, but smiled, and then went to her room.

There, she pulled out a child's charcoal drawing from a locked box in her desk. It was the most recent of the drawings, and had arrived about a month before. For a few uneasy days each month Gwen waited for the next drawing. She clung to each one because it meant the child was well. At first the foster woman had drawn them herself, but now Liyoni's small scribbles had taken their place. Gwen touched the charcoal lines. Was it a dog or a chicken? Hard to tell. She had always burned the woman's drawings, but the longing that had never completely left her meant she kept Liyoni's.

That night when Hugh was sick in his bed, Gwen thought it must be something to do with the three pieces of cake. She asked Naveena to bring the child to sleep with her. He was sick two more times and after that he slept, and she managed to sleep herself on and off.

In the morning Hugh shook and cried out that he was cold, but when she felt the back of his neck, it was fiery, and his forehead was burning too. She changed his night-clothes, but in no doubt that Hugh had a fever, she called Naveena to bring cold cloths. While she waited, Gwen opened the window for air and listened to the birds making their usual morning racket as they woke up the household. The unlikely combination of tuneful song and wild squawking would normally bring a smile to her face, but today it seemed loud and intrusive.

When Naveena came in carrying the cloths, Gwen placed them on the back of Hugh's neck and on his forehead, then after he'd cooled down a little, they looked him over.

"It wasn't the cake. The vomiting seems to have stopped, but he isn't well."

Naveena's nose twitched, but she didn't speak as she examined his arms and legs, then pulled up his nightshirt and ran a palm over his trunk to search for raised spots. When she didn't find any, she shook her head.

"Ask Laurence to call the doctor," Gwen said when the woman had finished. "Tell him Hugh's very sweaty, but complaining of the cold."

"Yes, Lady." Naveena turned to go.

"And tell him Hugh's skin looks a little bit blue, and he's starting to cough."

While Hugh slept in fits and starts, Gwen closed the shutters and paced the room. When Laurence came in, the concerned look in his eyes forced her to stay calm.

"It's probably just one of the childhood ailments," she said. "Don't worry. Dr. Partridge won't be long. Why don't you go to the kitchen and ask the *appu* to make us some chai?"

He nodded and left the room, coming back ten minutes later with two glass mugs on a silver tray. She smiled at him. The last thing he needed was for her to show her growing anxiety. She went to Laurence and took the tray.

While they waited for the doctor, Gwen sang nursery rhymes, with Laurence attempting to join in, but using the wrong words and jumbling them up in an effort to make Hugh smile.

By the time Dr. Partridge arrived, carrying his usual brown leather bag, Hugh was still awake but very drowsy.

The doctor sat on the bed.

"Let's have a look at you, old chap," he

said, and opened his own mouth wide to show Hugh what to do. But the room was dimly lit, and it was clear he was unable to see. "Laurence, open the shutters. Would you mind?"

With the shutters open, Dr. Partridge lifted Hugh and carried him to the light, then sat in Gwen's window chair and examined the child's mouth. He felt Hugh's neck, which looked a little swollen, then felt the pulse at his wrist. He took a deep breath and shook his head.

"Let's see if you can drink, shall we? Have you got a glass of water handy, Gwen?"

She passed him her own glass, and he sat Hugh up, then raised the glass to the child's lips. The little boy put a hand to his swollen neck and took a sip, but choked and spat it out, then coughed for several minutes.

When he had finished, the doctor listened to his chest then looked up at Gwen. "He has a rattle. Has he been coughing much?"

"On and off."

"All right, back to bed with you."

Gwen carried Hugh to her bed and covered him.

"He must have absolute rest. Even if he seems to recover a bit, don't allow him to move. His heart rate is fast, as is his breathing. If you put a couple of pillows behind him, it'll help the breathing, and get as much moisture in the air as you can. Then we just have to wait and see."

Gwen and Laurence exchanged worried looks.

"So what is this condition?" Gwen asked, trying to keep her voice level.

"It's the diphtheria."

She covered her mouth in shock and saw Laurence stiffen.

"I'm afraid the blue tinge to his skin predicted it. Several children in one of the local villages have recently contracted it too."

"But he was vaccinated," Laurence said as he twisted round to her. "Gwen?"

She squeezed her eyes shut and nodded.

The doctor shrugged. "Might have been a faulty batch."

"And the prognosis?" Gwen asked in a shaking voice.

The doctor tilted his head. "Hard to say at this stage. I'm sorry. If he starts to show lesions on his skin, just keep them clean. Try to get him to drink, if you can. And in his presence, you will all need to cover your mouths and noses with cotton masks. You'll probably have one or two in the house, but I'll have more sent down immediately."

"What if —"

There was a terrible silence in the room. Her voice had risen sharply and Laurence covered her hand with his own, holding it tightly, as if to stop her saying words that could not be erased.

"Let's not think of that just yet," he said in a gruff voice.

She knew by saying that he was hoping to stave off the inevitable and felt an explosion of heat in her head. "Just yet?"

"I meant let's wait and see; that's all we can do."

She wanted to give vent to her fear but forced herself to remain calm.

In the days that followed, Verity and Gwen wiped the beads of sweat that kept forming on Hugh's forehead, and tried to keep him cool. Naveena brought in a wet towel and hung it at the window, to moisten the air, she said. She also pinned a soaking wet sheet across the door. Then she arranged some small pieces of charcoal in a shallow bowl and poured a little hot water over them.

"What is that for?" Gwen asked.

"Whole trouble is to keep the air clean, Lady."

For the next two days his condition did not change, either for the worse or for the better. On the third day, his cough began to worsen; he struggled for breath and his color was gray. As she watched flies batter themselves against the window then drop to the floor, Gwen felt unable to breathe. She ripped off her face mask and, fighting back her fear for Hugh, laid beside him with her cheek against his and held him close to her. Laurence buried himself in his study, from time to time appearing at the bedside to relieve Gwen of her vigil. She kept a fixed smile on her face for Laurence's sake but barely left the room.

Laurence would not allow her to stay in the room to eat what little she could, saying there was no point her becoming sick too, and that she'd need her strength. While Gwen attempted to eat, Verity watched over Hugh, and with an anguished look offered to stay whenever Gwen came back in.

Naveena brought some sweet-smelling herbs to put in a bowl over a candle in an earthenware pot.

"This will help, Lady," she said.

But the fragrance did not help. When she was alone with Hugh, Gwen sat at his bedside, closed her aching eyes and, twisting her hands in her lap, pleaded with God to allow her child to live.

"I'll do anything you ask," she said. "Anything. I'll be a better wife, a better mother."

She went to the window while Hugh slept and had no idea how long she watched the colors of the garden change during the course of the day, from pale leafy green in the morning to deep shadowy purple by night. She stared at the lake with tears in her eyes, and the boundary between the water and the treeline blurred. While her child's condition deteriorated she listened to the household and, with a constantly heavy feeling in her chest, heard people going about things in the way they did. None of it seemed real. Not the liveliness of the mornings, nor the sleepiness of the afternoons. She asked Naveena to fetch some mending, Hugh's preferably, but anything would do if it kept her hands occupied.

Every moment that Hugh slept was a relief and, when he did, Gwen stitched, the tiny needle weaving in and out, pulling the silk thread in a long line of minute stitches. Verity and Laurence tiptoed in and out, but no one spoke. The more Hugh slept, the better chance he stood.

Night was different and not shared with anyone, and then the silence was unbearable. When Hugh's breathing became labored, it broke her heart to hear his small body struggling so, but at least she knew he was still alive. When it seemed to stop, she froze, and her heart only began to beat normally when the rasping breath started up again.

In the night, she was overwhelmed with memories of Hugh as a baby. Such a crying baby he had been. She refused to think that the worst might happen, or how she would be able to go on living without her darling boy.

She remembered him as a chubby toddler attempting his first wary steps, then later, how his thundering footsteps woke her in the morning. She thought of his first haircut, and the fuss he'd made at the sight of the scissors, so much so that Naveena had had to hold him down. She thought of the way he hated scrambled eggs for tea, but loved them boiled, with soldiers, in the morning. And his first words: Neena, Mumma, and Dadda. Verity had so wanted him to say her name too, and had sat with him for ages, saying "Verity" over and over. All Hugh had been able to manage was "Witty."

All Gwen's old anxieties flooded back. She remembered Savi Ravasinghe's painting of Christina, and what the woman had said more than three years ago. Everybody falls in love with him in the end. Was that it? She thought back to the ball, and the way Savi had escorted her to her room. She thought of Fran being with a man like that and ached for her cousin. And, as she watched Hugh's eyelids flicker in his sleep, her mind returned to the Sinhalese village where Liyoni lived. If this terrible illness could strike Hugh down, a child living in luxury, how vulnerable must her little girl be?

In the moments when she was neither awake nor asleep, she prayed for her daughter, as well as for Hugh, and entered an obscure luminal world. With her thoughts wheeling, she was torn between the village and her home. She thought of the lads washing elephants in the river and the simple way of life there, the women cooking over an open fire and men weaving on their primitive looms. Her own privileged life swam sharply into focus, now lacking even the most simple kind of peace.

Eventually one thought dominated her mind.

She had given up one child already. If Hugh's illness was her punishment for sacrificing her daughter's happiness for her own, the only way she would ever save Hugh would be by doing what was right. The truth in return for his life. It would be an exchange, a bargain with God, and even if it

meant losing everything, she must confess
or otherwise watch her son die.

16

For over a week everyone held their breath. Hugh was a much-loved member of the family, and even the houseboys and kitchen coolies walked around with long faces and spoke in hushed whispers. But once he had turned a corner and began to drink and sit up in bed, the household became a lighter place again, and the normal bang and rattle of daily life resumed.

As she watched over the child, unable to leave his side for long, Gwen's relief was as consuming as her fear had been. Laurence clattered about with a grin on his face and eyes sparkling with happiness. There was laughter as he sat with his son doing jigsaws on the bed and reading his best books while Gwen arranged for all Hugh's favorite foods to be made: a Victoria sponge, green macaroons, cardamom and mango ice cream — anything she could think of to tempt him, anything that might enable him to become once again the noisy, energetic child he had been.

Yet when he felt well enough to run around outside, she wanted to keep him with her.

"We mustn't smother the lad," Laurence said.

"Is that what you think I'm doing?"

"Let him run. It'll do him good."

"It is quite cold today."

"Gwen. He's a boy."

So she relented and watched for half an hour as he ran after the dogs, but when Laurence had gone in, she tempted Hugh back inside with crayons and a new pad of drawing paper. While she was watching him, her determination not to allow a moment's distraction grew. As long as she was watching Hugh, she was not worrying about Liyoni. In her room, he scribbled nonsense pictures of Bobbins and Spew and little Ginger, who was still smaller than the other two. In fact, it was Ginger being under his bed that made him happiest of all.

But the sight of the little boy's drawings made her feel ill at ease. Full moon had been and gone and the little girl's latest drawing had not arrived. Though she could barely breathe with the relief of knowing that her son would live, each day that he improved, she began to hear a trace of her daughter's voice as it breached the wall of noise in her head. The child's whispers pulled her through open doorways, beckoned her along the gloomy hallway and up the polished stairs. She thought she saw the girl silhouetted in one of the landing windows, but then the light moved and she realized it had only been a shadow cast by clouds against the sun.

What she could suppress by day became enormous at night. Liyoni's voice grew loud, demanding her attention, haunting her dreams and feeling so real, she believed the child was actually in her room. When she woke, sweating and shaking, it was with a feeling of reprieve that there was no one there but Hugh, or Naveena coming in with her bed tea.

She insisted on fresh flowers being placed throughout the house: in the hall, the dining room, the drawing room, and all their bedrooms. The moment any flower seemed to droop, the whole bunch had to go, and fresh ones were arranged in their place. But no amount of flowers could lessen her anxiety. Gwen had made a bargain with God, but she had not kept her side of it and now lived in fear of the consequences.

After Hugh returned to sleep in the nursery, Laurence found her sitting at her small desk with her shoulders hunched, playing solitaire. He stood behind and stooped down to kiss the top of her head. She glanced up. For a moment their eyes met in the mirror but, afraid the tell-tale shine of hers would give her away, she turned her face so that his lips only brushed her hair.

"I came to ask if you would like me to stay with you tonight?" He glanced at the cards. "Or play a game with you?"

"I would, but there's no point in neither of us getting any sleep."

"I thought you'd be sleeping, now that Hugh's so much better?"

"I'll be all right, Laurence. Please don't fuss. I'll be all right."

"Well, if you're sure."

She pressed her hands together to stop them shaking. "I am."

She didn't get into her bed when he had gone, but carried on playing cards. After an hour, she leaned back in the chair, but the moment she closed her eyes and the feeling of relaxation began to spread, her eyes flew open again. She brushed all the cards to the floor.

"Damn it. Leave me alone," she said aloud.

But the little girl would not leave.

Gwen walked around the room, picking up ornaments and putting them back down again. What if the child was ill? What if the child needed her?

Eventually, too tired to stay awake, she slept. And then the nightmares began. She was back at the Owl Tree, falling out of its branches, or riding in a bullock cart that never arrived at any destination. She woke and paced the room, then wrote a long letter to Fran telling her about Savi Ravasinghe. She put it in an envelope, addressed it, looked for a stamp, and then ripped the whole thing into dozens of fragments and threw them at the wastepaper basket. After that she just stared out at the darkness of the lake.

The next day she couldn't concentrate and lost the thread of things. Was this feeling that her world might be about to collapse around her God's punishment? Maybe the drawing hadn't arrived because Liyoni wasn't well, she argued. Some trifling childhood ailment. Nothing serious. Or had she been taken? Children were sometimes taken. Or had Savi found out and was now looking for the right moment to speak up? Each day that she waited, biting her nails, unable to eat, and not knowing, the feeling of dread grew.

She was short-tempered with Laurence, Naveena wasn't there when she needed her, and Hugh avoided her, spending time with Verity instead.

She took out all her clothes from her wardrobe and laid them on the bed, intending to decide which might be updated, and which she no longer wore at all. She tried them on, one by one, but every time she looked in the mirror, nothing looked right. The clothes hung from her, and she decided to remove her wedding ring, for fear it would slip from her finger and be lost. As she tried on her hats, she began to cry. Naveena came into the room and found her sitting motionless on the floor, gulping at air and surrounded by hats: felt hats, feathered hats, beaded hats, and sun hats. The woman held out a hand to her and Gwen took it, then stumbled to her feet. When she was standing, she leaned against Naveena, and the woman held her tight.

"I've lost weight. Nothing fits," she said through her sobs.

Naveena carried on holding her. "You've gone down a little, that is what."

"I feel so awful," she said when the tears stopped falling.

Naveena handed her a handkerchief to mop her face with. "Hugh is better. You do not need to worry."

"It isn't Hugh. Well, it is Hugh, but it's not just Hugh."

Unable to say the words, she went to her desk and took out the little box, found the key and unlocked it. She held up the drawings to Naveena.

"What if she is sick?"

Naveena patted her back. "I understand. You must not break your head. Put away. Next drawing will come. You call doctor for you, Lady."

Gwen shook her head.

But later that day, when she prickled all over, feeling as if her skin had been peeled away, she couldn't stand it any longer. Her deteriorating mental state, exacerbated by the lack of sleep, made her whole body ache. She jumped at the slightest sound, heard things that weren't there, felt unequal to the simplest task and found herself going round in circles, starting something, leaving it, then forgetting what it was she'd been doing in the first place. At the point where she felt she was losing her connection with everything she loved, she capitulated, knowing she would have to ask for help.

17

Luckily, the doctor had been able to call soon after Gwen had telephoned him and, knowing the powder he intended to prescribe would be on its way, she wanted to do something while she waited. In her troubled state, she was hardly in a position to attend to the cheesemaking and, in any case, she had trained one of the kitchen boys to do the job, so instead she turned her attention to the household accounts.

Over the years she had cleared up the discrepancies between the orders that had been paid for and the deliveries that actually appeared in the house. She'd insisted on seeing for herself when deliveries came, and had checked them off against the bills that were presented for payment. The irregularities had been sorted out, and though at one point she had suspected the *appu* of stealing, it was difficult to prove. She didn't expect to see any discrepancy now.

While Naveena looked after Hugh, she sat at her desk and forced herself not to think of her worries. As she rubbed her temple to try to ease the headache there, she noticed a payment for an unusual amount of rice, whisky, and oil, during the time Hugh had been ill. She went to the supplies cupboard expecting to see a much larger supply of the goods, but even less than the normal amount was there. Only the *appu* had the other key.

In the kitchen, she'd hoped to confront the *appu* about it, but McGregor was there smoking his pipe, with a pot of tea in front of him.

"Mrs. Hooper," he said as he lifted the pot and, holding it high, poured. "How are you? Tea?"

"A little tired, Mr. McGregor. No tea, thanks. I was hoping to speak to the *appu.*"

"He's gone to Hatton with Verity. She's taken the Daimler."

"Really? Why have they gone together?"

"A bit of business, she said."

Gwen frowned. "What kind of business?"

"She has been seeing to the ordering while you've been occupied with Hugh. I expect they must be picking up supplies."

"And she has been making the payments too?"

"I imagine she must have been."

"And are you the one who still goes to the bank in Colombo?"

"Yes, I bring back the laborers' wages and the money for the household expenses." He paused. "Well, usually I do, but we had a huge amount of tea to process this month, and with Laurence so preoccupied, Verity went in my place."

"In the Daimler, I suppose?"

He nodded.

Gwen settled Hugh for the night and, hoping the sleeping draft would soon arrive, she asked Naveena to come to her room.

As soon as the woman was sitting, Gwen looked into her calm dark eyes. "Why is this month's drawing late? I need to know."

Naveena shrugged. What did it mean, that shrug?

"Is she still thriving? Has something happened to her?" Gwen continued.

"Waiting a little longer, Lady," Naveena said. "If girl is sick I am already hearing by now."

Gwen felt so tired; it was hard for her to keep track of simple conversations, but she needed to know if Liyoni was safe.

As they were talking, Verity came in. "Hello. I've got something for you."

"Thank you, Naveena," Gwen said as she nodded a dismissal.

"We were in Hatton," Verity said after the woman had gone.

"I heard."

"I bumped into old Doc Partridge."

"Really, Verity, he isn't old at all. Just that his hair's thinning." She smiled weakly. "You know he's awfully nice. You could do a lot worse."

Verity blushed. "Don't be silly. He gave me a prescription to have made up in the dispensary. He was on his way to do it himself, but I saved him the bother. Shall I stir a dose into some hot milk now?"

"Oh, please, would you mind?"

"You just settle down in bed and I'll go to the kitchen and sweeten it with a good squirt of jaggery to take the unpleasant taste away. What do you say?"

"Thank you. That is kind."

"If anyone knows how ghastly sleeplessness can be, it's me. Though I was surprised, given that Hugh is so much better — I thought you'd be out like a light."

"It seems to have made me rather anxious generally."

"Right. Be back in a jiffy."

Gwen got out of her clothes and picked up the white nightdress Naveena had laid on her bed. She held it to her nose and breathed in the fresh flowery smell, then pulled it over her head and fumbled with the buttons. Her guilt had cemented her within a fearful inner space, but squeezing her hands together and wanting to think of happier times, she tried to banish the black thoughts. If Naveena was right, maybe Liyoni wasn't ill after all, but it was still possible that the drawing had been intercepted.

If she were to lose it all, the very best she could hope for would be to be sent back to Owl Tree, never to see her darling Hugh again. She trembled at the thought of her son without his mother, and pictured Florence and the other women with the same look of superiority on their faces if it all came out. With sly eyes they'd smile and congratulate themselves that it was she, and not they, who had succumbed to the advances of a charming native man.

By the time Verity came back, she was trembling with fear.

"Goodness. You are in a bad way. Here you are. It's not too hot, so drink it down straight away. I'll sit with you while you fall asleep."

Gwen drank the pink milky mixture, which, though bitter, wasn't as bad as she'd expected, and very quickly felt her eyes close. She drifted for a few minutes, feeling comfortably drowsy, realized her headache had lifted, wondered what it was that she'd been worrying about, and then lost all feeling of wakefulness.

The next morning, she could barely lift her head from the pillow, even though at the same time it also hurt to rest her head *on* the pillow. She heard raised voices going on in the corridor sounding a bit like Naveena and Verity arguing.

A few minutes later Naveena came in. "I am bringing bed tea earlier, Lady, but could not wake you. I was shaking you."

"Is there a problem with Verity?" Gwen asked, and glanced at the door.

The old ayah looked troubled but didn't speak.

Gwen felt cold and clammy, as if she was about to go down with influenza. "I need to get up," she said, and tried to swing her feet to the floor, just as Verity entered the room.

"Oh, no you don't. Rest for you, until you feel better. You can go, Naveena."

"I'm not ill, just tired. I need to look after Hugh."

"Leave Hugh to me."

"Are you sure?"

"Absolutely. In fact, leave everything to

340

me. I've already discussed the menus and paid the household staff."

"I wanted to talk to you." Gwen felt unfocused and drifted for a moment. "I can't remember. Deliveries, was it? Or something . . ."

"There's a daytime powder for you too. I'll mix it up with bee honey and tea. You probably don't need milk for this."

Verity went to the kitchen and came back in with a glass of cloudy reddish-brown liquid.

"What is it?"

Verity tilted her head. "Hmmm? Not sure. I've followed his directions exactly."

Almost as soon as she had drunk the potion, Gwen relaxed, feeling the most delicious floating sensation. Blanched of all distress and feeling wiped clean, she drifted off again.

Gwen began to long for the "magic potion," as she now thought of it. When she drank it, she floated in a mist, free from painful headaches and free from worry, but with the stupor came a complete lack of appetite and an inability to hold a normal conversation. When Laurence looked in on her one evening, she tried her best to be herself, but it was clear from the worry in his eyes she was not succeeding.

"Partridge will be here in the morning," he said. "God knows what he's been giving you."

Gwen shrugged as he took her hand. "I'm fine."

"Your skin feels clammy."

"I just said, I'm fine."

"Gwen, you really are not. Perhaps don't take the mixture tonight. I don't think it's doing you any good, and neither does Naveena."

"Did she say that?"

"Yes. She came to me worried sick."

Her throat constricted. "Laurence, I must have it. It does do me good. Naveena's wrong. It gets rid of the headaches completely."

"Stand up."

"What?"

"Stand up."

She shuffled her bottom toward the edge of the bed and lowered her feet to the floor. She held out a hand to him. "Help me, Laurence."

"I want to see you do it, Gwen."

She bit her lip and made an effort to stand, but the room was moving, dipping back and forth, and the furniture was shifting. She sat back down again. "What did you ask me to do, Laurence? I can't remember."

"I asked you to stand."

"Well, that was a silly thing, wasn't it?" She laughed, crawled back under the sheet, and stared at him.

18

In the morning, Gwen sat at her dressing table and opened a drawer where her mother's scent was preserved in an embroidered handkerchief. She took it out and sniffed. Fortified by the brief connection, she slipped on her silk dressing gown and some slippers, wrapped a fine woolen shawl round her shoulders, and then made her way out of the house by the side entrance.

Verity and McGregor were sitting on the verandah. "Darling, how are you?" Verity said with a broad smile.

"I thought some fresh air."

"Do sit for a while. Here's your drink."

Gwen drank the mixture but didn't sit.

"Won't you have some breakfast? It would do you good."

"I think I'll just take a walk."

"Hang on." Verity opened her bag and took out a folded piece of paper. "I'd almost forgotten, but Nick just reminded me," she said. "I've been carrying it around since Hugh was ill."

"Oh?"

Verity held out the crumpled paper. "Can you give it to Naveena?"

As she handed it over a door slammed somewhere in the house. Gwen felt as if her knees might give way, but she made a show of looking at it, while her heart raced and thoughts scrambled in her head.

"It's a drawing of some kind," Verity said. "For Naveena, from a niece or a cousin or something, in one of the valley villages. It's a bit blurred, and some of the charcoal seems to have rubbed off."

The blood drained from Gwen's face. She folded the drawing up again and, feeling emotionally buffeted, hoped the fear she was feeling didn't show and that the faint sound of voices was only in her head.

A God-fearing Englishwoman does not give birth to a colored child.

Nick McGregor, who hadn't spoken until now, looked up at her. "I caught the milk-cart coolie bringing it."

"Oh."

"I've made sure it's a different coolie doing the milk run now, with strict instructions not to carry messages."

"I'll give it to Naveena."

345

"I wanted to say before, but with Hugh ill . . ." He spread his hands in a wide gesture.

Gwen did not dare speak.

"And I know you haven't been too well yourself." He paused.

"Gwen, you look pale. Are you all right?" Verity reached out a hand, but Gwen took a step back. They knew. They both knew and were playing with her.

"Anyway," McGregor continued, "I really can't have my coolies delivering messages, not even for the ayah."

Gwen searched for words. "I shall put a stop to it."

"Good. We don't want the servants thinking they're entitled to send notes whenever they wish. With the current unrest, albeit minor, there can be no underground channels of communication."

"Let us hope the drawing really was from her relative, and not some activist," Verity said. "I always thought Naveena had no relations."

Gwen tried not to flinch, but she had to get away from the subject of the drawing and, clutching at passing thoughts, she began to speak. Luckily, McGregor stood up, interrupting her, and Gwen took her chance to escape.

The garden was aflame as she wandered past the bushes. With one hand she ran her fingertips over the red and orange blooms, and in the other she held Liyoni's drawing safely folded up. They would have to find a different method of receiving communications from the village, but at least she now knew what had happened to the one that had been overdue. Its absence had not been caused because she had failed to confess. Liyoni was safe and well and there was nothing to worry about on that score.

She walked down to the lakeside and thought about a swim, but the medicine was already beginning to take effect, and when the threads of gold in the water began to blur and the colors of the sky and lake melded into each other, she felt unsteady on her feet. She shook her head to clear her mind: the lake dissolved back into the lake, the sky into the sky. She walked to the boathouse. That was the place to be — safe and full of happy memories.

She opened the door and glanced around the room.

The fire was unlit, of course, and it was damp, but she was tired, so she picked up a knitted throw, covered herself, and lay back on the sofa.

Sometime later, she heard Hugh's voice.

At first she thought she was dreaming and smiled at the thought of him. Her lovely sweet boy. She'd seen so little of him lately. It was always "Verity this" and "Verity that." But when she heard Laurence's voice too, and then Hugh's once more, she was filled with the desire to see her boys. She wanted to touch her son's hair and feel Laurence's arms round her. She attempted to stand, but feeling as if she had an enormously thick head, she had to steady herself by gripping the arms of the sofa.

"Shall we see if Mummy is in there?" Gwen heard.

"Good idea, old boy."

"Daddy, can Wilfred come in too?"

"Just let me take a peek inside, and then we'll see."

Gwen saw Laurence's dark shape block the door. "Oh, Laurence, I —"

As he came toward her, he seemed to loom so large that he filled the entire space. He said a few words to her and then she blacked out.

When Gwen came back to consciousness, she heard Laurence speaking. They were in her bedroom now, and Dr. Partridge was standing next to Laurence by the window. She couldn't see their faces, but they stood close together, in silhouette, with their hands clasped behind their backs.

She coughed and the doctor turned. "I'd like to take a look at you, Gwen, if that's all right."

She tried to smooth her hair. "Well, I'm sure I must look an absolute fright, but really I'm fine, John."

"Nevertheless."

He looked in her eyes, then listened to her heart. "You say she fainted, Laurence?"

"I found her on the boathouse floor."

"And has she seemed confused?"

Gwen watched as Laurence nodded.

"Her pupils are as small as pinpricks and her heartbeat is fast." He looked round at Gwen. "Where is the last glass you drank the medication from, Gwen?"

"I don't know. Outside, I think. I can't quite remember."

Gwen closed her eyes and drifted while Laurence went to find the glass. He came back in and passed it to the doctor.

He sniffed, dipped a finger in the remains, and put it to his lips. "This seems rather strong."

"Where are the packets John prescribed?" Laurence asked.

As Gwen waved in the direction of the bathroom, Laurence went in and brought out a number of folded paper packets.

The doctor took them from him and his brow furrowed. "But these are far too strong."

Laurence looked at him, horrified.

The doctor seemed bewildered. "I'm so sorry. I don't understand how this could have happened."

"You must have made a mistake with the prescription."

The doctor shook his head. "Maybe they misread it at the dispensary."

Laurence glared at him and drew in his breath.

"In any case, Gwen must stop taking this immediately. It's not suitable for her constitution. She may have some reactions. Aches, sweating, restlessness. She may feel rather low. Call me if, after five or six days, it doesn't stop. I will look into it."

"I should hope so. This is unforgivable."

As Dr. Partridge bowed and made his escape, Laurence came over and sat by her bed.

"You'll start feeling better soon, sweetheart." Then he held out a piece of paper. "I found one of Hugh's drawings on the boathouse floor, near where you fainted."

"Oh, I wonder what he was doing in there," she said, trying to sound calm, though her stomach was churning. Did Laurence really believe it was Hugh's?

"We must have left the place unlocked, but it's an old drawing, I think. His recent stuff is better. At least now you can almost make out a face." He grinned as he handed the drawing to her.

She forced herself to smile as she took it. Laurence hadn't guessed.

19

For three days Gwen felt terrible. Furious with Laurence for involving the doctor and depriving her of her sleeping draft, she refused to speak to him. She took what little she ate in her room and felt very black indeed, so much so that even the sight of Hugh didn't cheer her up. More than anything she wanted to be at home with her mother and, wishing she had never met Laurence, she shed angry tears.

While she had been taking the medication, she'd had no worries and no headaches, but now something seemed to have got hold of her. Her head hurt so much she couldn't think, her hands were constantly clammy and, with sweat running down between her breasts, she had to change her nightdress three times a day. She hardly knew where she was, her body ached in every joint and, with a feeling of needles prickling her skin just under the surface, her muscles were so tender it hurt to be touched.

On the fourth day, in an effort to try to restore some semblance of sanity, she took out all her mother's letters and cried as she reread all the news. As memories of home flooded back, the gentle early sun danced a mosaic of light on the sheets of notepaper lying on her desk. She missed England: the frosts in winter, the first snowdrops, and the sweet summer days at the farm. Most of all she missed the young girl she used to be: the one who had been so full of hope, and who had believed that everything about life was going to be lovely. When she had done with crying, she had a bath, washed her hair, and felt a little better.

On the fifth day, still with shaking hands, she decided to get dressed and, not without qualms, take lunch in the dining room. She made an effort to appear to be her normal self and wore a pretty muslin dress with a long matching chiffon scarf. The dress fitted more loosely than before, but it moved nicely as she walked and gave her a pleasant floating sensation.

It was well past midday, but she decided to quickly check the supplies cupboard again, and when she unlocked the huge doors she was surprised to see the shelves groaning under the weight of rice, oil, and whisky. The *appu* had watched her do it, and while she frowned at him, he shrugged and muttered something she didn't understand. She scratched her head. It didn't make sense. What was wrong with her? Had she been so tired that she had imagined that the supplies weren't there when she had looked before? She shook her head, hating to feel so out of control.

The rains had not yet started, and because the weather had turned bright, Gwen went back to her room before going to the dining room and opened the window to freshen what, she realized, was very stuffy air. As she did so, she heard the gardener whistling in another part of the garden. Inside the house the phone rang, and someone started singing. It all seemed normal. As she left her room, she felt more confident that her abandoned bargain with God had become a thing of the past, had even begun to question whether she had a faith at all, but realized it mattered, for who else was there to forgive her?

In the dining room, lunch was laid for four. Laurence, Mr. McGregor, and Verity were already there, and two of the houseboys were hovering.

"Ah, here she is," Laurence said with a

wide smile.

As soon as Gwen was seated, they were served at breakneck speed.

"Apparently the soufflé will spoil," Verity said. "It's never very good at the best of times."

Over the meal, the talk was about tea, the upcoming auctions, and Laurence's mortgage on a neighboring plantation. Verity seemed in a good mood, and Laurence was happy too.

"Well, I'm pleased to report the recent incidents in the labor lines seem to have settled," McGregor said.

"Is Mr. Gandhi due to visit Ceylon again?" Verity asked.

"I doubt it. But if he does, it won't trouble us. None of the workers will be allowed to go."

"Maybe they should go," Gwen said, turning to Laurence. "What do you think?"

He frowned and Gwen had the impression this was a point of conflict between the two men.

"The question is hypothetical," McGregor said.

"What was the latest unrest about?" Gwen asked.

"The usual," McGregor replied. "Workers' rights. Union agitators come along, get the workers all riled up, and I'm left to pick up the pieces."

"I had hoped the new Legislative Council might have been enough," Laurence said. "And the amount of money and time the Department of Agriculture has spent teaching people how to improve their methods of farming."

"Yes, but that doesn't help our workers, does it?" Gwen said. "And John Partridge once told me he thought big changes lay ahead."

Laurence puffed out his cheeks. "You're right. The National Congress doesn't think enough has been done."

"Who knows what they think." McGregor pulled a face and laughed. "Or even *if* they think! It's all these intellectual types trying to ignite the workers. It's one thing giving women over the age of twenty-one the vote in England, but would you be happy to give the vote to ignorant natives?"

Gwen was intensely conscious of the butler and houseboys hearing this exchange, and it embarrassed her that McGregor should speak in such a tactless and unfeeling way. She itched to say something to counter it but found in her fragile state that she dared not.

Over the remainder of their lunch she

tried to find her way back to normality but only managed it in flashes. She joined in the conversation, following the thread, but then, when it moved on, her concentration lapsed and she floundered. She kept her eyes on Verity and McGregor, watching for signs that they might say something more about the drawing, but her brain still didn't seem to be working properly and nothing made much sense. The men discussed the political situation a little longer, but she was very relieved when a gorgeous-looking trifle was brought in, and the atmosphere in the room changed.

"How lovely," Verity said, clapping her hands.

There was silence as the trifle was eaten.

"Will you come for a walk, Gwen?" Laurence said and smiled.

She saw such warmth in his eyes it made her feel stronger. "I'd like that. I'll just fetch my wrap. I can't quite make out if I'm hot or cold."

"Take your time. I'll wait for you on the terrace."

She went to her room, opened out her favorite wrap, and threw it round her shoulders. Originally from Kashmir, with the beautiful design of a peacock woven into the paisley patterns on the back, it had been one of her mother's, though the green and blue wool had worn a little thin now. She was just about to close her bedroom window when she heard Laurence talking to somebody in the garden. The thick walls kept out the extreme heat and noise, but people never seemed to realize that when her window was open, she could hear what was said from as far as the garden room, and from that side of the garden itself.

"You mustn't take it personally," Laurence was saying.

"But why can't I come too?"

"A man likes to spend time alone with his wife sometimes, and she has been ill, remember."

"She's always ill."

"That is nonsense. And, quite frankly, after all I've done for you, it pains me dreadfully to hear you speak like that."

"Everything you do is for her."

"She is my wife."

"Yes, and she never lets me forget it."

"You know that's not true." He paused while Verity muttered something.

"I give you a generous allowance. I've transferred the deeds of the Yorkshire house to you, and I allow you to stay here for as long as you like."

"I'm polite to her."

"I'd like you to love her."

Don't think, Gwen told herself as tears came to her eyes. *Don't move.* And even though she felt truly stung, she remained where she was.

"After Caroline died, I had you to myself."

"Yes, you did. But you have to build your own life. It's unhealthy, this clinging to me. Now, apart from saying it really is high time you did your best to find a husband, I'm not going to discuss this further."

"I wondered when you'd get on to that, but you know very well there is only one man I wanted to marry."

During a long pause when neither Laurence nor Verity spoke, Gwen closed her eyes. Then she heard her sister-in-law again.

"You think I'm left on the shelf?"

"It seems to be where you have placed yourself." His voice was sharp, but hers, when she replied, was petulant.

"I have good reason. You think you know everything, but you don't."

"What are you talking about?"

"You know. Caroline . . . and Thomas."

"Come on, Verity, there's no reason anything like that should ever happen to you."

"You may be my older brother, but there are things about our family you don't understand."

"You're being melodramatic. Anyway, I think you're hanging around here far too much. It's time you did something else."

"Say what you like, Laurence, but . . ."

They moved away, their voices fading, and Gwen did not hear what else was said. She inhaled, then exhaled slowly through tight lips. After all the effort she'd made with Verity, she felt hurt. As she was walking back and forth thinking about it, Laurence appeared at her door.

"You look lovely, Gwen."

She smiled, pleased he had noticed. "I heard you talking to Verity, while you were in the garden."

Laurence didn't answer.

"She doesn't like me. I'd hoped she might, after all this time."

He sighed. "She's a complicated girl. I think she has tried her best."

"Who was the man she fell in love with?"

"Her fiancé, do you mean?"

"No, I'm talking of the one who didn't reciprocate."

His brow furrowed. "It was Savi Ravasinghe."

Gwen stared at the floor and kept her face rigid to conceal her shock. In the long silence that followed, the past came rushing back, and with it the image of her silk knickers on the floor.

"Did he encourage Verity?" she eventually asked.

Laurence shrugged, but his body tensed as if there was something he couldn't bring himself to say. "He met her when he painted Caroline's portrait."

"Where is the picture, Laurence? I've never seen it."

"I keep it in my study."

When he looked at her, she saw deep pain in his eyes, but also anger. Why? Was he angry with her?

"I would like to see it. Have we got time before our walk?"

He nodded but didn't speak as they walked along the corridor.

"Is it a good likeness?" she asked.

Again, he didn't answer, and when he unlocked the door his hands were shaking.

Once inside, she scanned the room. "I didn't realize it was on display. It wasn't there last time I came in here."

"I've taken it down a couple of times but always end up hanging it again. Do you mind?"

Gwen wasn't sure what she felt but shook her head and studied the painting. Caroline was portrayed wearing a red sari enhanced with silver and gold thread, and with a pattern of birds and leaves embroidered all along the section that fell from her shoulder. Ravasinghe had brought out Caroline's beauty in a way that hadn't been so apparent in the photograph Gwen had seen, but something fragile and sad in her face affected Gwen deeply.

"It's real silver, the thread," he said. "I'll take it down. Should have stored it away long ago. Don't know why I haven't."

"Did she always wear a sari?"

"No."

"For a minute there it seemed as if you were angry."

"Perhaps."

"Is there something you're not telling me?"

He turned away. Maybe he was angry with himself, she thought, or perhaps he still felt guilty that he hadn't had Caroline hospitalized? She knew very well how guilt could chew up your insides, how it could stick to you, invisibly at first, but gradually fester until it took on a life of its own. She was saddened by the feeling that Laurence might never fully recover from his first wife's tragic death.

20

Time passed by and, despite moments of intense anxiety when she still had to fight the panic, Gwen felt stronger every day. Hugh clattered about the place on his new bike and Laurence was cheerful. Gwen read her favorite books, sitting on a bench near the lake, where, listening to birds and the gentle lapping of water, she allowed nature to heal her. Gradually she started to feel like her old self, her worries about the drawing and the guilt about her broken bargain with God beginning to fade.

She knew she was properly better when she ate her first cooked breakfast in months. Sausages, slightly burned the way she liked them, one fried egg, two rashers of lean bacon, a slice of fried bread, and all of it washed down by two cups of tea.

Where the months had gone, she really couldn't say, but now it was October, and at last she was feeling bright. She glanced out of the window and down toward the lake, where a fresh wind was chopping up the surface of the water. A walk with Hugh might be just the thing. She called Spew and Bobbins, and then found Hugh sitting on his rocking horse and shouting "giddyup."

"Darling, do you want to come for a walk with Mummy?"

"Can Wilf come too?"

"Of course he can. Just wear your Wellingtons. It'll be wet."

"Not raining now."

Gwen pulled a face and looked up at the sky. During the last few months, the weather had barely registered. "Maybe silly old Mummy didn't notice that the rain had stopped."

He laughed. "Silly old Mummy. That's what Verity says. I'll bring my kite."

Gwen thought of her sister-in-law. There had been no trouble recently. Verity had taken Laurence's comments on board, and though she was back now, at least she had been gone for a while.

Neither Verity nor McGregor had mentioned the drawings again, and since McGregor had banned the use of the bullock cart to bring messages, Naveena had bribed the *dhobi* to bring them whenever he could. It no longer worked as a warning system, however, as the drawings now arrived erratically, rather than around full moon, and there was no guarantee that the *dhobi* would keep his mouth shut. But he was a greedy man and she hoped the money he received would be enough of a deterrent.

As Gwen and Hugh reached the lake, the path was still muddy. Gwen had not tied back her hair and enjoyed the way it flew in the wind as they ambled along and the dogs raced ahead. On the other side of the lake, a band of purple shadows darkened the water. Hugh was still at the age where every tiny speck was of infinite interest. With a determined look that brooked no argument, he picked up and examined each pebble or leaf that caught his eye, then filled his pockets, and hers, with treasures that ten minutes later would be forgotten.

Grateful for a return to her life after a long absence, she watched her son and her heart burst with love for his smile, his little stocky legs, his unruly hair, and his infectious giggles. The happy sound of chattering birds filled the air and, when she lifted her face to feel the warmth of the sun, she felt at peace; yet, despite that, one thing still nagged at her.

They went on a bit farther, but Hugh

cried when the kite got tangled up and would not fly.

"What's the matter with it, Mummy? Can you fix it?"

"I think Daddy will probably be able to fix it, sweetheart."

"But I want to fly it now." Livid with anger at his hopes being dashed, he threw it on the ground.

She picked it up. "Come on, hold my hand and we'll sing a song all the way home."

He grinned. "Can Wilf choose?"

She nodded. "If you're sure Wilf knows any songs."

Hugh jumped up and down with excitement. "He does. He does. He does."

"Well?"

"He's singing, Mummy. He's singing 'Baa Baa Black Sheep.' "

She laughed and glanced back to see Laurence coming down the steps. "Of course. Silly old Mummy."

"There you are," Laurence called out. "Better get back in."

"We went for a walk by the lake."

"You look absolutely wonderful. It has put the roses back."

"Have I got roses too, Daddy?"

Laurence laughed.

"I do feel better," she said. "And we both

have roses."

There was just one thing Gwen still needed to do to put her mind completely at rest, so the next morning she prepared herself, telling Naveena she wanted the stretch of a good long walk. At the back of her mind she knew the old ayah would object if she knew the real reason.

Naveena glanced at the sky. "It will be raining soon, Lady."

"I'll take an umbrella."

Once out of the house she followed the sweep of the road. Breathing deeply and swinging her arms, she was able to think more clearly when she walked. When the silver sheet of the lake could no longer be seen, she reached the part of the road where ferns laden with water almost brushed the ground. The smell of cooking fires from the labor lines still drifted across, and with it the distant sound of barking dogs. An expectant stillness hung in the air; the calm before the storm, she thought as she glanced at the approaching lines of black clouds divided by slivers of light.

She had always considered herself a good person, one who'd been brought up to know right from wrong. Since the birth of the twins her self-belief had been severely shaken, although her love for Hugh and Laurence was right; that much she did know. But what about Liyoni? Gwen didn't doubt the little girl was safe, now that the missing drawing had arrived, but what if she was not loved?

A memory came back of the day Liyoni was born and, as other images returned to her, the more sure she felt that going to the village was the right thing to do. She hated to think that Liyoni, cut off from her real mother, might be growing up with an inexplicable sense of abandonment. Shivering with the anticipation of seeing her daughter again, she imagined taking Liyoni home with her, but as the rain started up and grew steadily louder, her heart began to pound. Laurence might not be as offended by the color of Liyoni's skin as the rest of the European set, but he would be deeply hurt by her infidelity.

All along the road she searched for the turning, but now rainwater was dripping from the trees and into her eyes, making it difficult to see ahead. Eventually she found a track to the left, marked by a large lichen-coated rock, and there she stopped to collect her breath before continuing. She managed to break a path through the overhanging branches with her umbrella, but after just twenty or thirty yards the wall of trees became too dense. When the spokes of the umbrella caught in one of the trees, she tore at it and her hair knotted in the branches. Panting with the effort of freeing herself, it tangled even more and she panicked until, almost in tears, she pulled herself free. The trail had petered out and now the umbrella was ruined too.

She picked the leaves and twigs from her hair, and, as the rain became heavier, she made her way back to the road, straining to see through the thick white mist that had descended. Dark shapes seemed to appear and disappear at the edges of the road and she held out a hand to ward them off, suddenly feeling afraid. A bird screeched, there was a loud crash, and that was followed by the crackle of snapping branches.

She lifted her heavy wet hair from her neck and shook the water off. Now that she had started, she didn't want to stop. She wanted to see her daughter again: wanted to see what she looked like, wanted to look in her eyes and see her smile. She wanted to hold her hand, kiss her cheek again, and swing her round as she did Hugh. For a few moments she allowed herself to feel the emotions she had trained herself to deny. Instinctively she'd always known that if she permitted herself to feel love for her daughter she would not be able to cope with her absence. Now, as she allowed herself to want her daughter, she let in a little of that need, and it hurt so much that she doubled up with the pain of it. When she straightened up, she wiped her eyes, took a long slow breath, and looked about her. She'd never find the village in this. Dizzy from the rush of blood to her head, she sat on a rock in the pouring rain with her arms wrapped round herself and made believe it was Liyoni she was hugging.

She stayed until she was completely soaked through, then choked back a sob and let her little girl go. With her chest tight and hardly able to breathe, she stood. For several minutes she did not move but watched the huge drops of rain as they bounced off the road, and then, leaving her daughter behind again, she began the long uphill walk as the road slowly climbed toward home.

Laurence had not seen her arriving home drenched and swollen-eyed. In spite of her fatigue, she had lit candles and run a bath. Though the electricity supply from their own generator was unreliable during a storm, there had been hot water and she'd soaked in the scented bath so that the pain and tiredness might dissolve away. Then she'd taken two headache powders and splashed her face with ice-cold water.

Now as they both settled down to read after dinner, the oil lamps were lit. She sniffed their faintly smoky smell, hoping the gentle peace of the evening might stitch up the wound in her heart.

"Why did you go for such a long walk in the rain?" Laurence asked as he poured them both a brandy.

She shivered, fearing she had caught a chill. "I just needed fresh air. I had an umbrella."

He fetched the blanket from the other sofa, wrapped it round her, and rubbed the back of her neck. "You've only just got better. We don't want you ill again, my darling. We need you too much."

"I'll be fine."

The truth was the soaking had left her feeling drained, though more from emotion than the weather. However, she needed to appear her normal self, so decided to read for a while, then write to her mother. She'd been disappointed when, due to her father's shortness of breath, her parents had canceled their long-awaited trip to Ceylon.

"It's muggy, isn't it," she said, "now that

the rain has stopped?"

"It will rain again soon."

He went back to sit in his favorite armchair and picked up his paper.

Thoughts of Liyoni still threatened to spill over, but she swallowed back the distress and fought against them. She made herself comfortable on the sofa, not the one with the leopard skin. Gwen never felt at ease leaning against a dead animal. With a cushion behind her head, she put up her feet on one of the tapestry footstools and determined to concentrate on her book, but still the words swam.

"What are you reading?" he asked as he reached for his brandy.

"It's an Agatha Christie. *The Mystery of the Blue Train.* It only came out last year, so I'm quite lucky to get it. I do love Agatha Christie. It's so vivid, and so exciting, you really think you're there."

"A little unrealistic, though."

"True, but I like to lose myself in a story. And I can't bear those heavy tomes you keep in the library. Apart from the poetry, of course."

He grinned, raised his brows, and blew her a kiss. "Glad we have something else in common, then."

"Darling!"

She closed her eyes but the need to confess all to Laurence was still there. She imagined throwing herself at his feet and begging for mercy, like one of the heroines in the novels she so liked to read. But no, that was ludicrous. Her heart raced frantically and she put a hand to her breast as she rehearsed the words silently. She only had to open her mouth and speak.

"All right?" he said, noticing.

She nodded, aching not to have to keep Liyoni secret from him any longer. In that one night at Nuwara Eliya she had exchanged the love of her life for a drunken moment, but the price had been too high for too long, and she felt she could not go on. She tried the words again. *Laurence, I gave birth to another man's child; a child I have hidden away.* No. That sounded terrible, but what better way was there to say it?

When the doorbell rang, he raised his brows and she put down her book.

"Are we expecting someone?"

She shook her head, hiding the relief that washed through her.

"Who could it be at this hour?"

"I've no idea. Maybe when Verity left, she didn't take her key."

He frowned. "The door isn't locked. If it

were Verity, she'd come straight in."

They heard the butler's shuffling footsteps in the hall, and then a woman's voice. A woman with an American accent. That was followed by the sound of high heels briskly tapping on the parquet floor, becoming louder as she walked along the corridor.

"Christina?" Gwen said in a low voice.

"I don't know any other Americans, do you?"

"What can she — ?"

The door opened and Christina came in. She wore her usual black but was devoid of all jewelry. She looked as if she'd dressed in a hurry and had simply forgotten to put it on. While Gwen was coping with her misgivings at seeing the woman, Laurence had gone over and, with a smile on his face, was offering her a highball. She didn't smile back.

"No. Large whisky. Neat."

Gwen watched as Christina sat on a straight-backed chair at the card table. Her hair, usually so elaborately styled, was hanging loose over her shoulders, and Gwen could see from the color of the roots that it was dyed. Something about that made her look vulnerable.

Christina pulled out a packet of cigarettes and a lighter from her bag. She put the cigarette into a silver holder, but when she attempted to light it, her hand shook so much she couldn't manage it. Laurence stepped in, took the lighter from her, and reached over to offer the flame. She drew in a long breath, the cigarette lit, then leaned her head back and exhaled, sending rings of smoke to the ceiling.

"Is something wrong?" Laurence asked her with a concerned look, and touched her bare arm. Not a caress, not that, but gentle.

Christina lowered her head and didn't reply. Gwen noticed how the woman's face, stripped of makeup, was incredibly pale, and maybe because of that she appeared to be at least ten years older. Not a woman in her thirties after all. Not so glamorous either. But Christina looked so strained that the thought didn't comfort Gwen.

"You had better sit down, Laurence."

Gwen and Laurence exchanged puzzled looks.

"Very well," he said and pulled up a chair.

"You too, Gwen."

"Oh, I'm sure Gwen won't want to be bothered, if it's about business. She has been ill."

Christina looked up at Gwen. "I heard. Are you recovered now?"

"Thank you, yes," she said, smarting at

the thought that Laurence might want to exclude her. "But I will stay, if you don't mind, Laurence."

"Of course."

"I'm afraid there is no easy way to say this." Christina paused and with a strangled sound almost choked on her words as she tried to speak. They waited for her to compose herself.

"Is it Verity? Has something happened to her?" Laurence asked, looking alarmed.

Christina shook her head, but didn't raise her eyes. "No, nothing like that."

"What then?"

Another pause.

As Christina frowned, took a sharp breath in, and stared at the floor for a few minutes more, Gwen felt her heart jump. If it wasn't Verity, what was it? Was there news of Fran maybe or Savi Ravasinghe? It must be something serious for her to look so distraught.

Christina lifted her gaze and, biting her lip, looked from one to the other.

"Just tell us," Laurence said, drumming his fingertips on the tabletop.

She seemed to suddenly straighten up. "The simple truth is that the New York stock market has collapsed."

Laurence didn't speak but stared at her,

remaining unnaturally still.

"How does that matter to us, Christina?" Gwen said with a frown.

"On my advice, Laurence was heavily invested in Chilean copper mining."

Gwen frowned again. "Chilean copper?"

A smile hovered round Christina's mouth. Not a happy smile. "The shares are virtually worthless. And whatever they're worth today, it'll be even less tomorrow. You can be damn sure of that."

"So sell," Gwen said.

"You can't sell anything. I just said. They're worthless."

Laurence stood up, took a step away, and clasped his hands together behind his back. In the uncomfortable silence, Gwen wanted to ask questions but held her tongue as she watched Laurence.

"How could this happen?" he eventually said. "How is it possible? You said with the growth in the provision of electricity, copper was rock solid. You said that electricity would be coming to every house. That copper would take off beyond our wildest dreams."

"It looked that way. I promise you. It really did."

"But how did this happen?" Gwen asked.

Christina shook her head. "It started with

a bumper harvest. A glut."

"But wouldn't that be a good thing?" Gwen said.

"The prices dropped too low, farmers couldn't repay their debts to their suppliers, the labor, and so on. They hadn't the usual profits, so they had to draw cash from the banks to pay their bills." Laurence frowned. "You're telling me there was a run on the bank?"

She nodded.

"Your bank?"

Christina twisted her hands as she stood. "More people than expected wanted to withdraw. None of the banks keep that kind of money on deposit. There wasn't enough to meet the demand."

"I still don't understand," Gwen said, and looked across at Laurence. "We didn't want to withdraw money, did we, Laurence?"

"It's not that," he said.

"No. It's the knock-on effect. If there's no cash, interest rates will rocket. People will go bust."

"And one of the things that has suffered most is copper mining?" he said.

Christina nodded.

"And you're saying the rapid boom in electricity isn't going to happen?"

The American went across to him and put

her hands on both his shoulders. "I acted in good faith. It will happen, I promise you, but not now. Not until the economy picks up."

"It could take months," Laurence said, looking into her eyes.

Christina glanced down for a moment before raising a hand to caress his face, then left her palm resting on his cheek. "I'm so sorry, my dear, dear man. It will take years. How many years is anybody's guess."

"So what am I supposed to do?"

She let her hand fall, then took a step back. "Sit tight and wait. That's all you can do."

"But I was relying on those profits to fund the new plantation. The third one. I've already signed the contract."

Gwen swallowed the irritation she felt at seeing them so close. Christina sighed and dug out a tissue from her bag.

"And you," Gwen said, choking back her anger. "What about you?"

Christina dabbed her eyes. "Me? I will survive. People like me always do. I'm heading back to the States now. Once again, I am so sorry."

"I'll see you to the door," Gwen said.

"That's not necessary," she said as she turned to leave.

Gwen glanced over her shoulder at Laurence. "Nevertheless."

Laurence was now sitting at the small card table with his head in his hands. The irony of that was not lost on Gwen. Only it was not just a few dollars lost in a game of poker.

Out in the hall, Gwen stood tall. She opened the front door and, provoked beyond her limits, felt the urge to push the American through it. She restrained herself but spoke in a stiff voice.

"From now on, Christina, you are to stay away from my husband. Is that clear? No more financial advice and no more social occasions."

"Are you warning me off?"

"I think that's about right."

Christina gave a little snort and shook her head. "You really don't understand him, do you!"

As Gwen and Laurence left the house at first light, she pulled her woolen shawl tightly round her shoulders. After the storm, the path was littered with nature's debris: broken twigs and branches, flower heads, leaves. With the dip in temperature and the air full of moisture, the rains hadn't finished with them. She glanced ahead as they walked the hill in the direction of the tea factory. After Christina's shock announcement the night before, they had stayed up for hours, Laurence drinking brandy and looking morose, and Gwen wondering what Christina's parting shot had meant. How dare she imply that Gwen didn't understand her own husband, and what did Christina know about him that she, his wife, did not? Neither she nor Laurence had slept.

As they walked, the silence between them grew longer. She filled her lungs and with an overwhelming feeling of gratitude she thanked God that she had not confessed to Laurence. Christina's news as well as the truth about Liyoni would have finished him. Halfway up they stopped and looked at each other, as if searching for answers, or if not that, at least appealing for a glimmer of something to help them find a way through this. He was the first to look away.

Gwen glanced up at the massing clouds and felt her heart thump.

"I don't know what this is going to mean for us," he said.

The silence went on a little too long and she bit her lip, frightened to voice all her concerns.

He took her hands and held them between his. "Your hands are cold."

She nodded, and they walked on a little.

At the top, they turned round to look at the view. She took in the lime-green sheen on the damp tea bushes; the women pluckers in cerise, orange, and purple saris; the manicured garden and their light, airy house. It was all so lovingly cared for, but Laurence had explained that if the bushes weren't pruned, they'd grow into trees, and as she looked across air that shimmered in sunlight reflected from the surface of the lake, she tried to imagine what it would look like wild.

Laurence bent to pick some orange marigolds from the verge, then handed them to her.

She sniffed them and thought of their home and their life together. The times they went out in the boat, the flies in the hot months, the moths crisping when they flew into candlelight. A life filled with the sound of laughter. She listened carefully as pipe music from the kitchens floated up through an open window.

A cooler wind blew the trees about and, under the ever-darkening sky, they stood without speaking. When she could bear it no longer, she swallowed the lump in her throat and the words she had not wanted to say spilled out.

"Christina said I didn't understand you.

Why was that?"

"I have no idea."

"Was she talking about your attachment to her or to the plantation? Will we have to sell?"

"Other than friendship, I have no attachment to her." He paused for a second before he spoke again, this time with a crack in his voice. "And over my dead body will we sell."

"We won't have to lose our home?"

He sighed. "No. In any case, where would we find a buyer? And even if we did, the price we'd get would be laughable."

"So what are we going to do?"

"It's not the first time we've had our back against the wall. In 1900 when the demand for tea didn't keep up with production, the London price fell from around eight pence per pound to well below seven pence. Some plantations failed. My father found ways of improving his methods of cultivation, and he brought down the cost of production. But he also found new markets abroad. Russia was one and, believe it or not, China another. Three years later, exports had risen."

"So we need to do that again?"

He shrugged. "Not necessarily."

"We can look at making spending cuts," she suggested. "Draw in our belts."

"That goes without saying. If there are any household cuts you can make, do so."

It would probably amount to no more than a drop in the ocean, even if she budgeted hard, but now that their spending actually mattered, she was determined not to let Laurence down.

"Verity's car will have to go," he said.

"Oh dear, she loves that little Morris Cowley," Gwen said, but thinking it was only because of her beloved royal blue car that Verity had kept out of their hair at all.

"She may well love it. I'll need to look at cutting her allowance too, though I'll have to break it to her gently."

Gwen sighed deeply.

"My plan to expand the school for the plantation children will have to be delayed. As it is, fewer than half the children attend. I wanted to improve on that."

But for their footsteps and the sound of the birds, there was a painful hush, as if nature itself was on tenterhooks. Though so many thoughts were battling in her head and, she thought, must be in Laurence's head too, nothing more was said for a few minutes.

"The thing is, Gwen," he eventually said, "I will have to go away."

She stood still. "Must you?"

"I think so. First to London and then America. We can sit tight on the mining shares, but I have to buy time to work out how to fund the new plantation. And if, on top of everything else, the price of tea falls . . ."

"Will that happen?"

"It may. In any case, I'd like to be at the next London auctions, rowdy affairs that they are. I suspect we may be in for a bit of a bumpy ride."

As they walked the last few yards to the factory, his words sent a shiver up her spine.

"What about Hugh?"

"Well, he's not yet four, so I'm sure things will have improved by the time he needs to go to prep school in England."

Gwen stretched up to kiss him on the cheek. "We'll get through this, Laurence, and we'll do it together."

He didn't reply.

"When will you leave?"

"The day after tomorrow."

"So soon?"

He drew in his breath. "You are all right, aren't you? You'll be in charge. Just say if you don't feel well enough to handle it. Verity will do it, if you can't."

"I'm well enough."

"Good. I was hoping you'd say that. You'll

liaise with Nick McGregor, of course."

As she walked away, she thought about Hugh being sent off when he reached the age of eight: an inhuman thing to do to a little boy. Meanwhile, a voice at the very back of her mind whispered her hypocrisy. Then she thought about the challenge of being left in charge. She was well again, but this would mean dealing with McGregor on a regular basis, and reining in her sister-in-law.

Back at the house, Verity had arrived home and was parking her Morris. When she got out, Gwen gestured her to come over.

"I'd like a word, if you've got a moment."

"Of course. Is it about the crash? Everyone's talking about it in Nuwara Eliya."

"As well they might. Laurence is leaving me in charge while he is away. I think it would be better if we could all pull together at such a difficult time."

"Where's he going?"

"London, and then America."

"Blimey! That means he'll be gone for months."

Gwen drew her shoulders back. "And you might as well prepare yourself. Laurence says your car is going to have to go. We'll all share the Daimler. McGregor, you, and I."

"That's not fair. And anyway, you don't drive."

"I shall learn."

"How?"

"You're going to teach me. Laurence has lost everything in the crash. All his investments. Your allowance will be cut and, if we're to survive, we'll all have to tighten our belts."

Gwen left Verity standing on the gravel and walked off without another word. Once inside, she heard a clap of thunder and, glancing back over her shoulder, looked through the open door. Outside, sheets of rain bounced off the ground and ran in rivulets across the surface. She saw Verity climb into her car, rev the engine, and sweep back up the hill.

21

Though she hadn't realized it at the time, it had been a wrong move on Gwen's part to preempt Laurence's decision to inform Verity himself about the cut to her allowance, and that her car would have to go.

They were all together in the drawing room with their after-dinner coffee when Laurence brought the subject up. Verity acted shocked, claiming to have just landed her dream job, looking after horses up at Nuwara Eliya. Then she knelt beside Laurence and wrapped her arms round his legs.

"I need the car, you see," she said, looking up at him with moist eyes. "I'll be driving around to different stables every day. Laurence, please. This is such a chance for me to prove myself. You've always said I should do something useful, and now you're going to stop me doing it."

She lowered her head and began to cry, but he unwrapped her arms and stood up.

"I see. I hadn't realized about the job."

Gwen thought that Laurence was simply sounding more patient than he actually felt, and expected that at any moment he would deny Verity's plea.

"They aren't paying me to begin with," Verity said, raising her head and smiling across at Gwen. "If I prove myself, in a month or so they will. So you see, I really will need my allowance too, just for a little longer, and maybe a little extra to cover the cost of lodgings."

There was a pause.

"Very well," Laurence said after a moment. "For now your allowance will remain, but absolutely no extra."

He had made his decision without even a glance in Gwen's direction. She shook her head, appalled.

"No, of course," Verity was saying. "Thank you, Laurence. You won't regret your decision. Anyway, I must dash. Have a wonderful trip, my darling brother. Come back with oodles of money, won't you!"

As she skipped from the room, flashing another smile in Gwen's direction, Laurence looked satisfied.

"She does appear to be turning a corner, doesn't she? A bit of responsibility might help her grow up."

Gwen bit her tongue and kept what she hoped was a dignified silence. The only good that might come out of it was that at least Verity wouldn't be there.

Laurence must have noticed her expression. "What's up? You seem a bit jumpy."

Gwen looked away.

"Is it Verity? Look, don't be so down on her, give her another chance. She knows you don't see eye to eye."

Gwen kept her voice level but struggled to suppress her anger. "Don't you think you should have discussed that decision with me?"

He frowned. "She's my sister."

"And I am your wife. It really can't go on like this. I am not prepared to spend the rest of my married life sharing my home, and I might add, my husband, with his spoiled, indulged sister."

She left the room, narrowly avoiding trapping her fingers in the door as she slammed it.

Two days later, she accompanied Laurence as Nick McGregor drove him to Colombo. With the heavy monsoon in full force, it wasn't an easy journey, and in places small landslides almost blocked the road. Gwen gazed out of the window, and as she watched sheeting rain drench the countryside, sucking color from the world and obliterating the view, she knew an uncertain future hung over all of them. Nobody spoke. Even if they'd wanted to, the pounding rain on the roof of the car would have drowned out speech. Gwen felt tense, her stomach in knots. Laurence had barely said a word since her outburst, and neither had she.

The drive had taken far longer than it should have, but as soon as they had walked through the grand carved goddesses of the tall doorway of the Galle Face Hotel and climbed the few steps into the elegant entrance hall, a shutter seemed to have come down over what had passed. Without a word being said, they both knew what they would do next. The porters carried their cases, and while they waited Gwen worried that the charge of unresolved energy between them was obvious to all. She'd seen that look in Laurence's eyes before, and though it excited her, she felt herself tremble.

Upstairs, after racing up the right-hand staircase to the second floor, and before unpacking, they made love, though he was so fierce, she could barely breathe. Only when he shuddered at the end and his breathing relaxed did she realize that Lau-

391

rence was a man who needed sex to alleviate his fears. For a moment it shook her, this difference between them, but then she thought of all the times he'd been tender. At those times he had needed sex in order to feel his love for her, yet even then there were differences, for at those gentle times, she'd needed sex because she *already* felt her love for him. She closed her eyes and slept for an hour. When she woke, his eyes were open and he was leaning on one elbow, gazing down at her face.

"I hope I didn't hurt you," he said. "I'm sorry for the other day. I couldn't bear to go away still at odds with you."

She shook her head and lifted her hand to touch his cheek.

He got up and walked to the window. Laurence loved a room with a sea view and a balcony, so that was what they had, though Gwen preferred the view over the vast stretch of grass known as the Galle Face lawn. She liked to see the locals taking their evening walk there, and loved to watch the children playing ball.

When the clouds briefly cleared, they went outside and breathed in the salty ocean smell.

Laurence turned to her. "Do you think we might have just made another baby?"

She shrugged, staring over his shoulder at the twenty-foot white spray flying against the wall and bouncing back as foam. The fierce movement of the sea and the pounding noise echoed her own restless anxiety. He kissed the top of her head and seemed to be trying to keep the worry from his voice.

"What are you thinking?" he asked.

"Nothing," she said as they walked along the sandy carriageway that edged the lawn, and with their backs to the sea watched a perfect scarlet sunset. When they turned round the ocean had turned to liquid gold, though farther out black clouds were slowly gathering again.

"Please don't worry, Gwen. Just look after yourself and Hugh. I can do the worrying for both of us. Have faith. We will withstand this blow."

The next morning, the weather was too inclement to take breakfast on the long hotel verandah overlooking the lawns; the sunrise over the sea had been unexceptional and now they sat among the potted palms of the lounge. She listened to the clink of teacups on saucers and watched well-fed Europeans chatting as they sipped their tea and buttered their toast, smiling and nodding without a care. She had hardly slept. The ocean had been too loud and so had the thoughts in her head. She glanced at her own untouched breakfast, at the egg congealing and the bacon drying out. She attempted a bite of toast, but it tasted flavorless and felt like cardboard in her mouth.

She poured the tea and handed Laurence a cup.

For a moment she felt angry with him for listening to Christina. None of the other planters had followed suit, so why had he? Why did it have to be them who faced an uncertain future?

"Time is getting on," he said as he picked up his hat, and then stood. "Aren't you going to give me a farewell hug?"

She stood abruptly, ashamed of her flash of anger, and knocked over her full cup of tea. As a waiter hurried over to clear up the mess, Gwen hung back, keeping her eyes lowered to the ground and blinking rapidly. She had promised herself she would show Laurence a confident happy face, and under no circumstances was she going to cry.

"Darling?" Laurence said with raised brows. He held out his arms.

She barely noticed people looking, and wishing so much that he did not have to go, she ran to him then, clung on with a kind of desperation. They drew apart and his fingertips brushed her cheek, solicitous and loving. Her heart filled with love for him and she felt the pain of his going.

"We will be all right, won't we?" she whispered.

Did she imagine it or did he turn his head away before he answered? She needed him to be strong in a way that wasn't really fair. Nobody could be sure where the world was heading now. Only yesterday a New York banker had thrown himself from the roof of the stock exchange. And though she longed to tell Laurence about the sadness she felt, and how she dreaded the way it would slip round her heart the moment he was gone, she kept her mouth shut.

"Of course we will be all right," he said. "Just remember, no matter how you feel about it, there are set ways of doing things."

She frowned and, tilting her head to the side, stepped back. "But are they always the right ways, Laurence?"

He puckered his chin. "Maybe not, but now is not the time for change."

She didn't want to argue just as he was leaving, but couldn't help feeling irritated. "So, my opinion doesn't count?"

"That's not what I said."

"You implied as much."

He shrugged. "I'm only trying to make things easier for you."

"For me or for you?"

He put on his hat. "I'm sorry, darling, let's not quarrel. I really do have to go."

"You said I'd be in charge."

"Ultimately, you are. But allow yourself to be guided by Nick McGregor on matters of the estate. And, above all, remember I have faith in you, Gwen, and I trust you to make the right decisions."

He hugged her again, while glancing at his watch.

"And Verity?"

"I'll leave her to you."

She nodded, fighting back the tears.

He moved off quickly, then, with a wide grin, he twisted back to wave. Her heart lurched, but she managed to lift her hand in return. For a moment after he had been driven away, she pretended he'd just gone for a stroll round the garden. But then her shoulders drooped. She'd miss him so much. Miss the familiar pattern of his breathing, miss the little looks that sometimes passed between them and the warmth she felt when he held her close.

She gave herself a talking-to. There was no point wallowing, and their financial situation was something that had to be seen through until the end, though it seemed amazing that something that had happened as far away as America could have such a profound effect on her life, tucked away as she was on the little pearl drop that was Ceylon.

In the grand hall of the hotel, she glanced through the open doors again and, with some surprise, she saw Christina climbing into one of the new smaller-style Rolls-Royce cars. Part of her wanted to rush after Laurence to ensure the American wasn't traveling on the same ship. The other part of her knew it would only make things worse and Laurence would think she didn't trust him. She took a deep breath and decided to stock up on a few essential items for Hugh. Naveena skillfully cut down Laurence's clothes for Hugh, but the child needed crayons and paper.

A little later, and just before she walked through the doors of the fancy red-and-cream brick-built building that was Cargills, a gnarled and wrinkled Tamil woman sidled up to her. She spoke rapidly and opened her mouth, revealing a few black teeth with red tips. She spat on her palm, then rubbed it against Gwen's hand. The woman spoke again but still Gwen felt confused and glanced at the arched frontage of the store, itching to make her escape. As she turned away, the woman said "money" in English. Gwen glanced down and saw that the old lady carried a large curved bush-cutting knife under her arm. She delved into her purse and handed over some coins, then rubbed her hand on her skirt to remove the old lady's spittle.

The incident stayed with her as she watched the team of brass polishers working on the metal vacuum tubes that slid the money up and down to a cashier on a higher floor. She bought the crayons and left.

With a general air of depression in the streets, the hum of the city had lessened somehow. It still smelled aromatic, of coconut, cinnamon, and fried fish, but people looked thinner and more than usually dispirited, and fewer tea stalls lined the streets. She tried not to worry about what Laurence might be having to face alone — if he *was* facing it alone — but couldn't help feel he hadn't told her everything. She just hoped it was true that he would never have to sell the plantation. It had become her home, Hugh's too, and they all loved it. Much as she missed England in a nostalgic sort of a way, she couldn't imagine going back to live there, and could barely admit one of the reasons was that, if it happened, she would never know anything more about her daughter and would certainly never see her again.

As she walked through the Chinese bazaar on Chatham Street, she passed small fabric shops laden with silks, two or three herbalists, and several shops selling lacquered goods. Pru Bertram was sitting in the window of a tea shop and waved at Gwen to come in, but Gwen tapped her watch and shook her head. Further on, more shops displayed Sinhalese brassware and delicate patterned glasses. Eventually she stood outside a jewelry shop and from there could see McGregor drumming his fingers on the steering wheel as he waited in the car a few yards down from the clock tower. She glanced at the shop window and paused. She looked a little closer; surely it couldn't be, not after all this time? It couldn't be. She narrowed her eyes to see more clearly and held up a hand to protect her eyes from the sunlight. There had to be dozens that looked more or less the same, but still. She marched into the shop.

The jeweler handed her the bracelet for examination. She hesitated over the expense and haggled, but she could not leave it to be bought — and worn — by someone else.

Hang the cost, she thought as she handed over the cash, and, after examining the catch, she fastened the bracelet round her own wrist for safekeeping. Puzzled by how it had turned up like this, she carefully turned over each silver charm until she found Fran's little Buddhist temple. Perhaps it was a good omen.

22

On the drive back home, Gwen couldn't stop thinking about Fran. She missed her indomitable spirit and the way her chestnut hair shone as it swung. She missed her laughing blue eyes and would have given anything for a chance to bridge the gap that had opened up between them in London. Gwen felt as if something infinitely precious had been lost. She had no sister. Fran had been her sister, perhaps even more than a sister. They had, after all, shared much of their childhood, and had continued to be best of friends until Mr. Ravasinghe had turned up in their lives.

She wanted to get the thought of that man out of her head, so while the rain held off for most of the way, she attempted to engage Nick McGregor in conversation, but with the engine vibrating so much, especially where the roads had been affected by the weather, it wasn't easy.

"I'm sorry we haven't always seen eye to eye," she said during a lull.

"Indeed," he said, and changed the subject. "The state of these roads! They have improved over the years, but look at them. The monsoons break them up."

"So how are the labor lines in this kind of weather?"

"It can be difficult, I'll admit. The children do sicken."

She frowned. "I thought we provided a medical clinic."

"It's very rudimentary, Mrs. Hooper. Just an estate pharmacist really."

"It's not Dr. Partridge who runs it?"

He laughed. "Not for the Tamils. It's a Sinhalese chap, up from Colombo. They don't like him, mind, the Tamils."

"Why not?"

"He's Sinhalese, Mrs. Hooper."

She sighed with irritation. "Then get a Tamil doctor instead, one who maybe understands them better."

"Oh, he speaks Tamil all right."

She glanced sideways at McGregor. "I wasn't referring to their language. It was their culture I was speaking of."

"I'm afraid there is no Tamil doctor available. The next thing you'll be wanting is to provide them with sickness pay when they aren't able to work."

"Is that such a bad idea? Surely the welfare of the people matters."

"You don't understand the native mind, my dear. If you give them what you suggest, they'll all be complaining of some imaginary illness and lie about all day. We'd never get the tea plucked and processed."

Gwen realized that whatever she said, it would make no difference. Nick McGregor's obstinate conviction in his own rightness was absolute.

"And now with all the cuts I'm going to have to make, there's no money for anything extra. No, my dear lady, best leave the laborers to me."

"Cuts, Mr. McGregor?"

"To the workforce. We're going to be laying off two hundred, maybe more. A few have already gone."

She shook her head. "I didn't know. What will they do?"

"Go back to India, I expect."

"But some of them were born here. India isn't their home."

He glanced across at her and their eyes met briefly. "That isn't my problem, Mrs. Hooper."

She thought of the beggar woman with the bush-cutting knife and felt a little ashamed. Perhaps the woman was one who had already been displaced. "I should like to learn their language."

He inclined his head.

For several miles of tortuous hairpin bends and uphill roads there was silence, during which she looked out of the window at the heavy mists and thought of Laurence.

McGregor was the first to speak again.

"You will miss your husband," he said.

She nodded and felt the tension building round her eyes. "I will, indeed. But what about you, do you have any family?"

"My mother is still alive."

"Where is she?"

"Edinburgh."

"But you've never been back in all the time I've been here."

She glanced at McGregor as he shrugged. "We're not close. The army was my family, until I injured my knee."

"That's how you met Laurence?"

"Yes, he gave me a job here, then during the war he left me in charge. I'm sorry if I may sometimes appear a little brusque, but I know the plantation inside and out. I ran the place for four years, and it's sometimes difficult to accommodate the opinions of others."

"And you never married?"

"If you don't mind, Mrs. Hooper, I'd rather not talk about it. We are not all lucky enough to find the right partner in life."

The rest of the journey passed slowly, but they managed to arrive back by nightfall. Gwen was surprised to see Verity's car still parked outside, and as she stood in the hall, she heard voices in the drawing room. Verity and a man, it seemed. Heels clicking, she marched to the drawing room and flung open the door.

Spew steamed quietly in his basket on the floor beside Mr. Ravasinghe, who sat on a sofa, looking very relaxed and smoking a cigar. The shock of seeing him in her home jolted her, and, suddenly disoriented, she wanted him gone.

"Mr. Ravasinghe," she managed to say. "I didn't expect you to be here."

He stood and bowed. "We took the dog for a walk. He does rather reek."

She was shaking inside, so much so that she couldn't believe it didn't show, but when she spoke her voice remained level. "He normally stays in the boot room until he has dried off."

"Oh, that was my fault," Verity said with a smile. "Sorry."

Gwen turned to face her sister-in-law. "I thought you'd have already left for Nuwara

Eliya, Verity."

"Nuwara Eliya? Whatever for?"

"To start your new job."

Verity waved her hand in the air dismissively. "Oh, that! It all fell through."

Already rattled by the glimpse of Christina in Colombo, and now horrified at seeing Savi Ravasinghe, Gwen drew in her breath. She had worked hard to get over her illness, had ensured that life at the plantation ran smoothly again, meals happened on time, rooms were cleaned in the correct order, and the accounts all tallied, and yet Verity still managed to get under her skin.

"Is it all right if Savi stays the night?" Verity said with a wide grin. "I know you'll say yes, because I've already asked one of the boys to make up a bed in the room next to mine. It would be too embarrassing if you said no now."

Defeated for the moment, Gwen did not smile. She would have to choose her battles very carefully. She clasped her hands behind her back and dug a nail into the fleshy part of her hand, then, keeping very still, she replied, "Yes, of course Mr. Ravasinghe must stay. Now, if you'll excuse me I've had a rather long and tiring day. Is Hugh in bed?"

"Yes. I gave Naveena the evening off and

put him to bed myself. He and Wilf sang 'Baa Baa Black Sheep' together." Verity glanced at Gwen's wrist. "Goodness, that isn't your cousin's lost charm bracelet, is it? The one she made such a song and dance about?"

"I'm very surprised you recognized it. Doesn't one look much like another?"

"I noticed the temple, that's all. Was it here all the time?"

Gwen shook her head, making a mental note that Verity had paused before replying.

"So where did it turn up?"

"In a shop in Colombo."

"If you ask me, I think you should keep a watch on Naveena."

Gwen clenched her jaw and left the room, not trusting herself to speak. The gall of the girl, she thought as she walked down the corridor. *Naveena indeed! You might fool your brother, Verity, but I wouldn't put it past you to have taken the bracelet yourself.*

The next day the heat was building up earlier than usual, and the refreshing early-morning air had already thickened. Seeing Savi Ravasinghe had left a sour taste in Gwen's mouth and brought frightening memories flooding back. With her heart pounding for most of the night, she had barely slept, but, anxious to avoid seeing him again before he left, she wanted to keep busy.

Though her body ached with tiredness, she decided to check on the cheesemaking before it grew too hot. The kitchen boy who'd taken over from her while she had been ill had made a pretty good fist of it, but it was time she took charge again. In any case, she'd missed the sense of pride it gave her to actually produce something more than an embroidered cushion.

As she closed the side door and looked around the courtyard, it was with some satisfaction that she noticed the banks of bulbs she had planted were now in flower. It was surprising how well some of the English varieties grew here: roses, carnations, even sweet peas.

Hugh had come out with her and was pushing a trolley around.

"Come on, Hugh," she said, still feeling jumpy but doing her best to contain it. "Do you want to see Mummy make the cheese?"

"Nooooo. I want to play out here with Wilf."

"Very well, darling. But you know not to go into the trees, don't you?"

"Yes. Yes. Yes. Yes. Yes. Yes. Yes."

She laughed. "All right, I think I got that.

Come and tell Mummy if you want to go back inside."

She unlocked the door of the cheese room and then left it slightly ajar, so that she could hear Hugh, who was happily singing to himself. She looked about her. There was something indefinably soothing about making cheese and she smiled, happy to be in her own domain. Everything was tidy. The marble slab they stirred the milk on was spotlessly clean, but a faintly sour smell hung in the air and somebody had left the window open. *That's odd,* she thought, *we never leave it open.*

She closed the window to stop flying insects contaminating the milk, then wiped down the surfaces to be sure they were still hygienic. She went over to the heavy milk churn, and only managing to shift it to one side, she noticed a spillage on the floor, just behind where it had been. She cleaned up and then tilted the container to pour a day's supply of milk into the large pan they used for heating. Afterward she went out to ask a kitchen coolie to carry it for her, but once outside she realized the courtyard was quiet. Too quiet.

"Hugh, where are you?" she called.

There was no reply.

She told the kitchen coolie what she

409

needed him to do, then went to peer into the tall trees.

"Hugh, are you in there?" No reply.

She walked back to the house but stopped outside the door. He might have gone in but he would have said; and, she reasoned, she'd have heard the door. She crossed the yard and at the edge of the tall trees she heard barking coming from the path ahead. Hugh must have gone into the woods after one of the dogs.

She took a few steps through the tunnel of trees and, after a moment or two, lost her footing as Hugh charged into her.

"It's a girl, Mummy. A big girl."

She sat on the ground and frowned as Spew and Ginger jumped onto her lap and licked her face. She batted them away, then wiped her face with her sleeve.

"Is this somebody real, Hugh?"

"Yes. She can't stand up, Mummy. Spew heard, and Ginger and me go after."

"Went after, darling," Gwen said, standing up and brushing herself down. "Now look at the mess I'm in."

"Mummy. Come on!"

"Well, I suppose you'd better show me, hadn't you, if she's real."

He took hold of her hand and tugged.

As they walked along, Hugh spotted a

410

broken earthenware jug that lay abandoned in the middle of the path. He bent to pick it up.

"No. Best leave it," Gwen said.

He pulled a face, but did as he was told.

"Is she far?" she said, and ruffled her son's hair.

"No, she's near."

Gwen sighed, thinking of her cheese as they walked on. This was such a waste of time and would probably turn out to be a wild-goose chase. But then, a little farther on, she noticed a laborer bending over somebody sitting on the ground.

"He wasn't there," Hugh said. "She was all on her own."

"I think we'll turn back," Gwen said. "Now there's somebody to look after her."

"Mummy!" Hugh pulled a face. "I want to stay."

"No. Come on now," she said, and tugged at Hugh's hand.

She called Spew, but as they turned to go, a sharp cry halted them. They both twisted round to look.

"Mummy, you must help her," Hugh said with an obstinate look that reminded her of Laurence.

As she watched the man and the child, it was clear that the child could not stand,

and every time the man tried to lift her, she cried out.

"Very well. Let's see what's going on."

Hugh clapped his hands. "Good Mummy! Good Mummy!"

She smiled. Her son was repeating the way she often spoke to him when he'd been her "good boy."

He ran on ahead and waited a few feet away from the man, who was now bent over the girl.

"Her leg looks funny," Hugh said, wide-eyed.

The man glanced up at them, and Gwen was surprised to recognize the Tamil man she'd helped when she first arrived, the one who'd hurt his foot. From the look of distress on his face, it was clear he knew who she was too. He'd been in trouble because of their previous encounter, and she was well aware he might not relish her assistance. As she squatted down and looked her over, the little girl raised her head and gazed up with large brown eyes swimming with tears. Gwen's breath quickened. The child's eyes reminded her of Liyoni and instinctively she reached out with a surge of longing, the blood rushing to her head.

She did her best to draw back from the memory of her daughter and managed to steady herself. This girl was older than Liyoni, about eight, she thought, and she was Tamil, not Sinhalese, and much darker skinned. Her foot was lying at a strange angle from her swollen ankle, and her clothing was damp. At first Gwen thought the child must have wet herself, but when she sniffed, she realized it was milk.

"Go and fetch the jug we saw, Hugh. The broken one on the path."

When he returned carrying two pieces of the jug, the little girl shrank back and spoke in Tamil.

"She's sorry, Mummy."

"Can you understand her?"

"Yes, Mummy. I listen to the houseboys every day."

Gwen was surprised. Her own Tamil was poor, and though she knew Hugh was able to speak Sinhala, she hadn't realized about the Tamil. "Ask her why she is sorry."

Hugh spoke a few words and the girl said something, then burst into tears.

"She won't say."

"Are you sure?"

He nodded very importantly.

"Did she say anything?"

He shook his head.

"Well, never mind that now. Run to the kitchen and say Mummy wants two kitchen

413

boys to help her. Do you understand?"

"Yes, Mummy."

"And bring them here, straight away. Tell them it's an emergency."

"What's an emergency?"

"This is, darling. Now hurry."

The man was attempting to lift the girl again, but when the child shrieked in pain, Gwen shook her head and he seemed to give up. He glanced back in the direction of the labor lines and flapped his hands about, seeming anxious to be gone, but she couldn't let him take the girl in that condition.

A few minutes later, Hugh came back with two kitchen staff. They spoke in rapid Tamil to the man and he replied in the same way.

"What are they saying?"

"They spoke too fast, Mummy."

When Gwen indicated they were to lift the child, they did so, one holding her under her arms, the other by her legs. As she began to wail, they took a few steps in the direction of the labor lines.

Gwen told them to stop, and pointed back at the house.

The kitchen boys exchanged uneasy glances.

"To the house, now," she said, in what she hoped was understandable Tamil, and Hugh repeated it, sticking his chest out and trying to look like the master.

Gwen led them to the boot room, cleared the table of junk, and indicated they should put the child there. The man had followed them in and now stood shifting from foot to foot.

She pulled up a chair. "Hugh, tell the man to sit down. I'm phoning for the doctor."

The butler, hearing the commotion, appeared at the door with a houseboy but drew back at the sight of the Tamil father and child.

"These should not be here, Lady. There is pharmacist, out in the tea bushes. You must call the factory."

"I'm calling the doctor," she repeated, and marched into the hall, past the astonished butler.

Luckily, John Partridge was in his surgery near Hatton, and it didn't take him long to arrive. Gwen answered the front door and he came in huffing and puffing, and smelling of pipe tobacco. "I came as fast as I could. An injured child, you say."

"Yes. She's in the boot room."

"Really?"

"I didn't want to move her more than necessary. I think she might have a broken ankle."

When he entered the room, she heard him gasp quietly.

"You didn't say she was a Tamil child."

"Does it matter?"

He shrugged. "Perhaps not to you or to me, but still —"

"They say there's a pharmacist who deals with emergencies, but I thought she needed to see a qualified doctor right away."

She held the child's hand while the doctor examined her.

"You were right," he said as he straightened up. "If this had been allowed to heal without being properly set, she would have been crippled for life."

Relieved, Gwen let out her breath slowly. She couldn't admit that the longing for Liyoni had stayed with her, though she didn't believe she only wanted to take care of this girl because of that.

"Have you plaster of Paris in the house?"

She nodded and instructed a houseboy to fetch it. "Laurence and Hugh make models with it."

He then examined the child and patted her hand, before speaking to her in her own language.

"I didn't realize you spoke the language so well."

"I worked in India before coming here,

picked up a smattering of Tamil there."

"I'm ashamed to say I have little of the language. The household staff always speak to me in English, so I have almost no chance to practice. Would you mind telling the father what you're going to do? I'm assuming he is the father."

The doctor spoke a few words and the man nodded. He glanced up at Gwen. "He is the father, and he wants to take her home now. He has a job cutting back the overgrown areas and he's worried he'll be in trouble for bringing the child in here. He's right, McGregor won't like it at all."

"To hell with McGregor. She's just a little girl. Look at her face. Tell the father you have to set her ankle."

"Very well. Really, she shouldn't be moved for a day or so."

"In that case, I insist she stay here until she is well enough to be moved. We'll put a couple of camp beds in here and the father can stay too."

"Gwen, it might be better if the man goes back to the labor lines. He won't want an unexplained absence. Not only will his wages be docked, but there is a danger he'll lose his job."

She thought for a moment. "McGregor did say there would be job losses."

"Well, then. Is it agreed? I'll tell him he can go."

She nodded and the doctor explained the situation to the man. The father nodded and squeezed the little girl's hand, but when he turned his back and left the room, her face crumpled.

John Partridge glanced at Gwen and colored slightly. "I'm afraid I never got to the bottom of that mix-up over your prescription. I'm so sorry. I've never made a mistake like that before."

"It doesn't matter now."

He shook his head. "It has worried me. I've only ever prescribed the higher strength for people with terminal conditions."

"Well, there was no real harm done and, as you can see, I'm as right as rain. I'll leave you to your task, John. Come along, Hugh."

"I want to watch."

"No. Come with me now."

A little later she was jolted from her preluncheon rest by the sound of Verity and Savi Ravasinghe returning from a walk round the lake. She stood up and caught sight of her reflection in the window, with what appeared to be the shadow of a girl slightly behind her.

"Liyoni," she said, her voice no more than

a whisper. She spun round. Nothing. A trick of the light.

She had desperately hoped that Verity and Savi Ravasinghe would have been gone, and was barely able to look at the man as he entered the room.

"I hear we missed all the drama this morning," Verity said, then sprawled on a sofa. "Do sit, Savi, it makes me nervous when people hover."

"I really must be going," he said with an apologetic smile.

Verity pulled a face. "You can't go unless I drive you."

Gwen swallowed her anxiety and prepared herself to cope with the small talk that would get her through. "I'm sure Mr. Ravasinghe must be itching to get back to his work. Whose portrait are you currently painting?"

"I've been in England, actually. I had a commission there."

"Oh, I hope it was somebody terribly important. Did you see much of my cousin?"

He smiled once more and inclined his head. "A little, yes."

She tried to look at him dispassionately; thought again how attractive he must be to single women — good-looking, charming, and, of course, very talented. Women liked that in a man, the same way they liked a man who could make them laugh. She admired his skin, so beautifully burnished with a hint of saffron, but it brought back the horror of what she knew must have happened. It was followed by a flash of anger so extreme she felt as if she'd been physically attacked. She clenched her fists and turned away, a band of tension tightening her chest.

"Actually, it was your cousin he painted," Verity said with a smile. "Isn't that absolutely fabulous of him? I'm surprised she didn't tell you."

Gwen swallowed. Fran had not told her.

"Did you hear what I said, Gwen?"

She turned to face the man. "That is wonderful, Mr. Ravasinghe. I shall look forward to seeing it when I'm next in England. There seems to be so much else to do, I'm not always able to keep in touch."

"Like rescuing injured Tamil children. Is that what you mean, Gwen?" Verity had spoken with an innocent look on her face and raised her brows, then smiled at Savi, as if to communicate something Gwen was not intended to understand.

Something snapped in Gwen, so much so that she didn't care if they could see she was actually shaking.

"I didn't particularly mean that. I meant being a wife to Laurence, looking after Hugh and running the household, especially now that we have to keep a close eye on what we spend. The accounts, Verity. You know. And all the money that went missing. I wondered, actually, if you might be able to throw some light on that."

At least her sister-in-law had the decency to redden before she glanced away.

"Mr. Ravasinghe, Verity will take you to the station now."

"That's just it," he said. "There aren't any trains at this time."

"In that case, Verity will drive you to Nuwara Eliya."

"Gwen, really —"

"And to avoid any confusion, I mean right now."

She turned her back on them both and marched over to the window again, so taut she felt as if she might easily snap in two. She watched a heron fly low just above the layer of white mist rising from the lake and listened until they both got up and left. As she heard the squeal of tires she closed her eyes and took several deep breaths, the relief warming her skin and softening her muscles. She felt poised at the point when life shakes itself up, and you have no idea where you'll be standing when it settles in a new pattern, or whether you will be standing at all. What she did know was now that Laurence was not around, the battle lines had been drawn.

23

The next day was a Poya day, a Buddhist public holiday that happened at each full moon, and because it was so quiet Gwen overslept. Laurence always gave the household staff the day off, so that they could visit the temple to worship. For true followers it was a fast day or *uposatha*. For others, it meant shops and businesses were closed, and the sale of alcohol and meat was forbidden.

Most of the workers were Tamil, and therefore Hindu, but some of the household staff, like Naveena and the butler, were Sinhalese Buddhists. Laurence found it improved relations to close the plantation down on the twelve or thirteen times a year that full moon came around. And, of course, on the Hindu harvest festival too. It meant less division among the workers and ensured everybody had a break of sorts.

First thing, Gwen checked on the little

girl, with Hugh and Ginger at her heels. Hugh carried his favorite bear under his arm and, once in the room, held out his best cast-iron toy car to the girl. She took it, turned it over and spun the wheels, and then broke out in a wide grin.

"She likes it, Mummy."

"I think she does. Well done. It was nice of you to bring some toys for her." Gwen didn't say, but thought that the little girl probably had no toys of her own.

"I wanted to make her happy."

"Good for you."

"I've brought the bear too. And I asked Wilf, but he didn't want to come."

"Why was that?"

Hugh shrugged in that comical way little children do when they look as if they're trying to be adult.

She watched the two children for a moment. "I have some work to do. Would you like to play in my room?"

"No, Mummy. I want to stay with Anandi."

"You can, but don't ask her to move about. I'll leave my door open so that I can hear you. Be good."

"Mummy, her name means 'happy person.' She told me yesterday."

"Well, I'm pleased to see you two getting

on so well. Now remember —"

"I know. Be a good boy."

She smiled and drew Hugh to her for a hug before she left the room.

In the hall, she listened to her son and the girl rattling on in Tamil, followed by the sound of laughter. *He is a good boy,* she thought as she went to her room to catch up with her correspondence.

After an hour or so, the sound of raised voices disturbed her. Once she'd made out McGregor's Scottish accent, and realizing she should not have left Hugh and the Tamil child alone, she hurried to the boot room.

The door to the courtyard was open and Gwen could hear that the shouting was originating there. When she glimpsed McGregor shaking his fist at a woman wearing an orange sari, she took a breath and scanned the room. In one corner, Hugh sat on his bottom, arms wrapped round his knees. With a pinched face, and biting his lip, he looked as if he was trying not to cry. The girl was sitting up, tears spilling down her cheeks and dripping onto her open palms, almost as if she'd positioned her hands to catch them.

McGregor must have heard her come in,

because he turned round with a blazing face.

"What the devil is going on here, Mrs. Hooper? As soon as your husband turns his back, you bring a laborer's child to the house. What were you thinking?"

Gwen was surprised to see Verity come in, then squat at Hugh's side.

"I didn't realize you were back," Gwen said, ignoring McGregor, but she couldn't help feel that Verity had been waiting for an opportunity to alert the man.

Gwen went to Hugh. She leaned over him and ruffled his hair. "Are you all right, darling?"

He nodded but didn't speak. With a deep breath, she straightened up, took a step toward the man, and folded her arms. "You have frightened these children half to death, Mr. McGregor. Look at their faces. It's inexcusable."

He spluttered and she noticed his fists were clenched. "What is inexcusable is you interfering once again with the plantation workers. I've done my best to help you, given you gardeners, smoothed the waters for the cheesemaking, and you repay me like this."

She stiffened. "Repay you? This is not about repaying you, or anyone else. This is about a little girl with a broken ankle. Even the doctor said she would end up crippled if it was not set quickly."

"The Tamil do not use Dr. Partridge."

She felt her jaw twitch. "Oh, for God's sake, listen to yourself. She is just a child."

"Is there a reason you care about this girl?"

She stared at him blankly.

"Do you know who her father is?"

"I recognized him, if that's what you mean."

"He is one of the main agitators on the estate. You may remember he put a nail through his own foot once, in an effort to claim wages he hadn't earned. He probably broke the child's ankle himself."

By now Gwen was almost shaking with a mixture of anger and fear. "No, Mr. McGregor, he did not. She fell from the cheese room window."

"And you know this how?"

She held his gaze, wishing she hadn't said that. "Can we just concentrate on getting the child home safely?"

"What was she doing at the cheese room window? The workers are not allowed near the house. You know that."

Gwen felt her face burn.

"You'd better not tell him," Hugh piped up.

McGregor glanced into the room and spoke in a clipped tone of voice. "What had you better not tell me? What was she doing at the cheese room window?"

"I . . ."

There was a tense silence.

"I think she may have come for some milk."

"Mummy!" Hugh shouted.

"Come for some milk! Let me get this straight. You are telling me she was stealing?"

Gwen stared straight ahead and felt absolutely awful. "I didn't see her. It's just that she had milk on her dress, the window had been left open, and there was milk spilled on the cheese room floor." Hugh came outside to stand at her side. He slipped his hand into hers. "She took the milk for her little brother," he said. "Her brother isn't very well and she thought it would make him better. She's very sorry."

McGregor grimaced. "She certainly will be, and so will her father. No doubt he put her up to this. The father will be flogged and docked a day's wages. I will not have my workers stealing from the house."

Gwen gasped. The man seemed completely impervious to human misery. "Mr. McGregor, please. It was only a little milk."

"No, Mrs. Hooper. If you let one get away with it, they will all try. And I might add that I fail to understand why you are taking such a keen interest in this one girl. Remember how many there are of them. We have to rule them firmly or there will be chaos."

"But —"

He held up his hand. "I have nothing else to say on this matter."

"He's right," Verity said. "There are fewer floggings than there used to be, but even now they are sometimes necessary to remind the workers who is boss."

Gwen had to work to control her voice. "But they have rights now, don't they?"

Verity shrugged. "Sort of. The minimum wage order raised wages for plantation workers and made subsidized rice prices compulsory, but that's it. Mind you, we already provided subsidized rice three years before that. Laurence has always been fair."

"I know."

"But, you see, there's nothing in the ordinance to prevent a flogging."

The woman in the courtyard, who had hung back during this exchange, spoke again, and Gwen went over to her. She noticed her hair parted in the middle, her wide nostrils, her pronounced cheekbones, and the gold earrings in her long-lobed ears. Under the orange sari, she wore a clean cotton blouse. It looked like she'd dressed especially to come to the house.

"What is she saying, Hugh?"

"She has put on her best clothes and has come to take Anandi home."

"Tell her to go back. It's too far for the child to hop on one leg. Verity and I will take Anandi round in the car. She can put her leg up on the backseat." She glanced at Verity, who looked dubious.

"Verity?"

"Well, all right."

They spent the evening quietly. Nothing more had been said about Savi Ravasinghe's visit, though Gwen remained unhappy, partly because of that and partly because of the incident with McGregor. She assumed Verity had been the one to tell him, as there was no reason for him to be up at the house on a Poya day. It wasn't really cold, but a fire was comforting, so Verity made it up, and as the servants were off duty, Gwen prepared a simple meal of eggy bread, followed by jaggery pancakes filled with coconut and fruit.

Gwen left the curtains open, watching the

moonlight shining on the water. Something about its soft, silvery blue surface reminded her of the spirits in the Owl Tree and the dew pond at the top of the hill at home. Under a full moon it gleamed in the same way, and she'd always thought there had been a feeling of otherworldliness about the Owl Tree at night.

"Look, Mummy, I'm eating my carrots," Hugh said. "And so is Wilf."

She glanced at his plate. "Those aren't carrots, they're oranges."

"Don't oranges make you see in the dark too?"

Gwen laughed. "No, but they are good for you. All fruit is."

"Shall I play?" Verity said, rising from her chair.

While Verity played, Hugh sang along to wartime marching songs, making up most of the words when he didn't know them, and thank goodness he didn't know some of them. He wanted Gwen to sing too, and looked at her with eager eyes, but she shook her head, claiming she was tired, though really she was simply sick at heart.

After Hugh was packed off to bed, Gwen crouched by the fire, poking it to let in air.

Verity leaned back against the leopard skin. "I do like moon days."

Gwen didn't really want to talk, but if her sister-in-law was making an effort to be friendly, she had to try. "Yes. I quite like fending for myself. I just pray we don't end up losing the plantation. It's bad enough that Mr. McGregor will have to lay off so many workers."

"Oh, he's already done that. Didn't you know?"

"Really?"

"Yes, the day before yesterday."

"He told you and not me?"

"Don't read anything into that. He'd have told you if you'd asked, I'm sure."

Gwen nodded, but she wasn't so sure.

Because she'd felt so low, Gwen had taken to her bed during the afternoon while Hugh was resting, so there was still a subject she hadn't broached. She didn't know if McGregor had carried out his threat to flog the man, and tried to imagine what Laurence would have done if he'd been here. Would he have left it to McGregor, or would he have intervened? To her knowledge there had not been a flogging while she'd been living at the plantation.

She rubbed the back of her neck but could not rid herself of the tension. "Do you know if McGregor carried through his threat?" she eventually said. "Was the man flogged?"

"He was."

Gwen groaned.

"It wasn't pretty. His wife was made to watch."

Gwen looked at her, trying to take it in. "You surely didn't see it?"

Verity nodded. "The woman squatted on her haunches and made an awful moaning sound. She sounded like an animal."

"Oh God. You went? Where was it?"

"At the factory. Come on. Don't think about it. Shall we play cards?"

As she bit her lip to hold back her tears, Gwen felt raw.

Some hours later, Gwen lay awake and could not get the flogging out of her mind. Shadows played about the bedroom as she went over the part she had played. Had she only helped the child because of Liyoni? As the thoughts spun, she felt lonely and longed for Laurence's arms round her.

There was an unusual sound outside — a muffled noise — not loud enough for her to be able to make out where it was coming from. She went through to check on Hugh in the nursery, but he was fast asleep, as was Naveena, and as Gwen listened to the old ayah's gentle snores, she made a mental note to decide on a proper bedroom for

Hugh. Not a baby any more, he needed space for his growing collection of toys, plus a little desk to do his dinosaur drawings. Back in her bedroom, she opened the shutter and peered out.

At first she saw nothing unusual, but as her eyes adjusted to the moonlight she made out a trace of tiny lights, too far away to see clearly. She thought nothing of it, assuming it was something to do with the full-moon holiday, so she closed and fastened her shutter but left the window ajar.

She must have fallen asleep, because when she woke again the noise was louder. There was a faint sound of chanting, the voices rhythmic and almost musical. It sounded strangely magical and although it seemed to be coming from somewhere fairly nearby, she wasn't afraid. Now that she was awake, and still thinking it was part of a full-moon ritual, she decided to look. It was probably nothing; it might even be that the sound had simply carried on the breeze.

She opened the shutter to peer out, then stared at the sight of dozens of men marching along the path beside the lake. The dark figures looked deathly in the moonlight, but it was the smell of the smoke and kerosene from their flaming torches, and maybe some kind of pitch or tar, that really worried her.

She quickly shut the window, ran through to close Hugh's window, and woke Naveena.

"Take Hugh upstairs to the master's room, please, and wake Verity."

She ran along the corridor and into the drawing room, where she stopped short. Through the open curtains she stared out at the blue moonlit garden. Beyond it, the smoke and yellow flames of the torches lit the faces of the men and had turned the air above the lake brown. When it seemed as if the men were passing the house, she exhaled in relief and dashed over to close the curtains. Just then, a man came into view on the other side of the windowpane and, with a leap, his face loomed inches from her own. He glared at her, with wide eyes set in a shiny, dark-skinned face, dressed only in cloth wrapped round his lower body. His long frizzy hair stood out round his head, a living incarnation of the mask Laurence had given Christina.

As he raised his fist and stared back at her, she froze, too terrified to move, though her heart was pumping harder than ever. He carried on staring and did not move off. She couldn't bear to look any longer and, with shaking hands, forced herself to close the curtains to shut him out. She didn't know if there were more like him coming up behind, ready to surround the house, but if there were, what should she do? She felt sick at the thought of Hugh being hurt, and ran to fetch Laurence's rifle from the gun cupboard.

As the fear took hold, she could hardly think. There was no way to let McGregor know there were dozens of natives with burning torches who looked as if they were heading for his house. She pressed an arm against her ribs, as if to contain the panic, then ran up the stairs to Laurence's room, where Verity, Naveena, and Hugh were at the window.

"Look, Mummy. They are going past. They aren't coming here."

Gwen opened the window and pointed the rifle. She watched for a moment as the stragglers continued to move past the house. One or two turned to glance back at her. One man shook his torch in the air.

"Dear God, I hope McGregor will be all right."

"The noise will have woken him and Nick McGregor knows how to take care of himself," Verity said. "But, Hugh, you need to keep back from the window."

Suddenly a shot rang out and then another. A terrible shrieking filled the air.

"Oh God, he's shooting them!" Gwen

said. As Hugh jumped and ran to be folded into Gwen's arms, she passed the rifle to Verity.

"Turn off the light. I don't want them to see us."

"They've already seen us," Verity said. "Anyway, he won't be shooting at them. He'll be shooting into the air to scare them off."

"What if he hits one?"

"Well, he might hit one or two, but it would be accidental. He's got to disperse them somehow. Look, it's working."

Though she was scared, Gwen pitied the men, and feared McGregor's pursuit of them, but while the workers' wretched poverty moved her to tears, she realized that to Verity, they were too poor and insignificant to matter.

She looked across toward McGregor's bungalow, where a scene of immense confusion was unfolding. The men, like bees being smoked from a hive, were scattering; some had turned back and were already escaping. A few torches were burning out, some sizzling as they were thrown in the lake, and there was a sour, acrid smell spreading everywhere. Several failing flames continued to stain the air, but with relief Gwen saw that whatever it had been about, the men seemed to be taking the lake path and none of the stragglers appeared to be coming back up to the house. She prayed that nobody had been killed.

At that point, Verity, still hanging out of the window with the rifle, fired it into the air, the noise so loud it frightened Gwen half to death.

"Why did you do that, Verity?"

"I just want them to know that even though Laurence isn't here, we can still shoot."

Gwen took over the position at the window and remained watching until there was nothing left to see.

"I think we should all go back to bed," she said after a while. "I'll stay in here with Hugh. Naveena, use the spare room next to us. Now, good night, everybody."

"I'm not sure it's over yet," Verity said. "Please, can I stay here with you both? To help make sure Hugh is safe?"

Gwen thought for a moment. It probably would be better if they were together.

"I'll have the gun," she said, and though she would have done anything to protect her son, the thought of actually pointing the thing at another human being and killing them made her blood run cold.

Once Hugh had fallen asleep, Gwen

touched his soft warm cheek, then lay staring at the darkness with thoughts crowding her mind. She felt ill at ease with Hugh sandwiched in between her and Verity, and wondered how she was going to tell Laurence why the men were so angry and vengeful. It had to be because of the flogging, but McGregor might have been killed — they all might have been killed.

Just before dawn, she sat bolt upright in the bed. Verity was at the door, wrapped in a blanket and speaking with Naveena in whispers. She held a candle and the rifle, and turned when she heard Gwen getting out of bed. She gave the candle to Naveena and put a finger to her lips, then held the door open for Gwen.

"Quickly. Don't wake Hugh. Put on Laurence's dressing gown."

Gwen did so and then went through to the landing, closing the door behind her.

"Come on," Verity said, sounding excited.

"What's going on? Why is the smell worse than before?"

"You'll see."

Naveena led the way along the landing, down the stairs, along the corridor and to the boot room, with only the flickering light illuminating their way. Gwen heard the snapping and crackling before she saw the fire, then through the boot room window saw that the sky had turned a dull orange.

In a panic, she pushed past Verity and Naveena to unlock the side door to the courtyard. Her hand flew to her throat as clouds of blue smoke billowed from the left side of the building adjoining the main house. It seemed out of control, with so much smoke that it wasn't clear what was actually burning. There was a deep rumble followed by a loud crash as the main roof timbers of the cheese room collapsed, sending sparks and embers flying and black smoke exploding upward into the half light of the early-morning sky. Gwen's eyes streamed as the stench of smoke and burning cheese spread right across the yard, and it became impossible to breathe.

The noise continued, though the cheese room structure itself, built of stone with a concrete floor, was safe. Now the danger was that the flames might spread to the kitchens and the servants' quarters via the wooden ceiling beams that connected them, and then the whole house. Terrified by the thought of what might happen next, and worried for her son, Gwen ran forward, but despite covering her mouth and nose, she began to splutter and cough, flapping her arms wildly as she did so.

Verity came after her.

"Isn't it exciting! Look, the *appu* and the kitchen coolies are already fighting it. The houseboys are round at the other side."

As the men rushed about, shouting instructions to each other, she saw Verity's eyes light up, but as her sister-in-law moved closer, Gwen stepped back from the heat.

It seemed to go on and on as the flames consumed the entire roof structure. Then, spitting and whooshing, they died back as the men dampened everything with pots of water and a hose. Gwen watched in relief, but when, after a moment, the flames burst through again, seeming to grow even wilder, it shocked her afresh. She felt helpless as the wind dragged noxious black smoke to spiral across the lake and orange flames to rise into the air above.

Eventually, as they watched the fire surrender, the men smothered the embers with rugs and Gwen, breathing more freely, wiped her stinging eyes. When it was completely dead, the men grasped each other's hands, but as the *appu* checked to make certain that nothing more could catch, a heavy pall of smoke hung over the courtyard.

Verity shouted to him in Tamil.

He nodded, and said something Gwen couldn't understand.

"What did he say?" she asked.

"Nothing much. Just confirming the fire is out."

Everything was smothered in ash and Gwen felt contaminated by the feel of it on her clothes and in her hair. "I'm glad you woke me," she said, brushing off the powdery flakes.

Tears pooled in Verity's dark eyes. "Of course I woke you. Hugh means so much to me. I would never want to put him in danger."

Together they went indoors. As Gwen went back up to Laurence's room to be with Hugh, her eyes still smarting from the smoke, she shuddered at the thought of what might have happened if the fire hadn't been spotted so early. It wasn't the damage it had done that bothered her — the cheese room could be repaired — it was the damage it might have done. She wiped her face, and as the light slid across the room, she curled up in bed and stroked her son's cheek. Thank God he was safe.

The only person she trusted to judge if things had become really serious was Laurence. She thought of him and the day he had gone away. She wanted to cry. Really cry. As the image of Christina getting into the car outside the Galle Face Hotel came back, a ray of weak light illuminated the table where Caroline's face still shone out from its silver frame. *I wish I could talk to you,* she thought. *Maybe you'd know what to do.*

24

It turned into a golden morning, full of delicate light, and with a pale blue haze drifting over the lake. It seemed strange that after such a terrifying night everything should be so still and normal at the lakeside, with the fresh wetness of the trees and the dew coating the grass. However, the smell of burned cheese still hung about and at the side of the house, where the coolies were cleaning up, an air of desolation crept over the ash-covered yard. Gwen kept Hugh close to her and waited anxiously for McGregor to appear.

Verity came into the drawing room. "One of the kitchen coolies was hurt in the fire."

"How badly?"

"I don't know. The *appu* just told me. I'm going to find McGregor to ask if he knows."

"Tell me, won't you?"

"Of course."

Just as Florence Shoebotham turned up

with a bacon flan, Gwen spotted McGregor outside on the upper terrace, waving his arms about while he talked with Verity. Gwen bent her body back in an effort to see but not be seen, but when McGregor spotted her and stared without a smile, she tensed. It was as she expected.

Florence was the last person she wanted to see, but in a way, though she was worried about the injured man, Gwen was pleased to have a reason not to be bullied by McGregor just yet. They would speak soon enough, but in the meantime, she would not seek him out.

"I came as quickly as I could," Florence said, her chins wobbling sympathetically. "I heard your entire side wing burned down."

"No. Actually, it was just the cheese room."

"I am sorry to hear that."

Gwen was obliged to stay and entertain the woman, and on her instruction the butler brought tea served in the best china and a three-tiered cake stand. As Florence tucked into dainties that only smelled faintly of smoke, Gwen felt increasingly anxious. She would have to ask McGregor about the injured man sooner or later.

"Are we likely to be seeing your delightful cousin Fran again soon?" Florence asked.

"No, not soon, though she has promised another visit at some point."

"You will be missing her, and your husband, of course." The woman arranged her face to look concerned and lowered her voice. "I do hope everything is all right with Laurence. I did hear he suffered heavy losses in the Wall Street crash."

"You have no need to concern yourself, Florence. Laurence is fine, and so am I."

It seemed to Gwen that Florence struggled to conceal her disappointment that the gossip wasn't going to materialize in quite the juicy way she had hoped.

"We are looking forward to him being back with us very soon," Gwen continued; she didn't say that in fact Laurence had wired the agent that very morning, saying he might be away longer than expected, and that she had not passed on the information about the fire.

After Florence had gone, Gwen opened the window but with the smell of burning still lingering she rapidly closed it again, then went in search of Verity and Hugh. She'd wanted to keep Hugh with her, but he'd slipped outside during Florence's visit. She wandered among the trees and bushes of the garden, calling him, then stood on the bottom terrace, looking at the islands that dotted the water. A thin layer of mist still floated above the lake, and a gust of wind chilled her. When she heard footsteps on the path, and the sound of Hugh's voice, she spun round to see McGregor advancing, gripping Hugh by the hand.

"Mr. McGregor," she said.

"Mrs. Hooper." He released Hugh's hand and the child ran to her.

"How is the man?" she said, making an effort to appear calm.

"The pharmacist is with him."

"An unfortunate sequence of events," she said.

He shook his head. "Rather more than unfortunate. Deliberate destruction cannot be condoned. I hope that this is the end of it. I would advise, however, that for the time being you keep the lad close to you."

"Let's hope it was nothing sinister. It may have been an accident, don't you think? With all those flaming torches burning so close to the house."

"I doubt it. But you're very lucky it was spotted in time."

She drew in her breath.

He turned to go, took a few steps away, but then glanced back. "I knew something like this would happen. Lucky for you the man is still alive."

She held her hands together to suppress her rising anger. "What do you mean?"

"I mean that this is the sort of thing that happens when somebody interferes with the way of things."

"And by that, you mean me?"

He inclined his head and his face stiffened.

She took a step toward him and her efforts at keeping calm fell apart. "Actually, Mr. McGregor, I do not think I did anything wrong in helping that little girl. Only a person with a heart of stone could think otherwise. It was not I who caused this, but you. The days of flogging a man over a trifle are over, and if they are not, well, shame on you."

"Have you finished?"

"Not quite. You will be very fortunate if the Ceylon Labor Union do not pick this up. You are a mean-minded man who sees nothing but the bad in people. I believe in treating people kindly and fairly, whatever the color of their skin."

His face spasmed. "This is nothing to do with color."

"Of course it's to do with color. Everything in this country is to do with color. Well, mark my words, Mr. McGregor, all this will come back to bite you one day, and on that day none of us will be safe in our beds."

With that Gwen marched up the steps with her head held high and Hugh in tow. She would not give McGregor the satisfaction of seeing the tears that threatened to spill.

That night her dreams troubled her, with images of men brandishing flaming torches that seemed to rise from the surface of the lake. She dreamed of Laurence too, imagined he was there with her in the boathouse, a lock of waving hair falling over his eyes as he leaned over her. The hairs on his arms shone in the moonlight and freckles peppered his cheeks. She put her arm round his neck and he cupped the back of her head with his hand, but then she realized he wasn't looking at her at all — he was looking through her. It was a dark, unsettling dream and then, first thing in the morning, the news came that the man had died from his burns.

Gwen spent the day trying to find out who his family were, and wanting to see what she might do to help. She remembered the man in question, and it broke her heart to think of his life cut short in that agonizing way — he was not much more than a boy,

with a ready smile and a willing nature —
but when her path crossed McGregor's in
the garden, he insisted he would deal with
it.

"But he was one of my household coolies."

"Nevertheless, Mrs. Hooper, I can't allow
sentimentality at this delicate stage. We can't
rule out further repercussions."

"But —"

McGregor didn't reply but gave her a curt
nod and walked off in the opposite direction. She gazed at the lake, not knowing
what else she could do.

25

The weeks that followed remained tense, with a kind of gloom settling about the house. Gwen bravely attempted to behave as normally as possible for Hugh's sake, though it soon became clear Verity was drinking to excess. Almost overnight she became withdrawn, brooding in her room for hours on end, and at times Gwen heard her sobbing. At other times, she seemed brittle, even losing her temper with Hugh. Once or twice, Gwen had to admonish her, and afterward she heard her moving about in Laurence's room in the middle of the night. Melancholy hung about Verity when she did come down, and then, tall and thin, she loped around the house like a creature dispossessed.

There were no shortcuts to understanding her sister-in-law, and now Gwen worried for the girl's state of mind. Mood swings were one thing, but this! When she tried to ask what it was about, Verity squeezed her eyes shut and shook her head. It seemed as if her sister-in-law was trying not to give in to her feelings and, in the end, Gwen felt it better to let it run its course. If Verity's unhappiness could be regarded as her just deserts, equally Gwen's "revenge" — if that was what it was — was not so sweet, and something about the girl drew her pity.

Gwen also felt bruised by what had happened with McGregor and kept out of his way, though with Naveena's help she had managed to contact the dead man's family. In the empty detached weeks until Laurence came home, she attended to her household duties, approved the menus, ensured no laundry was being stolen, and kept a firm eye on the accounts. But still she tormented herself over the man's death and it left her feeling insecure and guilty.

On breezy days when the timbers of the bungalow creaked and groaned, she heard the footsteps of her absent child. Then she'd stand completely still as if waiting for the wind to bring some news, or, in order to break the spell, she'd compile a list of the contents of the storeroom, though anything mind-numbingly practical would do.

One morning she went to the kitchen and

found only McGregor there, looking morose.

"Mr. McGregor," she said, and turned to leave.

"Have a cup of tea with me, Mrs. Hooper," he said in a tone less brusque than usual.

She was surprised and hesitated.

"Don't worry, I won't bite."

"I wasn't thinking that."

As he fetched a second cup then poured the tea for her, she seated herself at the opposite side of the table.

"All my life, I've worked in tea," he said, not looking up at her.

"Laurence told me."

"I know these workers. But you come over here and you want to change everything. How is it that, knowing nothing, Mrs. Hooper, you want to change everything?"

She started to reply, but he held up his hand, and she smelled a trace of whisky on his breath.

"Let me finish. The thing is, the terrible thing is, the thing that has started to keep me awake at night . . ."

There was a long pause.

"Mr. McGregor?"

"Is that, after everything, you may have been right about the flogging."

"Is that such a bad thing?"

"For you, maybe not . . ."

Gwen cast around for an appropriate response. "What is it that really worries you?"

He hesitated and shook his head. There was another stretch of silence while his jaw worked, and he appeared to be thinking. With no idea what went on inside this man, Gwen had only ever seen his gruff exterior.

"What worries me, if you must know, is that I may not be able to adjust. I've given my life to tea, been part of the way it has been for so long . . . it's in my blood, do you see? In the beginning we never thought anything of flogging the blacks. We hardly even thought of them as people, at least not people like you and me."

"But they are people, aren't they, and one of them has lost his life."

He nodded. "I changed my view a long time ago. I am not a cruel man, Mrs. Hooper. I try to be fair, I hope you realize that."

"I believe we are all capable of change if we want it badly enough," she said.

"Aye," he said. "If we want it. I have been happy here but, like it or not, our days are numbered."

"We have to move with the times."

He sighed. "They won't want us, you know, when it comes. For all we've done for them, it'll be the end of everything."

"And maybe because of what we've done *to* them."

"And then I do not know what I shall do."

Gwen watched, feeling the sense of resignation in him as his shoulders drooped.

"How are things with the laborers now?"

"Quiet. I think the man's death shocked them as much as it did us. Nobody wants to lose their job."

"And the ones who started the fire?"

"No one is talking. I have either to make a big show of involving the authorities or make it widely known that I believe it was an accident. It goes against the grain, but I have decided to let it pass as an accident."

"You don't think there will be further trouble?"

"Who knows? But it's my bet the real trouble will begin in Colombo. The workers here have too much to lose."

She sighed. Neither of them spoke for a while after that, and, realizing there really wasn't anything else to say, Gwen got up.

"Thank you for the tea, but now I must find Hugh."

She spent most of her free time with Hugh.

Sometimes they played soldiers advancing on the enemy, usually one of the dogs. Sadly, the dogs didn't understand their roles as vanquished soldiers and ran round in circles instead of lying down to die. Hugh shouted at them and stamped his feet.

"Lie down, Spew! You too, Bobbins. Ginger, you're supposed to be dead!"

Today Hugh whirled around the drawing room with his arms outstretched, pretending to be a British triplane and making himself dizzy.

"Mummy, you be a plane too. You can be a German Albatros, and we can have a dogfight."

She shuddered at the thought of air-to-air eruptions in the skies. "Darling, I don't think I'm quite up to that. Why not let Aunty Verity read to you?"

Verity picked out a book and Hugh settled on the sofa beside her.

"Which book is it?" Gwen asked, and frowned when she looked over Verity's shoulder. Gwen preferred Beatrix Potter and claimed Verity's choice, Hans Christian Andersen's fairy tales, might frighten him. It was a long-standing difference of opinion.

Verity stood her ground. "He's not a baby. Hasn't he just been rushing around pretending to be a bomber aircraft?"

"Yes."

"Well, then. The Andersen stories are sometimes sad, but it's such a wonderful imaginary world. I don't want Hugh to miss out."

"And I don't want him scarred forever."

"But, Gwen, they are so much better than Grimm's."

"You have a point. Maybe when he's a little older."

Verity threw down the book of fairy tales. "I can never do anything right for you, can I?"

Gwen was taken aback and felt a little exasperated. "Why not try *Alice in Wonderland*?"

Verity shrugged.

Gwen passed the book over. "Come on, Verity. Please don't spoil things."

Verity stared at the book but didn't reply, and when Gwen noticed tears in her eyes, she wondered if she was missing her brother.

"What's wrong?" Gwen asked.

Verity shook her head.

"Nothing can be that bad, can it?"

As Verity hung her head, Gwen went across to her and held her hands, squeezing them gently. "Come on, old thing. Chin up."

Verity raised her head. "You do know I love Hugh, don't you?"

"Of course. It goes without saying." Verity sighed and no more was said.

A little later, just as Alice was sliding down the rabbit hole, the phone rang. All three looked up, but Gwen was first on her feet. When she answered it, a crackling voice told her that it was Laurence's agent in Colombo, and that he'd received a wire saying that Laurence would be arriving in exactly one week's time. Would McGregor pick him up from the docks? She said a silent prayer and went back into the drawing room. Watching her sister-in-law with her son, she wished she could keep the warm feeling to herself for a little longer.

Verity glanced up. "Who was on the phone?"

Gwen grinned.

"Come on, tell. You look as pleased as punch."

She couldn't hold it in. "Laurence is coming home."

"When? He's not already in Colombo, is he?"

Gwen shook her head. "He's arriving in a week. He wants McGregor to pick him up."

"No," Verity said. "We'll do it."

Not sure if she wanted to go with Verity, Gwen pulled a face. "You'd have to drive."

Hugh jumped up and down and clapped

his hands.

Verity stood up, lifted Hugh off his feet, and spun him round.

"I'd love to throw a party to welcome him home," Gwen said. "It's been so grim, and we all deserve a little fun."

"We're supposed to be tightening our belts."

"It doesn't have to be lavish."

As Verity put Hugh down and stepped back, Gwen considered for a minute or two.

"The food can just be canapés and we'll have massive bowls of fruit punch, with honey from the hives and plenty of fruit from the trees. That'll disguise the cheap alcohol. We don't need a string quartet, we can play the gramophone."

Verity smiled and Gwen realized she hadn't seen her sister-in-law this happy for weeks.

"We'll spend as little as possible. Laurence will be furious if he comes home to a big display. And we'll need to be here to oversee the preparations, so maybe McGregor had better fetch him after all."

Verity shook her head. "You don't want McGregor getting in first and telling tales. Because of the injured girl, he still blames you for the fire and the man's death."

"I thought he'd come round a little."

"Who knows? But do you want him speaking to Laurence before you have a chance to put your side of the story?"

"I suppose I could drive myself."

"Gwen, I know you've got the hang of driving out and about around here, but all the way to Colombo? It's not an easy route. What if you had an accident?"

She knew Verity was right.

"Tell you what. The servants are accustomed to the old parties here, those opulent, money-no-object affairs. Why not stay to make sure it's done your way? Keep an eye on the arrangements, and I'll pick Laurence up on my own."

"I want terribly to go, but I don't see how I can leave Hugh, when everyone will be so busy." And, not wanting to burst Verity's happy bubble, Gwen decided to let her go.

"Good. Now that's decided, let's draw up a list."

Two days later, Gwen rose early. She stood outside her bedroom in her dressing gown and gazed at the mist curling between trees of the deepest green imaginable. She loved the lake, the views of the hills around it and the sound of the water lapping against the small inlets. And whatever happened in the future, she prayed with all her heart that they would not have to leave Ceylon. It had become the most beautiful place in the world to her, and though she missed her parents, Hooper's Plantation was her home.

A little later she walked round to the top terrace, where the boys were already setting the table for breakfast. She sat down in a comfy rattan chair and watched the birds hop along the gravel pathways. Verity joined her briefly to say she was leaving for Colombo sooner than they had planned. She had some personal shopping to see to before she met Laurence at the harbor. In fact, while she was there, she hoped to see an exhibition of Savi Ravasinghe's. He'd been taken up by the New York art crowd, so he wouldn't often be in Ceylon now. It meant she'd be away for about five days and she hoped Gwen didn't mind.

Gwen shook her head. Though pleased that she was less likely to see Savi, she still felt a chill at the mention of the painter. "You go. Just bring your brother back in one piece."

"There's talk of another harbor strike, so that's another reason to go early."

Gwen sighed. The expanding population of Colombo had led to a scarcity of rice, which had caused a tramway strike earlier in the year, and another harbor strike would be even worse. But she was also well aware that Verity's early departure gave her no chance to change her mind about going too, unless she wanted to sit in a car alone with McGregor all the way to Colombo.

"So, I'll leave you now." Verity got up, kissed Gwen lightly on the cheek, waved at Hugh who was playing on the grass with Ginger, and she was gone.

Gwen had been living with her secret for so long that the initial heartbreak over the loss of her daughter had settled down into a dull but persistent sorrow. Occasionally it felt good to be alone, for, without Verity, she was free to allow her heart some space. She wondered what her daughter looked like now. Was she stocky like Hugh or fine-boned and petite like herself?

She longed to go to the village again and paced the room, crossing and uncrossing her arms, shaking her head and stopping to listen to the sounds of the house as she weighed it up. In her mind she pictured the peace of the village and all the noises of nature that surrounded it, but although she was tempted to try to find the way, the memory of the last time stopped her. She folded herself up in the chair by the window and, closing her eyes, imagined Liyoni swimming in the lake. Then she pictured her little girl running to her to be enfolded in a soft towel and smiling up at her mother as she gave her a cuddle.

She cried until the sadness passed, and then, after she'd wiped her eyes, she splashed her face. Maybe one day when Hugh was older and at school. Then she'd persuade Naveena to take her.

Gwen sent two houseboys up to the loft, instructing them to hunt for anything that might brighten up a party. While they were up there, she rummaged around a rarely used and rather shabby guest room. Under the bed she found the fireworks and, in a wardrobe, a pile of dusty paper lanterns. One or two were torn, but the others just needed a brush-down with a feather duster.

When she looked in an old chest of drawers, she noticed a large flat package that had been pushed to the back. She took it out and laid it on the bed, then slid off the string and paper. The most beautiful red sari lay folded inside, made of silk and embroidered with silver and gold thread. She lifted it to the light and examined the intricate pattern of birds and flowers all along one edge. This was Caroline's sari — the one she was wearing in the painting. She stared at it for a while, thinking of

Caroline and Thomas, and felt a little un-nerved as tears stung her eyes, but wanting neither to disturb the past nor complicate the present, she wrapped it up again and put it back.

The boys brought down bunting. It looked dingy but Gwen told them to wash it and hang it out to dry. The gardener dug up flowers from the banks coming into bloom at the side of the garden and replanted them in tubs on the back terrace, and Naveena brought out satinwood bowls full of spices and incense to dot around the place.

Gwen turned her attention to the food. They would keep it plain, using the typical breads of the Ceylonese: flower bread, coconut rice bread, kiri roti, and other simple dishes.

Once the household was sorted out, she considered what to wear. She wanted to look particularly nice for Laurence's home-coming and decided on a dress that exactly matched her eyes: a lovely shade of deep violet. Some time before, she'd bought the silk in Colombo, and had taken along a picture of a dress in *Vogue* magazine and asked the Sinhalese man who made many of their clothes to copy it. The finished dress had yet to come back from Nuwara Eliya, but if she had no opportunity to collect it herself, she still hoped it would be delivered in time.

In the exciting buildup, the few days passed rapidly, filled with last-minute adjustments, decisions, a minor crisis, and a servants' quarrel to deal with. Naveena took care of Hugh, while Gwen oversaw where the flowers would go and how many candles should be lit. She hoped the party would raise everybody's spirits, McGregor's included.

When the day arrived, Gwen spent it nervously seeing to final arrangements and choosing what Hugh would wear to welcome his father. When she put him in the light of the window and tried to cut his fringe with her sewing scissors, he could barely sit still.

"Don't squirm," she said, "or I'll have your eye out."

He giggled and pretended to remove an eye.

She laughed. It was the longest any of them had ever been apart, and Hugh's unrestrained excitement was infectious.

In the late afternoon, only an hour or so before the start time, Naveena rushed in with a large flat box. Gwen's dress had arrived. She opened the box, unwrapped the white tissue paper, and then held her breath as she carefully lifted the beautiful silk creation out. It was perfect. Not too short, flared, and with a bodice beaded with tiny pewter pearls. She would wear her matching pearl earrings and necklace. Luckily, she'd paid for the dress before their financial losses had begun, so she couldn't be accused of wasting money. She held it up against her and spun round.

Naveena smiled. "You will be looking beautiful, Lady."

Gwen saw to Hugh as he played with his boats in the bath. When he was eventually persuaded to get out, she enveloped him in a large towel and pulled his warm body to hers, but — not a baby any more — he wriggled away. After he was dressed in a little white suit, just like a proper gentleman, she sat at her dressing table with a fluttering heart.

On the dot of six, just as the light was changing, Gwen was dressed, with a spray of her favorite perfume in her pinned-up hair. The bunting was raised, the candles were lit, the punch concocted, and a delicate fragrance of burning cinnamon blew about in the air. As the guests began to arrive, the butler led them to the terrace and the outdoor room at the side of the house.

It wasn't a large party, just other tea planters and their wives, some of Verity's friends and Laurence's pals from the Hill Club in Nuwara Eliya. By seven most had already arrived. People were milling about and standing in knots around the house and down by the lake. Hugh went among them, offering roasted cashew nuts from a silver bowl and charming everyone with his perfect manners and beatific smile. The only person missing was Laurence — and Verity, of course. As they should have turned up well before six, Gwen began to feel apprehensive.

She played the part of a dutiful hostess, nodding at guests, helping them to mingle, asking Florence about her health and chatting with Pru. But as time went on, eight o'clock, then nine o'clock, her heart began to pound and she felt sick with nerves. The food had been served and there was still no sign of them. She now began to see that the evening might have been a dreadful mistake and struggled with the conflicting feelings going on inside her: her desire to see Laurence, her fear over what Verity might have said about the fire and the man's death, and her worry about whether she was doing the right thing by having a party.

The roads were treacherous, especially at night, and Verity drove too fast. Gwen began

468

to worry that something awful had happened to them. They were lying dead in a ditch after a collision, or upended in a ravine. With a panicky feeling, she sat down to gaze at the lake. Something about the timelessness of the lake flattened out her spiraling anxiety. And then, just as she was giving up the expectation that they would arrive at all that night, she heard a car pull up at the front of the house. This had to be them. No further guests were expected.

She ran round to the front of the house with a few guests in tow, Dr. Partridge, Pru, and Florence among them.

"There they are," Florence remarked.

"Better late than never," the doctor said.

Gwen couldn't speak. The sight of Laurence climbing from the car sent tears spilling down her face. He looked about stiffly and her heart seemed to still. She didn't move and what could only have been moments felt like an age. While nobody spoke, she held her breath. *Verity has blamed me, told him everything, and he'll never trust me with anything again,* she thought. Her whole life seemed to flash before her, hundreds of memories, thousands of moments. She clutched at excuses, tried to think of ways to explain her actions, but, when all was said and done, because of her a man lay dead.

Laurence took a few steps round the car and she felt so small she wanted to turn on her heels and run, or else for the ground to open up. She just could not bear for Laurence to think so badly of her. She brushed the tears from her cheeks, then looked at him properly. His face was soft and his eyes creased up as he broke into a wide grin. She released her breath and, instead of running away, she ran to him. He wrapped his arms round her, then lifted her into the air and spun her round.

"I have missed you so much," he whispered in her ear.

Gwen still could not speak.

"I see you have got me up a little welcoming party," he said as he put her back on the ground. "I ought to change. It's been an arduous journey."

"Never mind that," she said, and hugged him again through his dirty sweat-soaked shirt. "There are more people round at the back."

"Wonderful," he said. "The more the merrier."

Verity, standing on the other side of the car, looked on expressionlessly, but Gwen breathed a huge sigh of relief. It was going to be all right.

Later that night when Laurence and Gwen were alone, he told her how things had gone. Though the copper-mining shares were currently worthless, a partner had been found to invest in the new plantation. They were not out of the woods by any stretch, and the times ahead might be tough, but as long as they made the necessary changes, it looked like they would survive.

"You didn't tell me how bad it really was, did you?" she said.

"I couldn't, Gwen, and to be honest I didn't really know."

"So all that talk about never selling up . . ." He put a finger to her lips.

"I thought you said an investor couldn't be found in the current climate."

"And that was true, but this is someone you know well."

She raised her brows. "Surely not my father? He doesn't have that kind of money; he'd have to sell Owl Tree."

"Not your father."

She put a palm to his unshaven cheek, feeling the roughness as she stroked. "Then who? Tell me."

He grinned. "My new partner is your

cousin, Fran."

She pulled a face. "I don't believe you. Why would Fran invest? She knows nothing about tea. She doesn't even like it."

"One day she'll get a good return, but she did it for you, Gwen. So that we wouldn't lose the plantation. She's only investing in the newly acquired part, not my old family plantation, but by investing in the new plantation, it means I don't have to sell this one, and our home with it."

Gwen's relief was overwhelming. "Did you ask for her help?"

"No. We met for lunch, I told her about our situation, and there and then, she offered. Anyway," he said as he stroked her hair, "enough of that. How have you been here?"

"There was some trouble. I —"

He tangled his fingers in her hair and gently pulled her head back so that he could look in her eyes. "If it's about the fire, Verity's already told me."

She inhaled sharply. "Verity hasn't been happy. I'm worried for her."

"She seems all right. A bit unsettled maybe. But I am actually very proud of you."

"Really?"

"Gwen, you helped an injured child in the

only way you knew how. You are a good, kind woman."

"You didn't think I was interfering in labor business?"

"It was a child."

"You know about the kitchen boy then? The one who died."

"Any death on the plantation must be taken seriously, and it was very unfortunate —"

"It was awful, Laurence."

"But not your fault. You acted from your heart, and I shall speak to McGregor in the morning."

"I think he's struggling too."

"As I said, I shall speak with him. Sometimes events spiral out of control in ways we cannot foresee. It isn't necessarily a case for blame, but for realizing that even a slight lack of judiciousness can trigger something terrible."

"My lack of judiciousness?"

"No, Gwen, I don't think it was."

She felt so relieved he wasn't angry that all the frazzled nerves and anxiety of the past weeks finally seemed to unlock. He held her while she wept, and afterward when she looked into his eyes, she saw they were damp too.

"It has been a difficult time for all of us,

and loss of life is always very upsetting. I think my biggest task will be improving morale, beginning with you."

She smiled as he removed the pins from her hair and the ringlets fell past her shoulders.

"I tried so hard, Laurence."

"I know."

She touched the cleft in his chin and felt the stubble again.

"Shall I shave?"

"No. I want you just the way you are."

"You look very beautiful tonight," he said as he wrapped a ringlet round his middle finger.

At first Gwen held back, feeling self-conscious in the way that she had been when they first met all that time ago in London. She smiled, thinking of that, then yielded, allowing him to undress her.

He was gentle and tender, and they took it very slowly. Afterward they lay in each other's arms and, at last, she felt her heart settle in stillness.

"You are precious to me, Gwendolyn. I don't always express myself as I might wish, but I hope you know that."

"I do, Laurence."

"You are such a tiny thing, aren't you? Even after everything, as slim and sweet as a girl. You always will be my girl, no matter what."

She noticed his voice had taken on a serious tone, and with his eyes inches from hers, he seemed to be scrutinizing her.

Laurence summoned such a depth of love in her and that mattered more than anything. She smiled at the thought of those minute tokens of their life together: his warm hand when she was worried in the night, his off-key singing when he thought he was alone, and the strength of his trust in her. When he touched her heart in the way he did, she felt safe and completely protected against all misfortune. To think if she had not met him she might never have known what it was to love, and with that love she had flourished as a person and as a wife. The struggle had been worthwhile, and now they would face whatever lay ahead together. It would be a new start. She didn't ask if he had seen Christina while he was away.

■ ■ ■ ■

PART FOUR:
THE TRUTH

■ ■ ■ ■

27

1933

As Gwen bent down to pick up some pens that Hugh had abandoned on the boot room floor, she twisted her head to glance through the window at the men erecting a scaffold of bamboo outside her old cheese room. Though it had taken all these years for the work to begin, at least it was now underway. She couldn't begin to explain the delay, except that there had been endless discussions over alternative uses, and at one point it had even been on the cards to pull it down.

She went through to the dining room where the August sun, shining through horizontal blinds, had painted the walls with yellow lines. Outside the birds were singing, but poor old Hugh, now seven, was sitting at the table, scratching his head while poring over his sums. Gwen wanted him to be well up to the mark in maths and English grammar before he started school in Nuwara Eliya as a weekly boarder.

Laurence pushed open the door. "How's it going?"

Gwen pulled a face. "Arithmetic isn't his favorite."

"Wasn't mine either, I have to admit."

She smiled. "Actually, Laurence, his drawing is wonderful. What would you say to giving him private lessons?"

"I think private maths tuition would be money better spent."

She sighed. Hugh's drawings were so much more advanced than Liyoni's, but she'd kept all the little girl's attempts at human figures with overlarge heads and the strange-looking animals that didn't quite match up to any living thing. Only when she was alone at night did she dare look at them. But there had been a long gap since the last one, and Gwen, beginning to worry, had sent Naveena to find out if something was wrong. Children had been going missing from some of the local villages and turning up later as cheap labor in the paddy fields.

She looked up at Laurence and wished they could really talk. It always seemed to be about money ever since Laurence's "welcome home" party nearly four years before.

He smiled. "It's not all bad. One good thing about this damn Depression is that it's forced the union to moderate its demands. People are too worried about their jobs to persist in radical action. I know we need change but we have to find the right way to do it."

She rubbed her forehead. Despite more than three hundred of his immigrant workers having returned to India, overproduction and the Depression had caused the price of tea to plunge. She felt horrified that so many of the poor had lost their jobs, and with them what little they owned in the world, the extent of their poverty a truly dreadful thing.

"Our biggest problem at the moment is what to do about the plantation Tamils," Laurence continued. "It was a big mistake not to give them the vote too. Just adds to their sense of injustice."

Gwen nodded. Ever since the fire, tensions had rumbled on, with minor eruptions all over Ceylon, though more serious disputes had begun in 1931, when everyone but the Tamil workers had been given the vote.

"I don't see how they can still be considered temporary."

"Quite. As I said, it's made things worse," Laurence added.

Though Gwen kept a close eye on the household accounts and restricted spending rigorously, in comparison with the workers she still lived in the lap of luxury. Since she was a girl, every breath Gwen had taken, every word she'd spoken, every thought she'd had were geared toward being a wife and mother, and she had done her best. But it had been saddening to watch Laurence's hopes for new growth being dashed over and over. Although he'd grumbled when her father had offered to pay Hugh's school fees, just until they were back on their feet, she'd been happy to accept.

"Have you heard from Fran?" Laurence asked.

"She's coming in a few months' time."

"I'm glad. We owe your cousin a great deal." He ruffled his son's hair. "Now, you work hard for your mother, Hugh, and I'll take you up to the factory tomorrow. Is it a deal?"

Hugh's eyes sparkled.

"Laurence, why is Verity here again? She just doesn't seem to want to leave us alone."

Verity kept turning up like a bad penny, with a stream of unlikely excuses, from a burst water pipe preventing her from washing her hair to the smell of fish giving her headaches. Her marriage hadn't prevented her clinging to her brother, and now that there was a touch of desperation about it, Gwen felt something serious had to be fueling her behavior.

Laurence frowned. "Truth is, I don't really know."

"Can't you find out what's wrong? She's here far too often for a newlywed. Surely she needs to work through her problems with Alexander, not just run away to us?"

"I'll try, but I've got to make tracks now — I'm off to Hatton in the truck."

"Not the Daimler?"

He glanced away. "It's still in the garage waiting for repairs."

After Laurence left, Gwen thought about Verity as she settled down in the chair opposite her son. Despite her sister-in-law remaining a victim of mood changes, she'd eventually married Alexander Franklin, a decent but unexciting chap, and they lived down by the coast where he owned a fish farm. The marriage, six months previously, had surprised them all, but Gwen had been hugely relieved, and had hoped that married life might straighten her out. Now, it seemed, those hopes had been misplaced.

She watched Hugh chew the end of his

pencil, then scrub out his most recent answer. Arithmetic was a struggle for him and she worried about how he'd cope at school. His hair had darkened, and now fell exactly the same way that Laurence's did, with a double crown and a wave at the front. Hugh's eyes were the same dark brown as his father's too, though his skin remained fair, like her own. He still talked of his imaginary friend, Wilf, as if he were real, and Laurence didn't like it.

She was about to point out a mistake in his calculations when Naveena came in and hovered just inside the door.

Gwen glanced up at her.

"Lady, may I speak with you?"

"Of course, come in."

But Naveena nodded at the door, and Gwen, seeing the worried look in the old ayah's eyes, immediately went over to her.

Gwen sat on the bench under the curved top of the bullock cart and twisted her wedding ring round. Although it had been seven years since her previous visit to the Sinhalese village, she remembered exactly how it had felt. They passed the place she had mistaken for the track on her wild walk in the rain, and soon after turned down a potholed trail where dark trees had been permanently bent by wind.

In the almost silent forest, the light was green and gloomy, but when they came out into more open territory, the same smell of charcoal and spice filled the air, just as it had done before. When they reached the steep riverbank, Naveena did not stop but carried on through the village to a place where the banks were only slightly higher than the level of the water, and the river was wider. Today it looked brown and muddy, not clear and sparkling as it had been before, and there were no elephants taking a bath. Instead, several children were jumping about in the river, dipping earthenware pots and tipping the water over their heads.

Gwen dismounted and watched as the children called to each other while pointing at the bullock cart. After a few minutes they ignored the cart and carried on as before. The younger ones had round bellies and their ribs showed more than they ought. It was hard to tell their ages, but they seemed to range from about three to eleven or twelve. With sharp concentration, Gwen attempted to pick out a girl of seven.

"There is a strong wind blowing today," Naveena said, and pointed at the trees on the opposite bank, where a girl was pulling herself out of the water.

"Liyoni?"

Naveena nodded.

Unable to stop staring, Gwen saw that the child was too thin. She wore only a cotton sarong, dripping from her swim across the river. Her hair was tied back with some kind of ribbon and hung in a long wet column down her back.

"Apart from being thin, she looks all right," Gwen said, twisting her head to glance at Naveena.

All the ayah had revealed so far was that there was a problem. Nothing more.

"So what is the problem?"

As Naveena started to explain, Gwen was so absorbed in watching the girl slide into the water and begin her swim back across the river that she stopped listening. First the child's head was showing above the water and then, after a minute, her body was completely submerged.

"She swims like a fish," Gwen said, more to herself than to Naveena.

"Just wait, Lady."

As she followed the stream of water the child was leaving in her wake, Gwen continued to be amazed by the fearless way she swam and the ease with which she flew from the far side of the river to the nearer edge.

Naveena tapped her arm. "Now."

As the little girl climbed out of the water, Gwen narrowed her eyes in an effort to see, but it was only when the child began to walk along the riverbank that Gwen realized.

"She has a limp."

"Yes."

"What is the matter with her?"

Naveena shrugged. "That is only one part of the problem. Her foster mother will no longer keep her. She is sick, and her own two children have gone to live with their grandmother."

"So who is looking after Liyoni now?"

"Since last week, nobody."

"Call her over, will you?"

Naveena beckoned and called out. At first the girl carried on walking, and it looked as if she was going to ignore them, but then she spun round and stared. She took a few awkward steps toward them, then stood still again.

Naveena spoke to her in Sinhala, and the girl shook her head.

"What is it?" Gwen said. "Why won't she come?"

"Give her a few minutes. She is thinking."

As Gwen watched, she was aware of the little girl's uncertainty and realized that with the strong instincts of a native child, she must have sensed that something unusual was happening.

"Tell her she is safe, that we won't hurt her."

Naveena spoke again, and this time Liyoni hung her head but did come closer.

Gwen winced at the way the child's limp was hindering her movement. "Is she in pain, do you think?"

"I think, yes."

As thoughts swam in her head, Gwen closed her eyes for a moment. When she looked again she saw the little girl walk up to the cart and stop just a couple of feet away. The sun lit Liyoni's face and Gwen noticed that though the child's eyes were brown they were flecked with a similar shade of violet to her own.

"Is there no one to take her?"

Naveena shook her head. "I have asked, Lady."

"Are you sure?"

In the silence, Gwen tried to think, but the panicky feeling in her throat and chest stopped her brain from working. She thrashed around for solutions, but with her thoughts flying off in different directions, she kept returning to an image of her home. When she closed her eyes, all she could see was the plantation and everything she had built up over the years. It was not just her own downfall that frightened her, but the thought of the pain she would cause Laurence. She buried her face in her hands. She could never expect to be forgiven, never; yet if Naveena could not find a home for Liyoni . . .

When she looked up, she smelled burning wood and food cooking — but no one would be cooking for Liyoni.

"There is nobody?"

The ayah shook her head.

"Not even for more money?"

"They are afraid of the child, that is what. She is not one of them."

Gwen closed her eyes and listened to the sounds of life with just one thought spinning in her mind.

"We can't leave her to fend for herself."

As the truth of what she must do hit home, fear dragged the breath from her lungs. She wiped her clammy hands on her skirt and, despite the gravest misgivings, she made her decision. She could not leave her daughter on her own. That was what it boiled down to. With just the one choice, she braced herself and swallowed hard before she spoke.

"Very well, then. She must come with us."

Naveena's wrinkled brow showed her anxiety.

"When it's dry," Gwen asked, "does her hair curl like mine, in ringlets?"

Naveena nodded.

Gwen chewed the inside of her cheek and tasted her own blood.

"If we keep her hair plaited and tied back, and dress her plainly, nobody will guess she has anything to do with me. It's only an unusual eye color, after all, and nobody will be looking for similarities, will they?"

Naveena still looked uncertain.

Gwen managed to distance herself from her fear and momentarily gave way to a more primal desire: the desire to be a mother to her child.

"Then it is settled. We shall say she is a relative of yours, come to learn the duties of a housemaid and ayah's helper. Can you explain it to her, please?"

As Naveena spoke to the child in soft, soothing tones, Gwen watched carefully, focusing all her attention as if her life depended on it. At first the child shook her head and backed away, but Naveena caught hold of her hand and pointed to her bad leg. The girl glanced at her leg, and then up at Gwen, and said something in Sinhala.

"What did she say?"

"She wants to know if she will still be able to swim if she comes with us."

"Tell her she shall swim in the lake every day."

This time, when Naveena spoke, Liyoni smiled.

"I have explained to her, Lady. She knows that her foster mother has gone and that she is alone. Of course, she thinks of the woman as her mother and is very sad."

As a lump formed in her throat, Gwen nodded but could not speak. The little girl had lost her family. She gulped, and Naveena, seeing her emotion, allowed her a moment to recover while sympathetically busying herself with the girl. Gwen felt sick with guilt and shame. She tried to convince herself that it would work out but couldn't deny the very real current of fear that continued to run alongside her feelings for the child.

"Has she much to bring?"

"Only little. I shall go with her. You waiting here."

As Naveena and the girl walked away, Gwen scanned the compacted-earth street. Over in the trees beyond, a family of squirrels raced along the branches, sending out a high-pitched trill. Nearby, a couple of women wearing white tops and colored saris carried large baskets balanced on their heads. Another woman stopped at the bullock cart and stared in. She had thick lips but a fine nose and deeply shadowed eyes. Gwen quickly covered her own face with her shawl.

To Gwen, Ceylon was a place where British dreams had been built and fortunes made, where English families had lived and children had been born, and where her life had changed beyond her wildest dreams. Yet here was a different world, where girls ran about in simple cotton tops and threadbare skirts, where babies gurgled and crawled in the dirt, and people did not have enough to eat.

Liyoni was dressed like the other girls when Naveena brought her back, and she carried a small bundle under her arm.

Gwen glanced up at the sky. Heavy rain clouds had massed on the horizon and they'd be lucky to get back before the weather broke.

On the long journey back, Gwen had felt so sick that Naveena needed to stop the buggy twice for her to vomit in the bushes. But in between bouts of sickness, she and the ayah had concocted a plan.

Back at the house, Gwen helped the child

down from the cart and wrapped her shawl round her to protect her from the rain. She glanced at the front door and, heart in mouth, decided to duck round the house to the lakeside, and then slip in through her own full-length verandah windows. Less chance of being spotted, even if it did mean a soaking.

When Naveena turned to attend to the bullock, Liyoni attempted to follow the ayah. Gwen shook her head and took the child's hand, scared she might struggle, but the girl only hung her head and walked meekly by her side.

As the two skirted the drawing room, Verity was standing at the window wearing a flowing yellow dress, seemingly just staring at the gardener mowing the lawns. She raised a hand to wave and Gwen saw it freeze in mid-air, its stillness an exact mirror of the surprise on her sister-in-law's face.

A gust of wind cut through her and, teeth chattering with fear, Gwen nodded and hurried to her room, wanting to slip the girl through to the nursery as quickly as she could. Damn! It had to be Verity. The butler had kept an eye on Hugh all day and when she heard her son thundering about upstairs, she was relieved that he was playing with his train set, just as she'd hoped. How he might feel about another child being in the house she could only wonder.

She motioned to Liyoni to come with her and they went in, stopping only to lock the windows and the bedroom door from the inside. She picked up a dry shawl, removed the wet one from Liyoni's shoulders, and then, once through the bathroom and the door adjoining the small passageway, it was only a moment before they reached the nursery, and temporary sanctuary. Before she lost courage, Gwen closed the curtain against the daylight and any other curious onlookers who might have noticed their arrival, then she leaned against the wall with her head bowed. How would she cope under Verity's scrutiny? She calmed her breathing and closed her eyes to stop the tears. Naveena wasn't in the room, but Gwen knew she would be gathering her things to bring them to the nursery where she and the child would sleep.

In an attempt to get Liyoni out of her wet clothing, Gwen mimed what she wanted her to do, but the girl shook her head and stared at her.

"You, Liyoni," Gwen said, pointing at the child. "Me, Gwen. I am the Lady."

She tried a few words of Sinhala, but with no effect. She hesitated. Liyoni looked doubtful and sullen. Gwen herself felt wary. She knew nothing about the child. Nothing about her character, nothing about her life up until now. Nothing about what she liked or what she didn't like. She held out a hand to her daughter, but the little girl stared at the floor and didn't respond. Gwen felt a lump in her throat again. Whatever she did, she must not let her daughter see her cry.

She tried again to divest Liyoni of her clothes and was struck by how far the little girl might have to go to accept her new life, and how much further she herself needed to go to properly care for her. The feeling of unease grew as she heard her sister-in-law calling from the corridor outside her bedroom. She shuddered, terribly aware of the risk she was taking.

28

Still wearing her dressing gown, Gwen laid all her clothes out on her bed, plus a swathe or two of sari fabric that she'd thought particularly pretty. It was becoming harder to find an inexpensive dressmaker, and she was going to have to ask Naveena to alter some of her clothes. All round the world times were still hard, with some fabrics not only scarce but also expensive. A little while before, Fran had written about the new ready-to-wear clothes shops popping up all over London, and Gwen felt grateful that her relationship with her cousin had been at least partially restored, and no mention had been made of Ravasinghe.

Gwen read that, just as Laurence had found ways to streamline tea production, fashion houses had discovered less-expensive ways of manufacturing too, and were using new and cheaper fabrics instead of more costly materials. Fran was particularly keen on the new sheer stockings from America and had sent a saucy photograph of herself showing rather too much leg and wearing a new rayon dress.

Most of Gwen's best dresses were made of silk and awfully outmoded now; according to Fran, nobody in London or New York would be seen dead in a flapper dress. She'd included a recent American copy of *Good Housekeeping* to prove it.

Gwen studied the page where the magazine had fallen open. Some of the girls wore feminine two-piece outfits with simple blouses, or a little cardigan and longish wrap skirts. It was a lean look that she could imagine Fran bursting out of, though it would suit Verity well by lending a touch of elegance to her normally lanky appearance. If she curled her hair and wore some red lipstick, it could be the making of her. Being so petite herself, Gwen preferred the sweet short skirts of the twenties.

But her purpose today wasn't to work out how to get herself more up to date, it was to decide which dresses Naveena might cut down to make clothes for Liyoni. She picked up a few silk dresses but discarded them right away. A serving girl dressed in silk would attract attention. It was one thing providing for her daughter from a distance;

it was much more testing to actually have her living in the house. She hadn't slept a wink since the child had arrived, and most of the time the knot in her stomach had made it impossible to eat. She flinched at a noise outside her room and knew she'd have to find a way to iron out the dread that was building.

She picked out her old cotton day dresses — the fine wash-softened fabric might do well for the child — and created a small pile of sprigged cotton items: two or three skirts and a favorite but badly ripped red *broderie anglaise* dress. She rarely wore red but this dress was pretty. She folded the chosen items over her arm and carried them to the nursery.

Naveena was sitting on the floor with an abacus in front of her, and while the child moved the beads across and counted in Sinhala, Naveena was repeating the words in English.

"What about introducing her to the rest of the household staff?" Gwen said.

Naveena looked up. "Lady, do not break your head. I do that."

"I've told Laurence that you have had to bring an orphan relative to live here," Gwen said.

She'd had to force her legs from trembling

as she'd lied to Laurence, and when he'd looked up from his newspaper and frowned, she'd pinched her own flesh hard to keep from giving way.

"Darling, Naveena doesn't have relatives. We are her family."

She took a breath. "Well, it appears she does have this one relative, after all. A distant cousin."

There was a silence, during which Gwen fidgeted, straightening her skirt and tightening the pins in her hair as she fought to steady her nerves.

"I don't like the sound of this," he said. "Naveena has a good heart and I suspect someone has told her a cock-and-bull story about this missing relative and she has swallowed it. I shall talk to her myself."

"No!"

He looked surprised.

"I mean, you've always said that the household is my responsibility. Let me deal with this."

She waited and gave him a little smile as he paused before he spoke. "Very well. But I think we should do our best to find a more suitable home for her."

Gwen frowned at the memory and looked across at Naveena again. "Laurence isn't happy and Verity is curious as a cat."

Naveena shook her head.

"You don't think I should trust my sister-in-law, do you?"

"After his Lady die, the girl not happy. Unhappy person can be bad. Scared person too."

"Is Verity scared?" Naveena shrugged.

"What is she scared of?"

"I cannot say . . ."

Naveena's voice trailed off and there was silence.

The ayah would say no more. She rarely gave away her innermost thoughts, especially about the family, though Gwen wished she would. She couldn't think of any reason for Verity's fear, other than the dread of losing her brother, though that might explain her depression and the way she clung to Laurence.

"I haven't said anything to Hugh, and he hasn't seen Liyoni yet."

Naveena lowered her head and continued the lesson.

"Maybe you could take her round the garden later, when Hugh has his rest," Gwen added.

During dessert, Laurence opened the post. Nothing of real interest for Gwen, except another note from Fran enclosing a snapshot of the latest ladies' wear. Gwen was pleased that, judging by the tone of this letter, things really did seem to have completely returned to normal.

Laurence unwrapped a cylindrical item. A magazine rolled out, then lay, curled back on itself, on the white tablecloth.

"What on earth?" he said, picking it up and flattening it. "It looks like an American magazine."

"Can I leave the table, Mummy?" Hugh piped up.

"Yes, but no racing about until your food has gone down. And don't go near the lake on your own. Promise me?"

Hugh nodded, though Gwen had recently spotted him attempting to fish from a narrow promontory at the water's edge.

As Hugh left the room, Laurence's frown deepened.

"Is there a note with it?" she asked.

He picked up the magazine, and when he shook it, an envelope fell out.

"There you are," she said. "Who is it from?"

"Give me a moment." He tore open the envelope and stared at it with raised brows. "It's from Christina."

"Goodness! What does she say?" She tried to keep her voice level, but for the first time in years she felt discomfited by the mention of Christina's name.

He scanned the note, then looked up at her. "She says she has a marvelous idea for us, and that I should examine the magazine to see if I can guess what it is."

Gwen wiped her mouth and put down her pudding spoon. Her stomach was knotted and there wasn't any hope she could swallow another forkful. "Really, Laurence! Haven't we had enough of Christina's ideas for one lifetime?"

Laurence glanced up at the snappy tone in her voice, shook his head, and then flicked the pages. "It wasn't her fault, you know. Nobody foresaw the Wall Street crash."

Gwen pursed her lips but kept her opinion to herself. "So what's in the magazine?"

"Blowed if I know. It appears to be trash. Just endless advertisements for shoe polish, soap powder, and the like, strung together with an occasional article."

"Do you think she's bought the magazine?"

"Unlikely. All she says is that she has an idea that will transform our fortunes."

"But why would a magazine be of interest to us?"

As Laurence threw it down and prepared

to leave, Gwen asked if she could use the Daimler to drive to Hatton. With her fabrics now sorted out, she needed buttons and thread.

Laurence, standing by the door with his hand on the handle and his chin jutting out, paused.

"Well, can I?" she said.

He hesitated for a moment longer. "Actually, I haven't paid the garage bill yet."

"Why not?"

He reddened slightly and looked away. "I didn't want to say. We were a bit short last month and all the cash had to go on wages. Should be clear soon. After the next auctions, that is."

"Oh, Laurence."

He gave a brief nod and then, just as he was about to leave the room, twisted back and continued briskly. "I forgot, Christina also says she'll be arriving soon to discuss this idea of hers. And she has asked if she can stay here for a few days."

He shut the door quietly and Gwen sat alone, feeling appalled. She was already on tenterhooks trying to settle Liyoni without arousing suspicion, and now Christina would be staying with them. On top of everything else, how would she cope if Laurence fell under the American woman's spell again? Despite everything he had said to convince her otherwise, she did not trust Christina, and the suspicion that Christina still had designs on Laurence only compounded the strain she already felt. She leaned against the wall and closed her eyes.

As it happened, by the afternoon Naveena had developed a fever and was unfit to work, so with a sinking heart, Gwen had to look after Liyoni herself. At first it didn't go well. In an effort to control her nerves, Gwen was a little too brusque, and the child resisted, crying and clinging to the old ayah's bedpost. After Naveena stroked her hands and whispered to her, she eventually gave in and followed Gwen through the passageway. Gwen had no idea what had been said, but Naveena's instinctive sympathy must have settled the little girl.

In the bedroom, Gwen studied the child's possessions. Her clothing consisted of what she stood in, plus a beaded anklet, a spare top, and a ragged length of fabric.

She took Liyoni to the bathroom and showed her the bath. Though Naveena had washed the little girl, Gwen wanted to give her a good scrubbing before introducing her to Hugh. Self-conscious and hesitant, she tidied the towels and rearranged the soaps, and then — not wanting the little girl to pick up on her anxiety — she composed herself. She had expected Liyoni to resist, but when the water reached halfway up, the little girl jumped in fully dressed. With her wet clothes now sticking to her, she looked thin, with a painfully fragile neck and a head full of long curly hair that had matted in places.

Gwen took a breath, still not knowing how to behave. When she poured a small amount of shampoo on Liyoni's hair and rubbed the child's scalp to lather up, she felt as if she might lose her nerve. But the little girl giggled and Gwen's heart lifted a little.

After the bath, the girl struggled out of her clothes, and Gwen handed her a large white towel, then left her while she went back to the nursery to dig out an old shirt of Hugh's.

Naveena, poor soul, was fast asleep and looking pale. It was a lot for her to undertake at her age. As Gwen gazed down on her, feeling guilty, she heard a scream and rushed back through to her bedroom.

Verity, red-faced, was jabbing a shaking finger at Liyoni, while holding the towel by the tips of her fingers. Fear sliced through Gwen.

"I found her trying to steal this towel,"

Verity declared.

The naked child stood by the bed looking terrified, her arms crossed over her chest, her hair dripping water on the floor.

Gwen felt a stab of anguish, then squared her shoulders and felt so angry she had to fight her desire to hit Verity. "She wasn't stealing it. I gave her a bath. Give me the towel."

Verity hung on to it. "What! While you leave Hugh outside playing all alone?"

"Hugh is fine," Gwen said, brushing Verity's words aside. She marched over and snatched the towel, then squatted down to wrap it round Liyoni.

"Have you lost your senses? She can't be in your room like this, Gwen. She'll be absolutely crawling."

"What do you mean?"

"Lice, Gwen. Bugs."

"She's clean. She's had a bath."

"You said she was here to help Naveena. She's a servant. You can't treat her as if she's one of us."

"I'm doing no such thing," Gwen snapped as she stood. "And, Verity, as this is my house and not yours any more, I would appreciate it if you didn't interfere in what I do. Naveena is sick. The child is alone in the world. I am simply doing the charitable

506

thing, and if you can't find it in your heart to understand that, the sooner you go back to your husband the better."

Verity turned bright red and scowled but didn't speak for a moment or two.

Gwen squatted again to rub the child dry, then glanced up over her shoulder. "Why are you still in here?"

"You don't understand, Gwen," Verity said, speaking so quietly Gwen could barely hear. "I can't go back."

"What?"

Verity colored up, shook her head, and then abruptly left the room.

Gwen swallowed her anger. The timing of Liyoni coming to live at the house could not be worse. The place would be heaving. Just when she needed some peace and quiet to get to know her daughter unobserved, people would be asking questions, wanting to be fed and asking how she was. The last thing she needed was Verity hanging around watching her, or Christina hanging around watching Laurence.

She tried to look confident as she held Liyoni's hand, though inside she was quaking. She still felt awkward about the color of the little girl's skin, but whatever she felt could not be allowed to count; settling the girl was what mattered, and what was at stake if she dropped her guard.

The sound of Hugh thumping a ball against an outside wall carried through the house. He must have heard her coming too, for when Gwen turned the corner he'd already stopped throwing the ball and was watching with one hand on his hip. His stance, an exact replica of his father's, made her heart skip.

"This is Liyoni," she said, trying to sound perfectly normal as they walked across the terrace. "She is a relative of Naveena's and she's going to live here as Naveena's helper."

"Why does she walk funny?"

"She has a limp, that's all. I think there's something wrong with her foot."

Gwen was struck by Hugh's stocky legs and his shorts covered with grass stains. He loved rolling down the slightly sloping terraces, only stopping in the nick of time before the grass fell away. He gave her a toothy grin, and she smiled at his healthy pink cheeks and his strong nose with a streak of mud across it. Liyoni, standing not a yard away, looked fragile by comparison.

"Can she play ball?"

Gwen smiled again, pulled him to her, and gave him a hug. "Well, she's not really here to play with you, Hugh."

His face crumpled. "Why not? Doesn't she

know how? I can teach her."

"Perhaps not today. But she could go swimming with you tomorrow. She swims like a fish."

"How do you know?"

Gwen tapped the side of her nose. "Because I am a supreme and wonderful being who knows and sees everything."

He laughed. "Don't be silly, Mummy. That's Jesus."

"Actually, I have a rather splendid idea. Why not come inside and help teach Liyoni some English? Would you like that or are you too full of beans?"

"Oh, yes please, Mummy, but I didn't have beans for lunch."

She laughed at their little standing joke and gave him another quick hug, but Liyoni, who stood watching, only glowered. *Oh dear,* Gwen thought, *this might be tricky — I hope she doesn't think we're laughing at her.*

Despite her misgivings, Gwen had to admit that she hungered for more of her daughter. She watched her constantly, but the gap between who the child was and who she ought to have been was too great a distance to bridge. That her feelings for Liyoni were nothing like her love for Hugh pained her, though when she did allow them to surface and found herself craving to comfort the child, she did not know how. She wanted to understand how Liyoni felt about being there and what she thought about everything, but above all she longed to make her feel safe. She rubbed her smarting eyes with the heels of her palms. It tormented her to think of how she had abandoned her daughter as such a tiny helpless baby, and she knew that what her little girl really needed was love.

Once Naveena recovered, Gwen languished in her room imprisoned by her conflicting feelings and the fear that she might somehow give herself away if she was seen too much with Liyoni. Time dragged, and whenever she glanced at the clock, she was surprised the birds were still singing. Was this what life was going to be now — living with a shallow breath and looking over her shoulder? Yet no matter how long she remained in her room, she couldn't get away from the feeling she was stepping closer all the time to the chance event that would signal the end of everything.

Hearing Hugh's voice, Gwen went to the window to look out. He'd found a ragged skipping rope and she watched as he attempted to teach Liyoni to skip. Each time the little girl tried, she ended up tangled in the rope. It didn't seem to upset her, and she giggled as Hugh gently untangled her. For Gwen it was heartbreaking to see Hugh unknowingly playing with his twin sister and looking so happy.

When Naveena went outside, Gwen continued to observe, taking a step back so as to remain out of sight. Despite Hugh's protestations, Naveena led the girl away, and soon after she heard voices in the nursery. She waited and then went through to watch the ayah instruct Liyoni in the art of folding clothes. She stayed for a while, excluded from the pair as Liyoni began to sing in Sinhala while Naveena hummed.

"What is that?" Gwen asked when they had finished.

"A nursery rhyme, but, Lady, the child seems to tire very easily, and she does cough so."

"Give her some linctus. She's probably just getting used to the changes in her life."

When she heard footsteps in the main house corridor, Gwen hurried off, feeling unnerved.

The next morning, it was lovely outside. Gwen stood on the lower terrace and felt that the air itself was singing, not the

511

mosquitoes, the bees, or the water as it rippled across the lake. But then, as she watched the birds dive to the surface of the lake, she realized someone was actually singing. It was a tinkling, lilting sound, almost a low whistle, and it was coming from the water. She surveyed the scene but could see no sign of anyone.

Hugh came racing up behind her and called out. "I've put my swimmers on, Mummy!"

She spun round and caught him in her arms as he charged down the last few steps.

"I saw her go. I wanted to go with her, but she didn't wait."

"Who, darling?"

"The new girl."

"Her name is Liyoni, sweetheart."

"Yes, Mummy."

"And you're saying she's swimming in the lake?"

"Yes, Mummy."

Gwen felt a lick of fear and held her breath as she scanned the lake. What if Liyoni swam to the end of the lake and then found her way back to the river that led to her village? Anything might happen to her. The thought took hold as she gazed at the water and, as blood rushed to her head, for a split second she even wished for the river to take the child. But then, with her mind in turmoil and horrified at herself, she could hardly believe that she could ever think such a thing.

She felt a tug on her sleeve.

"Look, Mummy," Hugh was saying. "She's on that island. She just climbed out. Mummy, she is good at swimming, isn't she? I can't go that far."

Gwen sighed in relief.

"Is it all right if I go in now?" Hugh asked.

He'd been told he must always ask permission, and she wondered how she might find a way to allow Liyoni to swim unrestricted, while still maintaining the rule for Hugh. Water was like a magnet to the girl, and Gwen feared she could no more keep out of it than she could stop breathing.

Gwen watched Hugh's stocky little body as he leaped into the water with the biggest splash. What he lacked in fluidity as a swimmer, he made up for in noise, and his shrieks and yells continued until Liyoni swam back. Just before she climbed out, she twirled in the water, whirling like a dervish with her hair spinning out around her. Then, as they both got out and shook themselves, the little girl began to cough. Hugh stared at her, looking embarrassed, but beamed in delight when the coughing stopped and she smiled at him.

"Where's Wilf?" Gwen said.

"Oh, Wilf's boring. He doesn't like swimming anyway."

"Shall we go in and see if we can persuade the *appu* to make pancakes?"

"Can the girl —"

Gwen frowned.

"I mean, can Liyoni come too?"

"Perhaps just this once."

As Hugh reached out to take Liyoni's hand, she seemed not to mind, and as Gwen watched the pair run up the steps ahead of her, hand in hand, her heart skipped a beat and she felt a depth of feeling for the girl she had not experienced before. Her eyes watered, but just then she noticed Verity coming down the steps toward her.

"Laurence asked me to tell you he wants to speak to you in the drawing room."

"Why?"

Verity smiled, but it was perfunctory. "He didn't say."

Gwen hurried to the drawing room and found Laurence standing with a rolled-up newspaper under his arm. He turned at the sound of her footsteps, his face impassive. *He knows,* she thought in the short silence, *and he is about to throw me out.* She cast around for what to say.

"I —"

He interrupted. "I saw Hugh out there with the little girl. I thought we had decided."

Numb with tension, she forced herself to respond. "Pardon?"

He sat down and leaned against the back of the sofa. "I thought we had decided the child wasn't to stay."

Gwen struggled to suppress her relief. He didn't know. She stood behind the sofa so that she could rub his shoulders, but also to hide her face from him.

"No," she said, taking her time. "We agreed that I'd deal with it. And I am, but she isn't too well. She has a cough."

"Is it contagious?"

She steeled herself. "I don't think so, and Hugh is lonely."

As she stopped rubbing and took a step back, he straightened up and twisted round to look at her. "Darling, you know I'd be happy to help if the child really was related."

"I know, but can't you just trust me on this?"

"Come on, Gwen. As I said before, we already know Naveena has no relatives. And the thing is, I'd rather Hugh didn't get too attached to her."

She paused momentarily before she replied. "I don't understand."

He looked puzzled. "Isn't it obvious? If they become close he'll miss her terribly when she's gone. So, really, the sooner the better. Surely you agree?"

She could feel the pain racing to her temples as she stared at him. How could she possibly agree?

He reached out a hand. "Are you all right? You don't seem to be yourself."

Gwen shook her head.

"I understand you're doing your best, but —"

She broke in. "It's not fair, Laurence. It's really not. Where the hell do you expect her to go!"

Her heart splintered. No longer able to cope with the hurt, she felt as if all her efforts to protect Laurence and their marriage were beginning to crumble. She didn't want Liyoni to go, but he had no idea what she was going through; indeed, what she had gone through all these years. He was right — she was doing her best — but he did not know that trying to balance the conflicting needs of her husband, Hugh, and the little girl was more than she could bear. Completely losing control of herself, she left the room, slamming the door behind her.

29

For some time after that, Laurence was quiet. Whenever she came into a room he glanced up at her as if waiting for her to say something, but she was damned if she would apologize for her temper. Aware that bringing Liyoni to the house might turn out to be the worst mistake of her life, she had tried to look for alternatives but had drawn a blank.

On the pretext of going to a meeting of the Women's Charity Union, she visited an orphanage in Colombo, an overcrowded place reeking of urine. Afterward the memory of it gave her sleepless nights. Above all, she wanted to protect her marriage, but she could not bear for Liyoni to be sent there.

During the next few weeks, Laurence occasionally asked how her plans to find the girl another home were going, and so far Gwen had managed to change the subject, but it had strained her nerves to the breaking point. Meanwhile, Hugh thrived on helping Liyoni learn. She was now able to understand simple English commands and to ask for what she needed. But the little girl tired easily and, until Hugh started school in the autumn, Gwen still had to find ways to keep the children apart, for at least part of the time. Far from Liyoni's arrival causing jealousy, Hugh absolutely worshipped her, and on the occasion she was sick in bed with a bad cough, he had to be forced to keep away.

Verity was another matter. With no further clarification of her reluctance to return to her husband, she was still around on the afternoon of Laurence's birthday, and when Hugh came in for the birthday tea with Liyoni in tow, she glowered at her brother. Though Gwen thought it a shame when Verity spoiled her looks in that manner, her sister-in-law was looking quite chic in a long, slim-fitting outfit. It crossed Gwen's mind to wonder where she was finding the cash for expensive new clothes. Her husband wasn't especially wealthy.

"I put my foot down at this," Verity said. "That child is not a member of our family and this is a family birthday celebration. In fact, Laurence, why is she still living here? I thought you said you'd speak to Gwen."

"Let's not have a scene, Verity."

"But you said —"

Gwen stepped in quickly and, making a fist to contain her anger, she spoke to Hugh. "Sorry, darling, but your Aunty Verity is right. Tell Liyoni to go and find Naveena. She can find something for her to do."

Hugh pulled a sulky face but did as he was told. During this exchange, Verity continued to complain about Liyoni's presence in the house.

Still vexed by her sister-in-law's constant intrusion in their lives, Gwen interrupted again. "Actually, Laurence and I have discussed the matter, and he has left it up to me to deal with the situation. Let me remind you once again, Verity, that I am mistress here, and since your marriage you are merely here as a guest."

"Hang on, Gwen," Laurence said.

"No. I will not hang on. Not for you. Not for Verity. Either I am mistress here or I am not. I am absolutely sick of your sister poking her nose into my affairs. It's time she went back to her husband."

Laurence tried to put an arm round her shoulders, but, feeling shaken, she shrugged him off.

"Come on, darling. It is my birthday."

"I don't want Aunty Verity to go,

Mummy," Hugh protested.

Gwen glanced at the table, set for the four of them, with the best china and silverware, prettily arranged on a freshly starched damask tablecloth. She controlled her anger.

"All right, darling. Mummy and Daddy will talk about this later. Let's have the birthday tea."

But the days of free-flowing champagne were gone, and when the *appu* brought in Laurence's fruitcake on a silver platter, they washed it down with cups of tea. And the presents, once towering almost to the ceiling, now struggled to reach even a small pile.

"Let's not bother with the search," Laurence said.

"I think we should," Verity said.

Gwen sighed. If Verity wanted the blindfold, the blindfold she would have. She went to the sideboard, sifted through the remains of the party paraphernalia, and pulled out a long strip of thick black fabric, which she bound round Laurence's eyes, knotting it at the back.

"Now turn Daddy round three times," Hugh ordered.

The idea was that the pile of presents would magically vanish and Laurence, blindfolded, would have to find them all before he could unwrap any.

He dutifully stumbled around the room, play-acting the oaf, which sent Hugh into hoots of laughter. He was on all fours, tapping the floor round the open door, when they all heard clicking heels. Everyone froze.

"Well, I say, I hoped you'd be thrilled to see me, but bowing and scraping takes the biscuit. I never thought I'd see the day."

Laurence tore off his blindfold and smoothed his hair as he stood. "Christina!"

"The very same."

"But you're not due until next week," Gwen said.

Hugh stamped his foot and turned red. "She's spoiled it! Daddy didn't even find his presents."

"Ah," Christina said. "Maybe I can make up for that. I have presents too."

Laurence and Gwen exchanged looks.

"Did you know it was Laurence's birthday?" Verity said.

"What do you think? But these are for all of you, not just for Laurence. My man is waiting in the corridor." She spun round and snapped her fingers. A Sinhalese man in a long white linen coat came in, loaded with shopping bags.

"I'm sorry, I didn't have time to get them wrapped." She dug into one of the bags, pulled something soft out, still on its hanger, and then passed it to Gwen.

Gwen caught it, unrolled the beautiful fabric, and held up a two-piece outfit, just like the ones in *Good Housekeeping.*

"I thought it would complement your eyes," Christina said. "Such a lovely shade of lilac. And, Hugh, this train set is for you."

She put the box on the table and Hugh's eyes shone as he ran his fingers over the pictures of the engine and its compartments.

"What do you say to Christina, old son?" Laurence said.

Hugh only just managed to drag his eyes from the train set. "Thank you very much, American lady."

Everyone laughed.

"Verity," Christina continued, "I have a crocodile-skin bag for you. I thought you'd like it."

"Thank you. You didn't have to."

"I never do anything I have to. This was just for fun." She paused and winked at Laurence, then blew him a kiss. "And now for the birthday boy. I have something extra special for you, darling, though I'm afraid it isn't anything you can hold in your hands."

"Is it a car? Are you giving Daddy a new

car? He wouldn't be able to hold that in his hands."

"No, sweetie, do you think it should be a car?"

"Yes, I do!"

"Actually, if you all don't mind, I'm rather tired now. Your daddy's present will have to wait until after your bedtime."

Hugh started to complain but, still seething over Christina's unannounced arrival, which no number of expensive presents could atone for, Gwen silenced him with a look.

"It's almost time for Hugh's bath, Christina, so if you don't mind, Verity will show you to the guest room and I'll see you again at dinner. We don't dress these days."

"Oh, but you must. I insist. It is a special occasion, after all." Gwen nodded with a mix of annoyance and suspicion and took hold of Hugh's hand. "Very well," she said. "Off we trot. You can have your bath in my room today."

Hugh clapped his hands and chatted excitedly all the way to her bedroom. While she ran the bath, she couldn't help wonder how Liyoni had fared. Although she looked a little better, her limp seemed to be more pronounced each day. If it got any worse, the child wouldn't be able to carry out the few light household duties Gwen had found for her. It was work for appearance's sake and didn't really matter, but she had to maintain the illusion.

There had been an infected sore on the little girl's foot, which Naveena had treated with herbal tincture and then bound. Gwen had expected the limp to have disappeared once the wound cleared up, but it had not. Dr. Partridge would come to give Hugh the once-over in a couple of days' time, and she decided to ask him to look at Liyoni too.

They were enjoying coffee in the drawing room after dinner, when Christina revealed her great idea. Verity was sitting on the leopard-skin sofa next to the drinks table, Laurence stood by the mantelpiece, and Gwen was perched on an upright chair on the other side of the sofa, keeping an eye on the brandy bottle. They'd left the curtains open and the nighttime world outside was lit by an almost-full moon.

"Brands," Christina said, with a wide grin. She leaned back in her armchair and placed what looked like a picture wrapped in brown paper on the floor beside her chair.

"Pardon?" Laurence said.

"Brands. It's the way to go." She got up and went to stand next to Laurence, placing a hand on his shoulder and leaning against him. Then, with her face close to his, she looked into his eyes. "Didn't you look at the magazine I sent you, darling?"

"Laurence glanced at it," Gwen said, feeling like spitting but managing to maintain a calm exterior. "Neither of us had a clue what you meant."

Christina, who was smiling at Laurence, twisted back to face Gwen. "What *did* you notice in the magazine?"

Gwen eyed the room. As well as the presents, Christina had arrived laden with bouquets of flowers that were now elegantly arranged in four cut-glass vases, their perfume filling the air.

"There were an awful lot of advertisements."

Christina clapped her hands. "Well done you!"

"Are you suggesting we advertise?" Laurence said as he took a step away from the American. "That doesn't seem much of an idea, if you'll pardon my bluntness."

Christina threw back her head and laughed. "Darling, I'm American. Of course I don't mind your bluntness. How funny you English are."

Laurence jutted out his chin and Gwen wanted to rush across and smother the cleft with kisses. She restrained herself and addressed Christina instead. "Well, why don't you explain to us *funny* English exactly what you mean."

"Sweetheart, don't take offense. I'm not being unfriendly. I think you're all utterly adorable, and your husband, well, you know what I think about him — but yes, you're right, let's get down to business."

Gwen, who had been holding her breath, released it slowly.

"What is happening in America is that, despite the depression, some people are simply raking it in. The bigger the company, and the more ordinary the product, the better it is."

"You mean like the soap powders and shoe polish we saw in the magazine?" Laurence said.

"Yes, and here's my point . . . also like tea. Think of Lipton."

Gwen shook her head. "But there weren't any advertisements for tea."

"Exactamundo, *chérie.* My idea is that we develop Hooper's as a brand. You'd no longer just be a wholesale producer and manufacturer of tea, but actually a brand of tea."

Laurence nodded. "People are suffering in the Depression, but they still have to wash their clothes and polish their boots. That's your idea."

"Yes. And they have to buy their tea, week after week. But this only works if you go big."

Laurence shook his head. "We'd never be able to produce enough. Not even with the three plantations at full throttle. I don't see how it could work."

"Laurence. My dear" — she glanced round — "and *funny* Englishman, who I respect, admire, and love — that's where I come in."

Gwen swallowed her irritation.

"There won't be huge margins, but what you have to sell is the sort of thing people buy frequently and cannot do without." Christina paused. "Tell me, how are you coping in this Depression?"

Laurence coughed and looked at his feet.

"Quite. So we need to think of something new. There's a packet of tea in every house, and I want the name on that packet to be Hooper's. If we can come second to Lipton, we'll be flying."

Gwen's resentment of the woman seemed to explode in her throat. What did Christina really want? Was she toying with them, rubbing it in and showing that she had the power to do so? Had she come back to try again with Laurence? Gwen wanted to remove her from their lives as she had tried to do once before, but she was not keen to embarrass Laurence by causing a jealous scene. Her first instinct was to keep a rigid face and speak firmly.

"No," she said. "Let this be an end to your crazy idea. Laurence has already said we can't produce that kind of quantity."

Christina seemed oblivious. "Not you, darling. You will buy it in from all over Ceylon. Make deals with other plantations. We'll package the tea and advertise it like crazy. You don't need a big margin if you have the quantity."

"I don't have the cash for the capital expenditure," Laurence said.

"You don't, no, but I do. I'm suggesting I buy shares in Hooper's and you use that money to start up the business."

Gwen stood up on trembling legs and went to Laurence's side. Her voice, when she spoke, shook too. "And if it fails? What then? We can't risk anything more."

"It will be me who risks, not you. Mark my words, honey, this is the future. Advertising is really taking off in America. You saw the magazine, didn't you?"

"I'm not sure I'm all that happy about the way the future looks," Gwen said.

"Like it or not, you will stand to make millions. And it really is as simple as that."

"You may be right. Can we think about it?" Laurence said, linking his arm through Gwen's.

Gwen sighed. The woman was winning Laurence over, and there wasn't a thing she could do about it.

"You have two days. Then I'm off. We need to act quickly, and if we don't, someone else will get there before us."

She stood, smoothed down her very expensive-looking dress, and turned to Gwen with a persuasive smile. "Do you like my dress?"

Gwen muttered a reply.

"Off the peg, dirt cheap, not even silk. The world is changing, folks. You're either in for the ride or you're not. Now, I've had a long journey today, so I'm more than ready for my bed."

Verity, who had been quiet, stood too, though she appeared unsteady on her feet, and when she spoke her words were a little slurred. "I think it's a wonderful idea, Christina."

Gwen felt like saying that it had absolutely nothing to do with Verity but kept her mouth shut.

"Thank you. I forgot to say, Laurence, you

and Gwen will need to come to New York. It will help the brand to become known and respected."

"Really, is that necessary? For how long?"

"Absolutely necessary, and not for long. And, of course, I'll cover all your expenses."

"What about Hugh?"

"He'll be at school soon, won't he?"

Gwen frowned. "Why are you doing this, Christina, if the losses will be all yours?"

"Because there will be no losses. I am *that* sure . . . and also because I'm fond of you both. You've been struggling, and I felt so badly for Laurence's losses in Chile. Though I am sure, once this depression eases, you'll make your money back there too, and more besides."

Gwen nodded slowly. She had no choice but to let whatever was going to happen, happen.

"The campaign will be run from New York, and they'll need to see your faces. And talking of faces, I'd almost forgotten. Verity, if you don't mind, would you unwrap that small painting leaning against the sofa?"

"I wondered if that was going to be my present," Laurence said.

"In a way, it is," Christina said as Verity took off the brown paper.

"Well, let's all see," Laurence said.

Verity looked up at him. "It's one of Savi Ravasinghe's paintings."

Gwen's heart sank. She had never confronted Savi over what had happened that night, and gradually it had become easier to bury it at the back of her mind. But now, with Liyoni in the house as a constant reminder, why did he have to come back like this too?

Laurence frowned as Verity turned the painting round, then held it up so that they could see.

"It's a Tamil tea plucker," Laurence said.

Gwen took in the gorgeous scarlet color of the woman's sari, which seemed to shimmer against the luminous green of the tea bushes, and had to admit it was very beautiful. As she stared, she felt a flush spread from her neck to her cheeks and hoped nobody had noticed, though of course the one who did was Verity.

"Are you all right, Gwen?" Verity said.

"Just hot," she said, waving a hand in front of her face.

Laurence was silent as Christina explained that she thought it was the perfect image for Hooper's tea. It would be printed on the packets themselves, on the giant billboards, and in the magazine advertisements.

When she had finished, he shook her

hand. "You've certainly given us food for thought. We'll speak again tomorrow. I hope you have a comfortable night."

As they all departed for their rooms, Gwen thought about it. There wasn't much space in her mind for reason where Christina was concerned, and in that moment she felt as if the American would be the wind that blew her house down.

30

Over the next two days, Gwen heard Laurence moving around at night. With the renewed anxiety she was feeling at hearing Ravasinghe's name adding to her annoyance about Christina, she longed for Laurence to share her bed so that she could draw him close. But he did not. And also to Gwen's irritation, Verity, still very much on Christina's side, had remained. The brand issue had taken over the house, and the subject of Verity's leaving had not been broached again.

While everyone was preoccupied, Gwen allowed Liyoni and Hugh to play in her room. Sunlight poured through the bedroom window, and Gwen, sitting at the table in the window with Naveena, felt the warmth on the back of her neck. She watched the twins bouncing on the bed, while chanting something that sounded like a Sinhalese version of "Humpty Dumpty."

She was thinking about Christina, and the effect the woman's arrival had had on Laurence, who was becoming more remote.

Through the window she caught sight of them huddled together in the garden, and tried to convince herself it was only the brand they were discussing. But as a hollow feeling took hold of her, she felt out of place and excluded from her husband in her own home. She understood home wasn't a place. It was her daily relationship with everything she touched, saw, and heard. It was the certainty of familiarity and the reassurance of safe, well-trodden pathways. The fabric, the threads, the scents: the exact color of her morning cup of tea, Laurence throwing down his newspaper before heading off to work, and Hugh clattering up and down the stairs a thousand times a day. But now there was something extraordinary, the ground was shifting, and everything was different.

She felt a burst of heat and for a moment hated Christina almost as much as she hated Savi Ravasinghe; but more than that, she hated that they had turned her into such a jealous, fearful woman. What she longed for was some kind of escape from the shame she felt, but then she looked at the children and the anger drained out of her.

"Be careful, Hugh," she called out. "Remember Liyoni's bad leg."

"Yes, Mummy. That's why she's only bouncing on her bottom."

There was a tap on the door and Verity came in. "I thought you should know that Laurence has agreed to Christina's proposal."

Gwen rubbed her neck. "Oh my Lord, really?"

"They want your signature on a form. There will be more later." She paused and glanced at the children who were now sitting quietly on the bed. "I'd get rid of the brown girl, if I were you."

"I'm not sure I know what you mean."

Verity inclined her head and with a partial smile continued. "The servants are talking. They don't understand why the girl gets preferential treatment; you know what they're like."

Gwen frowned at her. "I was thinking you might be preparing to pack your bags."

Verity smiled again. "Oh no. You may be his wife, Gwendolyn, second wife at that, but I am his *only* sister. Now I'm off to play tennis with Pru Bertram at the club. Cheerio."

"What about your husband? Surely this isn't fair to him?"

Verity shrugged. "That really isn't any of

your business."

"Is it true?" Gwen asked Naveena once Verity had left. "About the gossip?"

The old lady sighed. "It means nothing."

"Are you sure?"

"I tell them it is good that Hugh has a friend."

There was a noise in the corridor and then the sound of footsteps. Gwen looked round, startled.

Naveena clicked her tongue. "Just one of the houseboys, Lady."

As Hugh and Liyoni started to bounce again, Gwen's attention wandered. Verity's warning had hit home. Since the day she'd brought Liyoni to live with them, her life had lost its cohesion. Trapped by her own fear, she jumped at noises and each time she heard the timbers of the house creak, she spun round expecting the worst, torturing herself with terrible outcomes until she couldn't see straight.

She needed Laurence to remind her of who she was, but instead of that they were slipping apart. She felt fractured, frightened to be near him in case she gave herself away, and at the same time needing him more than ever. When Laurence was nice to her, she was irritable and short-tempered; when he was distant, she worried about Christina's hold on him.

Suddenly there was a loud thump. Gwen glanced up and saw that Liyoni had fallen from the bed and now lay on the floor, not making a sound. She leaped from the chair.

"You pushed her, didn't you, Hugh?"

Hugh turned bright red and started to cry. "No, Mummy. I did not!"

As Gwen ran over, he climbed down from the bed. She picked up the girl and held her in her arms, and Hugh squatted right beside them.

"I'm so sorry, Hugh. It's not your fault. I had stopped watching you both."

She stroked Liyoni's cheek and looked into her scared eyes. The child blinked and a single tear fell. Gwen's heart almost stopped. She was looking at her daughter without seeing the color of her skin — truly thinking of her as her own flesh and blood for the first time. In that moment of utter clarity, time seemed to stand still. This was her own little girl, who she hadn't known how to love, and who she had given away like an unwanted puppy. The guilt over what she had done, and the pain of knowing that she could never openly acknowledge her own daughter, ripped her heart open. She made a strangled sound as she fought back the tears, then wrapped an arm round Hugh too, and drew them both to her. With her heart thumping wildly, she felt another rush of love and kissed Liyoni on both cheeks. When she looked up, she smiled at Naveena — but the ayah looked stiff, her eyes fixed on the door and her mouth slightly open.

With her back to the door and her attention on the children, Gwen hadn't heard it open, and only knew now because she heard Laurence cough.

"The girl fall," Naveena quickly said.

Gwen lifted Liyoni, then carefully placed her back on the bed, but her guilt cast a long shadow, and if Laurence had seen the fall, then he must have seen everything else too.

Laurence remained silent as he stood watching.

Gwen tried to think, unsure if she'd actually said anything out loud, or if she had simply been thinking. Fear blocked her mouth and airways as she swallowed and attempted to formulate a sequence of sounds that made sense.

Laurence cleared his throat and spoke directly to Naveena. "Phone Dr. Partridge. Tell him to come."

He came across to look at the child and Hugh took his hand. "She is my best friend, Daddy."

"She's just had a fall. Landed badly, I should think. That's all."

Gwen tried to keep the fear from her eyes. What had Laurence seen? What had he heard? Her skin prickled. She scratched her scalp, then the back of her neck and her shoulder blades. The scratching did not help. The prickle crawled over her until she wanted to scream.

"Partridge has seen her about the limp?" Laurence said, jolting her.

Gwen nodded.

"And?" Laurence asked.

She managed to find her voice. "He thought it was nothing. He said he'd be back. But how did you know? You weren't even here."

"McGregor said."

Though Laurence's usual expression was unchanged, there was something in his eyes. As he held her gaze, her stomach tightened. There were several moments before he spoke again.

"He said you seemed concerned about the child."

Gwen gulped. Why had she assumed McGregor was not watching her? "She is a sweet child, and I felt so sorry for her coming to live among strangers at such a young age."

"I went to boarding school in England at her age."

"And you know what I think about that."

For a few moments, Laurence gazed at her without speaking. She had no idea what was going through his mind. If she were to lose him now . . .

In an attempt to calm her nerves in the tense silence, she concentrated on her breathing.

"Hugh will be gone soon," he eventually said. "Then we'll decide what to do about the girl."

Gwen twisted her head away so that Laurence wouldn't see her eyes fill with tears.

"There are some papers to sign in the dining room. Come through after the doctor has been. And, by the way, we'll be traveling to America sometime after Christina. She's gone ahead today."

Gone. She was gone.

Gwen passed the hour that they waited for the doctor drinking tea and playing solitaire with Hugh. Liyoni slept, and when she did wake, she was silent and refused all offers of fruit or water. Gwen's heart jumped every time she heard footsteps in the corridor, frightened that it was Laurence come back, and by the time the doctor did actually appear in the room, Liyoni had grown quite weak.

The doctor put down his bag. "It might be an idea if the ayah takes Hugh out of here, Gwen."

"No," Hugh said and stamped his foot. "I want to stay. She's my friend, not yours or Mummy's."

"I've got lollipops in here. If you're very good and go with Naveena, I'll give you one."

"Are they yellow?"

"Yes, and pink."

"Only if Liyoni can have one too, the same color as mine."

"Absolutely agreed, old chap."

"And you promise not to hurt her?"

"It's a deal."

"And can we go swimming later? She likes to fly."

"Fly?"

Hugh nodded. "That's her word for swimming."

After Naveena had taken Hugh out to play ball, the doctor pulled up a chair and looked Liyoni over carefully, and very gently pulled and prodded.

Gwen came up to stand behind him, and when the little girl's eyes opened, she smiled. Gwen saw the trust that had begun to grow in her and smiled back. The look wasn't lost on the doctor, who glanced at Liyoni and then at Gwen. She prayed he hadn't noticed the color of the child's eyes, halfway between brown and violet, or her dark ringlets spread out across the pillow.

"Is there anything you want to tell me, Gwen?"

She held her breath. If only he knew how much she really did need to unburden herself, after all these years.

"About the fall, I mean."

Gwen let out her breath. "She rolled off the bed. They were bouncing. It was my fault. I should have known she isn't as strong as Hugh. My attention wandered."

"Very well. It's most probably a weakness caused by a deficiency of some kind. Feed her up, that's my advice."

"Oh, that is a relief. And there's nothing else? Nothing contagious?"

"Not at all. Just the shock of the fall."

A month later, Gwen was in her bedroom packing the last of Hugh's clothes for school. She'd given a great deal of thought to his leisure wear and had prepared for any changes in the weather. His school uniform had arrived from Nuwara Eliya the day before. Two sets of everything, the letter had stipulated, and the list was long. She was grateful her father was footing the bill, though part of her didn't want Hugh to have to go away at all.

Looking glum, he sat on his old rocking horse, which they now kept in Gwen's bedroom. "Can't I come to the wild west with you?"

"We're not going to the wild west. We're going to New York."

"But there will still be cowboys, won't there?"

She shook her head. "I think you're more likely to see a cowboy in Nuwara Eliya than I am in New York."

"It isn't fair. You can teach me arithmetic and spelling, can't you?"

"Darling, you have to receive a good education, so that you can grow up to be clever like Daddy."

"He isn't clever."

"Of course he is."

"Well, it isn't very clever to say I can't go to the waterfall with Liyoni."

Gwen knew there was a waterfall but had heard it was a bit of a climb and so had never ventured there. "I think Daddy thinks it's rather dangerous."

"Liyoni loves water. She would like it. I've seen it. You can actually drive there too.

Verity took me."

"To the top?"

"Yes, right at the top. I didn't go too close to the edge."

"Well, I'm jolly glad to hear that. Now, come on, help me with the catches on this trunk. I need a good strong man to help me."

He laughed. "All right, Mummy."

Later, while she was attempting to pack her own case, Laurence came in with a broad smile on his face. Since Christina had left to get things moving in New York, he'd been busy meeting with plantation owners and setting up deals. Gwen had barely seen him, a fact that she was grateful for. When he was there, he'd given no indication he knew anything more about why Liyoni was in the house, though Gwen watched him carefully for signs that he might.

"Hello," he said. "I've missed my two favorite people."

"Daddy!" Hugh shouted, and jumped off the horse to run and hug him.

"Careful, old boy, Daddy's tired. You don't want to knock me over, do you?"

Hugh laughed. "Yes I do, Daddy."

He smiled and looked over the top of Hugh's head at Gwen. "I've managed to make the arrangements for Hugh to board for the first few months."

"You mean not come home at weekends? Laurence, no. He'll hate it."

"Just while we're away. A trip to New York and back is quite an undertaking. By the way, it's all fixed. Christina has sorted the tickets."

"Hugh, run along now and play," she said. "Why not try out the new swing in the garden?"

Hugh pulled a face but did as he was told. In the way of all growing children, he was quick to sense a disagreement brewing between his parents.

Laurence stood with his back to the light. She looked up at him, shading her eyes from the bright sunlight streaming through the open window. "Can't Naveena look after him at weekends?"

"I think she'll have her hands full with the little girl." He sighed deeply. "I really had hoped we'd have done something about that child by now."

"I have tried."

"I'm sure you have."

"What do you mean by that?"

"Nothing at all, just what I said. Why are you being so touchy? I must say you have been increasingly tetchy since that child came to live here. Whatever is the matter?"

Gwen shook her head.

"Very well," he said. "I want to talk to you about Verity. I've told her she cannot stay here while we are gone. She must go back to Alexander."

Delighted by the news, Gwen breathed more freely. "Good for you. It seems you have thought of everything. Did she tell you what the trouble was between her and Alexander?"

"She hinted at difficulties."

"What difficulties?"

"Can't you imagine?"

"Really?"

"I told her she had to sort it out with him. The truth is this behavior of hers has gone on long enough. Added to which she's drinking too much again. She's her husband's responsibility now, not mine."

Hallelujah, Gwen thought, and managed to stop herself from applauding.

"We can decide what to do about the little girl when we come back. I know I said that we'd look after Naveena in her old age, but I wasn't planning on including her long-lost relatives, if that really is what the child is."

"Oh, Laurence, of course she is."

"There's something odd about it. I've sent for my mother's old family history papers, just in case there's anything that might tell us where she came from. Maybe some hint that might link her to Naveena."

"I doubt that will explain anything. Even Naveena didn't know of the child's existence."

"I know. I spoke to her."

Gwen's heart leaped into her throat. "What did she say?"

"Nothing more than we already know." He paused. "Gwen, you do look pale."

"I'm fine, just a little tired maybe."

She saw the concern in his eyes, but was relieved when he glanced at the dresses laid out on the bed.

"They all look lovely, but don't pack too much. I thought you might like to know Christina is taking you shopping on Fifth Avenue. She thinks you might like some more fashionable clothes."

She straightened up and, with her hands on her hips, she glared at him. "Who does bloody Christina think she is? I am not a charity case, and I do not need her to *take me* shopping."

His chin jutted out. "I thought you'd be pleased."

"Well, I am not. I'm fed up with being patronized by her. And by you."

"Darling, I'm sorry. I know you're upset about Hugh going away."

"I am not upset," she said.

"Darling —"

"Don't *darling* me! I am not upset at all." And then she burst into tears.

He came to fold his arms round her. She struggled, but he held her so tightly she couldn't break free. She couldn't tell him what she was really feeling about Liyoni, and although she would indeed miss Hugh terribly, the truth was he would probably enjoy himself at school. It was actually the thought of leaving everything in the lap of the gods for so long that sent a spasm of fear through her, and it didn't help that not for one minute did she believe Verity would stay away.

"We'll be back before you know it, sweetheart." He tilted her chin up toward him and kissed her on the lips, and she wanted him at that moment, so much that she couldn't speak.

"Shall I lock the door?" he said with a sly smile.

"And the window. Sound carries." She glanced back at the bed, littered with clothes.

"Don't worry about that," he said, and gathered them all up and chucked them in a shambolic heap on the floor, before heading to the door and locking it.

"Laurence! Those things had all been ironed."

He ignored what she had said, picked her up, tossed her over his shoulder, and carried her to the bed. She laughed as he threw her down and then began to help him remove her clothes.

31

Gwen pulled the heavy brocade curtain aside. From her viewpoint at the window of their apartment in the Savoy-Plaza Hotel, on their first morning in the great city, she was surprised to see trees and the rocky shore of a lake glittering in the September sunshine. She didn't know what she had expected, but it certainly wasn't this glorious shining morning, or such an enormous park in the center of New York.

She twisted back to survey the room. The glossy black, silver, and shades of green took quite some getting used to, but she decided she liked the geometric shapes and angular lines. A huge painting dominated one wall. She wasn't sure how to interpret the daubs of black on a cream background, apparently not representing anything in particular, but the painting made her think of Savi Ravasinghe. Christina had proposed a visit to see his latest show in a gallery in Greenwich

Village at some point, and Gwen was not looking forward to going. It was a series of paintings depicting the native population of Ceylon at work, not the usual portraits of rich, beautiful women. Although it was from these canvases that Christina had picked the one to represent Hooper's tea, Gwen had decided to claim one of her headaches as an excuse not to go and hoped that would mean Laurence would stay with her.

Free from the constant knot in her stomach she had grown used to at home, Gwen couldn't help feeling a burst of excitement. "Keep Young and Beautiful" was playing on the wireless. It seemed apt — New York was that kind of place. Laurence had already left for a meeting with Christina, and Gwen was considering what she might do in the meantime. To distract herself from thinking about Laurence spending time alone with Christina, she picked up a glossy copy of *Vogue* magazine and glanced through images of the new fashions, then picked up her bag, slipped a jacket on, and took the plunge. Laurence had promised to be back by twelve, which left her with over two hours to herself.

Out in the street, she glanced up at their hotel building. Christina had booked them in at the Savoy-Plaza because it was a livelier place than its older sister across Fifth Avenue, and you could listen to music in the bar at midnight. But when they'd arrived the night before, they'd been too tired to listen to anything. Gwen felt a little intimidated by the place: the series of arched windows on the ground floor, the Tudor-style slanted roof with the two chimneys and the masculine look of the edifice itself, so much more imposing than the buildings in Ceylon, which seemed gentle and elegant by comparison.

It was noisy, the horns of a handful of motor cars blaring as they wove round trolleybuses, a few double-decker gasoline-powered buses, and what looked like newer and smarter single deckers. She noticed a sign resembling an oversize lollipop on a stick, standing on what Christina called the sidewalk. On closer inspection, Gwen worked out it was a bus stop. She joined the troops of men wearing trilby hats and attempted to stroll as nonchalantly as them while she considered what to do. She decided a taxi was safer. A bus might be going anywhere. But then, before she had time to flag a taxi, she spotted a cream bus with a glass top and MANHATTAN SIGHTSEEING TOUR advertised on the side. Without a moment's hesitation, she queued to buy her ticket.

From her vantage point, leaning out of the window of the bus, she eavesdropped on a couple sitting in front of her, while watching street after street pass by. The man was complaining about a lawyer who had been indicted on a charge of hoarding gold. Two hundred thousand dollars' worth, the man said. Whatever next. His wife, if that was who she was, and Gwen was certain she was, muttered, "Yes, dear," in all the correct places, but Gwen could tell that the woman, as entranced by the sights as she was herself, did not care.

The subject of gold did, however, trigger thoughts of Laurence's reason to be in New York. However much she would like to think so, she and Laurence weren't here as tourists. Today he was going for meetings with Christina at the bank, and tomorrow they were all going to an advertising agency, and after that a solicitor's. Tonight, by way of celebration, they'd been promised an evening of nonstop entertainment. Even the idea of it took Gwen's breath away. Laurence was all for a visit to a jazz club, though Gwen would have preferred a show. They passed a series of billboards advertising *42nd Street* at the Strand Theater. That would be just the ticket, she thought.

That wasn't the only difference of opinion. There had been a continuing disagreement between Laurence and Christina over which advertising agency suited them better, so much so that they'd sounded like an old married couple. In the end it had boiled down to a choice between the James Walter Thompson Agency or Masefield, Moore and Clements, on Madison Avenue. The former had apparently invented the grilled cheese sandwich for one of its clients, and that impressed Christina no end, but it was rumored the latter were planning the first-ever commercially sponsored radio show, and that was even better. Accustomed to the slow rhythms of their Ceylon tea plantation, Gwen didn't know what to make of it all.

At the same time as she marveled at the succession of streets and tall buildings, she continued to be preoccupied by her thoughts and was surprised when the tour ended abruptly and she found herself back somewhere near the park. As she moved out of the bus and onto the pavement, she spotted Laurence guiding Christina by the elbow as they headed toward the hotel entrance. A woman in less need of guiding, Gwen could not imagine.

"Laurence!" she called, and, determined not to feel wounded, she swallowed her irritation. The noise in the street blocked the sound of her voice and he did not turn.

She ran and caught up with them a few moments later.

"How did it go?" she asked, slightly out of breath.

Laurence grinned and kissed her cheek. "We have a master plan in place."

"And we're seeing the advertising agency tomorrow at ten," Christina added, linking arms with them both as if absolutely nothing was wrong. "Perhaps we should lunch now. Gwen and I have some heavy shopping to get through this afternoon, Laurence. And a new suit for you wouldn't go amiss."

Later that day Gwen had just returned from the shopping trip to Saks and the House of Hawes. Outside, the daylight was fading, and as the electric lights came on, tiny yellow rectangles patterned the dark edifices of the looming buildings. In the sitting room of their apartment, Laurence smoked a pipe as he relaxed in one of two square leather armchairs. The bellboy carried in Gwen's packages and placed them just inside the door. After she'd tipped him, she sprawled on the other chair opposite Laurence.

It had been more exhausting than any shopping trip she'd ever experienced, but she'd come away with three wonderful new outfits that brought her right up to date. If she was honest, she'd actually rather enjoyed it. She had an evening dress in palest beige, with a slash of purple at the neckline and butterfly sleeves, and a beautifully cut two-piece in soft pea green, plus a business suit. All had the new midcalf-length hemline and sleek bodices. Christina had insisted on gloves and a hat to match the suit. With a brim, it was a style that flattered Gwen's face more than her old cloche hats had done. She was happy that she'd packed her fox-fur stole, as it lent a touch of class to the off-the-peg outfits.

"Laurence, have you noticed that hardly any of the bellboys and elevator attendants are white?" She rubbed her ankles and hesitated for a moment. "Some are very dark, but some are a sort of toffee color."

"Can't say I've noticed," he said from behind his newspaper. "I guess some people may well be descended from white slave owners."

"Was that common?"

He nodded and carried on reading.

"Are you reading about the lawyer who

was charged with hoarding gold?"

"Yes, and there's an interesting article about that Hitler chap in Germany. They've had monumental inflation there. Could be he'll be the one to sort it out."

"Do you really think so? I heard he's blaming the Jewish banks over there."

"You may be right. Where did you hear that?"

"I listen when I'm out and about."

There was a short silence while Laurence carried on reading, and Gwen bided her time.

"Shall I ring for some tea?" she asked.

As he didn't reply, she went ahead, then screwed up her eyes as she decided how to broach the subject that had been preoccupying her.

"Laurence, I've been thinking."

"Oh dear," he said, and grinned at her, then folded his paper and put it down.

"Since I am to be a director of the new company, even if it is in name only, you need me to sign the papers too, don't you?"

He nodded.

"I will sign everything you want me to, of course I will."

"I never doubted that."

"And I'll give the project my full support, but on one condition." Laurence's brows shot up, but he didn't say a word as she continued. "If we do make pots of money —"

"Not if, *when!*"

"According to Christina, yes."

"I think she's right."

"Well, if we succeed, I'd like to see conditions improve for our laborers. I'd like the children to have better access to medicine, for example."

"Is that all?"

She took a breath in. "No. I want to improve their housing too."

"Very well," he said. "Though I hope I've already improved things since my father's day. Dreadful to think of it now, but did you know that on a crocodile shoot, it was once common practice to use a chubby brown infant as bait?"

Her hand flew to her mouth.

"The hunters would haggle the price for the child, then tether him or her to a tree to lure the crocodile out of the water."

"I don't believe you."

"True, I'm afraid. The croc makes a rush for the child, and the hunter, hidden in the rushes, fires and shoots him dead. Child is untied and everyone smiles."

"What would have happened if the hunter had missed?"

"I guess the croc would have had a good lunch. Outrageous, isn't it?"

Gwen looked at her feet, shaking her head in disbelief. Laurence sighed and picked up his paper again but didn't unfold it.

She took a deep breath. "My point is that a school without good medical care and better housing is a waste of time. We have to improve all three to make any kind of difference to their lives. Imagine what it must be like to have so little."

He considered for a moment. "My father thought they were happy to have a job and be looked after."

"He believed that because it's what he wanted to believe."

"Why didn't you mention this before?"

"It's being here. I want to do something for our people if I can, that's all."

She waited while he opened out the newspaper and thumped it flat again.

"In principle, I do agree," he said. "But it would mean a huge capital expenditure, so only if our profits allow it. Now, my darling, please may I read my paper?"

"Is it one we'll be advertising in?"

"We'll find that out tomorrow."

"It's terribly exciting, isn't it?" she said, and leaned back in her chair.

She picked up a magazine and flicked

through, then, as she came across one particular article, tucked the magazine under her arm. This was something she needed to read alone.

"I'm just going to the bathroom," she said.

In the bathroom she bit a fingernail as she read, then she opened the cabinet, took out her nail scissors, and very carefully cut out the article before folding the magazine and throwing it in the bin.

At Masefield, Moore and Clements the next day, Laurence, Christina, and Gwen were ushered through to a meeting room with a bank of windows that overlooked the busy street.

William Moore was the creative director. He nodded at them all, while indicating some designs already pinned to two large easels. While the introductions were being made, Gwen gazed at the transformation of Savi Ravasinghe's original painting. She steeled herself not to reveal any unease at the mention of his name, but it was harder not to react to his work. The picture had been lovely before, but now, with the colors heightened and slightly adjusted, the image of the woman's red sari against the luminous green of the tea bushes shimmered with vitality.

"Sure will stand out," Mr. Moore said with a broad smile, showing startling white teeth.

"It is beautiful," Gwen said.

"Well, we have to thank Christina here for the idea. The artist has seen the images, by the way, and he's happy too."

"So that's how the package of tea will look. What about the advertisements?" Laurence said as he pulled out a chair at the large oval table.

They settled themselves and Moore handed out a sheet of typescript, while a girl brought in coffee and bagels.

"It's a list of the magazines and papers we're aiming for. Radio stations too. We'll be pushing out in the New Year."

Laurence nodded. "Very impressive."

Moore stood and flipped over the two sheets on the easels to reveal the design and layout for the billboards, and an enlarged version of a typical magazine advert. The smile never left his face.

"The idea is to carry the image through on everything. We want to implant it deep in the American mind, and color is by far the best way to go with Hooper's tea. The color of the woman's sari, the color of the tea bushes and so on, though it does work quite prettily in sepia tones too."

"And the exact launch date?" Christina asked as she lit a cigarette.

"At the start of the New Year. I'm just waiting to finalize the details. We want to emphasize the provenance."

"Pardon?"

He turned toward Gwen. "It's all about where it comes from. In this case, rich-flavored, pure Ceylon tea."

While they drank their coffee, an irony that made Gwen smile, Moore showed her other advertisements currently posted on billboards and in magazines. As she gazed at the pictures, she heard Laurence and Christina talking about the new investors she'd managed to convince. Gwen glanced across at her perfectly made-up face and glossy nails, and at her hair swept up in an elegant style. She wore black, as always, but with a red silk scarf knotted at the neck, and shoes to match. In a way Gwen admired her. She knew all the wealthy families and wasn't afraid to use her connections.

During a pause in the conversation the intercom buzzed.

"Excuse me a moment," Moore said, and left the room.

"So what do you think, Gwen?" Christina said. "Pretty exciting, huh?"

Gwen's smile widened. "I am dazzled, to

be honest."

"And this is just the start. You wait until we are the first commercial backers of a radio show."

"Is that likely?"

"Not yet, but you bet it will be."

Moore came back into the room with a sharp-looking younger man. His hair was slick and his suit immaculate, but he tugged at his tie and shuffled his feet. Moore took a deep breath and didn't smile for once. It was an awkward moment, and Laurence stood up, seeming to sense that something had changed and that it required a response from him. As the atmosphere shifted from excited hopefulness into a silent hiatus, Gwen and Christina exchanged looks.

"I'm afraid there's been a glitch." Moore held up a hand as they all fidgeted. "But it's nothing too serious, and I hope we can work around it."

Gwen glanced at Laurence, whose chin was jutting out.

"Like I say, I hope that we might still be able to proceed."

The tension grew, and Gwen, seeing that Laurence was irritated, was not surprised at the sharp tone of his voice when he spoke.

"Might? What do you mean? Just tell us what the glitch is, man," he said.

Moore, glancing at each one, pulled a series of faces, as if he was going over what to say in his head. "Well, the thing is, we've heard from our contact in another agency. Unfortunately another brand has bought up all the space we were going to advise you to take out."

"Brand of what?" Christina asked.

The man glanced at his feet before cracking his knuckles and speaking. "Tea . . . I'm afraid, it's tea."

Gwen's shoulders drooped. She'd known it was all too good to be true.

"There will be room for Hooper's in the marketplace. I do believe that. There are, after all, plenty of smaller companies selling tea. But this means we'll have to go later with our launch."

"And let them get the edge on us?" Laurence said, rubbing his chin.

The man did not smile, just swallowed awkwardly.

"If we want to rival Lipton, it's all about getting there first," Christina said. "I thought I made that clear at the outset."

"I do understand," Moore said, attempting a smile. "Unfortunately, we aren't party to everything that the other agencies are doing. We do our best."

"It had better not be one of your own

people who gave the other agency the nod about our plans," Christina said, tight-lipped.

Gwen stood up. "It is immaterial. Whoever told whom, we will not be going second with this."

Christina attempted to interrupt.

Gwen held up a hand to stop her. "Let me finish. We will not be going second. We will be going first. If you can arrange for our advertisements to go out in December, instead of the New Year, we still have a deal. If not, the whole thing is off."

Laurence was beaming at her and Christina was staring, openmouthed.

In the brief pause, Moore scanned all their faces.

"Well?" Gwen said, trying to ignore the butterflies taking flight in her stomach.

"Give me until tonight. Where will you be?"

The mood that evening was not as celebratory as they had planned. Christina had delayed the meeting with their solicitor, who had been none too pleased. All the contracts had been rushed through in double-quick time and were now languishing on his desk waiting to be signed. She'd managed to play down the delay; the last thing they needed now was investors getting cold feet. But they all knew that if Moore didn't come through and the launch of the campaign had to be delayed, they would lose an important advantage against their competitor.

Gwen, wearing her new evening dress, was in a quiet mood as Christina led them to the Stork Club on East 51st Street. Cab Calloway was playing later and, as a newly converted lover of jazz, Laurence brightened up as they made their way through the throng of people. As they reached the tables, Christina nodded at a woman in a floral satin gown.

"Who was that?" Gwen asked when they had passed.

"Oh, just one of the Vanderbilts. Nothing but money and glamour here, honey."

It was the intermission, and Christina, dressed in black satin and with her blond hair shining, sashayed up to one of three musicians sitting at a table at the back and kissed him, leaving a red lipstick mark on his cheek.

"Shuffle up, fellas," she said. "These are friends of mine over from Ceylon."

A bartender brought them a tray with several glasses of beer on it.

"It's weak stuff, less than three point two percent alcohol," Christina said, and winked at the barman. "Any chance of livening it up?"

Gwen listened as Christina chatted with her friends, and when the beer came back, discreetly fortified with vodka, she spluttered over her first sip.

"Prohibition is set to end soon," Christina whispered. "That awful beer is an interim measure."

As Gwen took another sip, the butterflies in her stomach had not subsided. Christina, however, managed to appear lighthearted and vivacious, no matter what was going on in her life, and Gwen sensed she hardly knew her at all. Here, in New York, she seemed more wholly American than she had in Ceylon. At first Gwen had been overawed, then jealous of the smooth way she had attempted to captivate Laurence, and then, with the loss of value in Laurence's shares, she'd been angry. Now that the anger had blunted a little, she was surprised to find she genuinely admired Christina's spirit and determination. It must have taken courage for her to come back to them with this new idea, after things had gone so badly wrong before.

One of the band got up and Christina came to sit by Gwen.

"I'm so glad we've buried the hatchet,"

she said, and squeezed Gwen's hand.

"The hatchet?"

"Come on, you must have known I was deadly jealous when Laurence came back from England with the news that he'd married you."

"You were jealous of me?"

"Who wouldn't be? You're beautiful, Gwen, and in that lovely natural way men adore."

Gwen shook her head.

"Of course, I had hoped Laurence would be happy with you as the mother of his children and me as his mistress."

"You thought that?" Gwen's breath caught in her throat. "Did he give you that impression?"

Christina laughed. "Not at all, though it wasn't for want of trying on my part."

"Did he ever . . . I mean, did you both ever —"

"After you were married?" Gwen nodded.

"Not really, though we came close once. At that first ball in Nuwara Eliya."

Gwen bit her lip and dug her nails into the fleshy part of her palm. She would not cry.

Christina reached out a hand. "Darling. Not that close. Just a kiss."

"And now?"

"It's long been over. I promise. You really never had anything to worry about, though I admit I wanted you to think you had."

"Why did you?"

"It was fun, I suppose, and I'm a bad loser. But believe me when I say I care about both of you now."

Gwen frowned very slightly.

"I do, truly. Anyway, I now have a bit of a thing with that rather delicious bass player." She inclined her head in the direction of the man she had kissed on the cheek.

Gwen laughed and Christina laughed with her. Ashamed that she had ever doubted Laurence, but overjoyed to hear that he really had not been tempted, Gwen felt more relaxed than she had in days.

Just as the musicians were standing up and gathering their instruments to continue the set, the bass player came across to Christina. She gave him a smile and he bent down to kiss her on the lips. Then, as the band members joked together, Gwen caught a glimpse of Mr. Moore heading their way, too far off for her to be able to see if he was smiling. Christina had noticed his arrival too, and reached out a hand. Gwen took it and was surprised how tightly Christina gripped. It clearly mattered as much to her as it did to them. They both kept their eyes on Moore as he advanced, ducking and diving through the jumbled knots of drinkers and dancers.

That night their lovemaking was powerful and largely silent. Afterward, Laurence looked at Gwen with so much appreciation in his eyes that she wondered how she could ever have imagined he might have still wanted Christina. When she tried to add up the small and large tokens of his love throughout the years — the jade necklace he'd given her for her birthday, the beautiful silk painting from India, and the dozens of small but thoughtful kindnesses — she saw the sum could never be totaled. Grateful for every single moment, she kissed him repeatedly.

"What's brought this on?"

"I'm a very lucky woman, that's all."

"The luck's all mine."

She smiled. "We're both very lucky," she said, then got up to go to the bathroom.

It had been a good night after all. Thank goodness the news had been positive, she thought as she ran the water to rinse her face. It turned out that Moore had managed to shift some of his other clients' advertising for December, and though the splash they would make might be a fraction reduced, it would still be enough, just. And they would repeat the whole show in February, sandwiching their competitor between the two promotions.

After turning off the tap, she dabbed herself dry, then heard the phone ring in their bedroom. The bathroom door was very slightly ajar so she knew that Laurence had already picked up.

"You know what I told you." He spoke in a low but audible voice. "Why is it so very important to talk now? I thought we'd reached an understanding."

There was silence while the other person was speaking, then Laurence was speaking again.

"My dear, you know I love you. Please don't cry. I care very much. But that's just not going to happen. Those days are over. I've already explained how it has to be."

Another short silence, though Gwen could hear her heart thumping in suspense.

"Very well, I'll see what I can do. Of course I love you. But you really must stop all this."

Gwen hugged herself.

"Yes, as soon as possible. I promise."

Gwen doubled over. She had been completely taken in by Christina.

32

On board the ship, Gwen had finally plucked up the courage to speak to Laurence about the phone call, but he had muttered something inconsequential about work and turned away. She desperately wanted him to admit that Christina was still obsessed with him and had felt bitterly hurt that he couldn't be honest, but a row at sea with no way to get away from each other was not a good idea. And then, when almost the first thing that happened after they got home was that Verity turned up smelling of tobacco, alcohol, and stale scent, everything else was swept aside.

The butler had opened the door to her and hadn't been able to prevent her stumbling into the sitting room where Laurence and Gwen were relaxing the day after their long journey ended. They'd already found out from McGregor that she'd flouted Laurence's instructions and had regularly arrived the worse for wear and stayed at the house for a night or two at a time. She had a key, after all, and by the time he, McGregor, had found out about it, she'd gone off again.

At the sight of his sister looking so unkempt, Laurence stood up. With his jaw working to control his distress, he asked what was going on. Verity collapsed into a chair and, her arms clasped round her knees and her head bent, she began to cry.

Gwen went to her and knelt beside the chair. "Tell us what the matter is."

"I can't," she groaned. "I've made such a mess of things."

Gwen held out a hand to comfort her, but Verity pushed it away.

"Is it Alexander? Maybe we can help."

"Nobody can help."

Laurence looked uncomfortable. "I don't understand. Why did you marry him if he doesn't make you happy? He's a decent chap."

She groaned again, this time with a note of real desolation. "It's not him . . . not him . . . you don't understand."

He frowned. "What then? What is wrong?"

"Please tell us, Verity," Gwen said. "How can we help if you don't say?"

Verity muttered something and began to

sob again. Gwen and Laurence exchanged worried looks. While Laurence continued to look uncertain, Gwen decided to take the lead and did her best to encourage her sister-in-law to speak. "Come on, darling, surely it can't be that bad?"

There was no reply in the long stretch of silence that followed.

Gwen stood up to look out of the window at the lake and in the silence thought about her sister-in-law. She'd lost her parents, true, but so had Fran, and they couldn't have been more different. Fran was full of life and ready to take on the world, but Verity was moody and very insecure. Now it seemed that whatever the indefinable thing had been, it was coming to a head. She twisted back when she heard Verity speak in a voice choked with emotion.

"What was that?" Laurence demanded. "What did you say about Hugh?"

Verity looked up and bit her lip. "I am really sorry."

She looked so pale Gwen felt sorry for her, but she hadn't heard Verity's words, and judging by the look on Laurence's face, he had. He marched over to her and pulled her up, holding both her arms.

"Say that again, Verity. Say it so that Gwen can hear."

He let go and Verity slumped back into the chair with her head in her hands. When she didn't speak, Laurence forced her up again.

"Say it. Say it," he growled, turning red in the face.

She looked at him for a moment, then with fluttering hand movements tried to hide her face.

"My God, you will say it or I will shake it out of you!"

"I'm sorry. I'm sorry."

Gwen took a step forward. "For what?"

Verity hung her head. "It's been driving me out of my mind. I can't forgive myself. I love him, you see. You have to believe that."

"I don't understand," Gwen said. "Is this about Savi Ravasinghe? Have you done something to him?"

Verity looked up sharply.

"What is it, Verity? You're scaring me."

"Tell her," Laurence ordered.

There was a pause, while Verity mumbled. "Louder."

"Very well," she said, raising her voice to a shout and emphasizing each word. "I did not take Hugh for his diphtheria vaccination!"

Gwen frowned. "Of course you did. Don't you remember? I had a terrible headache so

575

you went."

Verity shook her head. "You're not listening."

"But, Verity —"

"I did not take him. Don't you see? I did not take him! I did not."

As Verity began to sob, Gwen felt the blood drain from her face. "But you said you had," she said in a low voice.

"I went to Pru Bertram's and took Hugh along. There were some friends there. We had quite a lot to drink and I forgot."

Laurence let go of his sister and, with a push, drove her away, almost as if to prevent himself from striking her. Then he curled his hand into a fist and slammed it into the back of a sofa.

She clutched at his arm.

He pushed her away again. "Get off. I can't even bear to look at you."

"Please don't say that. Please, Laurence."

Gwen felt her breathing start to become rapid and shallow. Could it be true? The room seemed to blur, became featureless as the formless shapes of Laurence and his sister melted into their surroundings. She shook her head.

"Why didn't you say? He could have gone another time," Laurence was saying.

Verity began chewing her nails. "I was

scared. You'd have been cross with me. You'd both have been so cross."

Gwen stood motionless, choking with rage. In the stunned silence while nobody spoke, she knew she'd have to hold back or she would regret it. But even while the storm raged in her head she noticed a terrible look in Laurence's eyes.

"You're telling me my son nearly died because you got drunk?" he said in an icy voice.

He stared at his sister as she began to cry again.

"So rather than tell us the truth, you put Hugh's life at risk. You know how dangerous these diseases are."

"I know. I know. I thought he'd be all right. He was, wasn't he? I am sorry. I'm really sorry."

"Why are you telling us now?"

"I've never been able to get it out of my head. I haven't been able to sleep because of it. And then, when I looked at the sick native girl, it reminded me so much of when Hugh was sick . . . I couldn't bear it."

Gwen glared at her. "*You* couldn't bear it? You!? Have you any idea what it feels like to lose a child?"

Then, provoked beyond reason, she lost all effort at restraint and charged at her sister-in-law. With ragged, hopeless fists she started to pound on the girl's back. Verity doubled over, shielding her head with her arms. Gwen let her fists fall to her sides and began to heave silently until the loud gulping sobs finally erupted. Laurence instantly came to her side, and she allowed him to lead her away. As she sat down on the sofa and began rocking back and forth, he rang the bell for help.

Another thought now dominated Gwen's whole being. After a few moments, she glanced up. "My prescription, Verity, was it you who altered it?"

Suddenly Verity was shouting and crying at the same time. "You didn't belong here. It was my home. I didn't want you here."

Laurence froze, his face a picture of anguish. "You could have killed her," he said, his voice not much more than a whisper. And then Gwen screwed up her eyes and heard Laurence tell his sister to get out of the house, and never to expect another penny.

The second thing happened a week later, by which time they had already endured a trying seven days. It was almost the end of October now, and soon the rain would start. Laurence had spent long hours walking the dogs, returning very late, and Gwen resented his ability to escape the feeling of doom in the house. For her part, yes, she had wanted Verity gone, but not like this, and she was far too distraught to say *I told you so.* Despite her anger, she felt pity for her sister-in-law, and in all the turmoil and worry about what would happen to Verity now, she had not found it in her heart to confront Laurence again about the phone call she'd overheard in New York. She comforted herself with the knowledge that it would be some time before they saw Christina again.

Dr. Partridge stood at the window in the silent nursery, gazing out at the lake.

"It's a beautiful view," he said, and walked toward her where she sat in the chair beside the bed, holding Liyoni's hand and waiting for his diagnosis. She had called him the moment she noticed that Liyoni's posture had changed, but he'd been away from home and this was the first chance he'd had to call.

He lifted both Liyoni's arms and when he let go they seemed to flop. The same happened with her legs. He tested her knee and ankle reflexes. There was little or no response. He coughed, turned to face Gwen, then signaled that she should come to the

window. Gwen got up, glancing back at Liyoni, who was still staring at the ceiling.

"The news is not good," he said in a low
voice. "I'm afraid her condition is not what
I first thought."

Gwen looked out at the lake and attempted a smile that she didn't feel. "But
last time you were here, you said she would
be fine."

"This isn't a nutritional deficiency."

Her smile still hovered. "But she will get
better?"

"I believe this little girl may have a wasting disease. Does she sometimes find it hard
to catch her breath, or has she had any
respiratory infections?"

Gwen nodded.

"And you say her posture has worsened?"

Gwen bit her lip and couldn't speak.

"It's hard to be completely sure but I
think a degeneration in the spine is causing
withering of her muscles."

She covered her mouth with her hand.

"I'm sorry."

"But there is a treatment? You can still do
something?"

He shook his head. "If I am right, that
this is some kind of muscular atrophy, it
will probably only get worse. I'm afraid a

failure of the heart is the most likely prognosis."

Gwen, who had been holding her emotions tight inside, doubled over as if she had
been punched.

He held out a hand to help her, but she
didn't take it. If she allowed his sympathy,
everything she kept locked inside would
pour from her and she'd lose control. She
took a deep breath.

"Is there anything we can do for the poor
child?" she said, keeping her voice as level
as she could and gripping the back of a
chair for support. "Liyoni has no one, you
see. Just Naveena . . . and us."

"I will get a wheelchair sent down for her."

Gwen's lips parted as she shuddered.
"No!"

"If you want a second opinion . . ."

"She will still be able to swim, won't she?"

He smiled. "For a while. The natural
buoyancy of the water will reduce the pain
and the pressure on her spine and legs."

"But in the end?"

"I'll show the ayah how to massage her
legs." He made a small puckered movement
with his chin. "I'll leave you to it."

Gwen hesitated. "John, I just wondered, if
I'd been in a position to bring the child here
sooner —"

"Would this condition have been avoidable? Is that what you mean?"

She nodded, holding her breath during a short stretch of silence.

He shrugged. "It's hard to know. People are born with it. In adults it can be slow and chronic. We really don't know much about it. In one as young as this, the development tends to be rapid."

"So?"

"Well, in answer to your question, I doubt it would have made much difference."

As soon as he had gone, Gwen lay on the bed too. "It's all right," she said as she stroked Liyoni's hot forehead. "Everything will be all right."

The next morning, Naveena insisted Liyoni should remain in the nursery, where she could watch over her uninterrupted. The ayah was right. Gwen had other responsibilities to see to and could not be there every minute of the day.

Alone in her room, Gwen's thoughts returned to the night at the Stork Club. She couldn't help feeling New York had been a dream; a sleepless, brightly lit, and, apart from the phone call, wonderful dream. Whatever Christina had meant by that phone call in New York, at the moment

Gwen didn't care.

She glanced out of her bedroom window to look at the lake, hoping the stillness of the water might soothe her. Instead, against the pale water, she saw Laurence standing in silhouette, and it took a moment before she realized he was carrying Liyoni, with Hugh and the dogs following close behind. The sight of Laurence with the child provoked a depth of feeling in her that stripped her of fear. She grabbed her silk gown and, wrapping it round her, stepped out of her French doors and onto the verandah.

The air was teeming with birds and, together with the whine of mosquitoes, the noise was mounting. She stood for a moment, listening and watching the birds fly back and forth to their nests. A smudgy haze made the garden appear fuzzy, its colors running together like an impressionist painting. As an eagle flew across the horizon, she saw that it was a perfectly lovely day. She watched her little family as they reached the lake. Today it was silver in the middle and deepest green at the perimeter, with the reflections of the trees shading it in places.

Spew raced out of the water and ran up to Gwen, while Ginger ran around in circles chasing his tale. Gwen bent down to pat the dog, but he jumped up and rubbed against her, and every time she touched his nose, a pink tongue shot out and licked her hand. Her thin cotton skirt was damp from his wet fur and she'd acquired his doggy smell too.

Liyoni's arm was wrapped round Laurence's neck. After he had taken the last couple of steps to the border of the lake, he carefully unwrapped her. A fleet of cormorants took off as he laid her in the water, but for a moment nothing else happened. Gwen's heart almost stopped. The water wasn't deep at the edge, so the child was in no danger of drowning, but Gwen watched her absence of movement in dread.

Laurence stood at the ready, and Hugh had gone into the water on the other side of Liyoni, ready to help if anything went wrong. The child remained lifeless for a few seconds, then suddenly she turned over and began to flap her arms. After floundering for a moment longer, she seemed to find her equilibrium, and with a swift movement began to swim. As relief flooded through her, Gwen walked down the steps to the lake. Hearing her, Laurence glanced back.

"That was kind of you," she said with a smile, and felt overcome.

The look on his face puzzled her and his voice was gruff when he replied. "Partridge told me of her condition. I know you're fond of her. To be honest, I'm rather getting used to having her around too."

Gwen swallowed, unable to trust herself to speak. There was no reason to bring about this change in Laurence's attitude toward the child and, though pleased, she also felt confused. He came up and linked his arm with hers, and they both watched Liyoni's progress in the water.

"We mustn't let her swim too far," she said.

"Don't worry. At the slightest sign of a problem I'll be there. Once you've lost people you love it makes you realize how much family matters."

"Do you mind telling me what actually happened that day? To Caroline, I mean."

His voice was strained when he replied. "You already know."

"Yes. But I wondered . . . I'm sorry for asking, but you said it wasn't at the lake. I wondered where she drowned? You've never actually said."

"Because I hate the place. She slid into the pool at the bottom of the waterfall, holding Thomas in her arms. It would have been impossible for her to swim and hold a baby at the same time. Naveena witnessed it."

Gwen tried to imagine how Laurence

must have felt, but the sorrow was too dark and too nameless.

"Instinct told Naveena something was wrong. That's why she followed Caroline. If she hadn't, I don't suppose we'd ever have known exactly what happened. I sometimes wonder if it might have been better not to know."

Gwen thought about what he'd said, hesitating before she spoke. "Your mind might have invented things."

He nodded. "Perhaps you're right."

"Naveena wasn't able to stop her?"

Laurence looked at the ground and shook his head. "It all happened too quickly."

"Who found them? Was it Naveena?"

He placed a hand on his chest as he took a deep breath, then stared at her. For a moment he looked older. She hadn't noticed before the additional gray in his hair.

"I'm sorry. I shouldn't have asked. You don't have to tell me."

He looked down at her and, shading her own eyes from the sun, she gazed into his eyes.

"It isn't that . . ."

"What then?"

He shook his head. "Naveena came to fetch us. McGregor found Thomas, I found Caroline. The strange thing was she was

586

wearing her favorite dress. An oriental silk in vivid sea green. She was dressed as if for a party. It seemed like a statement."

Gwen's heart constricted at the thought of it, but she didn't speak, and for a while, neither did he. He seemed preoccupied. She felt he wanted to say more and waited.

"The rapids pulled them apart almost immediately. Thomas was found only twenty yards away, but already dead." Laurence wiped his forehead with the side of his hand. "Just before she left the house she had packed away all of his clothes in the trunk you found."

"I am so very sorry," Gwen said, and leaned against him.

Sorry in so many ways, she thought, and there was so much more she longed to say. She wanted to tell him the truth: wanted to tell him that when she'd overheard him on the phone she'd known it was Christina; wanted to, but did not. She concentrated on her breathing and kept it to herself. This was not the time.

On Sunday evening Hugh was packed off back to school, and early on Wednesday morning McGregor drove them both to Colombo to meet Fran. Once there, Laurence told Gwen to stay in the center as there had been one or two scuffles in the city's poorer outskirts.

She frowned. "I'm not frightened of a crowd."

"I mean it, Gwen. Just go to the store and come straight back to the hotel. No wandering in the bazaar."

While Laurence was busy arranging for the increased loads of tea to be shipped to the West Coast of America, where it would be packaged in a new facility Christina had organized, Gwen took care of some essential shopping. The last person she expected to see that evening was Verity, drenched in perfume and wheeling drunkenly onto the verandah at the Galle Face, waving a cigarette in the air.

"Darling, there you are," Verity said, giving her a twisted smile and slurring her words. "I heard you were coming, but I'm afraid you've missed your cousin. She left with her husband yesterday."

"What are you talking about?" Gwen said as she reluctantly walked over to her sister-in-law. "Fran doesn't have a husband."

"She does now," Verity said, and threw herself into a nearby chair. "Phew, I'm out of puff!"

An air of disorder hung about Verity: her thin brown hair, plastered to her skull, looked like it needed a good wash, and her clothes were crumpled.

Gwen stretched out a hand. "Get up. I'm taking you to your room. People are looking. You can't stay down here in this state."

"Haven't got a room."

"In that case, where did you spend last night?"

"This chap I met. Quite nice really. Had blue eyes." She paused, deliberately it seemed, for dramatic effect. "Or maybe they were brown."

Gwen bristled, as she knew Verity had intended she should. There wasn't a hint of contrition about her, and she was behaving as if the terrible scene at home had never happened.

"I don't give a fig about some chap, whatever the color of his eyes," Gwen said. "You're coming up to our room, right now."

She managed to maneuver Verity to the left-hand stairs without too much fuss, but when they were halfway up, the girl stopped and stood still.

"Come on," Gwen said, and gave her a push. "We're not there yet."

Verity, standing on the next step up, looked down at Gwen and prodded her in the chest. "You think you're so smart."

Gwen glanced at her watch and sighed. "I

don't think I'm smart at all. Now hurry up, I want you to sober up before Laurence gets back. You know very well he has refused to see you, and getting yourself in this state won't help him change his mind. About a gallon of coffee should do it."

"Nope. You need to listen to me first."

As they eyed one another, Gwen's spirits plummeted. This wasn't going to be easy. She was itching to see Fran, but first, after an afternoon in Colombo, with her hair and clothes full of dust, she needed a hot bath. As she thought of her cousin, she wondered if Verity could have been telling the truth. If so she really might know who Fran had married without whispering a word.

"So, are you listening?" Verity said, interrupting her thoughts and arching her brows.

Too close, Gwen smelled Verity's bad breath and sighed, unable to keep the sarcasm from her voice. "Out with it then. What startling revelation have you got for me?"

"You won't be laughing in a minute." Verity took a step and wobbled.

"Come on, let's get you upstairs double quick. Come on. Chop chop, before you fall down the stairs."

Verity stared at Gwen and muttered something.

"You are about as clear as mud. What is it?" Gwen said.

"I know." Her eyes narrowed as she smiled.

"Verity, this is becoming tedious. You've already told me about Fran. Now come on, before I lose patience."

Gwen attempted to push her up the stairs, but Verity nodded her head very slowly and, staring back with a look of intense determination, clutched the handrail and held her ground.

"I know that Liyoni is your daughter."

In the silence, Gwen stood absolutely still. Her mind seemed unnaturally clear. It was her body's reaction that was letting her down. The burst of heat, when it came, left her with bees buzzing in her head. She suddenly knew what it felt like to be consumed by the desire to kill. With just two little steps, and one little push, Verity would be gone. A drunken fall, a terrible accident. That was what the papers would say. As the strength of her feelings consumed her, she reached out a hand. Just a couple of steps up and one little push. Then the thought vanished as quickly as it had risen.

"That's shut you up, hasn't it?" Verity said, and began to climb the steps.

Gwen, now short of breath, tried to inhale,

but with the shock squeezing the air out of her, she'd forgotten how to breathe. She clung to the banister, opening and closing her mouth in panic. It flashed into her mind that, gasping as she was, she must look like a dying fish. The ridiculous image seemed to prompt her lungs to remember what to do and she managed to regain control.

She followed Verity to the landing, took a step forward, and pointed out their door, not trusting herself to speak. Verity barged past, her gait uneven, then sprawled in an armchair in the room, staring morosely at the patterned parquet floor. She glanced at Gwen, who was distracting herself by folding and unfolding Laurence's shirts in an attempt to stop her heart banging against her ribs.

"You've folded that one three times. I said you wouldn't be laughing."

"What?"

"I heard you talking to Naveena. Just before you brought the chee-chee mongrel child to live in Laurence's house."

"You must have misheard. Now I've called for some coffee and you're going to drink it and stop this silly nonsense."

Verity shook her head, dipped into her bag, pulled out a sheaf of charcoal drawings, and waved them in the air. "It was actually these that told me all I needed to know."

Gwen's heart jolted, and, conscious that her voice would shake and give away how frightened she was, she ran over and tried to tug Liyoni's drawings from Verity's hand.

"Oh no," Verity said, and pulled away. "I'm hanging on to these."

One ripped and Gwen bent to pick up the fragment, giving her a few seconds to compose herself before she stood and faced Verity again. "How dare you go through my private things! In any case, I don't know what you think you've found."

Verity laughed. "I read this fascinating article about a woman in the West Indies who had given birth to twins of different colors. She had slept with her husband, of course, but also with the master. I think Laurence would be interested. Don't you?"

There was a long stretch of silence, during which Gwen could hardly believe what she was feeling. Anger, yes, and fear too, but there was something else. A terrifying hollowed-out feeling she'd never quite felt before. From the drawings Verity would have seen that Liyoni had been learning to write in the tiny village school — and that on the last couple of drawings she had written about a white lady her foster mother had told her about. A white lady who, one day, might come for her. Naveena had translated it for her, but Gwen knew that Verity was able to understand Sinhala.

"If he asks Naveena outright, she will tell him, you know," Verity said.

"I've had enough of this," Gwen said, more to herself than Verity, and opened the window. She tried to calm her racing pulse by looking down at the long stretch of lawn that extended from the hotel, the road that passed through it, and the wisps of plants that grew in cracks in the sea wall. But when she heard the sound of children laughing as they flew a kite, it brought tears to her eyes.

There was a knock at the door.

"There's the coffee. Will you be mother?" Verity said. "It does seem rather apt, and I am just too tired to move."

When the waiter had left, Gwen poured the coffee.

Verity sipped hers. "I have a proposal for you. A way out, if you like."

Gwen shook her head.

"If you promise to get my allowance reinstated, I won't tell Laurence."

"That is blackmail."

Verity inclined her head. "Up to you."

Gwen sat down and scratched around for some kind of response that would put a stop to this. She gulped the scalding coffee and burned her lips.

"Now, changing the subject, wouldn't you like to know who Fran has married? I take it you don't already know?"

"If this is another of your hurtful lies . . ."

"No word of a lie. I saw them together, and when she saw I'd clocked the rings on her finger, what could she say? A massive diamond, the engagement ring, surrounded by sapphires, but also a telltale band of gold. The man had one too, though he tried to keep his hands behind his back."

Gwen folded her arms and leaned back, wondering what was coming next. "So who is he?"

Verity smiled. "Savi Ravasinghe."

Gwen watched the sunlight flickering on Verity's face and struggled to suppress her desire to throttle the woman.

Verity laughed. "The father of your brat — because he is the father, isn't he, Gwen? He must be. You don't know any other men of color. Apart from the servants, of course, and I don't think even you would stoop that low. You may have everyone fooled, Gwen, but I see through you."

Gwen felt like howling, and the only clear words she could hear in her head were: *Please, please — don't tell Laurence.*

"Florence said she saw you going up the stairs with Savi at the ball, and you went to see him on your own when Fran was ill. He now co-owns Fran's share in the plantation. Laurence won't be too happy about that, and if I tell him about your daughter too, well — I'm sure he'll let me come home."

Gwen stood up. "Very well. I'll have a word with him about your allowance."

"So it is true? Liyoni is your daughter."

"I did not say that. You're twisting my words. I just want to help you."

She knew her voice had sounded artificial, and it was confirmed when Verity threw back her head and roared with laughter.

"You are too transparent, Gwen. I didn't really overhear you and Naveena. One day the child was sitting near you, the sun lit your faces in a particular way, and I saw. She has your bone structure, Gwen. Then I noticed her hair. Normally it's tied up or plaited, but she'd been in the water and it had dried in ringlets, just like yours."

Gwen tried to interrupt.

"Hear me out. After that I watched you together and your feelings for her became obvious. I searched your room one day when you were in New York, and I found the box and the key. Now why would you hide the drawings of a native child, Gwen?

Why would you treasure them? Keep them under lock and key?"

Gwen felt the blood flood into her face as she bent down to pick up a piece of fluff from the floor.

"I felt sure when I found the drawings, but in any case your response now has told me all I needed to know. It was Savi Ravasinghe, wasn't it? He's the mongrel girl's father. Wonder what your cousin will make of that!"

When Gwen stood, she tucked a stray ringlet behind her ear and tried to keep her voice steady. "I don't understand why you want to hurt me so. Don't you even care how much you're going to hurt your brother?"

Silence.

"Well?"

"I care about Laurence."

Gwen feared she might not be able to hold herself together. "So why are you doing this?"

"I need my allowance."

"But why? You have a husband."

Verity closed her eyes briefly as she took a sharp breath in. "I don't want to end up like you."

"What do you mean?"

"Forget it. Just make sure you speak to

my brother."

"And if I don't, you're prepared to ruin our lives?"

Verity raised her brows. "I shall expect to see my allowance coming into my account on a monthly basis, starting next month. If not, Laurence shall know everything."

"You know very well that until the brand succeeds, Laurence won't be in a position to do that."

"In that case, I think you have something of a dilemma to resolve."

"I know you were stealing from the household budget. What do you think Laurence will make of that? I knew when I was ill. Supplies disappeared from the cupboard and then suddenly reappeared. You had the key while I was sick, and before I arrived. It could only have been you."

"It was good while it lasted. The *appu* and I sold stuff and shared the profits. What a joke when we saw you trying to make sense of the accounts! But you'd have a hard time proving it. I'll tell Laurence I was just borrowing, and anyway, when I tell him about your brat, do you think he'll care?"

"Tell me why you need money so badly. What about Alexander?"

Verity's face closed up. "I've already said. That is not an option."

"I could try to persuade Laurence to let you live with us again."

She looked at Verity, but her sister-in-law had fallen asleep.

Gwen knew she had to get Verity out of the hotel before Laurence arrived, and felt as if she was living on a boundary somewhere between her real life and a nightmare she had inadvertently stumbled into. She clung to the hope that Verity's threat was empty and only the result of a drunken excess, but in her heart she suspected her sister-in-law was capable of almost anything.

In order to keep an eye out for Laurence, Gwen paraded back and forth in front of the window, watching the clock and smoking several of Verity's vile cigarettes, which only intensified the nausea that was rising in her. Suffocated by fear, she longed to cry for the release it would bring but forced herself to suppress her tears, along with any hope that this would end well. Gwen didn't know if she really believed the story about Fran's marriage, but if it was true, her cousin was no longer the one person in the world she wanted to talk to.

33

By the time Laurence arrived back at the Galle Face, Verity had gone and Fran still had not turned up. Gwen passed a restless night listening to the ocean and going over what Verity had said until, just before dawn, she fell asleep for an hour or so.

Later, when they left without Fran, Gwen was relieved to curl up in the back of the car, while McGregor and Laurence talked business in the front. Laurence had been annoyed that they'd had no word from Fran but, knowing what a free spirit she was, didn't want to waste more time waiting. Gwen had not mentioned seeing Verity, nor her news about Fran's supposed marriage. She just wanted to sleep, if only to forget, but about a mile or so away from the hotel, some kind of commotion stopped the traffic. Rickshaw riders were managing to squeeze past, but the cars were at a standstill.

"What the devil . . . ?" McGregor said as he pulled up then wound down the driver's window.

The sound of shouts and whistles met them, as well as the usual smells and noises of the streets. It didn't seem much. Just a few people chanting. The shops were still open and pedestrians were still shopping.

"Can you see anything?" Gwen asked.

He shook his head.

But when Laurence opened the door on the passenger side, the noise hit them with full force.

"It's more than I thought. There seems to be some kind of demonstration. I'll get out and take a look. Nick, you stay in the car. You might get an opportunity to move it."

"Oh, Laurence," Gwen said. "After what you said! What if there's trouble?"

He shrugged. "I'll be fine."

While he was gone, they waited. She felt stifled, stuck inside a hot car with so much going on in her head, and asked McGregor to unlock the door so that she could look for Laurence. McGregor refused, the tapping of his fingers on the steering wheel only increasing her feeling of claustrophobia. As the level of noise intensified, Gwen heard the thump of drums coming from somewhere behind the car. She twisted back to look and saw another group of people shouting some kind of slogan as they marched along the road toward the car. When she glanced out of the front window again in the hope of seeing Laurence, she saw that the first group had turned and were also streaming toward the car, brandishing sticks. Shocked to see shrieking schoolchildren, dressed in white, swarming behind the mob, she shrank back in her seat, realizing their car was now hemmed in between the two groups.

"Make sure your window is wound up," McGregor said as a man thumped on the bonnet of the car and laughed. "Quickly. This isn't against us, I don't think, but you don't want to get caught in the crossfire."

"What about Laurence?"

"He'll be all right."

Now properly trapped in the car, they could only watch as the two groups faced each other just behind them. At the sound of breaking glass, Gwen looked through the back window.

"My God, they are throwing bottles. I hope they get the children out of the way."

Stones and lumps of concrete started to fly through the air. A couple of women screamed and there was the sound of a loudspeaker. A flare went up, and then another, followed by the sound of shopkeepers rolling down their shutters and people calling to each other as they fled into alleys and side streets. Smoke filled the air as somebody lit a bonfire in the street.

Gwen felt her neck and shoulders knotting up. "I'm frightened for Laurence."

"If he has any sense he'll have taken cover."

As she attempted to look for Laurence through the crowded street, three men ran up and leaned on one side of the car, rocking it with their weight.

Gwen could hardly speak, her fear almost choking her. "McGregor!"

"I'll fucking kill the bastards! They're trying to overturn us."

Shocked by his language, Gwen saw McGregor take out his gun and point it at them. It was enough. One of the men pulled the other two away and they joined the mob as it slowly shifted farther and farther behind them. At last the street ahead of them had cleared a little and McGregor was able to edge the car forward. A few people cowered on the pavement, some with cuts and bruises, but the situation behind them was growing uglier.

"Where are the police, for heaven's sake?" Gwen said.

She searched the street for Laurence, but it was only when they'd almost reached the school where it had all begun that she spotted him standing in a doorway with a woman who looked as if she'd been hurt. When they got nearer Gwen saw blood dripping from a cut on her forehead. She opened the window and signaled frantically. Laurence started toward them, guiding the woman by the elbow. By now, police on horseback had arrived and were threatening the mob with truncheons. Gwen breathed a sigh of relief to see the children being herded back inside the school.

As Laurence helped the woman into the back of the car, where she sat with her head in her hands, a shot rang out.

"Get us out of here, Nick," Laurence said. "Gwen, have you got anything to mop up the blood?"

Gwen squeezed the woman's hand. "I've got this," she said, and began dabbing with her shawl.

The woman groaned, then glanced up at her. "I am a teacher. It was supposed to be peaceful."

Laurence told McGregor to drive to the hospital, then spoke to Gwen. "It's about which language should dominate in the classroom."

"Really?"

"The educated Tamils have traditionally had the best government jobs and the Sinhalese think it's unfair. They want Sinhala to be the dominant language."

Gwen felt so upset, she couldn't hide it. First Verity and now this. "Why?" she asked. "Why the violence? Does it matter so much?"

The Sinhalese teacher looked at her. "When we have independence, which language is taught will matter very much."

"Can't they both be taught?"

The woman shook her head.

"Well, whichever it is, I hope it can happen without more bloodshed."

The woman snorted. "This is nothing. Someone like you who has never had to fight for anything can have no idea."

When they arrived home, Laurence said that in the wake of the riot he had letters to attend to and, so as not to disturb Gwen, he told her he would sleep in his own room. After a night during which Verity's threat left her with intense, disturbing dreams, Gwen sat at her dressing table gazing at her reflection. With her hair uncombed and no lipstick or rouge, she looked pale. She gripped her hairbrush and brushed furiously, then dabbed some rouge on her cheeks. Her dark hair stood out like a mane and the rouge looked startling against the pallor of her skin. She rubbed it off and braided her hair, then kept rubbing and rubbing her cheeks, as if by doing so she could rub away the fear. The woman was wrong. She might not have had to fight for a privileged existence, but she'd had to fight to protect it, and now that Verity knew the truth about Liyoni, she faced the gravest challenge of her life.

She took out the box where Liyoni's drawings had been hidden and, sure enough, when she looked for the key that she kept separately, it wasn't there. She rattled the box. There was nothing inside. She fumbled in each of her drawers, picking out the private contents, then dropping them, until the floor was strewn with pins, combs, and letters. She searched her desk, her bedside tables, and then her various handbags. Not that it really mattered now, but Verity had kept the key. Blinking away tears, Gwen gripped the arms of her chair and felt so invaded she wished that she had pushed Verity down the stairs.

The next day Fran called. Deeply apologetic for not coming back with them, and saying she was in Hatton and would be with them very soon, she did little to actually explain, other than to say there had been a hitch. Typical Fran, Gwen thought. Her cousin had also said that she had a big surprise for them, and Gwen prayed it wasn't that she was bringing Savi Ravasinghe with her.

While Laurence was downstairs immersed in his newspaper, reading about the riot, Gwen tiptoed into his dark bedroom. It smelled of him, soapy and lemony. She switched on the light and felt sad as she glanced round to see if the photograph of Caroline was still on the table. It was not, but Gwen still had the sense of Caroline being around, as if she had gone offstage and missed her cue to come back on.

She opened Laurence's large mahogany wardrobe and felt the row of clothes hanging inside. Trousers, jackets, evening dress, shirts. She picked one of his starched white shirts and pulled it out. Nothing of him remained on it, so she opened a drawer instead and found a blue silk scarf still with his hairs on it. She sniffed. That was better. If she was going to be forced to tell Laurence the truth, she wanted something of his to hold on to at night.

The light flickered and went out. She pocketed the scarf, found her way to the door by the light coming in from the hall, and slid her palm along the polished banister rail as she ran down. As she reached the bend in the stairs, she couldn't avoid seeing Liyoni's wheelchair in the hall. It had been received with such a mixture of disbelief and guilt that, since then, she hadn't gone near it. She couldn't stand the thought of the child's young body being crippled by illness, and still prayed for a miracle.

Restless, Gwen felt unable to remain in one place but went to join Laurence. Everything had become so confusing. Part of her longed to see Fran, but so far she didn't even know if it was true about the painter and her cousin. She picked up a magazine from the coffee table. It was the weekend and Laurence was still immersed in the paper, oblivious to Hugh getting under their feet.

Gwen prickled with irritation. "Laurence, can't you take Hugh off to make a model aeroplane or something?"

He glanced up and tapped his newspaper. "It became a mob, you know, in Colombo. People were killed. Hope it's not the start of things to come."

She closed her eyes at the memory of the scene in Colombo. It had been awful, but right now she had other concerns.

"On a lighter note, we'll soon be seeing our tea advertised in here."

"The aeroplane, Laurence. Must it always be me who notices? Hugh is bored. Can't you see?"

Hugh had three Hubley cast-iron planes, but while they'd been in New York, Laurence had bought one of the new die-cast toy planes and one in pressed steel. She knew he and Hugh were trying to copy them in balsa, a strong but easy-to-shape wood.

Laurence folded his paper. "You seem rather nervy, Gwen. Is anything wrong? If it's the riot —"

"No," she snapped. "Nothing that you getting Hugh out from under my feet won't fix. I'm just excited to be seeing Fran again."

He looked at her and nodded, but she could see he didn't believe her. "Very well," he said. "If you're sure. Come on, Hugh. Boot room for us, old chap."

She managed a half smile.

After he'd gone, she continued to pick up one magazine after another but couldn't focus on the words. At a loss, and with time hanging heavily, Gwen decided to examine the wheelchair. The longer she left it, the more dreadful the ghost it seemed to represent. She went out to the hall again, then stroked the leather arms, touched the head-rest, and tried out the metal braking system.

The thought of what Laurence would say if Fran really had married Savi Ravasinghe sent the tension that had knotted in her shoulders during the riot to travel to her temples. She rotated her neck in an attempt to ease it but felt as if she was sitting on a volcano that at any moment would go off, leaving the wreckage of her family in its wake.

Her thoughts were interrupted by the doorbell and, as she was already in the hall, she opened the door and found Fran standing on the step holding a small case. She wore a wonderful batwing coat, made up in a kind of tapestry fabric, and a ruby-red hat, but with no gloves. Gwen looked at her ring finger. A diamond surrounded by sapphires and a narrow band of gold. Verity had been telling the truth.

Gwen couldn't pretend surprise and glanced up at her cousin, seeing straight away that Fran's face was subtly changed. She looked softer somehow, as if love had blunted the edges.

Fran's smile faltered. "The bitch told you, didn't she?"

Gwen nodded.

"I asked her not to. I wanted to tell you

myself."

Gwen put her head on one side and scrutinized Fran's face. "And of course there are no such things as letters or telephones or telegraph wires!"

"Sorry."

"Look, Fran, I'm only confused why you didn't tell me before you got married."

"I felt sure you'd disapprove. I couldn't have borne to hear that in your voice when I was so frightfully happy."

Gwen opened her arms. "Come here."

After they had hugged, Gwen held her cousin at arm's length. "You are happy?"

"Blissfully."

"And you don't mind about —" She hesitated, not sure what she really wanted to say. "You don't mind about —"

"His checkered past? Of course I don't. This is the modern age, remember. In any case, I've had my fair share of experience, and you can wipe that shocked look off your face, Gwendolyn Hooper. We are well matched, Savi and I."

Gwen laughed. "Oh, Fran, I have missed you so much." She looked round. "Where is he anyway?"

"He's in Nuwara. I wanted to see how the land lay with Laurence."

There was a pause.

"And you're not worried that Savi might be attracted to other sitters?"

"Not at all. We've both had colorful pasts but now we just want to be together."

"Does Christina know?"

Fran laughed. "Christina doesn't want Savi."

"I know. She has a musician in tow now, but it was Laurence she really wanted. You know she has bought into the business too?"

"Yes, I saw her in New York, during Savi's exhibition."

"Christina didn't say."

"I asked her not to. I wanted to tell you about Savi myself."

They carried along the corridor to the room at the end, where Gwen flung open the door.

Fran threw her tapestry coat on the bed and looked round. "Fresh freesias. Mmm! And it has windows on two sides. How lovely."

"You can see the lake and the garden." Gwen paused, went to the chest of drawers, and took something out, then held out her hand.

Fran grinned, took the bracelet, and fastened it round her wrist. "You absolute darling, I could kiss you. Where did you find it? At the back of the sofa, no doubt."

Gwen raised her brows and shrugged. "In a shop in Colombo, believe it or not. I can't prove it but I suspect Verity took it."

"But why?"

"I don't know. To cause trouble perhaps. Who knows why Verity does anything?"

"Well, never mind. I am just so happy to have it back. Thank you. Thank you. But why didn't you go to Savi's exhibition?"

"I had a headache. In the end Laurence stayed with me."

"Savi thinks you've been avoiding him. Did he do something to upset you, Gwennie?"

Gwen swallowed and walked over to lean out of the window but didn't reply.

The following morning, a large brown parcel arrived for Laurence and now sat on the hall table, next to the ornamental ferns, waiting for his attention. Gwen thought he might not even have seen it, so she picked it up and examined what looked like English postal stamps, though they had been so heavily rubber-stamped in Colombo, and wherever else it had passed through, she couldn't be sure. Curious, she carried it to their sitting room and handed it to Laurence.

He got up from his chair, took the parcel

with a nod, and turned toward the door.

"What is it, Laurence? It's quite heavy."

He glanced back but carried on walking. "I haven't opened it yet."

"But do you know who it might be from?"

"No idea."

"Why not open it now?"

He coughed. "Gwen, I am busy. I have business to attend to in my study. It's probably something to do with tea."

Perhaps it was his curt tone of voice, but suddenly she could not bear it. "Why didn't you tell me Christina was still in love with you?"

He frowned, one hand on the door handle. It was just a moment of silence but it felt longer.

"Gwen, my love, I've told you many times. Christina and I are long over."

She chewed her cheek as he left the room, then looked out at the lake. She had wanted more reassurance than that.

Fran had gone for a long walk and didn't appear for lunch, so after Hugh went for his rest, Gwen decided it was time to tell Laurence about Fran's marriage to Savi Ravasinghe. He'd spent all morning enclosed in his study and the night before he had been out, so this was her first opportunity. She was surprised when he took the news in a better spirit than she'd expected, though he seemed preoccupied and she wondered if something else was bothering him.

It didn't matter if Savi was not a welcome guest at their home; in fact, Gwen preferred it to stay that way. Fran said that the bright airy flat he owned in Cinnamon Gardens, in Colombo, was where she had stayed during her first trip to Ceylon in 1925. Since then, their affair had been on and off, during which time both had continued to see other people. Though she would have loved Fran to be living in Ceylon, Gwen couldn't help feeling it would be better all round if they were as far away as possible.

She was lying on her bed thinking about it, when Naveena wheeled Liyoni through. It had become a habit for Naveena to bring Liyoni to her while the household was at rest. She lifted the child from the chair and placed her beside Gwen on the bed, then left the room. It was the one precious hour a day that they had alone together, and Gwen treasured it.

She began by reading Liyoni a story. She was working her way through all the fairy tales they had in the house; though Liyoni didn't speak much, she understood a great deal, and when Gwen picked up the book of Andersen's tales that Verity had once suggested for Hugh, Liyoni asked her to put it down.

"I like you speaking the story, Lady."

"Once upon a time," she said as she cast around in her mind for today's tale, "there was a wicked stepmother."

The child giggled and snuggled closer. Gwen brushed the hair from her daughter's face and gazed at her. She swallowed hard and carried on.

Gwen usually locked the door and made sure that she didn't fall asleep. Today she was so tired from the strain of worrying about Verity's threat that she hadn't remembered. She was thinking of getting up to do it when Liyoni fell asleep, and then she drifted too.

She woke to hear a knock on her door and, before she was able to answer, Fran had come in. She stopped just inside the door and stared in surprise.

Gwen stared back.

"Gwennie, is that the ayah's sick relative in bed with you?"

Her cousin's voice sounded awkward, and Gwen, struggling with her feelings, felt her eyes moisten but couldn't speak. She was unable to lie to Fran.

Fran came across and, with a puzzled

expression, gazed down at the little girl. "She's very beautiful."

Gwen nodded.

Fran sat on the side of the bed and leaned sideways to look in Gwen's face. "What's going on, darling? Why won't you tell me what the matter is?"

A lump came in Gwen's throat and she lowered her head, staring at the satin bedcover until it blurred.

"Is it really so awful?"

There was a stretch of silence that went on too long.

"I will tell you," Gwen eventually said as she looked up and brought her knees up to her chest. "But you must promise not to say a word, not to anyone."

Fran nodded.

"Liyoni is not a relative of the ayah."

For a moment more Gwen struggled with her thoughts, until the urge to unburden herself took over and the words came rushing out.

"She is my daughter."

Fran gazed at her. "When I saw how beautiful she was, I think I had an inkling. But, Gwen, who is the father? It can't be Laurence."

Gwen shook her head. "No, but she is Hugh's twin."

"Darling?"

Gwen felt a lump come in her throat.

"I don't understand," Fran said.

"I can't tell you any more. I would have before, but not now that you're . . ."

There was a moment's ghastly silence.

Then, with an appalled expression on her face, Fran's eyes widened. "Oh dear God. It's not Savi? Surely that isn't what you're concealing?"

Gwen bit her lip and saw the color drain from Fran's face as she rubbed her forehead in shock.

"I can't believe you slept with Savi."

They stared at each other and, when Gwen saw the judgment in Fran's eyes, her voice shook. "It isn't what you think."

"Does Savi know about the child?"

"Of course not. But please, Fran, it was before you two got together."

Fran shook her head in disbelief. "But what about Laurence? How could you do that to him?"

Gwen's eyes grew hot with tears. "I wish I hadn't said anything. I know it sounds ridiculous, but I don't know how it happened. I just can't remember."

Fran frowned and paced around the room, rubbing her wrists. There was a long pause during which neither spoke.

"Fran? I know you're angry, but please say something."

"I just can't believe it."

"I can't remember anything about it." Gwen hung her head for a moment, then glanced at Fran as she spoke. "It was at that first ball after we danced the Charleston. I was terribly drunk. Savi helped me upstairs and I remember he stayed for a while, but what he did to me after that I don't remember."

Fran's hand flew to her chest and she froze on the spot, her face rigid. "Jesus, Gwen! Do you realize what you're accusing him of?"

"I'm sorry."

The skin bunched round Fran's eyes and her face reddened as she headed for the door. "You're wrong. Completely wrong. Savi would never do a thing like that."

Gwen reached out a hand. "Don't go. Please don't go."

"How can I stay? He's my husband. How could you?!"

"I need you."

Fran shook her head but remained standing by the door.

"I don't even know if it's possible for there to be two fathers," Gwen said.

There was a long stretch of silence.

"It is possible," Fran said in a small, tight voice.

"How do you know?"

"I read something about it."

Gwen gazed at her.

"It was a case where a woman had twins, by two different fathers, somewhere in the West Indies or Africa. It was in all the newspapers."

Tears began to slide down Gwen's cheeks.

"Didn't you talk to Savi?" Fran said. "At the time, I mean. Didn't you want to know exactly what had happened?"

Gwen wiped her eyes and sniffed. "I didn't think anything *had* happened, at the time. It was only when the twins were born and I saw that Liyoni wasn't white. I had to decide what to do about Liyoni immediately. How could I confront Savi about it, so long afterward?"

"I would have."

"I'm not you."

"And so all these years you've assumed such a terrible thing about a decent man, when there has to be another explanation?"

"I had hidden the child away. What difference would it have made? In fact, it might have made things worse. If I had spoken to Savi he might have told Christina, and before long Laurence would have known too."

"It would have settled your mind."

"Anyway, even if I had confronted him, he could have lied about it."

Fran's face twisted in anger. "So now he's a liar too?"

Gwen shivered and bowed her head for a moment. "I'm so sorry."

As Fran rubbed her hands together and took a few steps toward Gwen, her eyes were moist. "Look, I know Savi. Sleeping with a drunk or senseless woman is not him. He may have had affairs, but he has morals."

Gwen opened her mouth to speak.

Fran held up a hand. "Hear me out. I know his morals may not be the same as yours, but he has them. In any case, I spent half that night talking to him, the night of the ball, Gwennie, after you'd gone to sleep. Do you really think he would have done that to you and then spent time with me? No. Believe me, it can't have been Savi. He's sensitive to women, that's why we like him."

"So what then?"

"So if we discount Savi — and we must, Gwen, we really must — how did this actually happen?"

Liyoni coughed and Gwen put a finger to

her lips. "Don't wake her."

Fran continued speaking in a whisper. "There has to have been some color in the bloodline. It's the only answer."

Gwen felt her heart lift and gave a shaky laugh. "Do you really think so? Is it possible?"

"Yes."

Gwen thought about it for a moment. "I did find an article in a magazine in New York, all about the interbreeding between black slaves and white plantation owners in America."

"Well, it can skip a generation or two. People don't like to admit it. The British try to pass it off as continental ancestry or they hide the person away."

Gwen gave her cousin a weak smile. "Oh, Fran, I hope you're right. But surely I'd have heard something about it if it were true?"

"Maybe, maybe not . . . but I do wish you'd confided in me sooner, or told somebody."

"Everyone would have assumed an affair, just like you did at first. People would never have accepted the child."

"I jumped to the wrong conclusion. I'm sorry."

"Exactly, and so would everyone. It would

destroy Laurence if he believed I'd slept with another man, especially so soon after we married."

"Nevertheless, something in the blood has to be the answer. We both know there is nothing in *our* family to explain this."

Gwen sighed. "Do we?"

Fran put her head on one side and a thoughtful look came into her eyes. "When I go back to England, I'll do all I can to find out."

Gwen checked her cousin's face for doubt. "But you still believe it has come from Laurence's side?"

"I don't know. What I think is that you have to talk to him."

"I can't. Not without evidence. I've already said that he'd believe I'd had an affair. He'd never forgive me."

"You don't have much faith in his love for you, do you?"

Gwen thought about it. "He loves me. It's just the way things are here. The shame. The disgrace. It would be the end of us as a family. I'd lose him, I'd lose my home and I'd lose my son."

She swallowed hard and Fran leaned over to hug her.

"There's something else."

"Take your time."

She gulped and fought back tears. "Verity has guessed and is threatening to tell Laurence if I don't persuade him to reinstate her allowance."

"Good God, that's blackmail. She'll have you where she has always wanted you. If you give in, there will be more demands. It won't stop, Gwennie. You'll live in fear of the wretched woman for the rest of your life." Fran got up and threw open the window. "Lord, I need air."

"Has it started raining?"

"It's blowy. But you've been cooped up inside for too long. You're terribly pale. We both need fresh air. Forget about it for now. Let's do something. A walk. You, me, Hugh, and his sister in her chair. I take it Hugh and Liyoni have no idea?"

The little girl began to cough again, this time waking up, and as Gwen murmured to her and felt her forehead, she thought about what Fran had said. Her cousin was right: the only thing she could possibly do was to talk to Laurence before Verity did. But without proof to back up the idea, the thought of doing it made her head spin.

A few days later, just as they were finishing breakfast, the first package of tea arrived. Laurence unwrapped the parcel, then held it up for them to see. It looked even more stunning on the packet than it had at the design stage.

"I think your husband's artwork has transferred well to the packet," he said, looking at Fran. "I hope we might see him here for supper in due course."

Gwen and Fran exchanged surprised looks.

"Thank you, Laurence," Fran said. "I really appreciate that. I know —"

Laurence held up his hand. "I shall be happy to welcome Mr. Ravasinghe to our home. I'm sorry we missed his exhibition in New York. We shall make every effort to attend the next, wherever it is, won't we, Gwen?"

She managed to smile but felt confused. Why had his attitude toward Savi changed so unexpectedly, especially as he still seemed so subdued?

After breakfast Laurence suggested a walk, while the rain held off. "I'll meet you at the front of the house," he said to Gwen.

First Gwen prepared herself, then went to the nursery and found Liyoni sitting up in bed, drawing a waterfall.

"She cannot draw for long," Naveena said. "But she did stand up for ten minutes to look at the lake."

"That's good. Can you help me put her in the chair? She needs fresh air before it rains."

"She is wanting to see the waterfall."

Ever since Hugh had mentioned the waterfall, Liyoni had been pestering to see it.

"I'm afraid that is out of the question."

Once Liyoni was in the chair with a blanket tucked round her legs, Gwen got ready to wheel her out. At the sound of a car leaving she glanced through the window and her heart jumped. Verity. She must have arrived earlier on and had come to carry through her threat. Gwen kept watching and saw Laurence pacing back and forth in front of the porch, raking his fingers through his hair. She felt her palms begin to sweat, but then an odd sensation swept through her and she realized it was actually a feeling of relief. If it was all over, there would be no more lies.

Laurence frowned when he saw her coming and he spoke stiffly. "Leave the child here in the porch. Naveena can take her back in. We'll walk up the hill."

All the way up, he didn't speak. When they reached the top and turned to look back, the view took her breath away, just as it had done on her first morning at the plantation and every other time since. Everything glittered. She inhaled the scented air and gazed at the luminous green of the plantation hills, now extending even further than they had before. She took in the L shape of the house, the back of it parallel with the lake, with the outdoor room on the right and, on the other side, the courtyard and the path that disappeared into the wall of tall trees.

"Was that Verity I saw?" she eventually said.

He didn't speak, just nodded.

"What did she want?"

"Her allowance, of course."

"Laurence, I —"

"If you don't mind," he interrupted, "I'd rather not talk about my sister."

There was a pause. She took a deep breath as she turned toward the view again.

"It's beautiful, isn't it?" he said. "The most beautiful place in the world. But are you happy at the moment, Gwendolyn?"

"Happy?"

"I mean with McGregor running things here, and me being in Colombo so much."

"Of course I'm happy."

"But something has been bothering you, hasn't it? It's as if I don't know you anymore."

In Gwen's sigh, her weariness revealed itself. This might be her best chance to tell him the truth, but when she squinted up to look at him, the sadness on his face almost unhinged her. And the fact was, although Verity had already been at the house earlier, Gwen didn't actually know what had or had not been said.

"It isn't Christina, is it?" he asked very gently, and drew her to him. "There's really no need."

She looked up at him, feeling uncertain.

He ran his fingers through her hair as he gazed at her, one arm round her waist. "Darling, really —"

Gwen interrupted. "In New York she told me it was all over before I even arrived here."

"Exactly what I told you."

"And I believed her, but really she still wanted you, didn't she, even then?"

"When?"

"Like I said. In New York. Isn't that what the phone call was about?"

He looked puzzled. "What call?"

"Just before we went to bed on our last night."

"Darling, that call wasn't from Christina. It was Verity."

Gwen took a step back and stared at him. "But Christina told me that she had hoped to continue as your mistress after we were married."

He pulled a face. "That was never an option. I know that she tried to give the impression there was still something between us, and she does like to provoke, but I swear there was no chance after I married you."

Gwen felt tears burn her eyelids.

"That's why, after our wedding, I was happy to travel back to Ceylon ahead of you. To put a stop to it."

"So it wasn't because of business?"

"She had been good for me after Caroline. I was a mess. She propped me up. I had to let her down gently."

"You didn't love her?"

"I was fond of her but it wasn't love."

"But why were you so distant with me when we first arrived here?"

"Because I did love you and I was afraid."

"Of what?"

"I'd lost Caroline. I felt I didn't deserve a second chance. I suppose I was afraid of losing you."

She swiped at the tears of relief that now dripped down her cheeks and then pinched the skin at her hairline where another headache was beginning. This was the moment. It was her turn. He reached over to brush her tears away. She held his hand, then opened her mouth to speak, but hesitated, and in that moment, in the split second that is all it takes to change a life, she knew she simply could not do it.

The world hung silently but for the cry of a lone crow. Dismayed at her cowardice, she sniffed the woody smell of the trees and tried to think. She just couldn't speak out and then watch everything fall apart. He had trusted her, had trusted her with his deepest feelings, his fears, his needs, his grief. But then something else occurred to her.

"Why have you changed your mind about Savi coming here?"

He took a breath. "I may have been wrong about him, that's all."

She glimpsed a look on his face that disturbed her: a look that suggested he was really hurting.

"Are you all right?" she asked.

He swallowed and turned away.

She weighed up what Fran had said. If Fran was right and Liyoni really was not Savi's child, then she would be able to tell Laurence the truth, but maybe not yet. After all these years she longed to shout out that she was a good woman and had not done the terrible, terrible thing she'd believed she had. But she needed to wait a little longer, just until she could find a way to prove it.

She touched his shoulder, feeling more certain that Verity could not have carried through her threat; after all, if Laurence already knew he would hardly be treating her so lovingly. "Actually," she said, "I was thinking it might be a good idea to reinstate your sister's allowance. It's clear she won't be going back to her marriage and she'll need something to live on."

He gave her a twisted smile. "Do you care? After all she has done . . ."

"She's still your sister. We could make going back to live in the house in England a condition."

There was a rumble of thunder and she glanced up.

He nodded slowly. "Once the brand takes off, it might be possible. But you do know the house in Yorkshire is rented out?"

"Yes, but when the lease runs out."

Gwen glanced up at the clouds again then down at her feet. It was almost November and late for the monsoon to begin. She stubbed the toe of her shoe in the dry ground. Soon it would be squelching underfoot.

"I received a letter yesterday. The English tenants have indicated they might like an extension on the lease."

She decided to push him over Verity's allowance. "Might we find a way to give Verity her allowance before the brand takes off?"

He gave her a long quizzical look. "I could raise a loan, I think, if you really believe I must."

Gwen hesitated. She didn't want Laurence to have to incur more debts before they'd even got off the ground with the brand, but it would be a way to get Verity off her back, and for now, at least, it would give her time.

Laurence glanced up. "Come on, time to scoot. The rain's here. Let's talk about Verity later."

34

March 1934

Now that the rains were long gone, the days were bright. Laurence had spent most of the last couple of months traveling, leaving McGregor in charge, though Gwen had had very little to do with the man. When Laurence was home he seemed a little cut off, as if he were troubled by something. When she questioned him he brushed her off and said that with so many plantations abandoned due to the fall in tea prices, far from riots being the biggest worry, it was the spread of the anopheles mosquito.

Fran and Savi were temporarily in Colombo while they decided what to do about a more permanent home, and Verity, delighted to have her allowance back, was staying with friends in Kandy until the rental lease on her home in England ran out. Gwen had made reinstating Verity's allowance conditional on her living in England.

It didn't mean she would not come back with further demands, but it gave Gwen a chance to catch her breath.

Fran had spoken to Savi and, while Laurence was away, Gwen agreed to meet up with them both in Nuwara Eliya. Savi wanted to talk to Gwen in private, so they decided to take a walk round a part of the lake there. She didn't really want to see him at all, but knew she must.

He walked toward her and held out a hand.

She gazed at the ground and did not take it.

"How are things in Colombo?" she managed to say without looking at him. "We saw the start of a riot."

There was a pause and she heard him sigh as she stood still for a little longer. When she glanced up she saw a tightness in the skin round his eyes.

"I'm so sorry," she said.

His nostrils flared and she could feel his pent-up anger.

"When Fran told me, I was appalled. I thought we were friends, Gwen. How could you ever think I'd have hurt you?"

She felt a burst of heat and bowed her head again. "I didn't know what to think."

"And yet you thought that of me. For

heaven's sake, Gwen. Can't you even look at me?"

She looked up and, devastated by the pain she saw in his eyes, shook her head.

He cracked his knuckles but didn't speak.

In the tense atmosphere she struggled to speak, her mind running over everything that had gone on, but after a few moments found the words.

"I didn't want to think that of you," she said. "It made me ill but I couldn't see how else it could have happened. I am so sorry."

"Oh, Gwen."

She felt a flash of anger, though more at herself than at him. "I am starting to love Liyoni. Do you know that? And all I've ever done is turn her away. Can you imagine how that feels? Can you even begin to understand?"

"And yet if she'd been white, even if I had actually done this terrible thing, you wouldn't have thought twice."

"That isn't fair. If she had been white I'd have had no cause to believe she was not Laurence's daughter."

Savi sighed. "He never did like me. I have no idea why."

"He's a reasonable man."

"Not where I'm concerned."

She reached out a hand to him. He did

not take it but walked over to the water's edge. Gwen swallowed rapidly and watched the birds gathering nearby. He turned abruptly and the birds took flight over the water.

"All these years, you must have been through hell. Why didn't you talk to me?"

"Back then I was very young and very frightened. I didn't know what to do. I hadn't been here long and I didn't know you."

She watched a vein pulse in his neck and waited for him to speak. When he didn't she continued.

"I thought you charming. More than charming, if I'm being honest. Laurence was being cool toward me. I was lonely. But then, once Liyoni was born, I hated you."

"I'm sorry if I gave you any cause," he said, with sadness in his voice.

She looked back at him. His sincerity was utterly convincing, but she didn't know how to cope with her mixed feelings. She felt immense relief that she truly believed he was not Liyoni's father, but also felt awful that she could have thought so badly of him.

There were tears in his eyes, but he smiled as he spoke. "Shall we draw a line under this? I'm married to your cousin, virtually your brother-in-law. Can we be friends again?"

"I'd like that."

He held out his arms and she went to him, trembling with relief as her tears fell. When they parted, she wiped her eyes. He took her hand and gently kissed it.

"If there is anything I can do to help . . . search the records, look through the Colombo archives. See if there's anything that might give us a clue as to Liyoni's heritage. By that, of course, I mean your husband's heritage."

She smiled. "Thank you. Thank you so much. I can't tell you what this means to me. I'm so sorry."

"I did wonder when our paths so rarely crossed again, and you didn't seem yourself when I came to the house with Verity that time."

"Verity only brought you there to undermine me."

"I think you should speak to the ayah. Quite often lifelong servants know more about a family than the family themselves."

With one hand she swept away the hair blowing in her eyes, then ran her fingers through the tangles.

"I don't think Naveena knows anything. She was the one who persuaded me to take

Liyoni to the village in the first place."

"I see. Well, the search might take a little while. These things are often well hidden, but I have good contacts and if there is anything to find, as I'm sure there must be, I will find it. I'll let you know the moment I have something concrete to report."

"Thank you."

"So now, what about lunch? Fran is expecting us both."

"Thank you, but I think I'll sit for a while."

He pressed his palms together in front of his chest, fingers pointing upward, and bowed very slightly just as he had done on their first meeting. It seemed so long ago.

After he had gone, free at last of the burden of guilt, she felt almost light-headed. But how oddly it had come about! If Fran had not got to know Savi and then married him, she would never have found out that she hadn't been unfaithful. Now that she was certain, she still had to find a way to approach Laurence. He needed to be told that Liyoni was his daughter, and the only question was whether to speak to him immediately or wait until she had dug up evidence of Ceylonese blood in his family.

She turned it over in her mind. It was better to wait. She pulled her shawl more tightly round her shoulders as the wind began to blow, hardly able to believe that this day had come. Yet despite her joy at no longer having to harbor the hate she'd felt for Savi, nothing could wipe away the fact that she had given her own child away. She sat on the bench watching the wind bending the trees on the opposite side of the Nuwara Eliya lake and had never felt so alone.

Once both Gwen and Laurence were back home, they heard that the new brand had enjoyed good sales after its launch in December and, despite the price of tea being so low, profits were likely to be reasonable. Christina had wired too, from America, her words encouraging them to stay positive because things could only get better. For the first time, Gwen heard Christina's name without the slightest wobble.

Hugh was also back for the weekend. He'd grown used to the fact that Liyoni could no longer play outside or swim in the lake with him, yet he spent hours at her side, reading to her and showing her how to do crossword puzzles.

Gwen came upon them huddled together in a corner of the nursery, giggling and looking so happy in each other's company that her heart skipped a beat. At eight years old, they were so different in appearance:

639

Hugh well-built and tall, just like Laurence, and Liyoni delicate and pretty. With every month that passed, she looked more like Gwen. Her English had come on, and she even spoke with a fairly authentic accent. And with Verity gone, this was a much-needed space for Gwen to spend a little time with both her children.

She found her voice and smiled. "What are you two doing?"

"Drawing, Mummy," said Hugh.

"Can I see?"

He pushed the two pieces of paper toward her, and she squatted down to look. Hugh had drawn a rather good aeroplane, a type used during the Great War.

"It's a German plane," he said.

"Very nice."

But when she looked at the other drawing she saw that, once again, Liyoni had drawn a waterfall.

"She only draws waterfalls, Mummy."

"Yes."

"Can't you take her to see it, Mummy? Just one time," he said in a wheedling tone of voice.

"I haven't come in here to talk about waterfalls, darling. I've come to say it's time to wash your hands before lunch."

"Can Liyoni have her lunch with us?"

"You know Liyoni has her lunch with Naveena."

"I really don't think that's fair."

"Don't you indeed. Well, perhaps you'd like to discuss the matter with your father over luncheon."

He grinned at her. "All right, Mummy, you win."

Gwen had never got used to sleeping in Laurence's room, so when he was back, more often than not, he spent the night with her in her room. On his final night home before he set off again, she was moved by his tenderness. After they'd made love, he kissed her firmly on the mouth and there were tears in his eyes as he stroked her cheek.

"You know you can tell me anything, Gwen."

"Of course. And you me."

He closed his eyes, but she saw that his chin was trembling very slightly.

They decided to let the candle burn itself out and she stared at the ceiling in the flickering light, thinking about what he'd said. Might it be better, after all, to tell him the truth about Liyoni now, even though she had not come up with anything yet? She began by saying something about Hugh.

Laurence murmured a response, but then, almost instantly, he fell asleep. She listened to his slow breathing, turned on her side, and folded her body up close.

They were woken by the sound of faint sobbing coming from the nursery. She fumbled for the switch to her bedside lamp, pulled back the blanket on her side, swung her feet to the white rug on the floor, and then got out of bed. She glanced at the clock. Three in the morning. She wrapped a gown round her shoulders, then pulled on some thick socks, glad that Hugh was back at school and wouldn't be disturbed.

She touched Laurence's face. "I'll go. You've got a long journey in the morning."

He grunted and rolled over.

In the nursery, Naveena stooped over Liyoni's bed. "She says her legs pain, Lady."

Gwen leaned over her daughter.

"Pull up the chair, Naveena. I'll have her on my lap. I know the doctor told you to rub her legs when they got painful, but I'd like to do it myself tonight."

Naveena pulled up the chair and, while Gwen settled with the child, went to the cupboard and took out a small bottle of aromatic oil. She poured a little into Gwen's outstretched palm.

"Rub gentle, Lady. Like a butterfly."

"I will, don't worry." Gwen had watched Naveena do it and knew exactly how much pressure to apply.

Liyoni continued to whimper and cough, but as Gwen massaged the child's limbs, she sang very softly. Gradually Liyoni closed her eyes and slept. Gwen didn't want to wake her, so stayed as she was for the remainder of the night, and only realized how stiff she had become when Laurence came through in the half light of early dawn.

"I brought you some tea," he said, putting the cup and saucer on the small table. "You must be exhausted."

"A little cold maybe."

"Here, I'll put the child into her bed. Will you let me?" He looked at her with such concern in his eyes, she could only nod.

After Liyoni was tucked up, he asked Naveena to fetch a blanket for Gwen.

When she stood, every muscle in her body seemed to be aching. She stretched and put a finger to her lips. "Let's leave her to sleep now."

"I'll call the doctor if you like."

"It's all right. There's nothing he can do. He's given me some strong painkillers for her. He said to use them sparingly, until . . ." She swallowed the lump in her throat. "She was such a wonderful swimmer."

He put an arm round her and led her to her room. "I think I'll phone the doctor anyway, if you don't mind. I'm afraid I shall have to be off fairly soon, if I'm to catch the train in time. But, before I go, I have something to show you."

"Darling, please can it wait? I'm so tired I think I'll try to sleep for an hour or so."

The doctor, when he came, suggested it was time to give Liyoni more painkillers. "Not all the time," he said, "but if you think it's necessary, don't hold back."

"She isn't going to get better, is she?"

He shook his head.

"How long?" Gwen asked, holding his gaze.

"That's impossible to tell. She could go on for some time longer . . . On the other hand . . ." He spread his hands in a gesture of uncertainty. "Can she still stand?"

"Yes."

As the realization sank in, a feeling of calm washed over her. Now that there was so little time, she would tell Laurence as soon as he returned. But before that, there was one thing she had to do for Liyoni.

After the doctor had gone, Gwen brought Liyoni through to her own bedroom, sat her on the chair in the window, and went to fetch some clean clothes from the nursery. Liyoni clapped her hands when she saw the dress Gwen came back with. It was one of Gwen's that Naveena had cut down for the child: a bright red, almost scarlet, *broderie anglaise* dress. She had a favorite red shawl too and some red socks that she wore inside her Wellington boots. Hugh always said she looked like Little Red Riding Hood.

Once Liyoni was well wrapped up, Gwen went outside to see if McGregor had already brought the Daimler back from dropping Laurence at the station. She grinned when she spotted the car parked just outside with the keys still in the ignition. She pocketed the keys. No need to even mention that she was taking the car.

Back in her room, Naveena was hovering around Liyoni.

"You think I'm doing the right thing?" she asked the woman. Naveena nodded slowly. "One time letting her see the water."

As they started off, Gwen hoped she'd find the turning Verity had once pointed out during a driving lesson.

Gwen had acted on impulse but didn't regret bringing Liyoni out. The little girl had asked so many times and as long as she was careful it would be fine. As she drove, she thought of Liyoni's time at the plantation: the way she'd shout, "I'm flying!" as she took off through the water and the way she'd twirl in delight at anything that pleased her.

Lost in thought, Gwen almost drove right past the overgrown turning. Specks of broken cloud flecked the pale sky and there was just a slight breeze. She stopped for a moment and rolled the windows right down so they could smell the fresh mint and eucalyptus and listen to the hum of flying creatures. Then she drove especially carefully so as not to jolt the child too much as they bumped over potholes and mounds of stone.

"Lean out, Liyoni," she said. "Can you smell the water? We can't be far."

The little girl leaned out and, glancing across, Gwen saw her daughter's dark hair streaming out behind her. She carried on driving, concentrating on the track, but when she heard the sound of falling water, she knew they were almost there.

"Do you hear it?" she said in a loud voice, twisting to look at Liyoni. The little girl's face shone with pleasure.

After Gwen had parked, she climbed down, walked round to the passenger side, and opened the door.

"I can't take the car any closer."

Gwen leaned against the side of the car while Liyoni sat on the edge of her seat, absorbing the sound of the waterfall. After a while the little girl tapped Gwen's hand, interrupting her thoughts. She bent her head to hear what Liyoni was saying.

"I cannot see. Get out?"

Gwen frowned. The doctor had said that although the child could still walk or stand for maybe ten minutes, any prolonged use of her legs would cause pain.

"No," she said. "It's dangerous."

"Please. Little closer. Please." Liyoni looked up at her with a pleading look.

"It's not a good idea. Just look from here."

"I be careful."

When she saw the longing in her little girl's eyes, Gwen gave in. If the disease progressed as the doctor expected, this might be her only chance to really see how the water fell.

"Very well, but you must let me hold you all the time. I'll carry you to where you will be able to see a little better."

The force of water had carved a horseshoe shape in the rocky surroundings, so Gwen carried her to a spot close to where the curve began. They stood far enough away from the edge to be perfectly safe, but near enough to see the water that fed the fall on the opposite side.

"Don't move at all. Hold tight. See over there," Gwen said, and pointed several yards over to the right. "See just over there where the ground is a bit crumbly."

"I be careful."

Gwen looked up. The clouds had thickened and the sun had gone in. The smell now was of damp vegetation, moist earth, and something indefinable coming from the water itself. Minerals, Gwen thought, or else something the water might have picked up en route. She heard a noise behind her and glanced over her shoulder, but it was only a couple of monkeys flying through the air and thumping as they landed.

"You do like water, don't you?" Gwen said, speaking loudly and tightening her hold round the child's waist.

Liyoni glanced up, her face flushed with excitement.

A few minutes passed as Gwen gazed at the rocky ledges opposite, where the water flew off before thundering to the pool where Caroline had drowned. The pool itself was out of sight, and Gwen could only imagine the foaming whiteness at the bottom and the despair her predecessor must have felt.

At that moment Liyoni threw back her head, giggling with joy, then stretched out her arms above her. A gust of wind snatched the red woolen shawl away. As Gwen bent to retrieve it, she relaxed her grip on Liyoni's waist for just a second or two. There was a burst of sunlight and, blinded by the brightness, Gwen stared into the torrent of glittering crystal water. A sudden gust of strong wind blew grit in her face, but at the back of her mind she was aware of the sound of an engine pulling up. With streaming eyes she reached out to catch hold of Liyoni, but the child had moved.

In the time that it took for Gwen's eyes to clear, the sun lit Liyoni's face as she turned, there was another gust of wind, and, startled by it, she wobbled. With her back to the waterfall Liyoni seemed confused and took a step backward instead of forward. As Gwen reached out, Liyoni stumbled, her red dress billowing out behind her with the wind forcing her back again.

In that split second Gwen felt the full force of her love for her daughter. Heart-stopping, absolute love.

Liyoni fell forward onto her knees.

"Stay down," Gwen shouted and, on all fours herself, crawled forward to grasp the little girl.

Suddenly Laurence was there. He scooped Liyoni up and tenderly carried her to the car. Gwen, still on her knees, looked down, winded by the shock. It had been too close. As the wind dropped, Gwen got up and ran to where Laurence now stood.

"Give her to me," she cried, then wrapped her arms round her shaking child.

Nobody had told her that being a mother would mean living with love so unqualified that it left you breathless, and fear so awful that it shook you to your soul. Nor had they said how close those two feelings were. At the back of Gwen's mind a single tiny dreadful thought crept in. If she had just had the courage to tip herself over the edge, it would all have been over. The years of guilt. The fear. The self-loathing. Everything. And then the thought was gone.

But Laurence must have seen something in her face.

"No, Gwen. Think of your other child."

Still reeling from the shock of what had happened, she had registered his voice in a disconnected kind of way. "What did you say?"

"I said, think of your other child."

She stared at him. Everything went silent. Isolated in the moment, she felt the wind brush her skin. She gazed about, seeing every detail of everything going on without really looking. The grass looked different, as if the wind blew it about more slowly than usual. And the insects — so many insects, hovering, hardly moving — and the birds swooping in slow motion from tree to tree. She heard a noise in the distance. Something calling. What was it? A goat? A bell? For a moment, her mind felt unnaturally serene, as if the world had come to rescue her from the pain of what she had done. But the pain had not gone. And, in the end, it came rushing back as the noise of the water came crashing in.

She looked at Laurence. "You know?"

He nodded.

"How long?"

"Not long."

"I thought you had already gone to Colombo."

Laurence shook his head, looking stiff and worried. "I needed to talk to you. I couldn't leave. Look, there are blankets in the boot of the car. I'm taking you both back now. Nick and I can pick up the truck later."

She twisted back to look at the spot where she and Liyoni had been standing, and trembled at what might have happened. While Laurence got out the blankets she held Liyoni and, stroking her cheeks, whispered all the things she had never dared say. Told her she was sorry, asked for her forgiveness, repeating it over and over. Though the little girl could not understand all the words, she gazed into Gwen's eyes and managed a smile.

As Laurence came back round, Gwen glanced up at him. "It was reckless. I shouldn't have brought her here, but she wanted to see it so much."

"It's the shock. She'll be fine. You kept far enough from the edge. The wind made it seem worse than it was, but you weren't really in danger. Come on, let's get you both away from here."

He took Liyoni and held her close, then placed her on the backseat and gently stroked her hair.

"You're all right now, little one," he said.

A bird screeched in the sky and Gwen glanced at the length of fabric she still held: Liyoni's red shawl. She lifted it into the air for a moment, then released her grip. The shawl spun gently and was carried downstream on the wind, like a red kite reeling and twisting as it surrendered to its inevitable descent. Then, standing out against the shining water, it fluttered momentarily before it disappeared.

35

Five weeks later, on a beautiful may morning, Liyoni died peacefully in her sleep. Gwen had spent most of the time at her side, stroking her forehead and keeping her cool. Afterward, she and Naveena gently washed her and brushed her hair. But as Gwen sank deeper into heartache, so far removed from anything she had known, she despaired of ever feeling normal again.

Soon after the incident at the waterfall, Laurence had wanted to explain how he'd found out. Something in the family records, he'd said, just as Fran had suggested there would be, but Gwen was so upset about Liyoni's deterioration, she wasn't ready to hear the details. *Later,* she'd said, *tell me everything later.* Then she'd burst into tears and hurried from the room, not at all ready to share the anguish she felt at having given their daughter away.

Now unable to speak, drink, or eat, she

knew her deepest regret would always be that she had discovered too late how much she loved Liyoni. She would never see her again, never touch her hair, never hear her voice, and she would never be able to make up for what she had done. That was worst of all. The ache for her child's lost life did not diminish. That she should live while her daughter was gone seemed like a physical impossibility. A terrible joke played out by an indifferent world.

In the nursery, Naveena laid Liyoni out in a long white dress. Gwen, standing several feet away, watched in numb silence. Several of the servants came in to place flowers around the little girl. Even McGregor came, and as he entered the room, Gwen's throat constricted. She glanced at him before he looked at Liyoni and she saw his face was white. She swallowed the lump in her throat and stepped toward the bed. McGregor looked at her and held out his hand, his eyes full of pain. She had never seen him look like that before, and wondered if he was remembering the day they had laid Thomas to rest.

Eventually, when they had all gone and she was alone, she touched her daughter's cheek, cold and so much paler than it had been in life. In that moment she welcomed how much it hurt. It was a just punishment. She kissed Liyoni's forehead, stroked her hair one last time, then turned and fled, hardly able to take a breath.

Hugh had been kept in the dark. Laurence thought it better for him to board for a few weeks, and only be told when he next came home in the school holidays. So when the funeral was held the next day, Hugh was absent.

Gwen felt her mind grow numb as she walked along the path the gardener had cut to the place where Thomas was buried, but almost fainted when she first glimpsed the deep rectangular hole waiting for Liyoni's coffin. Naveena walked beside her, with an arm round her waist, holding her up as she herself had held Liyoni. Unable to stand up straight, Gwen felt very old. Naveena's face did not give much away, and Gwen wondered what the ayah must be feeling. It flashed into Gwen's mind that all the servants must have trained themselves to be impassive.

When the coffin was lowered Gwen had to suppress the urge to jump in after it. Instead she knelt at the edge and threw in a bunch of large white daisies, which landed with a *thud*. She glanced up and, almost unbearably immune to any feelings of hope, heard the movement of the lake behind her. That was what would save her. Liyoni's water.

"I think I'd like to go swimming now," she said as Laurence helped her to her feet.

He spoke to Naveena, then came with her to her room, where he stood still, watching as she undressed before putting on her bathing clothes. As she struggled out of a badly fitting black dress, he was right not to lend a hand. She had resisted all offers of help, and now, it seemed, he understood that she must do everything by herself, because if she did not, there might never come a time when she would know how. When she was ready, he went to his room, changed, and then came back to collect her.

The water, as they stepped into it, was cold.

"Once you start swimming, you'll warm up," Laurence said. "Shall we head across to the island?"

She went farther in and began to swim, feeling as if she could go on and on and never stop. Halfway across, Laurence wanted her to rest at the island. She complied, but when they pulled themselves out of the water and onto the bank, it was far too cold to sit in the wind. She glanced back at their home across the lake, the place she loved but where so much fear had torn her apart.

"Let's swim to the boathouse," Laurence said, interrupting her thoughts. "As soon as you suggested a swim, I asked Naveena to organize dry towels, a log fire, and a flask of tea."

She nodded, swimming back more slowly as her energy began to fade. Her legs gave way as he helped her out of the water and then up the steps to the door of the little building.

Inside the boathouse, the logs were just catching and she sat on the floor beside the fire with her knees drawn up, holding out her palms to feel the heat. He came across and wrapped a large fluffy towel round her, and used another to dry her hair. As he rubbed, she leaned against him, and finally the tears began to spill. She turned round and, feeling his heart thump against her, she sobbed into his chest. She sobbed for her little girl's lost life and for Laurence never having been able to acknowledge his daughter. She sobbed that life could bring such incredible joy, while at the same time be capable of dealing a blow so cruel that it seemed impossible to withstand.

As she clung to Laurence, he stroked her back, bringing back feeling to her muscles and skin. It seemed to go on for a very long time. Then, as he dried her tears, she felt relief that she had been able to release a little of the pain and grateful for his generosity.

They sat on the floor together, Gwen gazing at the fire, while he poured tea into two cups, adding a splash of brandy to each.

"Is it time to talk?" he asked.

There was a long stretch of silence and then, when she was ready, Gwen looked up at him.

"How long have you known?"

"About Liyoni?"

She nodded. "I know you tried to tell me before. Will you tell me now?"

"You remember the parcel that arrived? The one you asked me about?"

"I'd almost forgotten."

There was a pause.

"I contacted our solicitor in England and asked him to gain access to a small apartment in our house. It's excluded from the tenancy agreement. A lot of old papers are kept there from the days when my parents lived part of the year there."

"What kind of papers?"

"Old family records. My mother loved that old house, had always looked forward to retiring there, which is why she kept the papers there."

Gwen nodded.

"I asked the solicitor to find them and send everything on to me. I knew Verity had seen my mother's records, but I had not. It was just an impulse, but Verity had once implied that there were things I didn't know about the family. At the time, quite frankly, I didn't believe her, but I wondered if there might be clues to Liyoni's relationship with Naveena. I wanted to know if they really were related."

"What did you find?"

"Photos, letters, documents . . . and a very delicate and much-folded piece of parchment." He paused. "A marriage certificate that recorded the marriage of my great-grandfather, Albert."

She waited.

"My great-grandmother's name was Sukeena. She wasn't English, wasn't even European — she was Sinhalese. She died soon after my grandmother was born and my parents never told me anything about her."

At last, she thought; here was the truth that had lain buried for so long. "You're saying the color of Liyoni's skin came from her?"

He nodded. "I believe so. If only you had

told me, Gwen, we might have been able to find that out from the start. We could have kept our daughter."

She shook her head. "We hadn't been married long and hardly even knew each other. If I had told you then, you would have sent me away. You wouldn't have wanted to, but that is what would have happened. You would have thought I'd had an affair."

The color left his face as he started to speak, but she put a finger to his lips. "It's true," she said. "We would never have got as far as looking for an alternative reason."

From the short pause that followed, Gwen knew her words had hit home and, for a moment, they stared at each other without speaking.

He took a deep breath. "When I persuaded Naveena to confirm what I guessed from the records, she admitted you had really given birth to twins. It took some doing, mind you. Naveena is very loyal to you." He hesitated. "What you must have gone through all these years. I am so sorry."

Gwen blinked rapidly to hold back the tears.

"When Verity came to me with the story of Liyoni and your supposed affair with Savi Ravasinghe and asked for her allowance back, I already knew it wasn't true."

"But you gave her the allowance then let me think it was because I'd asked you?"

He nodded.

"Has Verity seen this wedding certificate?"

"I'm so sorry, Gwen. I'm sure she has, but I didn't want to tell her I knew about Sukeena until I could find the way to tell you first." He frowned. "I just didn't know where to start."

She shook her head. "Verity knew the truth, but she still tried to blackmail me. Why did she need her allowance so badly?"

"I think she was afraid to remain married to Alexander in case she too gave birth to a colored child."

"But she fell in love with Savi?"

"I don't think she loved him. It was just that a mixed marriage would, in some circles, have been an acceptable reason for a colored child. She needed money to live independently. She's not strong like you, Gwen; the shame would have destroyed her. When you didn't give in to her, she came to me."

Gwen let out her breath slowly. "But I did give in. I asked you about the allowance."

"I don't think Verity believed you would."

Gwen paused. "She was taking money too, Laurence, by fiddling the accounts. Must have been stockpiling for years before I warned her that I knew."

He hung his head. "I can't begin to make excuses for her."

Gwen sipped the warm tea and thought about what he'd said.

He looked up. "I think on some level I had begun to see the truth the day I carried Liyoni to swim in the lake, though I denied it to myself. But once the records arrived and I really opened my eyes, I saw how much like you she was."

Gwen felt a wave of loss pass through her, so intense she didn't know if she could bear it. This was how it would be now, yet at the same time she knew she had to find courage for Hugh's sake.

"So where do we go from here?" she managed to say.

"We carry on. For now, only you and I and Naveena know the whole truth about Liyoni."

"And Verity."

"And my suggestion is that we don't tell Hugh until he is old enough to understand."

"Maybe you're right, though I think he'd understand perfectly well that his playmate was actually his sister." She paused. "What do you want to do about Verity?"

"Whatever you feel best, Gwen. I am

ashamed of her, but I can't completely turn my back on her. She's very troubled, I'm afraid."

Gwen shook her head but almost felt sorry for her sister-in-law.

"We can go back to England if you want," Laurence said. "It's still some years off, I believe, but we may have little choice once independence comes."

She looked up at him and smiled. "I seem to remember saying that if the plantation was where your heart belonged, it was where my heart belonged too. Ceylon is still our home. Maybe we really can improve conditions here. Let's stay until we're forced to go."

"I'll do whatever I can to make up for the past. All of the past."

"Can we keep the path to their resting places clear, and the view of the lake from there?"

He nodded.

"We can plant flowers," she added, with a lump in her throat. "Orange marigolds."

He took her hand. She leaned against him and gazed through the window at the deep lake, where water birds were gathering. Herons, ibises, storks.

"There was another thing I found in my mother's papers. Something I never knew."

"Oh?"

"Naveena's mother and my grandmother were cousins."

Gwen felt shaken. "Does Naveena know?"

"I don't think so."

There was a short silence.

"She's had a good life here," he said.

"Yes."

"But I feel heartbroken that I didn't have enough time with Liyoni, and that I never had a chance to love her."

Gwen took a deep breath. "I'm so sorry."

"I'm not blaming you. At least in the time she did have here she was happy."

"It could have been so much better."

Laurence looked at his feet before speaking again, in a low voice. "There is one more thing, and I don't know if you'll be able to forgive me for not telling you before."

Gwen closed her eyes. What else could there be?

"I was too ashamed. I'm dreadfully sorry. It's about Caroline."

She opened her eyes. "Yes?"

"And Thomas."

He paused and she watched a muscle in his neck pulse.

"You see Caroline's son, my son . . . Thomas. He was colored too."

Gwen's hand flew to her mouth.

"I'm so sorry for not telling you. I think that's what tipped Caroline over the edge. She was such a beautiful and sensitive woman, and I'd have done anything for her, but she was fragile emotionally. Soon after Thomas was born she had prolonged crying spells and terrible panic attacks. They were so bad she was actually sick. I sat with her night after night holding her, trying to find a way to comfort her . . . but it was impossible. Nothing I did helped. You should have seen the haunted look in her eyes, Gwen. It broke my heart."

"Did she talk to you?"

"No, though I tried to get through to her. Outside the family, only the doctor knew about Thomas, and Naveena. We'd kept him hidden from the rest of the servants, though, of course, McGregor found out when he retrieved Thomas from the water. Verity was home. It was the school holidays."

Gwen drew a little apart from him and shook her head. "Verity knew?"

"It had a terrible impact on her."

"That explains a lot."

He nodded. "I think it's probably why I've always given her so much leeway."

"Why didn't Naveena tell me?"

"I had begged her never to speak of it."

"But she was the one who came up with

665

the idea of sending Liyoni to live at the village."

"She'd seen what had happened to Caroline. She must have wanted to ensure you wouldn't go the same way." He paused and closed his eyes for a moment before speaking. "There's more, I'm afraid. You see, I'm to blame."

"It wasn't your fault."

He shook his head. "It was. When I first saw Thomas I felt betrayed and I accused Caroline of having an affair with Savi Ravasinghe when he painted her portrait. Even though she absolutely denied it, I didn't believe her."

Gwen pressed her lips together hard and squeezed her eyes shut in shock.

"I promise you I still loved her and tried so hard to help her."

She opened her eyes and scrutinized his face. "Good God, Laurence, there must have been something more you could have done?"

"I tried, really tried. But she'd lost all interest in her appearance. I helped her wash, I helped her dress, I even helped her feed the baby. I did everything I could think of to pull her out of the blackness, and I thought I had succeeded, Gwen, because just before the end she seemed to recover enough for me to leave her for the day . . ."

There was silence as he swallowed rapidly.

"But I was wrong . . . that was the day she took her own life. The awful thing is that even after she died I still didn't believe her denial of the affair. That might have been the one thing that could have made a difference."

Gwen suddenly understood what he was saying. "You think she killed herself because of you?"

He nodded. His face crumpled and his eyes filled with tears, but he brushed them away. "She had been telling the truth all along, though I only knew that after I sent for my mother's records and found out about Sukeena. I wanted to talk to you then, tell you everything about Caroline and Thomas . . . but I felt as if I had taken them to the pool under the falls and pushed them into the water myself. I couldn't bear to tell you."

Hardly able to believe what she was hearing, Gwen was in absolute turmoil. She watched him shudder as he tried to control his emotions. The moment seemed to last forever.

When he spoke again, his voice was shaking. "How do I live with this, Gwen? How can you forgive me?"

She shook her head.

"It's not only Caroline's death. She felt she had to take our baby with her, that she couldn't trust me to care for him. A tiny, defenseless baby."

As Gwen listened to the wind blowing the water about at the edge of the lake, she felt crushed.

Laurence took her hand. "I know I should have told you at the start, but I was certain I would lose you too."

She removed her hand from his and held her breath for a moment before speaking. When she did it was with sorrow in her voice. "Yes, Laurence, you should have."

There was a pause during which she didn't trust herself to speak again. If he had told her about Thomas at the beginning, would she still have married him? She had been so young, far too young really.

"I'm desperately sorry you've had to go through all this alone. And sorrier than I will ever be able to say for what I drove Caroline to do. I loved her so much."

Gwen closed her eyes. "Poor, poor woman."

"Can you forgive me for not telling you everything?"

While she tried to take it in, she opened her eyes and for a moment watched Laurence staring at the floor with his head in his hands and his shoulders hunched. What could she say? Outside the birds had silenced and even the wind had dropped. She had to make a decision that could mean the end of everything. She understood so much more now, but images from the past were crowding her mind and she felt such utter loss that she couldn't respond.

The silence dragged on, but when she glanced at Laurence again and saw the depth of his grief, that made her decision easier. It was not up to her to forgive him.

"You should have told me," she said.

He looked up and swallowed rapidly.

"But it was a mistake."

His brow creased as he nodded.

"There's nothing I can say to change what happened to Caroline. You have to find a way to live with that. But, Laurence, you're a good man and to keep on blaming yourself won't bring her back."

He reached out a hand but she didn't take it at first.

"You're not the only one. I made a terrible mistake too . . . I gave my own daughter away." Her eyes burned and she choked on her words. "And now she's dead."

She looked deep into his eyes and then took his hand. She knew what living with guilt and fear could do. It hurt. It hurt so much. She thought of all he had been through, and all she had been through too. The day of her own arrival in Ceylon came back to her, and she remembered that girl who had stood on the deck of the ship and met Savi Ravasinghe. Everything had been in front of her, with no hint of the terrifying fragility of happiness.

She recalled the moment of utter peacefulness when she had stared at the bruised and wrinkled red face of her newborn son, his baby hands trembling and juddering as he screamed. Then, as if it were only yesterday, she remembered unwrapping the warm blanket covering Liyoni. She experienced again the shock at seeing those little fingers, the rounded belly, the dark, dark eyes.

She thought of the years of guilt and shame, but also of everything that had been beautiful and glorious about Ceylon: the precious moments when the smell of cinnamon combined with blossom; the mornings when the sparkling dews of the chilly season sent her spirit soaring; the monsoons with their endless curtains of rain, and the sheen of the tea bushes when the rain had gone. And then tears spilled down her cheeks again, and with them a memory she handled with infinite tenderness: Liyoni, swimming like a fish across to the island, whirling in the water and singing. Free.

For such a small girl, Liyoni had left a long shadow; her ghost would not simply vanish, and Gwen wouldn't let it.

As Laurence stroked her hair soothingly, as you would a child, she thought of Caroline, and felt such an affinity with her it took her breath away. And, finally, she remembered the moment when she no longer noticed the color of her daughter's skin. She felt her husband's warm hand on her hair, and knew she would carry Liyoni's last words in her heart for the rest of her life.

I love you, Mama.

That was what the little girl had said, the night before she died.

Gwen wiped her tears away and smiled as she watched a flight of birds take off from the lake. Life goes on, she thought. God knows how, but it does, somehow. And she hoped that one day, maybe, if she was very lucky, she might find a way to forgive herself.

ACKNOWLEDGMENTS

I am indebted to Andrew Taylor at Ceylon Tea Trails, Sri Lanka, for his fantastic tour of the Norwood Tea Factory where I learned so much about tea, and also about the old days in Ceylon. Without the staff at Tea Trails who gave us such a wonderful taste of how colonial life might once have been, the book would have been less authentic. We stayed at beautiful Castlereagh situated beside a lake in tea country, where I had my nose stuck in one of the history books from their extensive library almost every day. Thanks particularly to our "butlers," and to Nadeera Weerasinghe for explaining the plants, trees, and birds of the beautiful Tea Trails gardens to me. Thanks also to our driver/guide Sudarshan Jayasinghe and Mark Forbes in Colombo for his City Walk, and to the staff of the Galle Face Hotel where we stayed when in Colombo. The whole trip was beautifully planned by Nick

Clark at Experience Travel.

I am grateful for the wealth of information that can be found on the Internet, especially YouTube for visual detail about Sri Lanka past and present. One particular memoir was very helpful: *Round the Tea Totum: When Sri Lanka was Ceylon* by David Ebbels (AuthorHouse 2006), which gave me fascinating insights into domestic life on a plantation, especially the bedtime customs and cleaning rituals.

Finally my warmest thanks go to my tireless agents, Caroline Hardman and Joanna Swainson, and to my editor, Venetia Butterfield, as well as the entire team at Penguin who work so hard to bring a book to publication. Thank you all.

Books that I found particularly useful while researching the novel include the following:

Dictionary of Sri Lankan English by Michael Meyler, www.mirisgala.net

19th Century Newspaper Engravings by R. K. de Silva, Serendib, 1998

Vintage Posters of Ceylon by Anura Saparamadu, W. L. H. Skeen, 2011

Ceylon under the British, 3rd ed. by G. C. Mendis, Asian Educational Services, 1951

Sri Lankan Wildlife by Gehan de Silva Wijeyeratne, Bradt Travel Guides, 2007

Sri Lanka in Pictures by Sara E. Hoffmann, TFCB, 2006

AUTHOR'S NOTE

The idea for this novel came as my mother-in-law, Joan Jefferies, reminisced about a childhood spent in India and Burma during the 1920s and early 1930s. As she told stories passed down by her family, which included tea planters in both Ceylon and India, I began thinking about attitudes toward race, in particular the typical prejudices of that time.

My next stop was the audio collection at the Center of South Asian Studies, University of Cambridge, where I found wonderful recorded voices which brought the period to life. Once I'd written the first draft of the book, I went to Sri Lanka. Although Hatton, Dickoya, and Nuwara Eliya are real places, Hooper's Plantation is an amalgamation of several locations and is placed at a higher altitude than Hatton or Dickoya really are. And while I stayed in a Ceylon Tea Trails planter's bungalow beside a reservoir, it is, of course, not the lake of the novel.

In the hills of a romantic tea plantation, swathed in mist, my "Tea Planter's Wife" would have lived an extraordinarily privileged life, but I created a predicament for her that would test all her assumptions about racial differences, and that would explore colonial attitudes and how they spelled such tragedy for her.

It is medically possible for two different men to father nonidentical twins, but regarding the birth of a distinctly dark baby to an apparently fully white couple, the best documented case is of Sandra Laing — born to white Afrikaaner parents in 1950s South Africa but who looked typically black in skin color, with tight curly hair and other distinctive features. To read more about Sandra, see Judith Stone's *When She Was White: The True Story of a Family Divided by Race* or pages 70–73 in *Who Are We — and Should It Matter in the 21st Century?* by Gary Younge.

In the early days it was quite usual for British men going out to work in India and Ceylon to take a "native" bride, as it was felt the men would settle and be better able to deal with the local population. This situation changed, however, especially with the opening of the Suez Canal in 1869. As more unmarried white women began to travel out to "fish" for a wealthy husband, those born of mixed race were less well tolerated; it was also thought that they might not be as loyal to the Crown.

Those familiar with the history of Sri Lanka will notice I have shifted the timing of a couple of events to better suit the purposes of the narrative. One was the riot over the language to be taught in schools and one was the battle of the flowers.

ABOUT THE AUTHOR

Dinah Jefferies was born in Malaysia and moved to England at the age of nine. She still loves Southeast Asia and the Far East and has been to Sri Lanka, India, and Vietnam on research trips for her novels. She once lived in a commune with a rock band and has worked as an exhibiting artist. After also living in Italy and Spain, she now lives in Gloucestershire with her husband and Norfolk terrier, where she writes full time. *The Tea Planter's Wife* is her US debut.

To find out more about Dinah, follow her on Twitter (@DinahJefferies) or visit her website, www.dinahjefferies.com.